PRAISE FOR The Catch

"As McCormack proved in *Six Weeks to Toxic*, she can subvert chick-lit convention without sacrificing the guilty good fun."
—*Chatelaine Magazine,* Top Pick for October

"McCormack's intoxicating love of language and funny quips... keep the story cruising, and the ending is unexpected yet appropriately feel-good."
—*Publishers Weekly*

"McCormack's flair, style and machine-gun wit are abundant throughout.... McCormack's writing is fun and edgy and contains oodles of raw wit and talent."
—*The Globe and Mail*

"McCormack provides a mature and nuanced outlook on matters dear to the heart, both personal and professional."
—*More Magazine*

"Author Louisa McCormack considers her writing (including her much-praised 2006 debut, *Six Weeks to Toxic*) not chick-lit but 'chick-literary.'"
—*Vancouver Sun* Editor's choice

"The characters in *The Catch* are an eclectic mix of laid-back island and Toronto on speed. Indeed, the first chapters of *The Catch* almost need scheduled 'breath breaks.'"
—*Halifax Chronicle Herald*

"While McCormack's first novel *Six Weeks to Toxic* looked at the dynamics and disintegration of female friendship against the backdrop of city living and career flux, *The Catch* is about an unapologetically 40-year-old's relationship with, well, herself and her singlehood."
—*National Post*

"Louisa McCormack's second novel is a fast-paced, accessible book, and McCormack employs colourful language and detail with authority and to good effect, particularly when depicting PEI's many splendours."
—*Quill & Quire*

PRAISE FOR Six Weeks to Toxic

"Far from the run-of-the-mill romantic-breakup novel, Louisa McCormack's witty debut, *Six Weeks to Toxic*, dramatizes the rarely explored yet universal story of a friendship's demise."
—*Vanity Fair*

"McCormack is a quick and deft writer. Witty, concise, controlled.... Louisa McCormack's smart-women's chick-lit works. It's fun, sassy, sexy, wild and self-indulgent."
—*The Globe and Mail*

"Louisa McCormack has written the perfect guilty-pleasure novel.... Funny and entertaining."
—*NOW Magazine*

"*Six Weeks to Toxic* is a sharp, sexy, and witty read that delves into the female psyche."
—*Weekly Scoop*

"Toronto author Louisa McCormack has more interesting things to talk, think and write about than boys.... On the surface, it looks as though [Maxine and Bess are] torn apart when they meet guys they'd actually like to commit to, but there's more to it than that. McCormack's plot touches on issues of family pressure to conform, class and money as dating issues and being a single woman in a world that fetishizes youth."
—*The Toronto Star*

"Louisa McCormack pushes chick-lit in a new direction."
—*Elle Canada*, Top 3 Books

"A treatise on the complex character of female friendship.... The writing, to be sure, is smart."
—*Vancouver Sun*

the
Catch

the
Catch

LOUISA McCORMACK

KEY PORTER BOOKS

Library and Archives Canada Cataloguing in Publication

McCormack, Louisa
    The catch: a novel / Louisa McCormack.

ISBN 978-1-55263-817-0 (bound)—ISBN 978-1-55470-209-1 (paperback)

    I. Title.

PS8625.C675C38 2009   C813'.6   C2009-901416-5

The author acknowledges the generous support of the Canada Council for the Arts.

The publisher gratefully acknowledges the support of the Canada Council for the Arts and the Ontario Arts Council for its publishing program. We acknowledge the support of the Government of Ontario through the Ontario Media Development Corporation's Ontario Book Initiative. We acknowledge the financial support of the Government of Canada through the Book Publishing Industry Development Program (BPIDP) for our publishing activities.

The author will be donating a portion of the proceeds from the sale of the novel to CODE, an organization that promotes and supports literacy in the developing world. For more information, please visit www.codecan.org.

Key Porter Books Limited
Six Adelaide Street East, Tenth Floor
Toronto, Ontario
Canada M5C 1H6

www.keyporter.com

Text design: Marijke Friesen
Electronic formatting: Alison Carr

Printed and bound in Canada

09 10 11 12 13 5 4 3 2 1

To the good people of PEI

... We look round and see that hardly anyone is too ugly or disagreeable to find a wife or a husband if he or she wants one, whilst many old maids and bachelors are above the average in quality and culture ...

George Bernard Shaw,
Pygmalion, the Sequel

Lobster

1

I uprooted myself one recent spring from a life of urban reassurances to an Atlantic island where the wind picks up quickly, the earth is rusted, and fools are ostentatiously tolerated. The island I am referring to is Prince Edward Island, home of Anne, home of a Green Gables simulacrum, where every local will be happy if they never see another carrot-topped doll again in their life. My mother had long escaped this island, escaped a father who had a taciturn way with a wrench and a mother who baked her own beans, both dying modestly of strokes in their sixties. She left PEI for an island on the opposite side of the country where the goat cheese is sold with little flowers embedded in it, by her, when she is not teaching high school physics. Coming as my mother did from the generation of women who just managed to miss out on feminism's major treats, Gail raised me to cherish autonomy, mobility and brute personal force as the three holiest graces.

As of last April, I had lived half of my life midway between my mother's island and my grandmother's island, in Toronto, a grid city where the walking is dull but the climbing is easy. I will admit that I was quietly ashamed of my last career bounce—from public radio to reality television. But I was saving for a condo. I was *saving for a condo*. I was not really saving for a condo; I wanted something more impractical than that. I wanted crumbling bricks, a stained-glass transom, sagging tulips, and a lugubrious grad student in the basement for whom I'd learn to bake cookies that didn't come in a chubby, refrigerated dildo. I am a proud homebody, or will be one day. I respect above all people with the capacity to get cozy. Picture ducks bobbing on November water: their drowsy blinks, calm wings and the relaxed collapse of their necks—whatever the glandular process at work, it's admirable.

What I most want to express is, just prior to my wild move, how I had been *thinking* and *feeling*. Because what do women want? They want to be intimately observed. There are men after men whom I have dated, whom we have all dated, who will court one, screw one and commit to one without ever displaying the slightest curiosity about a single snapshot studding one's photo album; not the pigtail and kneesock shots, not the strained prom portraits, not the zany college residence party (fedoras, boas, cigarillos). What's love without context?

What I had been thinking about a good deal last spring was *love*, about my need to conceive of love as a verb rather than a noun. The sort of noun many of my acquaintances seemed to have tightened their grip on, but I had always been too weak of finger, gesture and tactics to get a hold of. The best thing about aging is one's enhanced largesse: one can be truly happy for people regarding what they have because if one doesn't have it oneself already that means one probably never really wanted it.

The last cruddy bits of snow had melted, crocuses had peeped and gone, bike shops were swamped, a few patios, too. I was forty-and-a-half years old, a creature to my own eyes: a semi-confounded mix of non-negotiable habits and belated realizations. I was realizing that I would not *have* love, not in the form of a mate, spouse or domestic compact. Instead I would be *loving*. I would enact love wherever I went. I would love stray cats, escarpments, egalitarian principles. I would be a sieve for love, walking down the street to feel love sift through me: whenever I spied buddies cracking jokes over beers, mothers bending solicitously over strollers, even lovers, obvious lovers, owning each other's hands. I would love to avoid bitterness.

Definitely, I needed my moral health intact. One is very intimate with oneself, ethically, when one is single; one needs plenty of virtue operative to ensure one is bearable company.

Caught in April's grip, I would have liked to call my cousin, Desolée Gallant, to discuss all this, but I knew better. She is a florist, and Administrative Assistants' Day was on its yearly obliterating way. I would call Desolée too often to amble, conceptually, while she was spraying aerosol wax on greenery, pinching the stamens out of lilies, or telling some guy he was in deep for a four-hundred-dollar apology. Desolée's industry seems so sprightly, but it's all about death, travesty, covert envy, ingratiation and competitive righteousness. Desolée is my pigeon twin, born a week after me, doomed to keep me company forever.

My name is Minerva, but once Desolée began to call me Minnie other people did, too. Nonetheless, I am medium. I am of medium frame and medium height, and medium hat, bra and shoe size. My lips are thinnish, but curve upwards into a slight grin that has done wonders for my social standing. My eyes are muddy, only once in a while enlivened enough to qualify as hazel. I'm more pale than the typical Acadian, but my hair puts the black in Black Irish. My blunt cut hangs bone-straight to my triceps. Not that bones are straight. We Gallants in particular hunch.

I hunch over my tasks at hand, but my gait is quite marine-on-duty, actually: staunchness with a lacing of paranoia. One thing I do possess is physical fitness. The modern spinster's revenge is constant gym attendance. The gym is my spouse of sorts, providing me with regular engagements, regular duties, regular endorphins, regular demands on my purse and time, and cumulative payback. I enjoy the clarity of LifeCycles, the rhythmic promises of treadmills, the responsive clang of chest-press machines when you finally let them down. I like the way I'm hard to stir cardiovascularly, the way I have

sinews, flanks and buns, my hedged assurance of vigour, the conti-
nuity between my oncoming middle age and the carefree cross-
legged days of my childhood when my legs stretched brown and
sturdy from my sneakers to my shorts and I joyfully hollered *Tag,
you're It* at others. If it's any consolation, my calves are almost the
same size as my thighs, my arm veins are startlingly green, my shoulders are too hard to cry on, and if I flex muscle-man style, topless in
front of my dresser mirror, on a day that's stupid enough to offer
me that kind of a moment, my breasts thunk into these weird,
unsavoury, solid knobs.

On this fresh, bright evening, dusk coming almost apologetically, I was headed to spin class. I was looking forward to the blasted
tunes, the brow drips, the Roman delirium of it all. My day had not
gone smoothly and I was fighting to pretend I wasn't exhausted. I
was a senior producer on *Marry Me or Else!*, a brand new TV show
that united old maids with the men no one else wanted. We were
The Bachelor meets the *Golden Girls*, with a respectful nod to *The
Dating Game*. Each episode started off with a comical, in-studio
Compatibility Quiz for three broads and three gents at a time. That
was how we selected one of each to get to know each other better
on a *Fabulous Getaway*—a one-week vacation for the two formerly
unacquainted lonely hearts that we were coordinating with a camera crew so as to capture every tiff, snog and peccadillo. Very few of
our couples had deprived us of hilarious tension. In fact the couple
who had *Getaway*ed at Lake Louise had almost gotten in a food
fight, thanks to a piece of toast whipped across the breakfast table
during an argument about whether it was burnt or not.

The *Fabulous Getaways* would get edited together as the last
half of each show. No *Marry Me or Else!* television audience would
ever be in all that much suspense as to how things had worked out.
Just a little, as they waited for Episode 13 when all the *Getaway*
couples who'd since become engaged—at least four out of the
twelve, we figured—would fight it out to get voted most likely to
marry and stay that way. The winning couple would collect a poster

cheque; everyone else would have to rise above the disappointments they had brought upon each other. Roll credits (*Supervising Producer Minerva Gallant*).

Among my numerous executive duties I was wrangler-in-chief. We needed viable contestants, people who were willing to seek true love in front of thousands, preferably hundreds of thousands, of the glazed over and couch prone. All this sans hot tubs—we didn't insist on those. Although a couple of our ladies could have given next top models a run for their spa money, as I had been happy to see while screening tape of *Fabulous Getaways* from Episodes 1 though 10, most at Mexican and Panamanian beaches. All our raw tape could be snapped into shape over the autumn, meanwhile we had the spring to shoot, shoot, shoot. How did we find participants with crowd appeal sans youthful va-va-voom? Who were (somewhat) immune to humiliation? Yet (reasonably) sincere in their search for a loving touch? Through ads in free weeklies, network promos, website come-ons and hard-ass lead following. I led by example. No wonder I was glad to get home at night. No wonder I would somnambulate the minute I walked in my door. No wonder I needed to talk to no one for twelve straight hours.

Work had gone a lot better the week before when I had justified my huntress reputation at Myriad Television Co. by bagging Hardy Rutgers, a hale and merry fellow of fifty-two who had built up a Sudbury-based bow-tie and cummerbund empire (leopard prints, pastels, fake snakeskin, elastic inserts, your classic Cary Grant—all certifiably sweat-shop free). Hardy was a man so inexcusably optimistic that not even his sunburned pate, Tweedle Dum physique and luxuriant hand hair unsettled him. A man who had probably heretofore failed to pair-bond by rising too willingly to too many occasions.

With Hardy nailed down as comic relief, I now had all three males good to go, including an august research scientist from the Haynes Institute who would never know what hit him, and our prospective winner (the Applause-o-Meter rarely failed us), a Porsche-driving dandy with a corner office at the personal wireless device headquarters in Waterloo, Ontario. Mr. Device would almost certainly win our last quiz of the season, taping the following week. Joining Mr. Device—whichever lady could cavort with him just as photogenically on a southern holiday.

I had our grand cash prize winners picked out if I had my way, and I was paid to have my way, audience participation or not. I thought the chipper ex-nun and happy-go-lucky Okanagan vintner who had *Getaway*ed in Bocas del Toro should prevail. Not only would their siblings, cohorts and reverends surely soon be vouching for their engagement, but they would make everybody and their dog wistful enough to get us renewed for a second season.

The *Marry Me or Else!* debut was scheduled for early in the new year. Three years before, I'd convinced Juice Network to debut *The Urban Forager* in January and I had been coasting on ratings glory since. As long as I kept biting off chunks of the culture at its saltiest. As everyone nowadays knows, the more crassly intrusive the television, the higher the stakes. This was a good job; this was my best job so far; this was the best job I could hope for. Try telling that to my mother and believe her when she says she believes you. Let's just say I was as sad as you might be to know that I was wielding more power than a national news health reporter. Let's also say that my bank account appreciated my slum landlady ways. Money pays you compliments; money calls you back; money is hunky.

All that strugglesome day in question, before spin class set me free, I had been chasing something tantalizingly stern in Nicola Chalice, a librarian from Oakville. She was obviously intelligent: bad. But potentially oblivious to the cultural inflections of our show: good. I thought her terseness may well come off as hilarious. I could tell that pooled beneath Nicola Chalice's schoolmarm impatience was a dark, still reservoir of generosity that any audience would lap up given a chance. One of her young patrons, Patsy, a sweet high school treasurer type, not a conniving cheerleader as I had spent the morning verifying, had emailed in to recommend her. At this point the library district superintendent was game to release Nicola Chalice for one full day of skylarking—certainly we would ask no more of her than that. A production assistant sent out to scope matters reported that she was comely without being come-hither. No one seemed to have anything against Nicola Chalice beyond considering her more of an institution than a woman. I knew she would be able to give Mr. Device what-for without once referring to a sports car as a surrogate penis. In any case, she would leave everybody with a somewhat more complicated taste in their mouths than they had expected. And no one would feel bad for her because they would know that Nicola Chalice understood that she was less than soundly eligible. She was both shelver and shelved.

"We'd love to have you," I said to her. "Our contestants are finding the show a lot of fun."

"You say you run a televised competition?"

"Well, yes. It's a game, really. A matchmaking game, for people who seem unmatched but may well magically turn out to be very much so."

"Very much so matched?"

"Sure, ya."

"Affection as performance. Nothing new about that."

"There's a prize. Fifty thousand dollars to whoever gets engaged and then voted most likely to, like, stay that way."

Alas, the *like* disease. Linguists claim it's actually a form of fluency and that all languages provide a verbal pause for thought. *Like* is apparently a North American equivalent of *bof* and *pah* and any number of guttural European interjections. Nonetheless, I think it's a shame that as a society we're grasping after all these phantom similes, those of us born after 1970 and those of us susceptible to those of us born after 1970. Nicola Chalice was not dragged down by such conversational counterweights. But I had to, you know, like, keep things sounding somewhat ignorant. Any rarefied badinage and Nicola Chalice would usher us from my zone back to hers, where risky decisions did not get made.

"Fifty thousand dollars each?"

"Per couple. I mean, you can split it and each grab half, I guess. But supposedly you'll be, like, you know, together ..."

At least I was capable of honouring a silence, the possibly fruitful silence that was now blooming like ink in water between Nicola Chalice and me. I needed her.

"Would this engagement require cohabitation?"

"Oh, gosh no. Not if the couple doesn't want. I mean, if they wanted to, that wouldn't be a problem either. It'll all just be, you know, real."

To Nicola Chalice's credit, she snorted.

"May I ask, Ms. Gallant, are you married yourself?"

"No, not at all."

"Why do you think it would be worth this much trouble to be *matched?*"

Nicola Chalice had me there. Her authority was so pre-emptive that it left me with only one leg to stand on.

"Think of it as an adventure. Something a little out of the ordinary to tell, um, your library goers about."

"Oh, they wouldn't need telling. According to your plans they would all be able to watch for themselves."

I reached out with my free hand to grab tight to my desk. The Myriad offices are in the west end, in *Liberty Village* as the warehouse developers have it, nomenclature they justify with stray park benches and an upmarket cafeteria. Myriad is right on Liberty Street, in a bona fide industrial, sprawling, pillared workshop with original hardwood. Next door is the studio in a converted garage. I am the office asshole who sits on a stability ball. I felt my core muscles contract even more than usual as I tried to suck in everything that Nicola Chalice represented, and every possible benefit of our telecommunicatory connection. I tried to suck all that into the warm space of my desk lamp: a little Italian crane of a lamp thanks to my latest promotion, that placed a cosseting, honeyed cone of illumination upon my desk—a light that was fully enveloping if I could ignore the squabbles over the last chocolate chip muffin ricocheting out of the kitchenette, Barry, our executive producer, attempting the "Hallelujah" chorus, and Stephanie the intern's iPod swill.

"Everyone is going to have a television show sooner or later and I think this is yours," I told Nicola Chalice before our pause was impregnated with demon children.

"Fifty thousand dollars is a lot of money. I imagine you'll be selling this television show abroad?"

"We'll be taking it to the Banff festival and trying our luck for sure. We have high hopes. We've got a good track record. *Moms on Everest* airs in twenty countries. You can rely on the prize. It's legally stipulated."

"I'm quite alone," Nicola Chalice said. "I have no family whatsoever."

I could have said to Nicola Chalice that I was next to alone, considering that my dad had long been dispensed with and my mother made it a point of honour to be preoccupied. But Desolée made up for so much, and I adored her batty mother, too. Although Aunt Lee was just as far west as Gail, working as a masseuse in Ucluluet now that she had given up on registered nursing. But what would it be like to have no one expecting your annual Christmas call, better yet your April Fool's Day call? No one to send you a birthday card with lotto tickets that you'd never bother to check, no one to remember you hate ketchup and love mustard, no one to name as your beneficiary?

"I see," I said, but I knew I had only just glimpsed.

"There are advantages to solitude, Ms. Gallant." Worthily, Nicola Chalice failed to render herself further vulnerable. I am becoming my mother's daughter in one thing: I do not see the point of vulnerability. I wish inviolability on people.

"I imagine it's very, you know, liberating."

"It's certainly hard to feel ridiculous when there is no one to laugh at you."

"If a tree does a pratfall alone in a forest does it make a sound?"

"HA!"

It was like we'd had an argument that was entirely my fault, but I had acknowledged that and now Nicola Chalice got to decide if we were going to make up. Nicola Chalice, holder of my bacon. Nicola Chalice, who might just help sell the show to the Yorkshire Network, and the Harpo people, and librarians everywhere. I had scrawled PLEASE in block letters and hardened the outline of each letter and was just starting to polka dot the P when I overheard another phone ring at Oakville Public Library, disturbing what for Nicola Chalice must have been a moment of Magritte-calibre strangeness. I wanted her, this newfangled Miss Jane Hathaway. I would get so much credit for Nicola Chalice and all she had to do was be herself then endure second glances at the grocery store for a month or two post screen date.

"Will you think about this?" I asked.

"Oh yes, you can be sure that I will think about this."

I exhaled. Nicola and I said quick goodbyes, me admonishing her to call me Minerva, make that Minnie. She agreed to call back by late Friday with her decision. It was only after I hung up that I realized I had forgotten to double-check with Nicola Chalice exactly how old she was. Maybe little Patsy hadn't been completely correct when she'd said that Ms. Chalice was *old, like at least forty-five?* Despite photographic evidence to the contrary, for all I knew, Nicola Chalice was my junior. That would be bad news. For one thing, anyone younger than forty didn't suit our old-maid mandate now that thirty-eight-year-olds made it to the covers of gossip rags. Surely Nicola Chalice's voice was too full of challenges met and dealt with to be younger than me? I did not want to be envying that much wisdom. Not now that wisdom was something I wanted to luxuriate in the way smart women revel in French moisturizers. What I really needed to do was start reading again, the kind of solipsism-blasting prior-century novels that remind one: *others, too, always have, always will, same dilemmas, same joys, same natures.* I used to read at the gym, but then they attached television screens to the cardio equipment. Reading was rarely winning out anymore, not when a chick flick beckoned, or a trashy website called out for a clicking, or anyone else's elimination drama aired on whatever station. The West is a quagmire; one way or another, junk will get you.

I had been relieved to see from camera-phone evidence that Librarian Chalice did indeed wear glasses, propped on what looked like admirable cheeks. Nicola Chalice also had brain structure, and likely soul structure—in any case, far too much personal structure to succumb to social shorthand for long. She had cropped hair—wash-and-wear short, congresswoman short, don't-screw-with-me short. She had been spotted riding to work on a Vespa; we would have to get a shot of that.

Luce—an associate producer so stellar we often let her work from home—had already lined up a svelte real estate agent and a high-end department store manageress to go along with her. All I needed now to finish off my business day was to review the quiz questions for the next taping (*Would your ideal date be a) on a Saturday night, b) when the mood hit you or c) as soon as humanly possible?*). And I had to fine-tune some performance notes for our host, Angela, a perky morning radio DJ whom we were borrowing for Season 1. Angela struck just the right balance between snarky and soppy as long as no one else made any jokes (*"All right, buster, settle down, we only put half a Viagra in that coffee."*). Not good for Angela to escape the tyranny of cute, not good for us to have to concoct her charm in the edit suite. That was what I next spent twenty minutes emphasizing to Barry, our executive producer, aka EP. Barry would have to do the actual raking over a couple of coals, which he hated. Barry is the kind of team captain who never wants to haul anyone off the playing field.

"C'mon, Bar. Deal with this now and Angela'll be good to go for the hiatus," I said.

"Hiatus, you say? I've heard that word before. Too bad I don't know what it means."

Barry's office is a glass cage, the sole enclosed space in the loft, which he hated until I bought him Nerf balls in every available formation. Barry is the kind of guy who makes his way up a chain of command wearing souvenir sweatshirts, a man with reflexes so casual you might mistake them as luck—a regular sweetheart. Barry and his wife, Barb, had finally become pregnant on their sixth shot at in vitro and in celebration Barb had extended her mat leave from the premier's public policy office. Barry was in awe at Barb's stay-at-home skills; he didn't know how she managed. I liked Barb a lot and was happy for her, if fretful for my province now that no one else was going to be putting in a good word for Environment Ministry watchdogs, defending universal day care, ensuring good governance, and all the other nurturing predilections of feminine political power in action. Barry and Barb are the great parts/great sum kind of couple one wants the best for, their mutuality somehow guaranteeing all other kinds of magic while they're at it. No Barry and Barb—no leprechauns, or reincarnation, or signs from above, no mystery. Just cold, hard deduction; just objects and objectives.

"Okay, Bar, pardon my big fat fact crap, but listen up. We've got the *Getaway* shoot in Belize starting tomorrow—all the sponsorship is in place for that by the way, with product placement for Safe-T-Tan and Crantoony. Plus the Episode 12 quiz to tape next Friday. Chalice is looking very good to go as the female foil and Luce worked wonders with the other ladies. Let's assume Mr. Device and Ms. Remax scoop the last *Getaway*—"

"What about sending the guy from Waterloo away with the Nicola gal?"

"Barry, I love Chalice, but c'mon, show the woman some mercy. There's no way she's getting subjected to a *Getaway*, not while one of us still has a conscience."

Barry lounged while I usually paced. He had crammed as many places to sit down into his office as possible but I rarely made use of any of them.

"Okay, Prime Minister Thatcher. Your call."

"Thank you. Then we've got down-on-one-knees to shoot over the summer, budget permitting. The second unit can handle those, right? Fine, you win, scrap that. We can work question pops into the finale somehow, maybe just post-enact the suckers in-studio."

"Never gild the lily if you don't have to, kid. It costs too much."

"Juice is cool with a late October shoot for the finale by the way. They're thinking two hours, which should work. We'll have plenty of never-seen-befores to play around with."

"Great work, genius. Keep it up."

I perched on a sofa arm in honour of the tender moment.

"So, Bar. In the meantime, how's about I pound *Switcheroo* into shape? Once we get the green light for that—"

"I still don't know how you're going to finesse something so derivative. Hasn't everybody swapped everything already?"

"Swapped wives, not kids. C'mon, it's brilliant. Didn't you used to wish you were adopted? The kids themselves have to fill in the application form if they want to change families. Read the reaction survey—some of them want to swap with Mounties' kids and mayors' kids and CEOs' brats. It's not abusive, trust me."

"Don't count your chickens, chick."

"Our chickens, Barry, *ours*. *Switcheroo* is the best thing we have on the go right now, trust me. You might not want to bust ass, but I do. Think big for a change."

"Get out of my office, Feminazi. Go home. Go soak something, anything, just bring down the swelling."

I slid my clipboard under my arm and did the old winching up a middle finger routine. Barry loved that. At which point it was time to call a cab and get dropped off somewhere close to the gym but far enough to offer me a warm-up. The corner of Spadina Avenue and Dundas Street, I decided, so I could shop competitively amidst the hordes of Chinatown newcomers. I loved the bullying grannies, the catcalling guys with handcarts and chapped hands, the beautifully kempt young couples who never seemed to bicker. The less their English the more I loved these crowds for arriving to correct the depopulation stats we overly educated non-gestational social climbers had given rise to.

I had taken a cab because I never drove anywhere. Firstly, whenever possible I liked to arrive at my destination through expense of calories. Secondly, keep one's footprint small upon this earth. Thirdly, I was on my fourth learner's permit—the written test only. In order for one to learn how to drive there has to be somebody in one's life who really cares where one is going. At sixteen, while everyone else was piloting their family sedan, I was at a boarding school in Vancouver (I had begged to get off Saltspring since getting underarm hair). At the University of Toronto I was too busy prolonging my scholarship to study anything extraneous. Then I always seemed to hook up with men who were too urban to want cars or too demonstrative in their masculinity to own automatics. Desolée point-blank refused to teach me to drive; she said she wanted to stay cousins. And now I hated automobiles because I drove them as if they were bicycles. Rear-view mirrors are visual gibberish to someone who has spent four decades not looking into them.

Perhaps a bit more at this point about my *relationships*. It's a poor sign when something as complicated as the romance in one's life begins to subscribe to basic rules. I had developed unfortunate patterns; I understood that without talking to a professional. Constantly, I would tangle myself up with the kind of charismatic narcissists who are far more fascinated by the effect you have on them than by you. They're the ones who enjoy love as a toy, to be taken out and played with, but quickly stashed back in the toy trunk when the fun gets taxing. They'll have you over to their place to cook for you because that's actually easier and more flattering than following you to your own address—they enjoy the heroics of fetching you a throw and serving you a plate of fettuccine al vongole. But the moment anything gets remotely inconvenient an overgrown bachelor will back-pedal, retreat and clam up with the *I love you so much, gorgeous*. One instant too many that is less than completely on his terms and presto: rumbles, uprooting, a fault line opening in the crust, an abyss now yawning between you. And there is no way in hell he's pitching himself into that dark void because that's the way of sacrifice. Perhaps you attempt a chasm-spanning leap to rejoin him, your last-ditch attempt at union. But gravity is cruel. The light dims, you're dragging gravel under your front teeth, your chin and palms are lacerated, rubble tumbles towards your head, you're going down, down, down to where the suffering is. The worst of it is, you're going down there all alone again. Meanwhile buddy scampers for the sunshine. He doesn't know much about your kind of pain but he'll cry for help if he skins his knee. He will get help. No matter who raises them, males are raised entitled.

I was thinking maybe men prefer women with obvious designs on them, women who see them chiefly as procurers, agents of fertilization and validators. Those women are probably the easiest for men to parse, predict and answer to. But when you're not quite sure what you want from a man, when you're simply feeling him out, gently probing him for insight, kindness and morally valid ambition, then you're screwed.

I began to regret casual sex a lot less than my relationships because at least I rolled in the hay with the physically respectable. The men I committed to—based on their booming laughs, nicely cut jacket flaps, affection for their sisters or international development aspirations—were grody trolls after the fact, whom I never wanted to see naked again if my life depended on it, not their bare dicks and definitely not their bare toes. Then I began to have the kind of sex that gets worse as it goes along, no matter how Adonis the gentleman in question. Contrary to juvenile sex, the first time would be great. Then the juice would drain out of everything, neither of us being true receptacles for each other.

Maybe I was too palliative with my loved ones, too pampering, too *what's-the-point-of-jewellery, you-pick-the-movie, what-kind-of-flowers-does-your-mother-like?* Too prone to getting my uterus thumped when yet another one favoured going canine. Until I wasn't at all accommodating, either because I'd snapped shut or they had. I'll say this for the men I partnered with: they were all smart enough to realize I wanted a child more than them. I can't imagine I would have lasted long in Foreversville with any of my motley formers, taking turns sweeping the kitchen and paying the cable bill. I would have given every single one of them too many blank stares for that. Certainly, no man had *got away*. Nor did I wish for an instant that any of my friends' husbands were mine to work with. Definitely not Barry. Poor Barry, I'd have strained desperately towards unconditionality over breakfast, bedtime and weekends, meanwhile snipped off his ponytail in my sleep. At least Barry would understand this much: no man has ever been quite as interesting to me as watching a television show receive development funding, go into production and get ratings. Furthermore, I had inhaled, absorbed and ingested far too many poisons, toxins and out and out contaminants by now to think of steeping a bairn in such swill. My womb was actually not barren enough.

Incrementally, naturally, in my own good time, my default mode became singlehood. I had started off well disposed to relationships, but ended up less convinced they were my solution to anything. Don't ever try explaining this state of mind to anyone, however, because they will immediately tell you that it is *at times like this,* apparently *when you least expect it,* that *Mr. Right will sail into your life.* At which point I would think, *I fucking well hope not,* at which point I would say, "I fucking well hope not." I don't like to swear with that much verve, usually, but I found the *fucking* was necessary to hammer the point home. What I can safely say is that by last spring I had grown to love being single with the same tenacity and goodwill that one might show to a mate. And thanks to the gym, and despite my romantic and erotic fatigue, I stayed my sex weight. It's not quite the same as a fighting weight, but nice women don't have those.

Amid the Chinatown din, I loaded scarlet peppers, arboreal broccoli, plump mandarins, unidentified mushrooms, an Einstein of a cauliflower and the garlic bulbs I'd kept forgetting into two plastic bags. Desolée's boyfriend, Stash, is Polish so she is allowed to call plastic bags *Polish luggage*. Desolée rarely apologizes for anything.

She considers herself blanket exonerated since her very name means (feminine) *sorry* in French. It was the prettiest way Aunt Lee could think of to apologize to her parents for conceiving a baby way out of wedlock at a judgmental time, islands being inevitably judgmental places—continually running out of Mother Nature must get one in the habit of scrutinizing human nature, too. In the middle of the brouhaha engendered by Lee's condition, my slightly more pregnant mother, Gail, the responsible older sister (whose twerpy younger sister had simply had to divest herself of her virginity, too) got stuck at the end of a shotgun, got hitched to her teacher-college boyfriend. That would be Cecil, aka Cece, aka Dad, handily a Gallant as well but from two counties over and numerous family lines away. Gail and Cece remained married for ten months altogether and then Gail left it at that. Lee could not have married Desolée's father even if she had wanted to, her interlude having taken place on nickname basis only with an itinerant trombonist whose short-lived jazz band had played the Montague Legion before dispersing to the States. Both sisters swore to have been knocked up the *very first time*, as they never ceased to warn us. Desolée and I are contraception connoisseurs. We had to fight my mother off with our pancake forks when we were fifteen; she wanted so badly to serve the pill with our morning OJ.

Desolée and Lee used to come and live with us often. My mother and I didn't bother with extra bedrooms; sometimes we would share our double beds, sometimes we wouldn't. Gail would be at work during the day and Aunt Lee would do night shifts until she was *caught up*. It hadn't been easy for Lee to attend nursing school with a baby. It hadn't been easy for either of them to schlep infants across the country in Gail's VW bug. Grandma had packed them a week's worth of peanut butter sandwiches, a treat still resonant of luxury from a time when lobster was for poor kids. Grandpa apparently kissed everyone goodbye on the forehead, our first and last grandpaternal embrace. It was the last time either of them saw any of us. Expecting Grandma and Grandpa to visit BC would have been like asking the average person nowadays to go to Yemen. They were gone altogether by the time Desolée and I hit junior kindergarten.

Grandma's brother, Rex Arsenault, came out every Christmas, however, to add zip to his winter and ours. Grandma had inherited the family potato patch while Rex got the fishing boat and joviality genes. He toiled when the toiling was good, at which point there were traps to repair and herring nets to knit. But long, dark winter evenings were Rex's version of scratchy blankets, a serious cause of fidgets, which was how he found himself making his way out to an assortment of jumbo-treed Gulf Islands over the years. I got Rex's left knee and Desolée got his right knee, just like our mothers had before us. We thought Rex's striped suspenders matched his flannel shirts beautifully. We completely agreed that he was a *great* uncle. To this day, Desolée can barely forgive me that I always learned to tie Rex's sailor knots the fastest, and showed and told the fact at kindergarten.

Cece, my dad (Cece and Desist, Lee calls him) migrated to Maine, married properly, and worked his way up to a mailman job with no threat of going postal. He had never really wanted to be a teacher and he had never really wanted to marry my mother, but he had always wanted to be my father, as he would fervently guarantee whenever he met me at the Portland airport or saw me off. I could see that Cece was a darling, but I could also see how my mother found him ineffectual. I loved visiting him, his soft voice marvelling at my numerous skills, Cece and his plump new wife, Shelley, unable to conceive a semi-sibling as she'd apologize every visit, shuddering until I'd pat her quiet with an insistent pyrrhic tetrameter: pat-pat, pat-pat, pat-pat, pat-pat. I was relieved Shelley was American; it excused our lack of intimacy somehow, aloofness that persisted like a stubborn head cold on my part even when Shelley took me to outlet malls to shower me in discount logos. It's a *name*, she'd say, heaping my arms with polo shirts and suede sneakers. I would be polite; I would be too polite. Then all the Yo-Yo's, Ding-Dongs, Eggos and egg rolls on offer would upset my stomach by week two.

Cece made up for my mother's far-flung longitude by sending me bimonthly postcards in his sweet schoolteacher script. There were only so many postcards for sale in Deale, Maine. I got all of them, over and over again—the Farm Implement Museum, the stunned deer interrupted mid-graze, the cartoon bear picnic, the *Miss You in Maine*. I received them all in an unwavering succession that Cece never lost track of, right up until I begged him to go on-line, which he did, being a sweetly responsive father figure. With all Cece's gentility lapping at my ankles I'm not sure why I splash around so much when it comes to men. My father indubitably loves me. I guess the problem is that my mother and I terrify him.

Aunt Lee had her tubes tied and kept on having boyfriends: bearded men and younger men, skinny men and stocky men, a whole socio-economic smorgasbord to whom Desolée and I would give secret nicknames like Nosey, Furry and Fatty. No dates for Gail, however, even though she's the prettiest of all of us. "All men are babies," she says when questioned, and claims to prefer goats, although lately my spies tell me Rob so-and-so is more than just a neighbour. I wish my mother the best. I am much more interested in being an adult than I am in continuing to resent my mother. The way I see it, you forgive or flounder. Children must be somewhat hard to love. No wonder so many of them nowadays are so corpulent: they're stuffed full of misguided intentions. Easy for me to say; I've never had to deprive a child of a beverage that looks like chilled, liquefied cobalt. I can tell from some of our unsuccessful young job applicants (*"I won't start at less than 60K, I want to produce my own segments, I want top-flight dental …"*) that they anticipate a hell of a lot of unrestricted waltzing from one place to another. It's a shame because there is so much self-confidence implicit in humility. The boldness of admitting to others that your frame of reference is incomplete is what I admire most in the people I've learned the most from. Narcissists aren't really arrogant; they just wish they were.

Fruit and veg swung abundantly in my bags. I was right on time for the best, hardest spin class: the one in the small studio without windows but that was okay because Olympians in training surely endure worse. The gloaming had gone misty in a way that was more replenishing than uncomfortable. I waited to cross Queen Street inside a clump of squawking Goths with scuffed leather, double-dyed hair, spectral foundation, skunky eyes and gleaming black lips. It was the whole castle full from Walpole's *Otranto*. I remembered that crowd all too well from my Masters thesis, *Love and Fear: Early Eighteenth-Century English Literature and the Trope of Romance*.

I nabbed my favourite locker at the gym. I liked the one right by the door so I would be less tempted to scrutinize the miracle that is other women's bodies. No wonder there is a *male gaze*; we are limitlessly fascinating. My fascination is something most women can relate to whatever their leaning; we're highly curious about each other's variations. I don't think I could ever get into bed with boobs; they're too amorphous for me and some look like downright suffocation devices. Breasts are another one of those things for which we ladies must learn to be grateful. The chick to the left of me had pale downcast nipples the circumference of espresso saucers. She was probably the only person in the locker room who appreciated getting into her sports bra. And everything else about her was so beautifully tidy: her trim nails hand and toe, her matching yoga top and tights, her plastic basket of gym toiletries organized by function. There was no point in my pang. Her heart had possibly gone out to me due to my near bunions and boyish trunk. I had to get out of the locker room; the estrogen was going to my head.

I grabbed my favourite bike beside my best gym buddy, Bill, who defied the restrictions against scented products and dabbed on gorgeous, smoky cologne before class. Bill winked, already deep into his efforts. We liked second row centre: vaguely in view of the mirror, right out of view of the clock. Jeanette, the instructor, cranked her Majorcan disco tunes, shut us inside the room, straddled her own machine and we were off to the non-races. Soon Jeanette was hollering the sorts of things that Cotton Mather might have prided himself in uttering: *Be Strong; Do Not Give In; You'll Be Glad in the End*. Much pumping, much bouncing, several admonishments to the newbies to get their shoulders down, harder with the left leg, harder with the right leg, hill, sprint, hill, sprint. Fifty minutes later we were coasting towards our cool-down, upright again.

I needed a cool-down since I did not have time to shower. It was the last night of the In From the Cold program, where I volunteered every Thursday evening from mid-November until mid-April. Helping out at a homeless shelter is not hard work; there are too many other volunteers stirring tomato sauce and clearing dishes and checking names off lists for that. But to do any real good, I felt like I had to show up every time; whatever else I was to the clients, I also wanted to be a constant. Once in a while I was tempted to shirk, but not often. The dirty secret about volunteering is how addictive it is. I think our species must be hardwired to be altruistic much like we favour fat feel in the mouth. Having finally started to volunteer, I now knew that I could never go without it.

I hoofed it to the streetcar stop, the fastest way to get up Spadina to Bloor if my timing was good. It was. Window seat. Cast into a streetcar window, one's reflection stays so preternaturally young. Perhaps it's the look of inquiry you wear, and the lulling progress of the car, and the way your head seems to hover above the traffic with casual sorcery. I guess all vehicles are back-to-the-womb. Superior to that, I'd say. Wombs seem like terrifying places to me: dark, bloody flesh bags with no discernible openings or distractions. With all due respect to Gail, not my idea of Eden.

I dinged the bell to request my stop, hurrying past the Portuguese mother beside me so she wouldn't have to endure too much of my ass in her face, and exited by the front door. I bolted kitty corner through an amber light. I was headed to one of those big stone churches that are parked downtown like musty dowagers in hoop skirts, invited to but not welcome at the ball, never to be asked to dance again, encroached upon by slim, young, harder-selling buildings that unanimously ignore them. I said quick hellos to the In

From the Cold gatekeepers, men of professional football dimensions and demeanours. They had their purpose when brawls broke out or the truly strung-out tried to get in. I hurried downstairs to sign in, drawing a cross-eyed happy face on my name tag as usual, fielding queries as to how Desolée was doing as usual—she came when she could and let me stand in for her otherwise. I hung up my coat in the furnace room, zipped my messenger bag inside it, prayed my weekly prayer for the safety of my credit cards, gym gear and electronic devices, stowed my groceries up on a window ledge where they stood a chance of refrigeration, and scooted back up to the dining hall/dormitory, which always smelled of boiled tallow and second-hand parka, but only for the first five minutes. It's probably best to think of oneself as having several homes up and running; this was one of mine. Unexpectedly it was one of my favourites.

"Gabe!" I said. Good, Gabe was back. He had been missing for a couple of weeks, in Gabe's case not a good sign. With the Native guys, you could always hope they had gone up north for vaguely healthier times. But I had no right to begrudge someone like Gabe the city pleasures of anonymity, corner stores and a customer base. He sold his art on the street when he could, beautiful little miniatures with iconography he had inherited and then subtly revitalized. I had several of his pieces lined up on my mantel and wanted at least one more.

"Sit!" Gabe said. I sat and tried not to be disconcerted when the serving brigade kept offering me chicken dinners. One of the donating bakeries that night had provided wedding cake, disguised in slices but still evident; I wouldn't be partaking of that either.

"How's things?" I asked. Immediately I could see things were inebriated, but Gabe was so demure he could slip past the doormen without getting bounced.

"Good," Gabe said. "How's the arm?"

I had broken my arm the year before, skidding on ice just as I'd showed up at the church, landing on the hard stone steps with an audible crack, tumbling deep into the second seating dinner crowd pooled outside. I can safely say that I know a little bit about what it is like to be the pope. There was an immediate massive rush of concern on my behalf, a hundred hands stretched out in supplication begging to help. I had never broken a bone before and it made me cry, mostly because my volunteering was over for the night before I had even said hello. It was my left arm, more a sobering warning of what it would be like to break a bone than real incapacitation. I was soon back at the shelter. It turned out to be a great thing to have a glaring injury in such company. Now there was something I needed soothing for and advice about. Everybody likes to help. I helped by needing help. I did my best to prolong the effect.

"The damn wrist sure hurts in this damp, my friend."

"Old lady."

"Whatever!"

Gabe interrupted his supper to root in his tattered knapsack for his latest oils. I cleared table space and he laid them out in a northern row. Right away I picked the one with the moon etched high, splashing violet onto the snow. There was a howling wolf in the foreground with its jaws cranked so wide that I could almost hear wolf wail and smell wolf breath and feel a tongue licking up past my wrists. There was a pine tree in the background as hyper natural as a fractal. I paid up immediately.

"I knew you'd pick that one," Gabe said.

"I totally love it."

I gave Gabe a quick sideways hug and then Duardo wanted one, too. Duardo was an escapee from exploitive Honduran coffee plantations, Mexico City gangs and Texan border guards. He had a room in a frightening boarding house and visited the shelter for the quiet company of other Latin American cribbage players, all of whom let me practice Spanish so bad I hoped it was at least comical.

"Que tal, los guapos?"

"Bueno, Senorita Minnie, bueno. Estas loca esta noche?"

"Claro que si!"

No wonder I did not require a dating life with this fine glut of attention, weekly in times of frost. There was a lot at the shelter that scared my nose, but there was a base note of good old-fashioned testosterone. Leo tossed me a thumbs-up to start stacking chairs. We always began with the empty ones, then moved apologetically to the ones in use, carting some of them downstairs to the movie room for whoever was taking in the video of the night. By the time Pearl hit the microphone to call out the next batch of people getting in to see the street nurse—mostly for foot ailments since they all fought a kind of trench warfare—Leo and I had moved on to the tables. One of the guests jumped up to help me hold a table on its side while I kicked in the legs. Usually I urged the guests to relax. This time I was sensitive enough to share the job.

"Patrick," I said, reading his name tag, his in black, mine in red. He was short and wiry, with small, bright eyes and thick, feathered hair, wearing what Leo had taught me to refer to as a *Muskoka dinner jacket*. I doubted he had taken it off for days or that it had been warm enough to hitchhike in.

"You got that right." I could tell Patrick was his real name.

"Hey, you're from out East."

"Once I was. Now I'm coming from out west. Fort McMoney. So much for that. Fifteen hundred dollars a month rent if you're lucky. We were bunking up in shifts, the bed was warm from another man no matter when you got in it."

"You do what you gotta, I guess. Are you heading home?"

"You can call it that if you want to call it something."

"Where? Do you mind me asking?"

We weren't supposed to inquire too directly into any of the clients' circumstances, but sometimes that hardly seemed fair.

"Don't see why not."

"Hang on, let me guess. The Rock?"

I liked Patrick's sing-song enough to give him maximum credit; Newfoundland got half marks right off the bat for almost being County Cork.

"No, that would be the Island."

"PEI, the island?"

"That's the one."

"Oh my God, that's where my family is from! Tuck Harbour, do you know it?"

"I know of Buddy Donovan. Do you know him then?"

Tuck Harbour had actually sent a kid pro golfing, a boy who had spent summers as a caddy on public courses and now drank out of the occasional gold cup.

"No, gosh, sorry. I haven't visited all that much. My mother left when I was a baby and she never really wanted to go back. Once in a while my cousin and I go see my great uncle. The last time was, wow, four Christmases ago. The Donovans have that sleigh-ride business. I wanted to check it out, but my cousin hates the cold."

"No snow last Christmas or the one before."

"How weird."

"Lots is weird."

"So much is changing, I guess."

"No one likes change but a wet baby, that's what my good ma always said."

We laughed. Leo didn't mind when I paused to chat, but I didn't want him putting his back out.

"C'mon, Patrick, let's get busy." I motioned to the corner where we needed to drag the tables so there would be room for everyone to crash out.

"Right you are."

When I checked later, Patrick had found himself one of the worst spots to sleep: near the door and beside Izzy who was rumoured to have scabies. I managed to move him in beside the Guatemalans over by the radiators. I sneaked him an extra blanket, one that had been rejected for being pink.

"See you in Tuck Harbour some time," Patrick said.

"You got it!"

I waved a well-meant goodbye.

It was a wistful night, but there was happy conjunction in the air. Some of the clients were going to brave a hitchhike home. They had grandchildren to visit, wrinkled baby grandchildren that subsisted in well-worn snapshots from year to year showing small birthday cakes on highchair platters in tiny kitchens. William was off to High Park with a tarp, propane heater and rubber boots. Ernie's breath smelled of Aqua Velva and soft brown molars. There was no staying near him for long, but I managed a bit of farewell chitchat, wanting to provide him with one small moment that was in any way normal. If I could have, I would have thanked Ernie for reminding me there was such a thing as normal. I caught Dave's eye as he sprawled like a pasha beside his old lady, Shirl, and gave him a big wave, too. Then I sought out Gabe in the crowd and blew him a kiss goodbye so he'd have fun getting ribbed. I squeezed one of Leo's shoulders in silent farewell while he argued with a church rep about giving out a mat too many. Then I hurried downstairs to collect my coat and bags. I was ravenous; cab versus subway versus walking ravenous.

I was headed home to Concord Avenue, a couple of blocks north of College Street, to the main floor of a house belonging to a landlord who liked to garden, fortunately, so the perennials and shrubs were not my responsibility. I particularly appreciated the lilacs, which I was allowed to cull for bedside bunches. Tossing one's face into a pile of fresh lilacs feels like such a lucky thing to do: not only is it a ravishingly sweet aroma—the smell of promises made in spring—but the fragrance utterly matches the colour. My bedroom was a wood-panelled hexagon that had once been a dining room. This seemed to have given me permission to do a lot of eating in bed: grapes, baby carrots, pretzels. I had a bay window in there that provided a great close-up of the brick wall of the house next door: obviously, someone had at some point been very stubborn about something. The whole building had a belligerent air, actually, poking its head up above the rest of the block to show off its bulky bones and multiple chimneys. The declamatory manner had sold me on the place years before when the rent was not quite as reasonable as it eventually became. By the time the market caught up with my peregrinations my landlord, Mr. Krauss, was rewarding me for my longevity.

My apartment was furthermore a soothing place in that hot water was included. So I reminded myself every time I took a shower, setting the nozzle to pulse and switching shoulder blades for a good ten minutes while I breathed in steam. They say whatever has most recently upset a female gets lodged in her shoulder muscles; evidently we like our pain nice and close to our brains. I generally showered as soon as I got home from the shelter. They also wanted us to get regular TB tests, but nobody ever fussed about that. It was so horrible when there were fist fights, or deaths from exposure, that we suppressed any extra drama. This was the last night of In From the Cold until autumn because the church couldn't budget for more. In eight hours the last morning crew would mop the mats with bleach while the porridge simmered; banishing bedbugs like this kept us five star by shelter standards. I knew that many of the clients would be back again the next winter. It was infuriating when newspaper articles indicated anything to the contrary.

I was too tired to blow dry, no I wasn't, yes I was . . . I would blow dry while my pasta water boiled. Another Concord Avenue thrill was the gas stove, a regular miracle of reliability. Every time I switched on the burners they'd chatter in busy alarm then poof into action, a beautiful soft blue with an orange core that warmed me to my organs. Taking pronounced joy in basic Western comforts seems like the right thing to do. I wonder if we tend to have more lunatic dreams in the developed world because our subconsciouses strain to wrap themselves around our freakish plenty. It would make for a good doctoral dissertation—geopolitically motivated Jungian analysis. I had thought for a while I would surpass Gail and become a university professor, a plan Gail welded into rigidity every chance she got, muttering on about tenure and sabbaticals the way some mothers drop hints about grandchildren. But I'd stalled after my

Masters despite knuckling under sufficiently to write the thing in fluent academia (*Radcliffe reifies The Other as a transcendent agent of Selfhood, thereby extrapolating the polarities of Self and Other into a subsuming whole*). My least glorious battles always seemed to be the ones that took place the most publicly.

As usual I went for whole wheat pasta, one part pasta to three parts produce, all of it doused in extra virgin olive oil redolent of sun beating down on Italian pastures. Culinarily, I was my own Tuscan grandmother. One of my greatest flavour, passions is for rapini. Admittedly, it's a bitter flavour, but sometimes I want to chomp into steamed, oily swabs of it so badly my jaw aches. I appreciate rough foods for the way they take almost as many calories to digest as they provide; you can consume an extra plateful that way. I dine bright: oranges, reds, yellows, purples and multiple greens. To be honest, I've long been caught in a relentless upward spiral of health. That's what happens when a plate of nachos gives you a two-day hang-over—you relinquish. At the U of T residence cafeteria I annulled Gail's bulgur and tempeh casseroles for as long as I could, delving into breaded this and creamed that: deep-fried sweet potato, four-cheese pizza, breakfast links. But I simply don't enjoy goo or offal. My vegetarianism is autonomic rather than visceral in that I cannot for the life of me understand why people who eat lambs and chickens don't also eat kittens and sparrows; drawing distinctions between the edibility of one type of animal over another honestly seems specious to me. I did cling to seafood for a while, which even Gail consumes since they are, after all, *les fruits de mer*. Then I had to ask her why on earth she dines on something that has spent its life bottom feeding.

One more workday and it would be Saturday, which meant several hours at the office as a rule. Then there would be Saturday night to spend all alone at home—a divinely voluptuous pleasure. I'd rent movies I had too little gumption to catch in the cinema. I'd buy berries and stir them into acidophilus yogourt and spoon up the fruit in front of the tube with magazines in my lap. I'd do a grand tour of my appliances: washing and drying, toaster ovening, maybe scanning, colour printing, downloading, uploading, surfing. Perhaps I'd mop the kitchen floor with the music up, the beleaguered couple upstairs likely forced out to a bistro with a gullet-spraining tasting menu and wines tediously matched to courses. Say what you will, your concerns are all pressed to the forefront when you dine out. What will be truly delicious? Which table in the room is the happiest? What person at the table is the happiest? Who loves what and shows it? I thought alcohol was seriously overrated. The damn stuff is absolutely draining.

2

Friday afternoon Desolée called from her shop to tell me there was no getting out of it, I was invited over to her place for dinner on Saturday night. Stash was at home making vegetarian cabbage rolls as she spoke, especially for me. Administrative Assistants' Day was over for another year and she was fucking well going to celebrate, now that every suck-up bouquet had been sent to every executive secretary on Bay Street whose boss had a complex. Moreover, Rex was expecting a *How are my favourite girls?* call, including all the Tuck Harbour gossip delivered twice in a row, once for each of us. Not that Desolée or I had any idea who it was that had been caught fishing oversized lobsters or stealing an ATV.

"Rex says he has something special to tell us," Desolée snipped. Plus I could hear her snipping. Everything at Blooms Inc. was carefully processed: leaves stripped from stems, stems fed into tubes, fresh buckets sent to front fridges.

"Special good or special bad?"

"Minnie, calm down. Special good, I think."

"Sorry. It's just, you know."

"I know."

We had started to talk each other through the unbearable

thought of losing Rex. Desolée had warned me I was going to have to deliver the eulogy. I had warned her I would lose it at the Tuck Harbour pulpit, gulls screeching along out in the cemetery, stony-faced parishioners appalled at my fuss. At least Rex had quit smoking and stopped wheezing.

"Okay, you win. What can I bring?"

"Nothing. You. Okay then, something juicy."

"Once OPEC gets taken over by Islamic despots and oil prices go through the roof no one will be shipping mangoes to North America."

"Flowers neither, thank fucking God. I'll have to figure out how to sell dandelions."

"Stash will take care of you. He'll still be young."

"Then you better stay on his good side, too."

I loved Stash. He and Desolée had been together for years, ever since he had started doing deliveries for Blooms Inc. to finance his first chapbook. Stash wrote intricate poetry, every word a quintuple entendre, maximum meaning conveying minimum consolation. For a cheerful guy he seemed to be in a lot of agony, lyrically. I suppose poetry has always supplied far more problems than it has solved; predicaments seemed to be the whole point through the ages. As a sideline Stash took to writing out his sonnets, villanelles and sestines in flowery calligraphy on homemade parchment, then photographed the texts, blew up enigmatic chunks and corners of it, and sleekly framed the results. These artworks were now going for a pretty and prettier penny. Stash and Desolée were finding it useful to cross-promote and share a production studio. Desolée had always promised Stash that he would catch up to her. She was eight years older than him, currently the outer edge of negligible as an age difference. I thought Desolée might have missed the old days, when she had been a cradle-snatching firebrand rather than a sensible mistress of two opposing sexual peaks.

Friday evening I worked until past eight, fuelled by Nicola Chalice's agreement to do the show, faxed in without any of the usual nervous glee. Once I had all my Saturday toil wrapped up a day early, I cabbed straight home and went for a long and winding jog in tirelessly rustling overpants. Then I ordered in a sourdough spinach feta pizza, toggled between talk shows and a late night Hitchcock and crashed. I was allowed to sleep in on weekends. I was proud that I could still sleep in; hormonally, it was becoming a real accomplishment.

Desolée and Stash lived what I considered a walk away, but that was perhaps wishful thinking on my part by the time they were almost expecting my request to be buzzed up. They had bought a condo together on Wellington Street West, a snazzy building with ramparts and catwalks and a hint of moat and drawbridge about the front entrance. I wrenched myself away from my own hearth and strode to the twenty-four-hour supermarket in the hopes of ripe papaya. I already had the dignified weight of French champagne dragging me down by one shoulder. I found some starfruit and guavas that I thought would also manage nicely beneath the artful swipes of Desolée's knives. I entered the shortest line—and then I dodged it fast.

Roger, an ex of medium vintage, was ahead in line wearing a baby. Roger's wife—grim-faced as a piece worker at a sneaker factory—emptied their cart of its mass of jars and packets while he folk danced with the bewildered infant harnessed to his torso, its dimpled mini hands clenching his long thumbs. I had split from Roger when I couldn't convince him to get on board the baby express. At the time he hadn't been *ready*. I hadn't been ready to prick holes in the condoms, which had been Desolée's advice, delivered as if I'd needed help figuring out how to wash my hands. Evidently Roger was now *ready* to dress a baby up in an elf hat and croon loudly beside the gum rack while his wife did the heavy lifting. I loitered until they made their way to the exit—knowing Roger, out to what was either a cartoon car or something the UN would use to get from one Sudanese province to another.

Running late is not one of my preferred forms of selfishness. I didn't want to miss Rex's bedtime. Nine o'clock in Toronto was ten o'clock in Prince Edward Island—an absurdly late hour for that element of PEI society unfamiliar with nicknames for drugs. I jaywalked at every opportunity and sped through the park—no time to spare for the Morris dance club practice going on in the band shell or the poodle fight in the dog run. I used some of the approximately eighteen mirrors between Desolée's lobby and her apartment door to make sure my bangs were concealing my eyebrows since I was in no mood to get tweezed. I saw I was busy surmising as usual; I have a gaze that isn't easily put to rest. *No rest for the wicked*, Rex always says, which I have never really understood since from my point of view the wicked are more likely to lie around doing nothing. Dear sweet Rex, I could hardly wait to hear his aged lilt. I ding-donged. I mock glowered at the spy hole. Stash's tunes were seeping right out the door so I rang again and waited. Onward evening, onward nourishment, onward family history. I thought I had better not get completely out of the habit of eating with others. Chewing communally, coordinating digestion, subtly mimicking each other's body language: all these stacked duties we endure in order to convey reception and animal understanding.

In the time it took Desolée to click her way to the front door— she wears heels at home because they are so imponderable at work— my thoughts flashed in Patrick's direction. I could have taken Patrick with me to this dinner. It would have been great for Desolée to get a chance to dispense counselling to someone who truly needed it, that and protein. Alas, the longed for parallel universe. Space and time curve more gently there.

"Voila," I said, holding out the champagne bottle by its neck like a hunter home with a turkey.

"That was for you, jerk. You were supposed to keep it for social emergencies. God, Minnie, why don't you ever let me give you anything?"

"Sorry. I'm not crazy about champagne. I think it's overrated."

"Now you tell me. Here, give me your coat. Holy shit, this thing is plush."

"You look great. You always look great."

Desolée is as stunning as a Supreme while sharing nothing of their mod aesthetic or unison dressing. Her wardrobe isn't all that plentiful, but she creates compelling combinations: dresses over trousers, blouses over dresses, aprons over skirts and this evening, successfully, a camisole over a sweater. Desolée's hair is Bottecelli in scope: far-ranging curls that she weaves into thick braids when they get to be too much for her. Desolée is slightly shorter than me but there are other differences between us that ring louder. Where I am angular Desolée has give; she is more liquid, more generous with her slopes and dips and mounds, altogether more womanly and more liable to induce a swoon, in a man if not a fashion editor. All this and strength, too; I have always been able to run faster, but Desolée wins every arm wrestle, hands down. She is cocoa and I am low-fat milk; no wonder it has always been so advantageous to stir ourselves into each other. I would be shocked, in a way, to be told Desolée and I are different races. Desolée does me the favour of rarely reminding me of that, no matter how often she might be re-minded herself. Her features are always fully furled or unfurled, depending on her expression. Tonight her eyes were tightened and her nose was flared. I smelled trouble. I heard trouble. A hearty male laugh that was not Stash's—a good sport's well-trained laugh.

"Who the hell is that?"

"Our upstairs neighbour Frank. He's *very* nice. Divorced. Loaded."

"Damn it, Des. I am so not in the mood."

"Yes you are. Penthouse. Cute kid. Custody on alternate week-ends. Jack Russell puppy. Come on."

"Jesus. Why does *Frank* want to eat vegetarian cabbage rolls?"

"Only yours are vegetarian. Don't worry, Stash baked them in a separate dish. Stop shouting."

"I'm not shouting."

"Well you're hissing. It's hurtful to Frank."

Desolée hurried back to her party basics. I was stranded alone in the foyer with ten seconds of tranquillity to my credit and then a threesome to broach, up to me to yank it into a foursome. I had been romantically ambushed. I had probably been keyword searched. Lord only knew how I had been described. This never worked, this never ever worked. People need to hunt each other on terrain they roam, not get introduced in cages. Since when was forty not too old for this? When exoneration? When release to the bleak tundra? When my own ice floe?

"Hello, I'm Minnie." I strode into the room like a surgeon on rounds, shaking the hand of a man who looked very nice, of course, since Desolée was not completely without tact. Nice as in twinkly and harmless.

"Frank!"

He was immediately to his feet despite an airplane-pillow-sized layer of something abdominally subcutaneous that I was sure he was inclined to forgive himself for, being such a nice guy. He had on glasses that were too rimless to suit him. He had very smooth, round, rosy cheeks. Frank was going to be Smooth Cheeks forever-more whenever I needed him as a reference point. All over the culture, men were being reduced to common nouns. Frank had on a mock navy turtleneck with a distinct whiff of investment about it— to go along with all his other no doubt numerous investments, real, mutual and emotional. Unfortunately I was wearing an almost identical sweater. Not that I shop in the menswear department, but I shop based on touch. A Saturday evening towards the end of April was the perfect send-off to everyone's favourite cashmere.

"How do you do, Frank." Was that a question? Because I had not intonated it as a question—more like a prognosis. Tune the social instrument, Minerva, for crying out loud.

"Nice to finally meet you, Minnie. Desolée tells me you're in television."

"Yes I am. Excuse me for that!"

Chuckles all around. The worst of it was that I would now have to drink. And having a drink would deprive me of the acuity I needed to stick to one drink. And Desolée had drummed up cassis for the champagne. And in anticipation of the friendly feast I had not eaten all day, another spinster privilege. Clutching my cold flute, I took the only chair that wasn't a loveseat and left poor Frank the whole couch to himself. That was after I had hugged Stash, lean and limber Stash of the ever-changing beard and moustache formations like silt in a very active estuary. Lately he'd gone Fu Manchu. Stash was shamelessly hogging the party dips and jumping up to fast forward through his music files.

Desolée loved to run her fingers through Stash's mop, which was always clean enough to cascade from one side of his forehead to the other, probably because Stash never ran his own hands through it, just shook it out of the way. There would be no more running of hands through Frank's hair, which was perhaps all for the best since it seemed to have been a bright, wiry russet.

"Frank is in finance," Desolée called over from the kitchen bar where she was tossing a meaty-looking spinach salad like a woman in an advertisement for granite countertops, or savings accounts, or the latest hopeful breast cancer medication.

"Money markets," Frank specified. "Currency trading."

"Hey, back off of my zloty!" said Stash with a fake Polish accent.

More chuckles, still all around. It was going to be hard not to get trashed and shag Frank just to spare everyone's feelings what with the onus on me to keep pride soothed in every direction.

"Finance is very ... inevitable," I tried.

"Oh, honey no!" said Desolée. Stash had reached for his baggie. The man loved a pre-dinner joint. The new condo upholstery was already fragrant with sweet weed, the price Desolée paid for an extra helping of calm.

"I'll open a window," I said, happy for any excuse to jump up, happy to spare myself more of the sad, stabbing sight of Frank accepting the proffered stub and sucking on it with Daffy Duck lips, his fingers Versailles dainty, his eyes alive to his unexpected mischief. Obviously, the night no longer belonged to anyone but Frank, the brave veteran from the divorce wars who might as well have come to dinner wrapped in bandages. Little did he know, Frank's intoxication was now going to make him even more forlorn. I wanted to stay out on Desolée's balcony. Lake Ontario glimmered as enormous as ever, forgotten as usual by anyone who was not looking right at it. From this vantage point the Toronto skyline looked concentrated rather than dribbling—a children's chorus of towers gathered together to sing of the glory that is post-colonialism.

"Minnie, get in here, we have to call Rex before we have any more bubbly," Desolée shouted.

"Their great uncle," Stash explained to Frank in the clamped voice of a man unwilling to exhale.

"Gotcha," Frank muttered. He sat as pert as a canary, ankles crossed; it was the comfort of a man who had no need to use the facilities, but knew there would always be facilities should he need them.

"Honey, don't you dare get out your conga drums while we're on the phone, you know how it confuses Rex. He gets scared I've gone tribal."

"Excuse us," I said to Frank, who beamed up at me, his grin digging into his wadded cheeks. I had meant it every which way. Excuse us for inviting you to an event that has caused you to gush expectation like blood from a world war wound. Excuse us for the misinformation: I am not available, I offer you nothing that can be ticked off a list. Excuse us for eventually discussing you in a way that it will not occur to you to discuss us, and if you do we won't care.

"Well?" asked Desolée once we were within the confines of her cream, off-white, ecru bedroom that bore nothing floral.

"Well what?"

"He's nice, right?"

"Sure he's nice."

"Honestly, Minnie, you are too fussy. Compromise. Fucking com-pro-mise. The rest of us do it, maybe it's about time you did, too. I always thought you'd make a great second wife. Well, here he is, and his kid is really sweet, and you should see his place, it's totally Italian up there. Kind *and* successful, how often do you get that in one package? He's into you, I can tell."

"I warned you, I've given up."

"Fine, be an idiot then. See if I care."

"Let's just call Rex. Pass the phone, I'll go first this time."

Second wife. Stepmother. Mrs. Frank So and So. A life larded with guarantees, trussed up with safety nets, punctuated with *just checking in, honey.* Frank's shoes lined up in a neat Noah's Ark row at the bottom of his arithmetically stocked closet, with that smell men's clothes always have of being a bit burnt. I'd be someone to gripe to about the chairman. Someone to inveigle into eating T-bones at the steak house before catching the latest art house hit. Someone who'd share the ceiling fan during heat waves. Would I love Frank back if he was in a wheelchair? I'd always thought that was the clincher, but then Desolée said the clincher was adult diapers.

I knew Rex's number off by heart, a rare recommendation lately. It whirred repeatedly in my ear, which was no cause for alarm, rather the contrary; Rex never answered right away now that he took care to cross slowly from rug to rug.

"Well hello!" Rex always said hello as if he was congratulating us for existing.

"Hi, Uncle Rex, it's Minnie. How are you?"

"Fine, fine, fine. I'm moving out, dear. Would you by chance like to move in?"

"You're what?"

"I'm moving into the old age home in Montague. I want to give it a try. My legs are bad, dear, you know that. They have a nice room empty on the main floor. I'm going to see how I like it is all."

"A nursing home?" I asked this of Rex and Desolée at once. She stopped punching her pillows and thumped down beside me. Any second she would grab the receiver. Whatever was happening, I had to work fast to get it straight in my head.

"For the summer just to start with, dear. These legs, you know."

"You used the furnace this winter, right? You didn't exhaust yourself chopping?"

"I only chopped what I wanted to, I promise you that."

There was a big wood stove in Rex's kitchen. Rex's kitchen was huge. Rex's house was huge: an old farmhouse that he had purchased fully furnished as a young man and never stocked with a wife and children. It had old linoleum in the hallways printed to look like carpet. It had five bedrooms, each with a bed, each bed with just one blanket. It had a parlour with wing chairs, a musty American encyclopaedia set and engravings of nineteenth-century farm life that seemed pinpointed but had probably always been generic. The house had a terribly grave air, which, thanks to Rex, had long gone somewhat ironic. It was yellow with red trim, the same as the barn.

"Is this what you really want, Uncle Rex?"

"Oh yes, dear, I'd love to see you in a place you can count on."

"What about Dosie?"

Dosie was a nag of twenty-eight that Rex had bought when he was sixty-six. She had never been properly trained, but she had always been well treated so at this point she was just very, very boring.

"That's the thing. Dosie can graze as she likes. Colin will look in on her to see her fountain is working and her salt lick is good."

"Rex, I don't think I can—"

"Uncle Rex? It's Desolée. How are you?... No, no you're right, *I* can't but you never know, maybe Minnie will be able to. Can you go ahead and move to Montague for now?... Yes, I think it will be loads of fun. And lots of chickies to flirt with!... You're a fine specimen of manhood, Uncle Rex, just ask the church ladies... Oh, the condo is great. You would love it. You have to come and visit. We'll put you in the TV room... No, we never use it... uh-huh... oh yes, Mother's Day *and* Father's Day, no mercy for me... Great Uncle's Day, good one! I'll see if I can get that going... For sure... Don't forget your bathing suit!... Okay... Sounds like a plan..."

To be fair I knew Desolée worried about Rex as much as I did, but in their conversations she always managed to dingle jester bells as opposed to my fretful interrogations about his electric blanket, blood pressure and holiday activities. And now I would have to add to my regular slate of worries this baffling new headline of worry— Rex wanted me to toss aside everything I had going for me in Toronto and spend the summer or longer in Tuck Harbour. For ages we had all been warning Rex to bequeath everything to his charity of choice, haunted house included.

"Minnie wants to say goodbye. Bye, Uncle Rex, love ya." Desolée held out the receiver. I was scared to move; my heart felt like a big blood blister.

"Hi, Uncle Rex, me again."

"Are you okay, Minnie, my dear? You sound like you've got yourself tired."

"Oh no, not really. I'm busy as a bee, but you know me, I like it that way. I'm just worried about you."

"I'm fine, dear. Colin is coming with his truck to move my things. Shall I take the encyclopedia with me?"

"Very funny."

No one read the encyclopedia anymore; absolutely everyone was allergic to whatever spore had grown in the bindings. But I had sneezed through a lot of it when I was little, back when Gail and Lee and Desolée and I had been back to the Island for funerals 1 and 2. I got as far as the J's. Jackal, Jack-knife, Jack'o'lanterns. Gail taught me how to read when I was a toddler; I went pretty well straight from pabulum to flash cards. My pediatrician was angry that I'd been ushered so hurriedly into my own little world, but I respected Gail's impulse. I was grateful to her for making so much so legible for so long.

"I'll leave K for you, shall I, dear? You can take another crack at it this summer."

"One step at a time, Uncle Rex. Right now we want you safe and settled."

"I'll call you both from Montague next week then. Cheerio!"

Rex never said formal goodbyes, he was more like someone on horseback: a fast adieu and then off to trot.

"Don't worry, Min." Desolée put the phone back on the bedside table, her side. "You can't move to PEI. Rex knows that, he's just being stubborn."

"How can I not worry? I don't want him to feel, shit, repudiated."

"Let me top up that drink. It's the only thing that's going to help right now."

There was nothing to do but traipse back into the living area. I sat beside Frank this time, my fleshy anchor for the evening. I asked him what his little girl's name was and how she got along at nursery school and where he had grown up. I asked him to please pass the crackers. I ordered Stash to get out the bongos after all. I complimented Desolée on her new throw pillows. I tried to distract myself with everything in eye's reach that was in any way incidental. To disappoint Rex, of all people. Never had I thought I'd see the day, not with all my city sins filed far away, not with my innumerable promises to Rex himself that I would *take care*. I had never experienced self-interest so badly cross-referenced with panic. But there was no point discussing this, not even if Desolée had let me get away with it. Not with my tongue thickened in my mouth, my eyeball ligaments loose and my inner ears sloshy. I was slightly hammered on my way to totally smashed.

We wended our way to the dining table: a horizontal pane of frosted glass that allowed us to spy on our hazy bottom halves while we made busy with our top halves. We were soon devouring bread sopped in tomato sauce and trotting out stories we were used to telling.

"How did you get your latest job, Minnie?" Frank wanted to know.

"I was headhunted," I said. "My first time, but I'm sure you're used to it."

"Minnie was the brains behind *Nude Radio*," Desolée bragged, bless her for that. She spooned the last of the salad onto my plate.

"The retooling of CBC Radio Two on Saturday nights," I specified. "No more concertos. It's all talk and new music now."

"She's very BBC." Stash had programmed the BBC radio website to play out the condo speakers and could now imitate the accents of about fifteen different British deejays.

"How did you neighbours meet?" I like to keep people guessing when the obvious questions will come.

"Stash and I were looking for the utility room. We thought it was on the top floor." Desolée did her wrong-answer-in-a-game-show buzzer noise.

"His Highness here directed us to the sub-penthouse." Stash offered Frank a court bow as he got up to clear the table.

"Who gets to live up top with you, Frank? Besides your dog?"

"A big-time basketball player." Desolée was bussing small bowls into bigger bowls with the speed of a three-card monte shyster. "Frank says he's a total slut."

"Right, men can be sluts, too." If I had scored the last of the salad then I figured I could nab the butt end of the bread, too. "Now that women can be assholes."

"My cousin never behaves herself, Frank. I forgot to warn you."

"At least you warned me she's smart!"

Frank wiggled whenever he had an enjoyable announcement to make, his pelvis sprung loose by festivity. I could picture him playing with dinky toys way back when, making putt-putt noises in the rec room. Stash and Desolée looked to be doing a slow form of salsa dancing over by the dishwasher. Whenever they tipped they laughed.

"Cheers, Frank. It's great to make a new pal."

Desolée and Stash inevitably whipped cream once people's weaknesses had set in. After five loud minutes with the beaters we had gloops of cinnamon-dusted butterfat overlaying our fresh fruit. And we had cumulus cream clouds bobbing in our coffee. Then Stash concocted a round of frothy shooters that had me belying my rule number one: never drink something I can't see through. When Stash started trotting out Polish jokes it was time to go. At the coat closet Frank slipped me his card, which specified his managing direction. If ever I needed currency traded by someone with an eye out further than normal for my welfare, I certainly knew where to go. I went home. I watched the tail end of *Klute* on the movie classics channel with my left hand over my left eye to keep the television from pitching back and forth inside my whirling apartment, then slept with my sweater and socks on all night long.

⌒

Sunday afternoon my brain felt like it was full of fried eggs, my thoughts slipping on the grease. I carted around the front section of the newspaper like a security blanket, crumpling it up but not reading it. I did not jog. I did not check email. I barely moved.

With so little mental traction, I didn't worry as much about Rex's odd invitation. Rex had allowed himself to get used to the idea of having me nearby, true. But the rest of us could make such a huge distracting fuss over what Rex *did* have going on, rather than what he didn't, that he'd soon forget I had failed to show. We'd up the ante on the joys of getting all his meals prepared by experts in geriatric digestion. We'd emphasize the fun to be had in regular bingo afternoons and dissecting other people's visitors. Rex's life would soon fill back up to its brim. Desolée's number rang mid Sunday afternoon while I was sitting on my bathtub ledge eyeing the toilet. I paid her the courtesy of not calling back. By evening I was able to get down a banana and honey sandwich. I sat at my kitchen table with my face cupped in my hands for half an hour afterward, amazed at how small faces are when one gets right down to them. The best thing about the day was making it to bed before midnight, a pleasure as infrequent as a good date and probably more beneficial to the psyche. Monday morning I was back on the job.

The latest *Fabulous Getaway* shoot was wrapping early with plenty of canoodling and bickering in the can. Luce had the upcoming Compatibility Quiz finalized with adaptations in Nicola

Chalice's honour: (*Your preferred romantic tactic is a) Persuasion, b) Pride and Prejudice, c) Sense and Sensibility or d) ripping out pages and starting all over again.*) All the quiz participants were booked to arrive at the studio Friday 9 a.m. sharp. We had plain shirts and blouses on hand in case anyone had ignored our instructions not to wear houndstooth. Hardy Rutgers was flying in from Sudbury on Thursday afternoon and renting a car. Mr. Device and Scientist Gent were driving themselves. The real estate agent and department store manageress had taken us up on limos. Nicola Chalice was scootering; I shushed everyone after one too many jokes about losing her on the highway.

Luce was on the job in person now rather than telecommuting, answering my line in her industrious monotone so I had a bit of time to do prep on *Switcheroo*. I was convinced we'd soon have takers. Pinpointed questions were starting to come in from Kiddo Network execs and the CBC. Sure, we'd had some rejections early on, from programmers who failed to understand that this was not purely kids' stuff, that those of us who were the deepest soaked in life's bitter juices stood to learn the most from youngsters getting a second chance at defining themselves. What's more significant than one's identity? Admittedly, I was biased as a first-world citizen; we expect each other's identities to assume maximum volume in the West. I thought maybe *Switcheroo* should send some North American kid to live with Kalahari tribespeople or outer Mongolians—any nomadic nation lacking a bedroom-poster tradition. By Thursday afternoon the CBC bailed on *Switcheroo*, citing insurance concerns.

"Morons," I said to Luce.

In her dreams Luce Lee was a wasp-waisted film noir secretary; in reality she just cleared five feet. She did not actually belong to a Japanese fashion cult so much as look like she belonged to two at once: manga super heroine on the bottom and schoolgirl up above. Luce was the oil on my water. She could calm me down even when the interns sent emails hopping with emoticons and *there* for *they're*.

"Don't sweat it, man. You haven't got the final word from

Kiddo yet. By the way, I did remind Angela that Mr. Device and the real estate lady should scoop the *Getaway*."

Luce hated my double-checking, knowing it was a waste of her time. She had a corner desk and used the bulk of her shelves for dictionaries and spider plants. I could tell she wanted to get back there, not microscopically examine the likelihood that Kiddo would get back in touch with me with a doable offer by the end of Friday.

"You know what? I need some air. I need a lot of air. Hold the fort if you would. I'm out of here."

Luce grew an inch and gleamed. The interns promised to go easy on the *Reply All* button. I told Barry I would be in extra early in the morning and he waved goodbye. I headed out into the urine-coloured late April afternoon. When the cabbie asked where to, I was surprised, in a way that he wasn't, to hear myself ask for my old college. I'd always loved the crackle in the quad air during exam time. Desolée had gone somewhere western and bracingly modern for Communication Studies but I'd wanted lore, tradition and Oxbridge airs and graces—found in Toronto's dead centre. Traffic did not necessarily rush right through my old campus but it had not been diverted very far. I felt as vacuumed in as ever. The quad was still otherworldly; sound here carried on the air differently. All of a sudden there were birds chirping, and university girls chirping, too, congregated in duos and trios with leather sacks hanging from their shoulders. University student bodies were now two thirds female; no matter how academic one's goals, that had to be a downer for a feminine eighteen-year-old humanities major. There were some boys around as well—young men in hoods despite their alpine grade point averages. They were starting to drop into the dining hall, easily mistaken for a minor cathedral. I decided to poke my head into the library.

I'd forgotten that I'd need a student card to pass through the wickets. I was going to get quite the bruise on my groin from the brutal little stile. There were no librarians to look up in alarm; too much was now computerized for that. I was about to slink out when

I caught sight of myself, of myself as I had never become, of myself as another woman my age had become—after a no doubt arduous dissertation process and numerous fights for lecturing positions and an eventual habit of bringing in top drawer student evaluations. Eager undergrads were detaining her in the library foyer before she could get to her office. I pictured a top-of-the-line laptop and a correspondingly ancient carpet plus wraparound book-shelves with a shelf across the radiator for more books. And photos, of course, silver framed portraits of her and her man and their boy and girl. My professor self was casually yet stylishly yet cozily dressed, like someone in the Scottish gentry, with thick dark hair chopped off at her neck bone and a side part. She was holding a heavy leather briefcase. She was holding everyone's attention, teasing them about her no extension policy maybe, or the idea that every seminar that term should be delivered in olde Saxon. Then a note of seriousness settled over the little crowd. Someone had asked advice about how to give agency to the marginalized in a time of teleological fascism perhaps. Or how to take Chaucer as seriously as Al Qaeda. I could picture her at the chalkboard, the way her hips swung a little bit, the way her handprints showed up for the rest of the hour lightly dusted on her ass. Her face was a combination of fresh and weathered, like a first read of a great text. She was still supple enough to stick her feet up on the desk in front of her when the deconstructing got good. There but for my lack of grace went I. She sensed that someone was mesmerized and so did a couple of her students, turning to look at me just as my phone buzzed. That was my excuse to bolt with a forlorn smile as if I hated to leave them.

It was Luce calling to tell me that Hardy Rutgers had dropped by the studio a day early—with fudge.

"Maple," said Luce. "I'll save you some."

I was going to tell Luce not to bother then I shut myself up. Fudge would last in my desk drawer until I needed to do a little buttering-up of my own.

"I'd ask you what he's like but I doubt I need to."

"He's a doll. He made Angela blush. Should we report it to a medical journal?"

"How on earth did he do that?"

"Just by being nice to her, I guess."

"Luce, time to go home. Big day tomorrow."

"Screw that. My mom is baby-sitting. I've already called in my order at the Hog. Over and out."

Luce was the proud single mother of Cordy, short for Cordelia, a whip-smart three-year-old who was going through a lot of dollar-store tiaras. Luce bought her toy soldiers to no avail. The Hog & Dog was the ersatz pub where a klatch of Myriad staffers did happy hour, eschewing weekends out now that the most attractive nights to hit the town came early in the week, climaxing on Thursday. Plodding north towards Bloor I put in a quick call to my cousin.

"Has Rex moved yet?" I asked.

"Minnie, hooray, you're alive. I haven't talked to him. Let's do that tomorrow. Drop by my place after work. Stash'll get a movie."

"I'll try. We're taping."

"What did you do to Frank? Stash says there's elevator strain."

"Nothing. Literally nothing. Romantic miscarriage, very sad, it happens all the time."

"God, you're a pain. Always have been. Good thing I'm used to you."

Desolée needed to stop berating me in traffic; it made it hard to compute the meaning of flashing green. I'd crossed too soon and been honked at. An elderly couple in matching camel coats tut-tutted to see me dither, their hackles raised in perfect tandem that had taken years of patient newspaper section trading to accomplish. "I've got to go, Des."

"Me, too. Some bigwig is retiring, Centrepiece City."

I wanted to catch the organic boutique before it closed, grateful as ever for discus-sized portabellas and avocadoes that took a dent, every country of origin posted by the in-house calligrapher. By going organic as often as possible I figured fields were going to end up healthier if not me. But I wanted to end up healthier as well, now that vitality was my primary source of erotic satisfaction. Hence my walk the whole way home, faster the closer I got.

I stripped to my underpants as soon as I got in the door and draped myself over my Concord Avenue stability ball, this one red. I could go a day without serious cardio only if it was a day in which I stretched beyond human reason, stretched in ways that filled my head with blood, stretched until I gasped at how hard it was to bend to my own purposes. Sleep came that night as it often did: like opium. It was becoming less easy to admit to myself, but impossible to hide from myself, the fact that I sleep entirely undisturbed.

3

Friday morning, the office at Myriad was quiet, but the production studio was hopping. Audience members were pooling in the foyer: friends and family of the contestants and friends and classmates of the interns. The interns' main task was to plump up our in-studio audience, so I had bitched to them at Monday's all-staff meeting. I said I did not care who the hell they corralled as long as they were sentient. This time I wanted every row filled. Finally, I had been obeyed. Numerous kids were streaming in who looked like they'd skipped Production 101. And Graffiti 101. We could snatch close-ups of the cute ones. Kevin, our best cameraman, sturdy, shaggy and gentle, was outside gathering arrival shots to edit together later for the episode intro.

Luce was already on set wearing her studio poncho; the temperature in there was North polar to subdue the tetchy equipment. Nerves usually kept me warm until I noticed my teeth chattering. I loved the operating-room urgency at play. Soon the set would be lit as necessary, wired for sound as necessary, dusted and dressed as necessary—pop art on the walls and red shag carpeting on the floor, three twisty blue stools stage right for the male contestants and three twisty pink stools stage left for the ladies. Angela would start off in the middle, but was wirelessly miked in order to wander over to whoever needed the most attention. Hal, the director, was barking at Danny, the audio guy. There always had to be at least one bud microphone that wasn't working properly right up until the last minute. I would have preferred not to see Danny balled out to the point of quivering; within an hour he would have to clip a mike to the bodice of Nicola Chalice. I made my way to the green room to find out which of our guests had shown up.

Hardy Rutgers was pre-eminent: slapping his competitors' backs in a way that turned up the noses of Mary-Jane and Dawn, the real estate agent and department store manageress respectively. The ladies retreated to a corner, to bond whisperingly over water sipped from bottles blotched crimson. They should not have sneered at Hardy; he was as dear as a nursery rhyme character. He had on a linen suit and polka-dotted socks with a matching kerchief and bow tie. His neck was so subtle he was Babushka shaped; if we were lucky there were going to be Hardy upon Hardys contained within.

"Yummy!" Hardy had been presented with the muffin tray. "Breakfast cake! A plate? Wonderful, I would love a plate. Carrot, blueberry or bran, yum yum yum, which one should I have?!"

"Carrot's my favourite," I stepped forth to say.

"Is that so? Carrot it is then. Good for the eyeballs. Now who is this I might ask?"

"Minnie Gallant," I said. "We spoke."

"Minnie! You're the reason I'm here, you enchantress. I have you to blame for everything."

"I'm so glad you could make it." I patted Hardy's arm to let him know that I was solid, too.

Jack (Mr. Device) Drentz was more cursory with his greetings as befit his front-runner status, which had been hard for any of us not to intimate by inference and inflection. He was wearing a polo shirt with a golf club crest that suggested petty nobility. Thinning seemed to be improving his hair, making him look less crested, less determinedly in season. Jack had not been lying when he'd said that he was six feet on the nose. He had the proud nose of a man who was exactly six feet, a nose without pity that would never really get pity. It was not at all like Hardy's nose, which looked like a bump in a buttery bun. In fact, Hardy was buttering his muffin; I had not thought anyone did that anymore. Our research scientist, Richard Munk, was deductive enough of mentality to realize that he had taken a wrong turn to somewhere very puzzling. I had promised him that we were in the *factual entertainment* business. He was slightly taller than Jack, but stooped until he was shorter, with hands that were nervous about whether they belonged in his pockets or not (Jack's did). His palm was moist. I would ask Luce to ask Angela to go easy on him.

Not so the ladies, who were straining like little bulls ready for the arena. Possibly they had both just treated themselves to hair extensions for the occasion, for the price of a third-hand car—tresses that had been donated by a needy maiden to a temple in the hinterland of India. The braid would have been bleached and treated in Italy, then shipped stateside. Hair was glued to a customer's head in time-consuming rows using small blobs of melted protein that would have to be professionally cracked apart three months later, entailing another small fortune. I had learned all about it on Sunday afternoon, glazed in front of *Fashion Television*. Obviously, we needed a vanity tax and we needed to set it high. Both the ladies had also taken advantage of some new millennium denim, their posteriors carved into bold new shapes thanks to rear seams that worked like brassieres.

I sent the men into makeup first. Jack looked grim but expectant, as if he had been warned about this by other reality show studs. Richard had been forewarned in detail, I had seen to that myself, but he nonetheless seemed totally perplexed by the foundation airbrush, although if anyone had asked him about the interaction of coloured pigment with a focused light he would have had a quantum answer.

I made my way back to the ladies to thank them once more for coming and to double-check that Mary-Jane had a certain *nous ne savons quoi* over Dawn. They both looked up from the false comfort of the green-room sofa; not in obvious alarm but I could tell from the arching of their waxed brows that they had been startled. Not by me. Nicola Chalice had just walked into the green room wearing a big white scooter helmet, the strap still snug under her chin. Luce hurried over to take her coat. Nicola Chalice said thank you, then fully emerged. Her head only seemed small now because her hips were in evidence despite serviceable grey flannel trousers. We all awaited the requisite hat head fuss. Instead Nicola Chalice tugged a tissue out the end of her left sweater sleeve and briskly blew her nose. Mary-Jane and Dawn relaxed. Mr. Device was theirs, all theirs. Whoever did not nab him today could email later to suggest drinks.

"Morning. Nicola," we were told one by one. Nicola Chalice was so tall that her nods were not obsequious, in fact almost the opposite.

"Minnie Gallant," I said. "Welcome."

"Yes, well."

Nicola Chalice's grip was as presidential as the other ladies' had been maidenly. Everyone's great beauty is their eyes and Nicola Chalice's eyes looked like they had garnered oracular truths over the ages. They were Wedgwood eyes, inkwell eyes, an illuminated new blue to take account of. Although Luce came close to mimicking them when she freaked everybody out by wearing blue contact lenses. Reading glasses hung around Nicola's neck. I doubt it bothered her that she had hips minus a bust; she probably felt more balanced that way.

"You found us all right?" I cursed my inanity.

"Thanks to your expert directions, yes." She was forgiving.

"We'll pop you ladies into makeup soon. We should get taping within an hour and we'll be all done by lunch." I hugged my clipboard close to my chest. Now that I had met Nicola Chalice my notes were more off limits than ever.

"You didn't warn us we could make it back to work today, Ms. Gallant. That hardly seems fair." Nicola evidently liked to drag people out of the deadpan into the fire.

"Oh, I'm not going back to the office today!" said Dawn.

"Cocktails!" said Mary-Jane.

The aged babes risked a high five, which failed to make proper contact, one little beringed and manicured hand not quite slapping the other.

Nicola Chalice accepted a cup of tea from Luce, and I saw that she had big bony hands that were perfectly clean of freckles, the kind of hands one might see in an instructional diagram. I made a mental note never to bother pitying Nicola Chalice for anything and in turn to pity anyone who insisted on pitying Nicola Chalice. Pity seemed to have taken over from flirtation as my most complicated energy. I smiled once more at Nicola before I headed to the studio. She had the kind of face that didn't really need to smile back. I still wasn't sure how old she was.

It was taking longer than usual to get the taping underway due to the swollen studio audience. Finally we configured the kids and settled them down. *The Marry Me or Else!* theme music bubbled up and halted while starting positions got confirmed. With an unprecedentedly loud cheer from the audience, the contestants were shown to their stools: Jack and Mary-Jane on the inside for improved sexual tension, plus they would show up over Angela's shoulders. Hardy and Nicola were given the outside flanks. Richard was nicely buttressed. Dawn was mistakenly happy to get the middle. Everyone had their blue or pink clipboard in hand, and blue or pink marker to jot down their Compatibility Quiz answers. We could have gone with wireless styluses, but I'd argued that something retro would suit our *vibe*, and besides that erasing would soothe our guests. Luce had on her headphones, catcher to my umpire. Barry had a live feed to his office to keep an eye on us, but for the most part we were stuck with our own competencies. Now Angela wanted a word.

"The taller guy and the dirty blonde, right, boss?"

Unlike Luce, Angela frequently ingratiated herself by double-checking, but to her counter purposes she left it to the last minute. Angela always spat out her gum right before we rolled. I was worried one day she wouldn't, thereby forcing me to take charge to the degree that I would thoroughly become my mother. Not that I had all that much against Gail, but Gail herself was a firm believer in never becoming your mother. As of New Years, poor Angela had a gum habit and a pack-a-day habit both. She was too scared to relinquish herself to a non-smoker's metabolism to quit, constantly loitering outside the building as if she had never really got the job. I'd hired Angela because I wanted someone who ultimately wanted people to make fun of her.

"That's right, Ange. And please go easy on the scientist if you could."

"The droopy-looking guy?"

"That would be him."

"We gotta have a couple of 'em way past their prime or what's the point of the show, right?"

"You got it."

Angela had not been too proud to sidle up to a number of our gentleman also-rans after the tapings. She had defied enough familial expectation already in becoming a potty-mouthed wisecracker with a collection of T-shirts better suited to a fourteen-year-old boy, her double D's be damned. Angela was not now also going to go without a mate.

"Is my outfit okay, boss?"

A ruffled hot-pink blouse with more of those teen jeans and boots with toes that looked like weaponry—we had hired a stylist to get this right. Angela was not allowed to keep her outfits. There was no way we could have afforded that now that a wardrobe full of ladies' play clothes cost the same as a cargo of wheat.

"You look great. Go have fun."

Out with the gum. On with the theme music for real. We were rolling on the last Compatibility Quiz, later to be aired as the first half of Episode 12, with the last Fabulous Getaway to follow. As the crane camera worked the crowd, I saw Danny jump to lower the sound levels on the audience. Hal scrutinized his monitors like they were trained on a war zone. Angela beamed while she waited for Luce's voice to penetrate her earpiece and coach her step by step. Hardy was laughing already. Nicola Chalice was grinning, too.

Things started off as planned in that Jack warmed up to Mary-Jane when they both answered that they would rather fly their own plane than first class (Dawn and Hardy's choice) or in a helicopter (Richard and Nicola's choice) or in a balloon (Hardy's final choice on second thought). Jack and Mary-Jane's bond was further solidified when they both thought that a mink coat was an appropriate gift from a man to a woman, that a Big Bertha golf club was an appropriate gift from a woman to a man and that a ring ought to cost the same as two mortgage payments. Everything was going fairly well, provided Dawn did not burst into tears if Angela accused her one more time of peeking at Mary-Jane's answers. Dawn was getting the brunt of things because Richard was going largely unscathed as directed and Nicola and Hardy were the crowd favourites. Especially when they both admitted to eating saltines in bed, they both claimed to think sex was better if the dog was watching, and they both decided nothing ruined a date except for a bad case of the trots. By the end of the final round, Nicola and Hardy were tied with Jack and Mary-Jane on the *Marry Me or Else!* Compatibility Scale—comically indicated with an animated calculator I'd asked Barry to invest in knowing playful graphics were essential to our brand. Nine Compatibility Points each. Of course, the audience knew best when it came to matters of the heart. Cut to commercial. Time to coax the rowdies into clapping for the obvious. No worries there: Danny could adjust the sound afterwards to back up my executive decision. I made my way over to the hooting rows. Heretofore, my authority had been expressed aloofly. Now I was in charge.

"Thanks, guys, you've been great." We are all of us *guys* nowadays.

"We know," said a little thing in a shrunken pink parka with pink fuzz trim.

"So after the break you're going to clap for the couple you want to win. Not just, you know, the one that's the most fun but the one that's the best bet."

"Go Har-dy, go Har-dy!" A young Turk with an indoor/outdoor toque.

"But let's clap for the couple who fit together the best, okay?"

Their boomer parents had raised them to be their little friends; now they were going to have to get wheedled into everything forever, especially the ones whose boomer parents were no longer friends with each other.

"Nicola rocks!"

"People." My hands were in prayer position. "I think we all know who's a real match here today so I'm going to trust you to make the right choice. You've accumulated a little power of deduction, right? A tiny bit of reason? All those video games must have taught you something. Quiet off the top please. Thanks again for coming, everyone."

The *Marry Me or Else!* visual convention was for the camera to pan all over the crowd while our Applause-o-Meter graphic pulsed mid screen, tallying votes. Previous crowds had been so meek that in order to get a real winner the camera operators had had to veer around maniacally and Danny had tapped the sound library for extra claps. Not so this week. Richard and Dawn were nowhere near the running, but they each got a loud hand. Jack and Mary-Jane were not outright spurned, but merely politely congratulated. Hardy and Nicola brought the house down. Not just fingers-in-the-mouth whistles, but riser pounding and fists in the air and spontaneous hula dances. I looked over at Hal, who shrugged. I could have put in a call to Barry to ask him if he wanted circumstances manipulated, but I knew he would blame me for *control freaking*, for not letting instinct *have its way*, for being insufficiently *raw*. Hardy was elated, peering from his outermost blue stool towards Nicola's outermost pink stool, sending her merry waves. Nicola was as calm in her victory as if it had been the ordered result of a task no less intentional than the Dewey decimal system. Still, her eyes flashed sky.

I nodded feebly at Luce. Luce spoke to Angela and Angela charged over to Nicola. She grabbed Nicola with one hand, then Hardy with the other, escorted both of them centre ring, and told everyone at home to stay right there because they'd find out how the happy couple fared on their *Getaway* coming up in the second half. Angela step back; happy couple arm link; cut to a jubilant crowd member; cut to stunned Mary-Jane, one more wide shot, one more blast of theme song and we were wrapped.

It didn't seem like Cozumel would now be the ticket. In-pool margarita bars would have worked for Jack and Mary-Jane, but Hardy looked like he had endured one burn too many in his lifetime and Nicola was unlikely to stay still long enough for a chaise longue shot. As for side-by-side beach gazebo massages, forget it. Where on earth we should send the pair of them to keep them happy enough that they left with their dignity in working order I was not sure. Nicola Chalice shook a fist good-naturedly at a wolf whistler who disappeared back under his baseball brim and clomped down the bleachers. Of course Nicola Chalice could handle antics and monkey business; she had been reading picture books aloud in a children's nook all her professional life.

Happily for Mary-Jane she made a plan with Jack to go out for a consolation bite. Unhappily for Mary-Jane, Jack invited Dawn as well. He wanted to prolong his choice as usual, or he wanted to choose neither by pretending to want both. Richard was shell-shocked, but the two tweenage nephews he had brought along distracted him; he probably hadn't caused their faces to shine so brightly since he'd made a lucky guess at a toy store. Angela was distributing signed postcards of herself in a rock pig stance to every little lout who would take one on his or her way out. I was not about to leave the studio until the entire hoodie brigade had exited. Cold as it was, the air in there had never before been quite so scented: half animal, half cosmetic.

Then I headed back to the office and slumped under my little desk lamp like it was an umbrella. I had multiple emails and blinking phone messages, all manner of incoming, which was for the best. If professional stimulation kept on coming I would survive on vocation buzz for another quarter century. The first phone call was from Desolée, reminding me to drop by after work so we could ring Rex. Then someone from Juice calling to say they had the *Marry Me or Else!* ratings projections finalized, if I was interested. Then came a message from Liz at Kiddo Network referring to her email with an invitation to call her if I needed to discuss anything, but she doubted it. Where was that? My inbox was two thirds bold. On top was an email subject headed *Cozumel?* from Nate, our sponsorship manager, asking if we should see about getting Hardy some sugar-free Crantoony instead of regular. Then an email from Barry championing me for going with the flow; he would back me up *no matter what*. An all-staff from Stephanie wondered who stole her hole puncher. And there it was, an email from Liz at Kiddo turning down *Switcheroo* with instructions to keep her in mind whenever I had something else to pitch. I forwarded the email to Barry with a bulbous red exclamation point attached to the header, then made my way straight to his office, like a broken-necked victim of a car accident flagging down oncoming traffic before collapsing roadside. I heard myself beep into his inbox just as I got to his door.

"Check out the latest." My tone was sepulchral. I was pale for now but soon I would be crimson.

Barry's finger tapped on his mouse as he read, as if he would rewrite the thing for me if he could. "Ah, kid, *c'est la vie*. Don't think I'm too shocked or anything. I had my doubts. Shut the door. Take a seat."

"No. Everyone will think I'm in trouble."

"Not if you laugh. Laugh right now. Ho ho. Hee hee."

"Oh God, Bar. Maybe I'm losing my touch?"

Barry had wisely stocked his office couch with extremely puffy cushions; he liked to see what happened when people got too comfortable. I sank.

"*Switcheroo* was kind of on the brutal side. Deep down you know that."

"Was?"

"I have to pull the plug, slugger."

"Damn it, Bar. I was so sure I was going to break us into the children's market. Nothing would have stopped us then. Fuck, fuck, fucking shit."

"No hard work ever goes down the drain, genius, remember that. Speaking of, you've been slave driving yourself since you got here. Take some time off, crazy woman, or we'll owe you a fortune in holiday pay." As usual, Barry was occupying his office chair as if it was a lawn chair. I shivered.

"Time off?"

I had gone from one job straight to another and on reflection I had done that for years. I always took cash over lieu days.

"Between you and me, Minervy, we need to chill expenses this quarter or up top are going to be on my back for months. Hell, take the whole damn summer. I know you can afford it. Luce and I can baby-sit *Marry Me*. If anything big busts loose I'll haul you back here in a flash, you know that. You're the brains of this operation. I like my brains fresh."

Now I was my own personal forest fire; I'd have to rage all afternoon and douse at home. "Barry, please, give it to me straight. What are you saying?"

"I'm merely saying take a vacation, Minnie. A nice, long one. It's considered to be a very pleasant experience."

"Then why are you attacking me with it?"

I intercepted the little Nerf football Barry had aimed somewhere above my head and scrunched it to death.

"Good catch," he said.

Desolée was expecting me at her place that evening, but I took advantage of the fact that Barry had walked me out to my taxi and given the cabbie my address to steer her to mine. Ordinarily, I would not have preyed on Barry's paternal energies, but the moment he took my arm I felt ridiculously frail, like I'd lost my bonnet and been struck with consumption. Not that I had knocked off work early. I was so punch drunk there had been nowhere for me but the ring. Nate and I spent the better part of the afternoon plotting Hardy and Nicola's *Getaway*. Nate called Nicola and I conferenced with Hardy and together we decided on Cape Breton. Nate had plumped for Bermuda, but Hardy and Nicola both liked hiking and scotch. I hoped Canadian content would make up for the lack of a salt-and-pepper Ken doll and a Barbie *d'un certain âge*. Nicola asked to wait until the end of the school year to travel and I agreed to that, hoping to sex up the Cabot Trail by then with establishment shots of day trippers in halter tops. Nate found a small spa outside Baddeck and a few more sugary inns along the way. I booked nearby motels for the crew. Shortly thereafter, I'd boarded the freight elevator and jerked downward fast.

Desolée was heading over right away. We were calling Rex that night whether I liked it or not. So she said when I talked to her again from the cab.

"Chill, Minnie. You know how much it upsets Rex when we're freaked out." Desolée bullied any given cellphone into delivering clearly.

"How do you know I'm freaked out?" I asked.

"You're going all tight in that Minnie way, like you got less than an A on your report card. Go ahead and hang up, Min, or you'll rip something. See you soon."

I watched flophouses that had been turned into boutique hotels flip past and wondered where the rats had gone. I was a rat. All I ever did was scuttle and carry diseases and get claimed as a pet by people with odd tastes.

"Minnie, put down the vodka, now!" Desolée had a spare key to my apartment. She was hot on my heels.

"You're right, I am so nerve-wracked it hurts, what the hell, what the hell."

I sought the crook of my couch like a blind woman.

"Poor Minnikins. It isn't easy sharking up the waters day in day out, I know. Oh boy, oh shit." Desolée marched into my bathroom for a toilet paper roll and tossed it my way before sticking the vodka back in the freezer and hanging up her coat.

"Crying on May Day, you lapsed socialist, you should be ashamed."

"Des, I *am* ashamed. I have the most untrustworthy politics imaginable. Just when I think I've stooped to conquer it turns out I've fallen right on my face, in the slime. I stink, I totally stink!"

"Dang, sorry, Minnie. I'm starving. Hold that thought."

Desolée found the box of gruyère sticks I bought just for her. Finally, she sat down beside me, with the same expression she'd worn when I got chicken pox and she didn't.

"I thought the TV biz was full of humiliation. Where's the shame in one little setback?"

"The shame is that I am so out of touch with my advantages that it's sick! It's evil! Granted, my best reality television concept ever just went tits up, possibly bludgeoning my credibility. But how dare I suffer, you know? What about Bangladesh?"

My sinuses were clogged piping hot. The tip of my nose would be telling tales on me for days.

"Damn, Minnie. I forgot to nominate you for sainthood on my way over here. My bad."

In socks, Desolée's feet are pointy and triangulated. And often aching—her excuse to warm them up against me. My feet are blunter objects, on this day pathetically encased in my striped lucky-day socks. What had I drunk to cry so much? All my tea had been from a cup of innocence thus far. I had been ignorant of true failure and I missed that ignorance now with dread. Desolée and I had not been brought up to panic.

"Welcome to my travesty festival, Des. I'm my own pariah. I mean, I got children's hopes up, innocent little kids! Fuck me."

"You know, Min, we think all we really need in this life is a sense of humour. I find things go a lot better when you develop other senses, too. A good sense of time, that's a biggy. And a good sense of treats, for sure." Desolée enjoyed snacks even more than lavish meals.

"A sense of sadness."

"A sense of love. How about that one, Minnie, huh, huh, huh?"

"Ouch, don't kick."

"Bony butt."

Finally, things were draining and there was no more to blow.

"Sorry I got so upset for a second there. It's just that I don't date much anymore so I'm poorly prepared for disappointment."

"Oh, Minnie, you'll pick back up the habit. Getting disappointed is easy peasy. Just ask Frank."

Eating something salty always put Desolée in a good mood, as did cheering me up. Gail and Lee had always made a big fuss over her ability to do so, the way some kids get congratulated on their piano recitals. I unwedged myself and claimed my half of the couch.

"Why does everything have to be so goddamn perilous all of the time, you know? Silly me, I was really feeling bang on for a while there. My mistake."

"You'll get through this, Minnie. You're a total professional. That's why you get the big bucks."

"I keep saving, but I can't figure out how to spend. Let's call Rex. I'm ready but you go first."

"Good girl. Rex loves you whatever you do."

Now my eyes were too full to blink again. So much of crying is in the chin; if you can steady that then little else contorts. But your breath will still catch on hooks and your temples still throb full of woe's chunder.

"Holy crap, maybe you *do* need to get away, Minnie. I always say if you get out of town when you're feeling stupid, chances are you get to come back smarter. God, these cheese sticks are greasy, pass me some of that TP, the phone's going to slip right out of my hands. I've got his new number here somewhere. . . . Hiya, Uncle Rex! How's Montague treating you? Wait a sec, it looks like Minnie wants a word. She's tugging on my sweater like a mad woman. You know she's crazy, right, Rex? Here she is."

Desolée was bang on; I did need to get away. I was screeching through a turning point. A change was purportedly as good as a rest.

"Hello, Uncle Rex."

"Minnie, my dear. It's lovely you girls called. I was just telling Doris you would."

"Is your house key still under your front porch mat?"

"Yes, dear. I had it under the flower pot for a change and then I put it back under the mat for you. Will I be seeing you soon?"

"You will indeed. Say in a week or so? I can hardly wait, we can talk then. Here's Des, with her mouth full as usual."

As soon as Desolée left with the rest of the cheese sticks, I called Gail, not wanting to frighten her with what might have seemed like a frontal lobotomy if she'd heard about it second-hand. But it made sense to Gail that I summer in Tuck Harbour. She reminded me that I had always said the Atlantic was the real ocean, the one that other oceans get defined by. Then she forgave me for having been so supercilious. Apologies sprouted easily in my quaked state. Gail had been concerned enough about Rex to think about a trip out East herself, but now I had spared her the worry. She asked me if finances were an issue because she could help if they were, but I promised her they weren't, or that I would not let them become so, but thanks. Gail did well by goat cheese.

Monday morning at Myriad, everyone nodded sagely upon hearing my plans. Many of them probably found Toronto too incessantly convenient and wished that they, too, could retreat to a fishing village on the southeastern shore of Prince Edward Island where kids took turns jumping off the one bridge into oily harbour water and the sign outside the corner store had once bashfully advertised a sale on chicken *chests*. Barry let it slip to the office gossips that in a way I was headed out there to supervise the Cape Breton shoot; hopefully there would be no nervous breakdown scuttlebutt for anyone to wash down at the water cooler. By the end of the week, my last week at work for a while, Barry quietly mentioned he was more proud of me than ever. No pressure, but he knew I'd come back with great stuff on the go. Absolutely, I should email him whenever I had something to bounce around, meanwhile I'd be cc'd on every loose end. I reminded Luce she was a rock. She thanked me repeatedly for sparing her a hiatus and swore she owed me forever. I encouraged her to borrow my desk lamp and hugged her tight. Obviously, Luce was the Myriad ego, mediating between our dreams and our televised reality. Barry was the superego, staving away taboos. Off splashed the primitive id, unsure where exactly, but I was determined to be expletive not retentive. Desolée backed me up on that.

"Whatever it is, Minnie, just hide out there and shit it all out. You'll feel better, I promise."

Desolée and Stash drove me to the airport, my suitcase full of utilitarian wear and running gear. And the designer rubber boots that Desolée had found for me as a going-away present, black with sparkles as if every wet step I'd take would also be intergalactic. Desolée came right up to the Air Canada wicket with me to get my seat switched to a window. She was right; I wanted to press my cheek up against the cold pane the whole trip, unintroduced to whoever was headed to Charlottetown to set new benchmarks for aquaculture profits. When we came in for the landing, I wanted to spy red soil rife with oxide, red as if one could hack bricks straight from the ground, red as if the earth was shouting. I was headed to a province laid out in cuts and gashes. An island that had cut itself shaving.

4

I told Rex that a taxi was going to be cheap at the price, he wasn't to worry, I could make my own way from the airport seventy ziggety kilometres south and east. The truth was that a cab from Charlotte-town to Tuck Harbour would cost me eighty bucks minimum. Unusually for the cabbie, I would not be five teenage girls at four in the morning after a bunch of rum-and-cokes plus a late-night burger from the Chinese restaurant, crowing about who'd humped who after last call at Velvet Underground. I said my goodbyes to the Air Canada flight crew who were delivering Perma Press grins by the cabin door, shoulder to shivering shoulder. I said hello to the wind. The breeze had a slapstick sense of humour and the rain was in on the joke; PEI May had been crossed with February. The grass beside the runway was as drab and mucky as a basement carpet after a house flood. Nothing had budded. Hopefully, the summer started late and ended late, but possibly it was just short.

Arriving at the Charlottetown airport entailed a stroll across tarmac: no getting digested through a shaky tunnel and then dumped into a concourse. There was the usual Celtic din at the sole baggage carousel, families noisily reabsorbing their prodigals, cracking funny to alleviate the reunion joy. There was definitely no Rex on hand to be ordered not to lift anything, which was all for the best. Rex knew well enough to stop driving just like I knew well enough not to start. His truck was long gone and his Oldsmobile had followed. I grabbed a cart. I had a coin ready to insert for the privilege, but it was free. My bags obediently showed up, packed to their outermost pockets. I liked the tortoise sensation of travelling with a couple of months' worth of essentials. I could have gone anywhere temperate without cocktail parties.

A man who looked to be near my age except with much rosier cheeks bounced into view, looking strangely amused when he spotted me.

"Minnie. It's Colin. I seen your picture at your uncle Rex's place so I knew it was you. I got my rig parked out front. Let me help you with that. Wheels, we like that!"

This was Colin McTeal, who had built a house across the road from Rex's place. Compact, clear-eyed, brush cut, broad-browed and brawny—speedy of gesture on the way home, maybe not so much when he got there. I knew that Colin was father of two sets of twins, that he assisted his fisherman brother for a living, that he had a serious biography addiction and was Rex's best friend in Tuck Harbour, fifty years his junior.

"Aren't you supposed to be fishing?"

"I was until a couple of hours ago and I will be again before I know it. Don't you worry, Minnie. The wife wanted me to stop in at the Superstore anyway for some fresh basil. I got tarps in the back for your bags. Off we go."

I had to get used to the country economy, where favours are done rapid fire, where there is no shame in small-scale giving and getting—cast-off board games, a handful of rhubarb, last month's magazines. I would find a favour fast to do for Colin or his wife, Etta. Or the eight-year-olds Pierre and Elliot. Or the five-year-olds Joan and Bette. I had quickly racked brains with Desolée to sort through neighbour names on the way to the airport and then memorized en route, a task made easier by the thousand miles of cloud cover. Once Colin and I got outside I felt sea in the air, only slightly, but I was sensitive to tang. Perhaps the whole purpose of this trip had been to give my thoughts a good salt scrub. I wasn't going to suggest anything so whimsical to Colin. He had probably decided by now that I was quiet and nothing would persuade him otherwise. I certainly wasn't going to tell Colin that I was tired. He had hauled traps out of the gelid ocean for eight hours straight beginning sometime between 3 a.m. and 4—three hundred traps containing blackish-green aquatic insects doomed to be boiled red in pots. Like most men, Colin's truck gave him energy. This was a proud King Cab with kid clutter in the back. I filed my ecological concerns elsewhere.

"What a nice truck," I said.

"Does the job. Stick your computer on the back seat there. I'll make sure to lock up. There are crackheads all over this town now, poor fools. All over this little province."

At least PEI had fewer pimpmobiles on the road than Toronto; extravagant engineering here was industrially based. Islanders with a fondness for inessentials had left for more superficial pastures, leaving behind the hard-nosed, less imaginative and secretly sentimental. Of course, this was a great place to *raise children*—so said parents, but I wondered if the children would agree. I was going to have to deactivate the verbal lobe of my brain for a while or risk saying something pretentious. In downtown Toronto we owed pretension to each other as a social duty. Not here, unless I also wanted to play the buffoon, which might not have been a bad idea. I'd be better at it than Desolée, who usually spent her time on the Island in people's vegetable gardens pulling beans and weeding radishes, showing off her red-stained fingernails on the flight home.

"How's Rex?" I asked Colin as he shuttled us towards Charlottetown's most mammoth grocery store, presiding over a thicket of take-out restaurants.

"Happy as can be. I know it was a big surprise, him moving out to the Manor. To Etta and me, too. But now we seen him all settled in with company around all the time, we can see how the old guy made sense. He's got someone there to remind him to take his heart pills now. And video nights, he's looking forward to that. And the theme dinners, he gets some jollies out of those, I tell ya. We told old Rex we'd bring him home to the Harbour whenever he wants, all he has to do is ask."

"Thank you, much appreciated."

"He's a good man, your uncle Rex. What you don't want is an end like Steve McQueen's, young and already fighting the inevitable. James Dean ordered Steve McQueen to brush his hair once, and Steve did it. Can you picture that? No thank you, Mr. Dean. Brush your own damn mop."

Another four-way stop sign. There seemed to be a lot of them on the Island.

"It's wonderful that Rex has neighbours after all these years. A real blessing."

"We all love Rex, Minnie. The kids miss him big time. Etta and I don't have enough hours in the day for Checkers and Snakes and Ladders."

"Desolée and I haven't been doing so well in the offspring department."

"Never say never, Minnie, my dear."

Colin told me to take my time at the Superstore and meet him at the big box bookstore next door. I needed to pick out produce that had more going for it than the frail stuff in the Tuck Harbour Clover Mart, and get my hands on whatever was tropical or came in whole wheat. I grabbed multi packs of tofu dogs, several boxes of flaxseed porridge and a flat of multigrain penne. I sought olive oil and balsamic, a pepper grinder, herbed chèvre, tins of coconut milk and a big jar of sundried tomatoes. I got anything I could possibly have wanted for myself plus boxes of frozen hors d'oeuvres and bags of gourmet cookies for those who might pop in. The Island enjoyed a grand culinary tradition to which the supermarkets were highly responsive. For the foreseeable while, I would not be able to buy a designer garment, but I could get Arborio rice, German chocolate and kumquats. As long as I could hitch a ride. In Rex's day there had been trains to take from town to Charlottetown, but now the population base was considered too minimal for even a bus line. My grocery bill amounted to an astonishing $286. I could not remember when I had purchased bread to freeze and tomatoes that weren't ripe. *Culture shock*, I heard myself tell Desolée, Luce and Barry.

I spotted the back of Colin's head surveying the New in Non-Fiction. I promised I really did want to buy the latest Alexander Graham Bell text he was eyeing. Then I admitted I just wanted to borrow it when Colin was done. I got a head shake, then a grin. Then we were across the Hillsborough Bridge and zipping along the Trans-Canada Highway, on the lookout for our side road with Charlottetown behind us. There were suburbs on the other side of the bridge. I knew from Rex that they were growing, but were not yet extensive enough to have their own junior school. The sky was watery, but it had cleared in patches and the most stubborn clouds had gold linings. *Island climate*, I heard myself say. But it seemed to me I was merely performing my knowledge, that I simply collected jargon and recited it. I probably didn't really know anything. Unlike the sturdy Tuck Harbour folk. There were genuine church ladies, formidable ones who weighed ninety-nine pounds and lived on tea and tea biscuits.

"They got rid of the oldies station." Colin was the kind of driver who could fiddle with dials. Finally he made do with some poppy rap, or one of its mysterious sub-groups.

"You grew up in Tuck Harbour?"

"That I did. My brother and me. I was at university in Halifax for a while there."

"What did you study?"

"Business mostly. Some computer courses. History."

"I should have done more history. I like how it's officially sanctioned gossip."

"And who alive doesn't like gossip, right, Minnie? Oh, we love gossip here on this Island."

"I hope I get some gossip going."

"Don't you worry about that, Minnie, my dear. Don't you worry about that."

There were clusters of birch trees by the side of the highway, like slender girls in white dresses too shy to dance. The clumps of roadside forest kept bursting into fields of undulating red, ploughed and seeded all the way to the shore in the good old PEI way. The sky was steely again and the sea played along, getting more credit for hue and mood as it always did. I thought the spring landscape was plain and striking at the same time, like a pretty woman first thing in the morning. When I had walked into the bookstore, a girl far enough ahead to make it totally optional had held open the door for me: a smiling teenager willing to donate 6.8 seconds of her time to a stranger. I was still touched twenty minutes later. Of course, bad attitudes make for big news on an island. Defective merchandise has to be returned with good humour, boardwalks hum with hellos and doors get held open for who knows who. Colin switched stations. At 4 p.m., PEI mothers were starting to make dinner: time for Island Call-In. Someone had always lost a cat or had a bedroom set to sell. Rex was probably listening. I was looking forward to bringing him his new moccasins from me and his new teapot from Desolée. She had gone to a fire-it-yourself pottery place and hand-painted a pot that said *Rex's Brew, Hands Off*. Etta was going to drop me off at the old-age home in Montague the next morning on her way to work as a Royal Bank teller. I had sent word I was offering babysitting in return, but been told Mrs. McTeal Sr. had that covered.

This was likely the least talkative Colin had been in years, but my mouth had gone slack while my eyes gulped down landmarks. We had passed Aunt Milly's Island Treasures and the gay-friendly B&B with the plucky rainbow flag. I was on the lookout for the Potato Museum and Glad's Dairy Bar. "How's the catch this year?" I tried.

"Minnie, I have to tell you it's not good. I'm afraid it's damn bad."

"Oh no. I'm so sorry."

"Worst numbers in the Strait in God knows how many years. Something's going on. Something raunchy is going on. Something more than just a *cycle*. Joe will get to the bottom of it, I know that much."

"Joe is your brother?"

I already knew from Rex that Joe owned and controlled the fishing boat, licence and profits. Colin earned a seasonal salary, living thaw to thaw.

"That's right, Minnie, Joe is my big brother. In this life anyway. Maybe in the next one I'll get to be boss. He's the Fishermen's Association rep for Section 26A this year, voted in pretty well unanimously, I'm happy to say. I'll say it for him because he won't say it himself, not unless it scores him a point when he needs one. Meanwhile the guys up on the north shore are going gangbusters. They catch canners up there in the gulf, the smaller lobsters. They're grossing 300K this season if they're on the ball. They aren't going to have much sympathy for us whiners, and why should they? The Strait is mostly markets. Used to be. But now those guys up there in LFA 25, sorry, Minnie, lobster fishing area 25, they're getting more of those, too. They're getting it all."

"Markets?"

"The bigger lobsters. For diners, for home use, for your fancy restaurants there in Toronto. We used to catch plenty of those in the Strait, back when our licenses were worth the half million bucks they still cost even though there's too many of them. The government's got to start doing some buy-backs, soon. Trouble is, no one wants to be the one to give it all up, the boats they've named after their kids, the skills they've learned the hard way, the mortgage due one way or another. No, Minnie, these are not easy times. I'm sticking with my brother, though. He's always been fair by me, I'm going to be fair by him. Etta says so, too."

"It can't be easy with kids."

"Four kids and the Game Boy bust, you better believe it. Recognize anything, Minnie?"

"Yes!"

I recognized the postage-stamp-sized post office. I recognized

the little white church face-off: Anglican versus Presbyterian. I recognized the Eats n' Treats diner, the Clover Mart, the Petro Can gas
station and the bridge you could sneeze your way over if you were
going fast enough. I recognized what was well and truly called Main
Street. Vinyl siding had outweighed shingle for years. Up the hill was
the community centre cum library, and the house with little lighthouse flowerpots. And now the fork in the road. The road to the
right looped back around the village. To the left was Tuck Point
Road—the road that kept going far enough to deposit a house or
two immediately sea side amid surrounding fields. This was Rex's
road, called as such by most. He rented out the fields to potato farmers and reserved one beside the house for hay, plus Dosie's seaside
meadow. Rex's house was a teetering ochre edifice with red trim that
looked like it had jaundice and a skin condition both. There I would
endeavour to make myself comfortable, for how long I was not sure,
but it was time to store the last of my resistance in the bacon-fat jar
that I was sure to find stashed on the top shelf of Rex's fridge. Neat
Rex, capable Rex, calm Rex. It occurred to me I might have to buy
Rex's house its first television set.

"Can you get high-speed Internet out here?"

"Not yet. You might want to write to complain about that. Lord
knows Etta's tried. Home sweet home, Minnie. Dosie must be round
back."

Colin's big truck had come in useful. He hauled my suitcases
out from under the tarps with a lobsterman's adroit strength while
I tried to grab one grocery bag per finger. We piled everything into
Rex's kitchen at the back of the house, a very wooden kitchen by city
standards thanks to its pine table and chairs, wood pile by the stove,
and big oak sideboard displaying serving bowls, serving plates and
to each cup a hook. Colin offered to start a fire, but I promised I'd
manage. Gail had reminded me to burn the creosote out of the
stovepipe with a good hot fire off the top.

"You drop by anytime, Minnie. Stop in if you want some company for dinner or a bit of the TV."

Across the road, a standard saltbox with beige siding and sleepy-eyed windows had emerged between Rex's house and Tuck Point: the first dwelling ever outside Rex's windows that was not his shed or barn. When Rex had decided to sell off some land we had all encouraged him to do so and it seemed to have worked out well for all concerned. I for one was not as prepared to be country alone as I was to be city alone.

"Will do, thanks."

"Cheerio then. Etta will be here at eight sharp. Unless you want to get going early?"

"No eight's good. Bye for now."

Colin was off with a toot, off but not far. I had to stick my perishables into the old avocado-green fridge with its seventies side-by-side doors, then find a raincoat with a hood and say hi to Dosie. I wanted to go for a walk now that I was living somewhere where there was a walk to go on. I needed to head down to the beach and see how my favourite rock was doing—the sandstone promontory that made me feel like I'd spot any whales for miles. I had never arrived in Tuck Harbour without Desolée before and I was missing her pragmatism—but the boots helped. It's hard to feel helpless when one is wearing rubber boots, especially ones with round toes and give at the calf. I was not too old to clamber, gulping air as fresh as Evian.

Dosie looked up, surprised enough to stop chomping for a second or two, then she was back tugging on new shoots with her old teeth. Dosie was a bay, vying with the soil for clarity of red, which Rex always joked made for less grime. I slipped under the electrified string of wire that kept her off the back lawn. Lazily, she let me pat her from her withers to her haunches; I was tall enough but just. At some point I'd brush her clean, but only if she wanted. Dosie's hocks were sensitive beneath her sprays of hoof hair. It always looked to me like Dosie was wearing the kind of après ski boots favoured by Italians. Like most cart horses, she was gentler than a pony. I felt bad that I had no carrot peelings or lettuce hearts, but there was not a lot of accusation in Dosie's inquiring eye when she finally lifted her head back up above mine and looked chewingly down on me. I gathered I could have the house to myself and she would stick to the meadow and I had her permission to head to the beach.

"Thanks, Dosie."

I swished through wet grass to the edge of the field, then scissored over the far stretch of fence. A small sandstone cliff overlooked Rex's rocky plage: it was Rex's beach down to the high-tide mark. The north shore of the Island had rolling dunes and surf with crash, much of it under park protection. The southern shores overlooking the Strait were rockier, brighter red and less prone to waves, with Nova Scotia often visible. If I became a local, I would probably stop swimming altogether. Gail and Lee had lost two high school friends at Blooming Point, their bodies retrieved by fishing boats, the white coffins his and hers. PEI license plates said *The Gentle Island* but Lee preferred *Rip Tide Island*.

I ran down the crumbling slope with my heels dug in as far as they would go. The beach looked clean even when strewn with kelp. I knew the sea was going to churn up a haiku poem of debris every day—fish bones, a barn door, scraps of netting, rusted engine parts and the occasional dead seal—but crumbled bits of buoy never really looked like garbage to me. I promised the beach I would take a waste bag down the next time and collect whatever wasn't biodegradable. The beach and I would be good pals. Every day there would be fresh shells to crush under my boots, the closest I had come in a long time to carnivorousness.

I found my rock amongst rocks and mounted it, feeling like a carved maiden nailed to a prow. I looked for Damson Island in the mist. If you could distinguish it clearly from the Nova Scotia mainland that meant rain was on the way. I could not see further than a dozen waves away and the wind was getting under my hood, Rex's hood, which smelled of lawnmower gas and deeply vegetable proteins. It was time to pick a bedroom and unpack, then call Bell to request a connection to the World Wide Web no matter the rustic speed. My Toronto cellphone definitely wasn't working.

I chose the south beach view with the double bed—the bedroom I always had to flip Desolée for and lost out on. Rex's bedroom looked out on the lane—he preferred to sleep vigilant of comers and goers. I would not so much as peep into Rex's room, not just yet, not with the tsunami of affection it would unleash to see his plaid blanket, coin tray and bedside copy of *Robinson Crusoe*. The south bedroom was above the kitchen so it had the benefit of the stovepipe as well as a water view and morning light. Soon waves would be murmuring in the open window all night long. I unpacked all my clothes into the chubby chest of drawers, squirreled my empty suitcases under the bed and bustled downstairs. I built a fire with kindling teepeed over newspaper balls just like Gail said. Then I pumped up my new green Pilates ball; along with the Tuck Point Road it would have to suffice as a gym. Shortly afterwards I realized I had forgotten something back in unthinking, uncaring Toronto. The AC adaptor for my laptop was half plugged in at Concord Avenue. Rex had a red kitchen phone hanging on the wall. I called Luce.

"Myriad." Luce had a separate work line at home that rang with a continental ring-ring.

"Luce, it's me."

"Minnie, where are you?"

"In a country kitchen looking out a side window at some twisty little trees with lichen growing all over them."

"How are things?"

"So far so good. Chilly. It was raining when I got here, then it cleared up, then it started raining again, now it's clearing up."

"Yikes."

"Island climate, what can you do? Things are changeable around here. Weather in Toronto always feels like it starts in Toronto. Out here it goes whipping past on its way somewhere else."

"You sound great. Relaxed, kind of."

"I have a feeling I'm going to be in bed early. A lot early, early a lot."

"Good for you."

"Listen, I forgot my damn laptop plug. From the socket under my desk at home. My house key's in my top office desk drawer."

"No problem, I'll grab your key and courier out your plug."

"Thanks so much, Luce. That's the bad news. The good news is that I want you to keep the key and use my place whenever you want. It's crazy to leave it empty and it's not like I'm paying rent here. Please."

"Seriously? Because I wouldn't want Cordy getting into your stuff, but I would love to get my mother out of my hair for a while. Secretly I know she would love a break even though she won't admit to it."

Luce's father had died young, not long after Cordy was born. Luce's mother needed company just when Luce and Cordy needed a home and the situation had stabilized, tensions and all.

"Totally up to you, Luce. I trust you whatever."

"God, thanks, Minnie. I love my mom for all she's done, but this will make things so much easier for a while. Your power is on the way, woman. I'll send it express."

By the time Luce and I hung up there were crows collecting on Rex's fences, trees, eaves and pastures. Every evening big black birds flocked from across town, over the river, and up and down the point, to lurk like shadowy guys in black leather jackets at the back of a bar. The crows were riled often by hawks, potato truck traffic and skunks, or just the strain of roosting. Gail called it the Edgar Allen Poe Chorus and timed her calls to Rex to coincide with it. The evening was setting pale reddish. The strip of conifers at the edge of the hay field was the first thing to go dark. Dosie retreated to her stable, looking morosely out the door at the way blue was turning to indigo and green to grey. The moon over the water was as bright as an amateur theatricals backdrop, with that silvery road poured beneath it that always seems to lead from somewhere lunar rather than to. A jewellery box of stars remained in effect; for years I had forgotten to check. When I'd walked along the beach that afternoon I spotted seven ducks indeed in a row, one exemplary guy with a neck so green that emeralds would cower. I had also seen a dead gannet, rotted into jagged angles. And I had stomped over a bed of beached seaweed as puffy, smelly and massive as some derelict giant's unlaundered old duvet. In a month or two there would be purple jellyfish blobbing everywhere—that same giant's fried eggs.

I flicked on a light or two, an outdoor light included so that I wouldn't be accused of moping. I dared brew some Earl Grey, knowing I was tired enough to crash nonetheless. I dug into Rex's jam stash, polished off five pieces of rye toast with lime marmalade, set the crumby plate in the dishpan and climbed the twisted back stairs with crazy tall treads that led off the kitchen. The bathroom sink had separate hot and cold faucets. I had forgotten there was simply the big tub: no shower. All the water came from Rex's well and all the sewage was headed to his septic tank. I thought it was going to prove morally useful—to be reminded that nothing really gets flushed away.

In the night, stumbling for the toilet then back in bed, I spent a moment in sheer amazement at where I was before sinking asleep. My dreams were immediately hectic, as they usually are once tranquillity sets in and my psyche can afford to dump its junk. I dreamed of Rex, happy as usual then clatteringly fallen on the kitchen floor, of trying to call 911 on my deadened cell, of Rex's face going from pink to blue and back again as long as I kept my eye on him. Hard to do when you're ordered to drive the ambulance and you have absolutely no memory of what's brake and what's gas.

⌒

Etta was at Rex's kitchen door promptly at 8 a.m., calling my name with maternally efficient decibels. I was ready to go and had been for an hour, aware as I was of the widespread Tuck Harbour habit to wake up early in case the morning weather was better than the afternoon. This morning was brilliantly sunny, complete with bright white caplets in the Strait, the kind of sunshine that commands gulls to circle and seeds to sprout. I had jumped feet first into the morning as soon as I caught sight of it. Another bonus to staying at Rex's house was the permission one received to wear the same thing two days in a row or more. Not that Rex didn't have a trusty washing machine and a long clothesline, to which Etta was now fixing fallen pins. She looked to have a good forty pounds on Colin, an increasingly common PEI wife-husband ratio. She bore her heft with good cheer. Etta also had half a head over Colin. Her hair was a thick, tinted auburn, tugged into a blobby bun.

"Minnie, finally!"

"Finally!"

Etta's smile was as wide as her hips. I sensed she was a woman who felt her happiness as substance, not ether. She was like a big helping of warm berry pudding soaked with cream. She had very small feet. Her maroon slip-ons made my track shoes look like ski boots.

"The girls are beside themselves to meet you. We'll have to drop them off first. The boys prefer the school bus. They said to tell you so. Braids are Bette, pigtails are Joan. What's that you've got there? Presents for Rex? Isn't that nice, girls? Minnie's got presents for her uncle Rex."

"I want a present!"

"I want a present!"

Bette and Joan were squished into child seats in the minivan's second row. They were both wearing palm-tree-and-sunshine-rays sunglasses, Joan's pink and Bette's yellow.

"Are you a celeberty?" one of them asked me. Joan.

"Gosh no," I said. "Are you?"

"I have pesto breath." Bette had the slightly upturned nose.

"We all have pesto breath! All except for Minnie."

"All except FOR MINNIE!"

"Smell our breath, smell our breath, haaa, haaaaaa HAAH!"

"What did we say, girls? Politely does it. Minnie isn't used to you banshees."

Etta reversed with the same speed with which she drove. Rex

had a long lane, the better to deposit him sea side. It was rutted; I'd do some patch work with flat red rocks from Dosie's field. Meanwhile I had children to impress.

"Bye, Dosie, see you soon," I said. Dosie was of course disinterested as ever.

The girls took my cue. "Bye, Dosie!" they chirped. I loved the way their chubby little legs looked stuffed inside their striped leotards, the way their raincoat hoods had beaks, and the way they wore dime-store rings on their index fingers like mini Elizabethans. I assumed that they were going to be more easily won over than their big brothers, even though I had very little lip gloss to pass around.

"It's ABOUT TIME one of you women came to visit Rex," said Bette.

Mighty Etta neither blinked nor blushed, at least not that I could see out of the corner of my eye. I wasn't sure what was being transmitted via the rear-view mirror.

"Mom, you said so!"

"Gosh, it's about time, I completely agree. Well, here I am."

I reached around and grabbed Joan's glasses to try on, then gave them back again when I was told I looked like a silly dum-dum.

When Etta dropped the girls off at their schoolyard I was pleased to see they were not as plump once contextualized by their portly classmates. So many kids were coming from a half an hour drive away rather than a hike, bike ride, or hopscotch. The Island was at the wrong end of the worst of the new obesity stats. Statistics are barely worth trusting until one sees them complacently brought to life. Before long I would be told I needed *more meat on my bones*. Not true by any stretch in Toronto but gospel in Prince Edward Island. For breakfast I had fished my plate out of the dishpan and enjoyed another three slices of toast and marmalade. More jam would come when I needed it, although I suspected Etta was too new guard to produce preserves or teach me how. She whizzed us past the Royal Bank, past the hardware store with new bikes lined up out front the colour of army vehicles and warning signs, and past the Montague Superstore, smaller than Charlottetown's but still super. We zoomed up to Montague Manor, Rex's new home, perched snidely on the highest hill in town like a mansion in a Bugs Bunny cartoon.

"Thanks so much for the lift, Etta. I can grab a cab home."

"How long do you think you'll be?"

"The morning, I guess. I'll tire Rex out if I linger."

"He'll want you to stay for lunch. Here." A brown bag with multiple items. "Don't worry, all vegetarian. You need some meat on those Minnie bones."

"Wow, thank you."

"Colin's brother Joe is headed to the hardware store this aft. Why don't you meet him there at two? He'll give you a ride back. Look for the red truck with traps in the back."

"I don't want to be a pain."

"You're not a pain, Minnie. Not much of one anyway."

"What does Joe look like?"

"Good. Joe looks good."

Etta was off, leaving me standing on the Manor steps with my cucumber and cream cheese on whole wheat plus a Saran-wrapped date square and a cored and quartered Granny Smith. I had Rex's booty in the other hand—moccasins, teapot, cashews, All Sorts, and the latest *National Geographic*. The Manor front hall smelled of wax and antiseptic spray. On the desk was a bell with a sign that said *Ring Me!* I wasn't sure if there was much point considering the elderly ruckus emanating from the dining room. I poked my head in there to see a dozen circular dining tables, most in use. As a courtesy I generally try to avoid looking directly at people in wheelchairs, but that would have been impossible here. Some had canes hooked on the back of their dining chairs instead, or walkers waiting for them tableside like the aluminium equivalent of guide dogs. Everyone who had been peckish had an empty egg cup in front of them. There had also been bacon as I could smell, the intelligent feeding the senescent. Of course, no amount of snark was going to protect me now. I needed to rip away my scrim of spin fast, go forth without protective attitudes and fully feel out Rex's new living situation in all its reduction and pathos.

I saw him before he saw me, alone but not lonely, his *Guardian* neatly folded at the editorial page beside his oatmeal bowl. Hopefully someone was espousing proportional representation or an elected Senate, or even better arguing against them. Rex only gave in to anger when it came to gerrymandering and partisan appointments. Apparently even the liquor store salespeople in PEI were politically appointed—all very toadstools in Wonderland until one considers how far a twelve-dollar-an-hour job goes in a place where a house and acre can be had for a low five figures.

"Uncle Rex, hello. Don't get up! Here, we can still hug this way. You look great. I can't tell you how happy I am to see you, I mean it."

"You can't tell? Minnie without words in her mouth, now there's a new one."

"Don't start teasing already!"

Rex was more gnarled, more age spotted, wispier, more veined with blue and in some places he was mauve. He was still Rex, though, with eyes that stayed still and a mouth that sagged open a bit, then snapped shut when the thought he had been enjoying completed itself.

"We saved you some pancakes, dear."

"Oh no, that's okay."

"Doris made them for you special, here they are." Rex's hand trembled as he lifted the industrial white plate that had been hiding three silver dollar flapjacks, all with a burned-in M.

"Uncle Rex, fabulous, thank you!"

"That Doris is full of tricks."

"Yummy."

It was worth choking down chemically preserved mix that had been diluted with tap water, fried and then doused in maplesque sauce, just to see Rex bask in what he'd provided.

"How was your trip then?"

"Just fine. Colin came and got me at the airport. And Etta drove me here today."

"You use that telephone at the house anytime you want, Minnie."

"Oh, Rex, I would have called you when I got in, but I knew I was going to be seeing you so soon. I'm sorry. I've missed you. We all do, Uncle Rex, so much."

"Don't you go missing an old guy like me. That's no use for busy ladies like yourselves. I can't understand why you're not married, Minnie. A lovely young woman like you, it doesn't seem right."

"Show me your room, Uncle Rex. Just wait until you see what Des sent you."

Rex needed help getting to his feet, or at least was unwilling to decline it. He still worked up speed once he got going, but his challenges were now horizontal as well as vertical, every hallway the equivalent of a foothill. I gathered the thing to do was ignore the fact that he was winded from a race all his own. Doris was our first stop, beaming despite her hairnet and rubber gloves, happy to be a pet. Rex's suite was more than adequate, I was relieved to have that to report. He had four tall windows looking out onto the back lawn where coyotes had been known to prowl and the first robin spotted. For visitors there was a choice of hard-backed chair, footstool or rocking chair, and a wing chair for Rex. The floor was warm wood and there was a nice quilt on the bed, which was not horribly front and centre. Rex had a cane now, in his umbrella urn. He still wore green work pants with vaguely coordinating flannel shirts. There was still a good deal caged in by his ribs. He still went without a sweater.

No shutting the door—it was too much fun peeking out at the corridor and beckoning people in. I sustained niecely pride throughout every introduction, admitting to my Toronto achievements while playing them down. I met Penny, Jenny and Donny—all of them tending to the geriatrically vulnerable in body, mind and spirit with sweethearted dispositions while they ordered stretching exercises, organized small prize-winning games or mopped around the toilet. I had not known Rex needed physiotherapy, but I was glad Penny worked in-house and that if it came to it, there would be knee surgery. Most of Rex's fellow residents lacked mobility, but I was glad to see that none had lost their wits. Dementia called for specialists based elsewhere.

After gabbing about Gail, Lee, Desolée and Stash in as much detail as I could muster—not that I had breaking news, but my outdated chat was refreshed by face-to-face delivery—Rex and I shared my date square in the dining room over lunch. This time he was at a busier table. Lydia, Gladys, Shirlene and Sally were Rex's clique of choice, all of them with fluffy white perms, shrunken shoulders, pronounced knuckles and advanced opinions.

"Nice young woman like her not married?" wondered Shirlene.

"That's what I say!" That is what Rex had obviously said well in advance of my arrival.

"You never married either, Uncle Rex."

"I missed the boat. Then I sold it!"

"Hush now, all of you. Minerva can do as she likes."

I liked Sally's asperity. I hoped to have that much vinegar to spout at her age—enough to spill into a conversation and change its flavour. Sally had a wheelchair for just-in-case days, this being one of them. She let me wheel her back to her room for her early afternoon nap. Sally's husband, Don, had been a ministry man, the Department of Agriculture and Fisheries, forced behind a desk by a game leg. He had won the heart of this woman of nervy decorum shortly before his second promotion.

"He helped put in place the lobster licence cap in nineteen seventy-six. There was a lot of resentment at the time, Minerva. But they're thanking him now."

We toured Sally's cavalcade of family photos full of nuclear groupings. On Sally's top shelf there was one small but dazzling black-and-white wedding photo. Don Driver had his hand barnacled over Sally's as they cut into their arctic-white cake, his eyes looking outwards but his ear tipped down to his bride's matte mouth, her lips intently pursed.

"You look like you really admired him." Now that I had reached for the picture, Sally also wanted a closer look.

"Indeed I did, Minerva. That was important to me and I made sure it was possible. I admired my husband and I loved my children. But I felt I had other duties and I did them."

"Did you work? Outside the house?" She had been a nurse or teacher perhaps, maybe a secretary.

"I raised funds. I believe that's what you call it nowadays. I saw things that were needed and saw to it that there was rallying round and that they got done."

"You're Sally from Sally's Place?"

Sally's Place was the first women's shelter of its kind on the Island, formerly anonymous, now a hub of Charlottetown post-feminist activity with midwifery alliance offices and space for single-mother support groups and prenatal yoga sessions.

"Yes, Minerva. Now put this back, this young woman and her cake that made her so happy."

"That picture makes *me* feel old."

"Nonsense."

"I'm forty."

"Then you're less than halfway to me. Put age out of your mind, Minerva. It's no way to judge yourself."

Sally was tired and it was getting on to one-thirty. I said a quick goodbye after refilling her water glass. Then I said a longer goodbye to Rex, who claimed the moccasins were a perfect fit. He wore them out to the Manor porch just in time for a sunbeam to make it to the bench. He had taken his cane this time. I reminded myself that Rex's wave goodbye was a minimal farewell. I had promised to come back in a couple of days and drop by three times a week. I sensed Rex wanted me kept too busy for that, with lawns to mow, floors to mop, Dosie to pat, milk to fetch from the Clover Mart, and Etta and gang to drop in on, to welcome, to feed.

I arrived at the hardware store just short of two. My attention got snagged on the jagged row of new bikes outside, smelling of rubber and get-up-and-go. There was one nice girl's bike—not something I insisted on in a bicycle—but it was the only blue one, something I insisted on for sure. I began to feel new-purchase fizz bubbling from my solar plexus up to my brain stem. A bike would be the perfect thing for getting around the Harbour! This was the perfect bike! I was getting the hang of making the most of things! It would make Rex so happy to think about me settling in, fat tires, coaster handlebars and all. I hurried inside to grab my prize before anyone else did, love quickly making me neurotic.

"I want that blue bike!" I told the first *sales associate* I could find. He was hanging out by the doorknobs, a man my age stuck at the hardware store, which was a shame because although he was short, my height fairly exactly, he was handsome steered well clear of pretty. This kind of default career would never have happened to him in Toronto where pulchritude, even male, reaps improved destiny. I thought he must have been a father employed at any cost. But I had my own worries. "That blue bike outside, I want it."

"Okay."

"They're all locked up to each other. But I can buy the one that's assembled, right? I need one that's assembled. I want it now. You take debit, right?"

If "Joe" had a pickup truck, then "Joe" could surely fit a bicycle in the back of it. I checked my watch. I definitely didn't want to keep "Joe" waiting. I couldn't afford to get a reputation as a woman who held anyone up.

"You're sure you want the bike?"

At least I had the man's attention, for what is was worth. Whatever sociological currents had led this island to be less than thoroughly mercantile of spirit I was not sure. Maybe it was only this slumper who lacked a nose for gain, this man dressed entirely in denim with eyes unnecessarily the colour of American-dollar-bill green.

"Yes, I'm *sure* I want the bike." Chrrrrrrist. "Let's go."

"You're sure you want the *blue* bike?"

"Is there some kind of problem? Yes, I want the blue bike. Right away." Minus the Socratic dialogue if he didn't mind.

"Okay then."

"Okay then?"

"Okay, let's find you someone who works here so you can get the blue bike."

It was funny, I could see that. I had been given something, not robbed of anything. Just because Rex was more vulnerable than I had ever seen him before and I had only just seen him that way did not mean that I now had to droop and blubber. The bike was as shiny and promising despite taking its first wrong turn. Since when had I stopped getting a single thing right? Damn it, not again. My *Switcheroo* humiliation had tapped into a dark reservoir of anguish, obviously. I was going to need days of beach wind to dry my tears.

"Shoot, sorry, here," said the man who was not a hardware store employee.

We were halfway down the household paper aisle and he had punched open a box of tissues. Now *he* was horrified. I had to be an agent of consolation, fast. I'd manage provided he refrained from any more kindness. Another kind act at this point would feel worse than assault and battery. Did women with children break down like this? Surely Etta would never burst into tears at Home Hardware. One more kind word and I would be a total goner.

"Don't be nice to me."

We were the same height so I had to look down rather than away.

"What's that, dear?"

"Don't be nice! I need you not to be nice. To me. Please don't do anything nice, don't say anything nice. Don't even think anything nice. Just don't."

What was he supposed to do, now that it would be nice of him not to be nice? No point asking me—he had got us into this. Once upon a time all I had wanted was a bike.

"Can I help you?" I dared to look up. This time a man in a Home Hardware uniform and name tag wanted to know.

"The lady wants the blue bike, the one that's outside and ready to go."

"No problem!"

"Oh, I also need a basket. For going to the Clover Mart."

They had no reason to care, but at least I was talking—improvised adult speech.

Jim sped away with another *no problem*.

"Would that be the Tuck Harbour Clover Mart?"

This from the eastern heartthrob in jeans and a jeans jacket. His hair was probably too long in his opinion, which was a shame because it curled in dark little tendrils around his temples and neck. His lips were delightful if you looked past the emergency-room-doctor stubble. His eyes seemed tired, but not from taking things in.

I nodded yes and winced out a smile.

"Well, you better get a light for that bike then. You don't want to be running into skunks at night. They love Rex's road. Truck's round the side. Let me know when you're ready to go."

"Joe?"

"Sorry, Minnie, I should have known it was you. Etta said you'd stick out nicely."

Joe apologized but he had a bunch of phone calls to make on our drive back to the Harbour. To men called Ted and Reg, and a secretary called Peggy he was doing battle with to get through to someone called Dave Devine at DFO. There was some talk of his going ahead and calling Ottawa, then a decision to hold off but to schedule a Web conference for later. Then Etta rang and Joe was able to report that, yes, we had found each other all right. He dropped me off right at Rex's door. I said a watery thank you, which I meant sincerely but could barely taste in my mouth. Did I not want my bike after all? Gosh, yes, yes I did. Joe had originated the McTeal brothers' grip and stance; it was like their dexterity had spread to their whole bodies. Before Joe's phone rang again he told me that he would see me *around*. I went inside to call Desolée. In Toronto it was not yet 2 p.m. I had hoped being an hour ahead of Ontario would make me feel wise; instead it was making me feel uncorrected.

"Minnie, you goose. How the hell are you?"

"Fine. Rex is good. His room is actually really nice. He loves the teapot, but I think he's going to treat it as décor."

"That's okay. Is he eating?"

"Seems to be. The food isn't bad. There are handrails all the way around his bathroom. He has loads of new lady friends. He's on fire."

"How about you? Flirted with any farmers?"

"All the single guys here are twenty-three, remember? Except the neighbour's brother. But he thinks I'm a head case."

"Perfect. He'll love you for who you really are."

"Nice, thanks, I needed that."

"Someone has to criticize you, Minnie. If not me then who?"

"Barry has his ways."

I reached over to my satchel and dug out my cardigan. I had to learn to put on a sweater as soon as I stopped moving. Desolée asked if I had a moment, she had big news. She knew it was corny, but she wanted to make sure I was sitting down. She didn't sound distressed, just careful: the verbal equivalent of walking blindfolded. I tucked up my legs and contracted around the phone.

"What is it, Des?"

"Stash and I are getting married."

"Oh my God, that's incredible—"

"Minnie, you're sweet but don't bother, it's not that big a deal. The thing is, we can't get married *yet* because I've applied to adopt a baby from Haiti. Couples need to have been married for at least five years so I'm adopting as a single person. Once we get the kid, then we'll get married. Nuts, I know."

It was such big news from so many sudden miles away. Desolée was in her lily-crammed boutique beneath a bank tower; I was watching Dosie chomp her way from west to east.

"My God, Desolée, this is amazing. When do you think you might receive your child?"

"That's just it, we were assigned a baby boy today. They think we can pick him up in about nine months. Ironic, huh?"

"That's beautiful."

"No kidding because he'll be sleeping through the night by then. Apparently, 81 percent of people request girls. We said we'd take a boy gladly. Harder for Stash maybe, but easier for me. Boys always love their mothers, right?"

"Of course they do. Desolée, this is wonderful. You'll be a fantastic mother. Why didn't you tell me sooner?"

"I was scared I'd back out. I didn't want to disappoint anyone."

"Do you guys not want a baby of your own? Sorry, you know what I mean."

"Who knows? No, actually. This seems right. They get tested for HIV and what have you before you're allowed to bring them to Canada."

"What's his name?"

"Bernard-Louis. I think we'll keep it. Stash says he looks like me. He's got my nose anyway. He's got the cutest Afro. He's three months. They sent us a picture. Right now we're calling him Boo."

"Oh my God."

"Minnie, please stop calling on the Lord, He's got nothing to do with this. Although I'm telling everyone in Port-au-Prince who'll listen that I want to keep the little guy in close contact with Jesus Christ our Saviour. The orphanage is seriously Christian. Maybe I ought to brush up on some voodoo just to cover his bases? Wait, that can be your job, Minnie. We want you to be godmother, honorary aunt, anything you want to be. How about maid of honour while you're at it? No wait, best woman."

I had never thanked anyone for so much. Out West, I had experienced the way mountain cliffs warn you never to be too presumptuous. Atlantic beaches, however, seem to give permission to stop at nothing. As soon as Desolée and I hung up, I hiked to my viewing rock. I sat there and engaged in some athletic introspection while the waves sloshed. I pictured Bernard-Louis and myself in various joyful states of play and nestling. I would work hard to be a cool aunt, unafraid of the latest musicians or body modifications. I pictured Desolée being the one Boo ran to when his knees were skinned or his finger painting was ready for viewing. Now she would have to put up Christmas trees and hide Easter eggs. She was Mom forevermore. I checked, more carefully the braver I felt, and it turned out I was not jealous of anyone for anything. I hate envy for the way it's like cholera, poisoning what we need to drink from in order to survive. Sweetly, Desolée had said I could be the one to tell Rex.

Just as I got back to the house a FedEx truck arrived. It was my power adaptor, delivered from capital to capital then from Queen's County to King's. Soon I'd be clicking hither and yonder. Desolée had promised to forward the picture of the baby right away. Rex would be pleased about that; boasting at the Manor was best done with visual aids. I thanked the delivery man, wondering if I should tip him for coming so far, but he seemed to have too much job satisfaction for that, hopping back into his van like it was his Ferrari. I was surprised by how well I was coping with my Myriad leave of absence. My heart was growing fonder of absence by the day. But I needed exercise.

It was perfect jogging weather. I kept to the left in order to face down traffic rather than joining it. As I dodged a monstrous farm machine that was lumbering between potato fields, I had to wonder what the farmers made of my profligate expense of effort to no good end other than the state of my end. I ran past a field of mama cows and clingy baby cows, all melancholy with their cow worries. Warmed up now, I ran out Rex's road onto Main Street. I ran down over the bridge where Tuck River darted inland like a long, flat tongue. I bypassed the flotilla of fishing boats—*A Salt Weapon, Frayed Knot, Fishful Thinking, Owen Mor*—and wharfside huts. I passed lawns and dwellings tidied to perfection—their owners having run out of house to be proud of. Then I looped all the way around the back of the village where the houses shrank to trailers. I rejoined Rex's road and made it home in fifty-nine minutes. If I stayed in shape this route would take me exactly fifty-nine minutes all summer long; my pace was regular if not mighty. I filled the tub while there was still sun shining in the bathroom window. Afloat, I was an island upon an island. Exercise endorphins were easing my way with my own nudity. There was not all that much of me, really. Somewhere or other, there would always be room for me. I just had to stay flexible enough to fit in.

5

I was grateful to PEI's advanced recycling system for the pride-tickling challenges it presented. One false move and one's refuse was mortifyingly left roadside, not something that would have ever happened to Rex, not in this aeon. It was almost too much to handle—separating paper towels from newsprint and tubs from bags and jars from lids—but then Etta sent over Pierre and Elliot to explain what bin took what. The boys were not identical. Pierre had shot taller faster so now he was also stringier, with a heap of sandy curls up top, the sides shorn by request, and a nose dense with felt-tip freckles. Pierre's air was precociously sober. Elliot was darker, scrappier and more insinuating when he was not being sarcastic. He was much less interested than Pierre in setting up my laptop to dial into my Island server. Finally contact was made with old-fashioned robot beeps, the boys five dollars richer. Then Elliot wanted a double ride on the blue bike and to show off his handstand and to pretend Dosie was a Trojan horse, c'mon, c'mon. Secretly, shamefully, he was quickly my favourite. He had placed a grimy little hand on my shoulder while we waited for the picture of Bernard-Louis to download and was just as entranced as me by the little potentate—the back of his head propped in the crook of a missionary's pale arm, pouting to have been hoisted mid baby dream, dribbling formula, staring back at Desolée with her own marshy eyes. Was I going to cry *again*?

Elliot was the only person around at all interested in helping me collect beach garbage. We set off with two waste bags and two cookies each.

"My mom says you're going to get more attention than a widow with a pension."

"Don't think so, Mister Man."

"Dad said she got that right. He says you're a real looker. What does that mean, Minnie?"

"It means I look hard at stuff. Trade you a chocolate chip for a gingersnap?"

"Okay. Race ya!"

"Careful of Dosie! No running behind her rear."

Dosie was turning out to be far more expressive of hind than fore; she barely blinked but she farted any degree of distress. For the most part this resulted from visits by Secord, the ardent McTeal collie cross. Secord lived to bully Dosie out of her clover-centric daze, yapping at her evangelically then jackrabbiting home. There had been a series of barn cats to keep Dosie company over the years, but Rex had thought it best not to replace the last one. A few months before it had been literally potato trucked flat but for a lump of skull. Now Dosie's only pals were mice and me. To make it up to her I plied her with treats. She got the last of the California strawberries, which was fun for both of us, her velvety muzzle twitching, licking sweet red out of my hands too fast for my second thoughts. Dosie also got my brown bananas and corn husks. I loved practicing country economies—manure to the garden, paper scraps to the fire; bread to the crows, care to the winds. Carefully managed, these policies were the closest I came to prayer. Oscar Wilde once said anyone can be good in the country. I hoped he had a point.

One day, in Technicolor animated glory, I saw a hummingbird dive-bombing a fence post. Then it turned out he was dive mating his missy. Not easy to do: they had to keep resting and have a cluck.

Meanwhile the bees were almost as big as the birds: fuzzy, bobbing, dark ping pong balls that droned as if they'd been militarized. So I thought and then I was backed up by an above-the-crease headline in the *Eastern Graphic*: Bumble Bees Bigger this Year. Daffodil season was also banner. Rex's kitchen was soon heaped with them, and the big south bedroom, and Etta's kitchen, and Rex's room at the Manor. I threatened to Lydia, Gladys and Shirlene that I was going to bike all the way to Montague and back one day. Etta gave me most of my rides in, an Eye Spy tournament with the girls ensuing. There was no more mention of Joe giving me a lift home. I thought maybe I had spotted his truck once or twice while I was out jogging. It was smaller than Colin's.

I was starting to get honks and waves from pickups, tractors and sedans whenever I jogged forth. Evidently the road was like a pub. I rarely had any idea who was driving but I always waved back. Otherwise I kept my eyes on the view—the sweep from field to shore to Nova Scotia gone violet in the distance, the various greens of various crops as subtly different as a Parisian eye-shadow palette, the five-storey swarms of starlings. I'd take it all in as greedily as a gourmet diner leaving no room for dessert. The fields soon turned from rusty red to red striped with wasabi green. I missed flagrantly red earth, the furrowed tracts upon tracts of it, once I figured out that red dirt was the most, and only, notably sensual thing about PEI. Daily life had a sex dream tinge when one walked around on soil that was bright red, meanwhile there was little eroticism from the ground up and absolutely none in the air. That was okay; I could wait for new potatoes, coming early in July. I'd boil them by the pot load with mint plucked from the patch by Rex's back door. *New* in potato terms meant picked too young for thick skins. By then I would have shed a skin or two of my own and be in a position to relate.

I finally took a look in on the parlour, to peruse the good old bookshelf and remind myself to dust the ships in bottles, the ancestral pipe rack, the World's Greatest Uncle trophy and the loose-lipped conch shell. I took a sniff at the encyclopedias, but K-L was stuck to M-N and didn't want to be budged. Of course, Rex had the entire Lucy Maud Montgomery oeuvre amassed. Gail and Lee weren't around to make cracks about Matthew and Marilla's Dry Cleaning. Or about the Green Gables store in Charlottetown where the sales ladies wore outsized pinafore uniforms that made them look like members of a cult that would hole up in Montana with shotguns and a polygamous leader. I wasn't interested in little orphan Anne, but teenage Anne intrigued me enough to transport *Anne of Avonlea* bedside. I conked asleep quickly without television to harass me. Every so often the kitchen got lonely, but the bed didn't.

I did not miss Toronto; instead I missed the Island already, more sensitive to the fact that I would have to leave it than that I was there. Barry and Luce had things nicely under control at Myriad Productions. As promised, they were cc'ing me on absolutely everything strategic. I feared no coup d'état.

↜

By early June Rex came to an unexpected conclusion; I needed an occupation to keep me busy over the summer in the way that being busy kept me happy. So I was told over lunch; shepherd's pie for everyone else and grilled vegetables on panini from the Superstore deli for me.

"Doris's cousin Trudy owns the Eats n' Treats," Rex said.

"Owns and runs." Shirlene loved to qualify.

"And it's been some busy." Rex put his fork down. I didn't want that.

Doris was summoned from the kitchen to corroborate. "It's been nuts," she agreed. "People sit themselves down faster than she can clear the tables."

At first I thought I was being chastised for not dropping in for a cup of soup.

"I'll have to check it out. Sounds like quite the scene."

"Trudy could do with some help, Minnie. Day shifts from ten until three." Rex had fork in hand again.

"The morning coffee crowd and the lunch rush," Doris specified.

"This is darn foolishness if you ask me. Minnie has her job in Toronto to keep her busy if busy is what she wants. She's working on the email." Lydia had asked me as many questions about television production as I might have asked her of sweater knitting. From thorn in side to saviour in one jab.

"I'm actually—I'm kind of, you know, enjoying a break." I dared to shrug in vague defence of my status quo. I looked over at Sally. Surely Sally understood that I'd fail miserably at proletarian employment? That I'd confuse diet cola for regular and forget to brew decaf?

"If Minerva really wants to get to know the community, then she couldn't pick a better way." Rendered prim with determination, the traitor.

"You go see Trudy tomorrow, Minnie." Rex dug into his potato topping.

"Okay then."

I figured there was no harm in playing along for a while. Then I had a dangerous vision, of serving outsized waffle cones to the twins and giving people the leftover milkshake that hadn't fit into their cup, of cutting pies into eight slices instead of ten. Lobster catches in the Strait might have been down, but I could be on duty behind a diner counter sneaking extras to whoever would take them.

"I'll tell Trudy," Doris said. "Better make it quarter to ten at the latest, Minnie."

That evening I saw my first skunk, waddling across the back lawn before dusk had cajoled day into night. I knew there were skunks in downtown Toronto, but in their proper habitat they seemed more exotic. I followed the punky waddler's path for as long as I could—kitchen window to parlour—then phoned over to Etta's to tell her to whistle Secord indoors unless she had an oil drum of tomato juice handy. Local calls were a lot more exciting than long distance. Gail had called twice already, which was nice of her, but I hinted at her the second time to cool it. Too much BC was going to disrupt PEI. Gail had to know that I completely forgave her for preferring her own island, and was aware that she forgave me for preferring mine.

I woke up early enough to make it to the beach for a quick tramp. The boots were on duty again. As usual, my footprints looked like someone else's on the way back. I made it home in time to do some weeding: the Tuck Harbour equivalent of a pedicure. I loved it when the interlopers came sliding all the way out from the pointy tips of their pale roots—the give and the cowed slither. It must have been the same frisson that Desolée had enjoyed when popping her zits years before. I had refused to let her do mine.

I finished off in the garden, washed my hands with the kitchen scrub brush, had breakfast in its second stage and then pointed my fat bike tires towards the village. I got to Eats n' Treats at nine-thirty. The diner was identifiable mostly by its enlarged parking lot. The breakfast rush was over; no rigs cramming the road, just a few smokers connoitering on the veranda. I stashed my bike around to the side. No one had warned me to buy a lock.

I jingled indoors. There was a long counter with wooden stools. There was a bench along the front wall and large booths down the sides to the back. There was an ice cream fridge and a pop fridge and an old-fashioned cash register with a ding.

"You must be Minnie," said a woman whose youth was not completely over. She had probably captained her school basketball team, or been one of the first girls in the midget league to play hockey with boys. She had the kind of face that people call striking when they want to imply that in the long run that's better than pretty—more captivating, more enduring and more authoritative. Her brows were dark and deft, her cheeks were subtly concave, her hair was longer than it would have been if she had lived in Toronto. "I heard you have Rex's eyes. Hang up your coat and pull up a stool. You might as well start off by relaxing. I'm Trudy."

I was poured a coffee before I knew it. I took a sip. As usual it tasted like hell to pay. I wondered if it would be keeping me up past midnight fifteen hours later. Only if I finished it. Maybe I could turn down "my" job fast enough not to have to do that.

"So business is good," I said.

"Too good. I can't crack eggs fast enough and the take-out is nuts. If I leave the phone off the hook, people call my house. I'm fried like fish."

Trudy had on a T-shirt that said *Danger Band*.

"You're not wearing a polyester blouse with your name over the pocket," I said.

"Oh, we can get you one of those if you want, Minnie."

"The thing is—"

"You come round and make the next pot. I can see the boats getting in. Any moment now there will be a lot of whiny fishermen looking to warm their hands around a cup of something hot. Large is a buck, small is seventy-five cents. So's in-house, but keep it to one refill. Use these white mugs here, clean ones in the back."

I decided not to go to my grave without ever having womanned a diner counter. Really, I should have been paying Trudy for the crazy highlight with which I'd spike my next phone calls back to Toronto. I made my way around to the back of the counter where there were maroon aprons hanging, one of which was "mine." There was a wide doorway through to the kitchen.

"This is Minnie, girls. She's come to help out."

"Wicked."

"Lovely to meet you, Minnie."

It looked busy in the kitchen, but I found out later this was a lull. Deep fryers crackled, soup bubbled, peas defrosted and a shiny skin of gravy clutched at a ladle. Verna, a teenager, and Debbie, a grandmother, looked pleased to see me. Something about Verna warned me not to get those names mixed up, no matter how excusable. I said my hellos. The door jingled.

"Go get 'em, Minnie. You pour, I'll ring in. If you can't find anything, just ask. Don't forget to keep the tips separate, you girls split those between you."

The door chimed, chimed and chimed. Every spare stool and front bench filled up with men with red hands and loud voices. There were a couple of equally burly fishing wives. No one was wearing Aran knit sweaters. Almost everyone took cream and sugar and no one asked for decaf. Pie was $2.95 a slice. Fresh pies were stashed in the fridge in the back, behind bags of carrots, trays of eggs and massive plastic sacks of fat-yellow soft ice cream base. Apple pie, pecan pie or strawberry rhubarb: every slice that wasn't right out of the oven had to be microwaved gooey for thirty seconds before being served. So I found out the hard way.

"Jeez almighty, my teeth just froze!"

"Let me warm that up for you, sir."

I pretended to sit my ass down on the nutty wedge. Lenny Bruce would have envied the reaction.

I made two old guys flip a coin to see who got the last butter tart. I kept the three coffee pots in slick rotation: filled, filling and all poured out. I rubbed elbows with Trudy to make change from the till. I slapped high fives with Verna and if we kept at it we would be adding hip bumps. It was absurd what I was so busy doing, but I couldn't escape the feeling that it was something I had to date missed out on doing and it was great that I had gotten around to it, the way some people finally make it to theme parks. I had just asked one massive and chivalrous fellow with oil stains from his wrists to his elbows and a gut the size of a Santa sack to help me open my latest stubborn packlet of coffee, then blown him a kiss of thanks, then had him wheezily offer to help me out any time, general harty har har—when the door jingled and Joe walked in, turning heads and receiving nods.

"Large?" I asked him.

I had not meant to get another laugh. Joe was no laughing matter. Joe was as serious as filling out forms or giving blood.

"Got yourself a job then, Minnie, did you?"

Joe knew my name and now everyone knew that. It was as if the mayor of Toronto had just bought me a shot of tequila.

"Maybe so. I like to keep busy. Mug for in or take-out?"

"In, thanks. Good for you, Minnie. I'm impressed."

Joe straddled the empty stool that had materialized. He spooned up a lot of sugar. All eyes were on us.

"Hungry?" I asked.

"That I am. How about a grilled cheese?"

"Whole wheat with tomato," Trudy called into the kitchen from over by the milkshake machine.

"Nice choice," I told Joe. It was honestly what I would have ordered.

But Joe was already talking to Herman Walker, about the latest theory that the bridge between Prince Edward Island and New Brunswick had altered the tidal currents in the Strait. The pilings were funnelling the current infinitesimally faster, potentially fast enough to rough up the lobster spawn was the thought. I wanted to hear more, but Debbie needed help in the dish pit, loading dirty cups and wiping the clean cutlery with vinegar solution. By the time I got back out front, Joe had left. Most of the fishermen were gone. A recently retired American couple wandered in, exclaiming over how absolutely darling the place was. I sat them at a booth in the back and convinced them to order lobster rolls. I decided to be honest about my status as a mere summer timer but one with legitimate local ties for as long as my "job" lasted. But I would not split the tips; that was going too far. I would volunteer to count them up and then sneak off without taking a share if I was going to preserve any sense of justice. There was no sign of Joe's truck at the wharf when I pedalled past. I had no idea which boat was his.

When I spotted Etta getting home from her own job, I hurried over to tell her about mine. She was loading a baking sheet with fish fingers—processed fish, caught by Portuguese trawlers dragging indiscriminately vast nets through international waters, flash frozen on board, sent to Asia for processing, then shipped back to eastern

Canadian grocery cases for the sake of harried parents. Suppertime was six sharp at the latest in the Harbour, with or without young-sters. Colin was dozing on the couch waiting for the PEI television news. It was rated high, locally, I suspected because it featured so many second cousins and former classmates. The sportscast extended to junior high softball and kiddy soccer. The anchorman was as stout and cheerful as a guidance counsellor.

"That sounds like fun, Minnie." Etta emptied a bag of frozen fries onto a second sheet. "Trudy's a real nice lady."

"What's the deal with her?"

Bette and then Joan were using my lap as an armchair while they pencil crayoned landscapes for Rex's fridge. I was recognizable by my anvil of hair, the girls were disproportionately lofty, and we were all grinning to be holding bunched hands beneath suns with yellow spokes and their own smiles. I supposed I had been that optimistic as a child, too.

"Trudy was living in Moncton for a while there managing the Fish Barn, but then her mother got sick. We've got a cancer cluster here, Minnie. Three guesses why."

"Nitrates!" the couch shouted. "Run-off!"

"Col, quiet with you or help cook!" Etta countered. "Where was I? Oh right, Trudy moved back for a while to help her dad run things at the diner. When her mom passed he didn't have the heart to keep going with the business so Trudy took over, jazzed it up a bit, got that new sign painted for out front. It was Trudy who added those salads to the menu. Then her dad died, too."

"Mommy, are you going to get sick?"

"No, pet, mom is as healthy as that horse next door and will be for a long time."

"Trudy hasn't got a man?"

"No, thank God, because she was with Fibby Trask for a long time and he's just an A-hole."

"MOM!"

"Oh, for crying out loud, I can't get away with a thing around here. Go wash your hands and tell your brothers to set the table."

"What makes him such an A-hole?" I hadn't figured out whether swearing on PEI caused half or twice the offence that it did in Toronto.

"God and nature!"

"Can I not tell a story around here without getting interrupted? Sorry, Minnie. As I was saying, Fibby bought a licence for the north shore back when they were a lot cheaper because that was all he could afford at the time. That was when the Strait guys were raking it in. Now things are the pits down here and try as he might, Fibby just can't resist lording it over everyone."

"Why's he called Fibby?"

"For one it's short for Filbert. For two, he told some tall ones when he was little. If you piss your pants when you're seven around here you're Pissy Pants until you're seventy-seven."

"So what's, um, the deal with Joe?" A whisper, my mistake.

"Colin! Minnie wants to know what the scoop is with your brother. Get in here and tell her. And set this table because your children refuse to."

"Set the table for what?" Colin stretched his limbs by the breakfast bar. "What the hell is that stench?"

"The sooner you get back to cooking the better, hubby of mine. All the best chefs are men, right, Minnie?"

"How long does lobster season go?"

"Until the last Friday of June, Minnie, my dear." Colin was much shorter than Etta in sock feet. Anyone indoors in Tuck Harbour was undoubtedly in sock feet, the culture was very Japanese that way. Anywhere but Rex's, since Rex knew urban Gallant women could not think properly without their shoes on.

"It's June already. That's not so far away."

"At which point my dear brother will busy himself talking to every bluefin tuna committee member from here to the Mediterranean. No one fishes for a tuna these days without eighty-five meetings going on beforehand."

"I'm sure he'll do what he needs to do."

"The deal with Joseph, Minnie, is that he's married to his work. Good thing, too, because no one else would have him. Not the way the ladies want me. Especially the fat ones."

"Thanks a helluva. Ouch!" Colin liked to bite Etta's earlobes, which Etta claimed to hate, but Colin loved to think she really loved it. He obviously loved to wrap his arms around her soft circumference and sniff, a good way to check if she was still using her Mother's Day perfume. Colin and Etta seemed to slide into each other as reasonably as six and seven.

"Am I setting a place for you, Minnie, my dear? You say the word and we'll call up that brother of mine and make it an even eight."

"Gosh, thanks, but I still have email to get through, maybe go for a run."

"Priorities, I remember those." Etta still had priorities, of course, in that she woke up every morning thinking *family, my family, my precious family, what does my family need to keep breathing, thriving, loving?*

"Can't a father get some help in this house? When Bob Hope was twelve he won a Charlie Chaplin look-alike contest and went right out and bought his mother a stove!"

I left Colin to bellow and Etta to butter the beans, after I'd tickled the girls and run upstairs to say goodbye to the boys, manic-thumbed in front of their bedroom television conducting a high-speed chase in a dark urban jungle. When I bent to give Secord a pat on my way out, he dropped to the ground in play death; his latest and favourite trick that he could not now be trained out of.

On the way back to Rex's house I checked for whales and eagles—not this time of year but I never knew. There was so much northerliness to the summer evening light that six o'clock beamed as gloriously as 1 p.m. I had time for a slow jog, the fields now rivalling couturier Italian textiles in their subtle combination of rust, yellow and eighteen different greens. I backtracked to Tuck Point to start with. The Tuck Point lighthouse had been one of the first to receive an SOS signal from the *Titanic*. I reminded myself to pick up a postcard and drop my father a line. Cece had grown up on the western wing of the Island, the somewhat less prosperous zone where all the jokes about inbreeding came from and more barns had half disintegrated. When Cece's vacation time came along he preferred to head south where beaches came with rental umbrellas. By the time I got back from my jog, a spider had built a heartbreaker of a web across the back door. There were screens on all the windows and the front door was locked so I was forced to poke my hand through the sticky fibres. That was after some contemplation as to predators' eternal faith in prey. Perhaps that was why I was vegetarian—I lacked devotion.

Everyone's Eats n' Treats habits were so ingrained that I quickly became used to them. There was no need to ask how anyone wanted their burger cooked: well unless ordered otherwise. Most Tuck Harbour teenyboppers ordered fries with gravy, but once in a while a kid would ask for chowder instead, mixed seafood or pinky lobster. Verna would scowl through the kitchen door at the alpha tweens, one or all of her three little brothers usually among them. A few short years before a similar gang had completely failed to comprehend Verna's punk aesthetic: purple nail polish, purple highlights, black on black attire with black ruffles, black lace and black flounces, fishnets *unter alles*. Verna had boycotted proms even in a place where proms were practice weddings with dresses the colours of candles that kept seamstresses and portrait photographers flush.

"Soon as I can, Minnie, I'm headed off Island." Verna would perk up at the thought of Montreal campuses, film school and a possible internship at Myriad. She was videotaping as much kitchen activity as she could, spending the summer perfecting her close-ups.

"You got a package today, Minnie." Debbie only moonlighted

at Eats n' Treats; she was also the mail lady, hoisting mailbox flags all over the village. I could lift the flag myself and leave a stamped item in my mailbox for Debbie to post: Tuck Harbour's only stab at concierge service. I would never have dared, however, not with a mail lady back home in Toronto who barely cracked a smile at Christmas tip season.

"Who from, Debs, did you notice?" I was not expecting anything.

"Looks like it's from your cousin."

"Minnie, counter please." Trudy was mid-hurtle, from the front through the kitchen back to the bottle room, her ponytail, which was actually the length of a pony's tail, bopping.

At first I thought another of those youngish Tuck Harbour gents of wholesome suavity had walked in, the kind with oxen shoulders and halting glances. Men of that ilk had begun to unburden themselves to me about the hardships of divorce while I filled their toddlers' cones with single scoops of Island Fantasy: vanilla with biscuit crumblings and caramel chunks.

"Who are you?" This guy's gaze was as blunt as his diction.

"I'm from Toronto," I warned.

He would have been handsome with smaller nostrils and ear rims that weren't so burnt red, and eyes that were a little bigger, higher, brighter. His hair gel had malfunctioned, flattening most of his hair except for one hiked sheaf towards the back that would pain him once he saw it in one of his no doubt numerous mirrors. I wouldn't have wanted to smooth it down; his 'do looked far too crispy. Right away he seemed like the kind of man whose dick is long and skinny, a cervix bruiser to no good end.

"Why'd you get this job then? Didn't some local kid need the money?"

"Dumb luck, I suppose."

"Large, two creams, three sugars."

I chose a take-out cup and tossed him a lid. He tossed me a dollar, then he tossed me a quarter. I let it lie.

"Herman," he nodded.

Herman Walker had paused halfway through his special treat piece of pie, not wanting to sour the last of his whipped cream.

"Fib," Herman nodded back.

"Filbert Trask, I presume?" I extended a hand, courtesy twisted so far up my arm it was rolled inside my underarm. "I'm Minerva Gallant. Your reputation precedes you."

His grip moistened and weakened as we shook on this, then his gaze tumbled into the wastebasket for stir sticks. He was gone with a screen door bang and tire squeal.

"Wednesdays Fibby comes down from North Lake." Verna had slid up behind me. "Weekends, too, worse luck." PEI fishers knocked off en masse on Sundays, family time worth organizing collectively. "Quel jerk."

"Coast clear, gals?" Trudy rubbed her tall brow with the back of her hand. She was pretty; it showed up when she worried. We would protect her virtue from the rapacious male. There might be pursuit but there would be no more capture.

"Minnie scared him off big time."

"Nice work, Minnie-Poo. I knew I hired you for a reason."

Herman caught up to me on my ride home and offered me a lift in his truck. I thanked him, but explained that in Toronto I paid over a hundred dollars a month to sit as often as I could on a bike that went nowhere. I sped the rest of the way. I grabbed a bubble envelope addressed to me in Desolée's block capitals out of the mailbox and stashed my bike in the old henhouse. Desolée, the twerp, had sent three boxes of condoms. She reasoned I would not want to be "caught" buying them at the Montague drugstore. I hurried to email a thank you—and remind her what a relief it was to spend some time in a place where one is judged for having sex rather than not having it. My laptop laboured over the connection, then Luce appeared exponentially in my inbox. Hardy and Nicola were headed to Cape Breton in early July as planned, so cooperatively it was making Luce edgy. I wrote back to tell her that sometimes reliability erupted and it unnerved me, too, but you had to go with the steadfast flow. Luce replied right away. Her mother had been using my place on Tuesdays, Thursdays and Saturdays. Luce was extremely apologetic, but her mother had bought me some houseplants and waxed my floors.

It was lovely the way everyone was thanking everyone else. I was tempted to write back to Luce one more time to tell her that I had a new job so she could go ahead and steal my old one if she wanted. Then I decided against tempting anyone to detect truth in the jest. A kid had ordered an old-time float that afternoon. I'd spent a fascinated moment staring at the glob of dairy product melting in cola fizz before handing it over. High calorie temptations and Fibby Trask aside, working at the Eats n' Treats was a good job.

Toward the end of June Rex told me to expect the Perkins boy to come and mow the hay before he left for air cadet camp in New Brunswick. I'd spotted Perkins Junior using his tractor as wheels, trundling up and down perimeter Tuck Harbour roads. When I got home from the diner one afternoon, Etta was incensed at the results. Young Perkins had left mounds of cut hay scattered high and low that were going to suffocate the second growth. I told Etta not to worry; I would grab a rake and get busy declumping. It was quite the phenomenon to set myself a task that encompassed thousands of square feet and made me look—to myself from afar—like a peasant in a maudlin watercolour. I appreciated living somewhere that so many metaphors came to life: back-breaking labour, pitching in, tough rows to hoe. I was also enjoying the way time was measured out in tasks rather than events. The raking loomed interminably, for days it was not done, not all done, not yet done, then suddenly done, at least until the Perkins boy mowed again. My shadow had kept me company out in the pasture, a more salubrious place for shadows than sidewalks. I dragged my shadow beachcombing whether it was in the mood to charge ahead, hang back or shrivel. I found a fifth piece of washed blue glass waiting out low tide. It was hard to understand where such blue glass came from, unless a lot of fishermen in the Strait were smashing Milk of Magnesia bottles overboard. By the third week of June, wind was finally blowing in my bedroom window all night long. I was tucked in bed counting waves in the dark when Desolée startled me with a late-night call.

"What's wrong?" I answered, slapped with worry that Bernard-Louis might not be on his way to Toronto after all, that Gail had choked on a lump of spelt bread, that Lee had been bitten by a rabid bat.

"What do you mean what's wrong?"

"It's so late."

"It's ten o'clock your time, you freak. I just got home from work. I've been looking forward to this all day. Be nice."

"Sorry, ten is the dead of night here. And it's ten twenty-two."

I'd answered the phone too quickly to turn on the kitchen light, but milky moonlight was seeping in the windows, softening the black to greys.

"How's Rex?"

"Good. He's corrupted the bridge club, they're all playing Texas Hold 'Em. I had to zip out to Etta's bank the other day and buy another thirty rolls of pennies. I found some lobster suspenders on-line for Rex's eighty-eighth. They should be here any day. I'll tell him they're from both of us. How are you?"

"Work is nuts. Tons of sympathy arrangements, which is weird because not that many people ordinarily die in the summer. Lots of closed-card high jinx that you'd get a kick out of, guys sneaking in here biting their pens and going for orchids. I'm sourcing tons of stuff locally lately, which is great. But my hard good costs are through the roof."

"How's Stash?"

"Fab. He's been decorating Boo's room. We're working with a train theme. I think we're going to go au pair rather than nanny. They have boy au pairs now. Nice kids from Guadeloupe and Martinique. How's your love life faring out there in lobster country?"

"I've already told you, the available ones have mothers our age or thereabouts."

The moon was so full it was smudged. I widened my eyes to fit all of it into my irises. I was gleaning so much lunar energy that my cycle had regularized for the first time in years.

"What about that guy who gave you the ride back from Montague that time?"

"Who, Joe? I barely see him."

"Don't pickup trucks make you want to get picked up?"

"No."

"Your loss. Eaten any lobster yet?"

"Cockroach of the sea."

"Frank has a new lady friend."

"That's nice."

"She's a dentist. They met over his teeth. She has a cottage in Haliburton."

I thought about telling Desolée it was lupin season and that luxuriantly mauve, purple and pink swaying stalks had colonized Island ditches. I thought about telling her how everyone of any vintage in Tuck Harbour seemed to have neat schoolteacher writing, as if they had all been hypnotized into replicating cursive script posters. I could have told her about the step dance end-of-year recital that Etta had taken me to in a boat barn: the little twins hopping hopefully with sideways glances at their pretty teacher, Pierre and the big boys far more confident as long as no one informed them that there was something entirely effeminate about their moves and outfits. Elliot was wise to that, a step class drop-out who sneaked cookies from the paper plate selection on the potluck table.

"The girl at the diner who I work with is going to score us some moonshine," I said instead.

"Oh my fuck, Minnie, you are so going to get poisoned."

"No I'm not! The retired RCMP guy who gave Verna's buddy her driving lessons explained how to tell if the stuff's okay. If you pour shine on a pane of glass and light it and it burns without colours, then it's fine."

"No funerals, that's all I ask. And if you do kill yourself, I promise there'll be hydrangeas. The Victorian look is very big this year."

"There's not as much fashion out here. You get to be yourself more blatantly than that." I was wearing a pair of boxer shorts that I had bought for Rex. I would have to fight with myself not to use them for underwear as well as pyjamas.

"Okay, well that's good I guess."

"Don't get me wrong, there's skateboards and lap dogs and bikini waxes. They haven't failed to join the century or anything."

"Maybe you can write a self-help book about all this when you're done, Minnie? Home Truths from the Potato Patch."

"You're the one who thought it would be a good idea if I came out here."

"Sorry, Min. I'm glad you're having a good time, seriously. Thanks for keeping such a good eye on Rex, we all thank you for that. Just promise me you won't get lonely, okay?"

"Okay."

Little did Desolée know that I had wind, waves, fields, sunshine, gulls and gannets, grass, Dosie, the house, the kitchen radio and an entire community to keep me company, besides my own mental thunder. Admittedly, I sometimes imagined being held by a loving man—in an armchair in a dark room, or in bed right after I'd turned out the light—a man I imagined far from particularly, only ever hazily, someone I sensed mostly over my shoulder who offered embraces no warmer than smoke. Longing did not bring him on; he was more of a reminder that I belonged to something large, general and grand. There was no sign of him by the time I had hung up on Desolée and got back into bed.

I suspected that Joe didn't make as many Eats n' Treats appearances as everyone else because whenever he walked into a room the impact was similar in scope if not effect to that of a parish priest. Once in a while, however, Joe would pop into the diner, usually with his cellphone pressed to his ear, sometimes with twenty minutes to spare to make Herman Walker feel like he had never retired. Joe ate fast, four chomps per sandwich half, his temples pulsing like they were timing an Indy 500 pit stop. He drank fountain diet cola, large no ice, which disappointed me in the way the Marlboro man would have if he'd turned out to smoke menthols, which was unfair of me so I tried not to show it. That was hard because Joe had great clarity of eyeball. He had unquestionably beautiful eyes; in fact, Joe could have been a glass-eye eye model. I also liked the way Joe's voice defied his height; he had a very bass grumble. As for that hair—Byronic. To myself I could admit that taken as a whole Joe made my breasts buzz and my lungs hot. There were things I wanted to tell him by breath alone.

With one week of school to go, kids were getting off the bus with their sweaters stuffed in their knapsacks. Most sipping took place out on the front porch. I'd go out there with paper towel and Windex to wipe the front windows when I wanted to join in on the chat. Usually the talk had to do with how well the Donovan kid was doing on the Gateway Tour—he'd had a beer with Tiger Woods in some Californian country club after winning a key tournament—or whether the chilly June was going to delay the strawberry crop, or what the total suspended solids level had gotten to be in the Strait. "Siltation happens," I suggested, and got a few laughs.

Verna's bulky father, Archie Doiron, was warning everybody off the latest science since the government had never known jack shit and never would, and who did they think they were taking money out of fishermen's pockets to monitor catches when the best rules had always been set by fishermen for fishermen? Archie wasn't naming names, but if anyone was going to get it into their head to fish undersized or oversized, they damn well knew what they were in for, he'd see to that. I knew that buoys could get cut loose from traps, and that traps could go missing at a hundred dollars apiece. The word was out that some of the fleets working the dead centre of the Strait had petitioned for short-term government loans to bail them out of the dismal season. Joe had let it be known that instead he was pressing hard for fleet reduction. But who would give up and sell out? It seemed to me like the fishing equivalent of unloading the family farm.

Joe and Colin ambled up to the diner porch one morning looking relieved. They had pulled in five hundred pounds that day—good for this year, if not five years earlier. "Minnie, my dear, make me a coffee milkshake would you? And don't tell my wife."

"Anything for you, Joe?"

It was the first time that I had said his name aloud, a caress of sorts. I thought it would be good to really touch Joe, just once, to see what it was like. I guessed he would be smooth, hirsute, hard and soft in all the appropriate places. Given the chance, given Joe naked, I thought I would place my hand on the small of his back first, emphatically as a plate on a tray. From there I would rub in circles down to his ass, so atavistically full of female-over-the-shoulder muscles, so nice and bundled. With one hand wrapped tight around Joe's hips, I could press the other to his breastbone until I felt heartbeat. Then I'd slide that hand up to his neck and around the back of his head into his thick, dark curls. I'd take a nice fistful, but I wouldn't pull, not hard, just for a second, if only to then smooth Joe's brow clear of worry as tenderly as a mother checking for a fever. Then I'd slide that hand back down his ribs, swivel it, and send it right down to his ..., wrapping my fingers around, squeezing, fiddling, rubbing, more squeezing. Damn. Finally, I would pitch forward and fucking kiss the man, finishing off with small pecks where the corners of his lips tucked into darling little lumps. It was time to bless males again, for their addictive geography, and the way they smell deep inside one's brain, the wakeful dream of them; the foolish pheromonal elixir; the crush. As for Joe's hands, they would be madness, his fingertips brutalized over the years by ropes and salt. What it would feel like for me to be touched by Joe, or feel like for Joe to touch me: those were burning new questions.

"No thanks, Minnie, I'm fine."

"My brother has the sweetest teeth known to science, Minnie, my dear. He just doesn't want to admit to it." Colin came inside to keep me company while I scooped and squirted.

"Maybe Joe's seasick," I said.

"Nah. Our father warned us he'd slap our face with a wet mitt if we got sick out on the boat when we were little. That's what his father did to him."

"Really?"

"Probably not."

Joe and Colin's parents, Charlie and Dolly McTeal, were jolly and timorous respectively, the kind of father who notices when a light bulb needs replacing, the kind of mother who bakes casseroles with potato chip crusts.

"Here you go, neighbour. One coffee milkshake, extra coffee, extra shake."

"What do I owe you, Minnie, dear?"

"It's on me." I dug in my pocket for change to toss in the till.

"Come on now."

"Okay then. Take me lobstering. I want to know what all the fuss is about."

"Did you hear that, everybody? Minnie wants to go out on the boat."

Colin had headed back out to the porch; I followed. Bob and Linda MacPhee and Thane Donovan were out there, and Darlene MacDonald who always brought her own lawn chair, and Herman. Joe remained at the bottom of the porch stairs, tossing his keys and catching them with a happy *kachink* sound that satisfied me, too.

"Better make it snappy." Thane Donovan was the golf pro's youngest uncle, cocky by association. "Season's over Friday, that only gives you two days."

"How about tomorrow?" My face was a calm sea. Trudy had promised to give me a day off whenever I wanted.

Joe's keys were quiet now. "There's a northeasterly, it'll be choppy."

"Miserable slop," said Bob MacPhee.

"No problem," I said. "Really, I want to try this out. It'll be exciting for me. Believe me."

"Okay then, Minnie, if you say so. Colin can pick you up. Dress warm."

"I'll be at your door at three, Minnie, my dear. With Gravol!"

Laughs all around. Colin tossed his empty milkshake cup and they split. I found Trudy in the back kitchen eviscerating roast chickens for sandwich meat. She smiled when I told her my plan to go fishing, then smiled harder when I told her who with.

"Joe McTeal?" Verna overheard. "Oh my God, he's so iconic."

Debbie giggled into her latest pie crust.

"He looks just like the father in the *Bicycle Thief*, don't you think, Minnie?"

"I don't know about that. I just think of him as Colin's brother."

"Ya right," said Trudy. "I call bullshit."

Giddiness is as pure a form of confession as they go. I cracked up so hard I thought I might pop apart a couple of vertebrae, the kind of laugh after which little needs to be said to get everyone howling again. If I hadn't already been dragged off my high horse, base desire—that great leveller—had done the trick. All everyone needed now was to get Joe and me up in a tree.

Then Verna and I invented a new game. We all had to take turns imagining that we were going to have sex with the next person who walked in the door. I got a church lady. Verna got one of her brothers. When Trudy got Herman Walker she said game over. On my way home I found extra-strength Gravol for sale at the Clover Mart. Beth at the front cash advised me to take two as soon as I woke up. It was a bizarre circumstance to set my alarm clock for an hour that I might conceivably be heading to bed in Toronto if I had caught last call at Desolée's latest *boîte* of choice. I was ready for Colin at a quarter to 3 a.m., wearing the sparkly boots and two layers of fleece under my windbreaker, with a peanut-butter-and-banana sandwich, and a tray of bear paw cookies from the Clover Mart bakery section to make up for that.

Colin was as cheerful in the dead of night as he was waking up from an afternoon nap, tuning in to the country station just to bug me and cranking it when the tune got pious. The Tuck Harbour wharf was bustling in a subdued way when we got there, the anchor clanks loud in the dark but voices lowered with elves-and-shoemaker secrecy. Colin offered me his hand getting from the dock to the boat, not Joe's boat but someone else's over which we had to clamber to get to the *Darling Dolly*. Joe had been smart to name his boat after his mother, his version of a *Mom* tattoo. Most were named after wives and Harbour lore had it one bitter divorcé had tried to rename his boat *The Slut*. By the time I landed on Joe's deck my equilibrium was my own. He was busy with his dashboard gizmos. I thanked him again for having me. I was told to beware coiled ropes on deck, I could help myself to pop and there was a head in the cuddy if I needed it. Colin momentarily teased Joe about tidying up for the first time in years, but there was little shooting the shit while three hundred traps waited miles out and fathoms down to be hauled up and checked for money-makers.

Once we had chugged out as far as we needed to, the brothers hopped into bibbed overpants and grabbed matching zippered jackets. I had expected traditional lemony gear, not slickers the same green as cottage cheese mould. It was hard to tell in the dark, but it looked like Joe had been assigned pink buoys. There was a hydraulic system hanging off the side of the boat to haul the traps up onto the starboard gunwale. Colin shoved the traps aft to Joe, who emptied them of bugs (lobsters) and slime (seaweed), then baited them again. I felt bad for the squirming perch, their little faces so sad in the first place.

Colin saw to it that the traps plunged back overboard, the first one shoved, the next five following fast, one after the other. Joe hustled onward to the next dump while Colin looked over whatever lobsters Joe had just set aside. Anything undersized or egg-bearing got tossed back in the water in a wheeling arc and plop.

It would have been nice to help out, but insinuating myself into such a well-worn system just seemed rude. And I didn't really want to grab hold of a lobster's abdomen, its claws uselessly waving, its territorial instincts thrown hopelessly out of whack, and hold a metal Fisheries Department–issued ruler up to its carapace. The past few hours from a lobster's point of view would have gone from claustrophobic to agoraphobic, then incarceratory—if I cared to anthropomorphize what it was like to be trapped, sorted, have an elastic band snapped around my claws, then get plonked in a writhing crate with dozens of other captives.

Colin had warned me the tiring part was going to be bracing against the pitching: walking down the boat when it was downhill, up when it was uphill, plus up when it was downhill and down when it was uphill. The gradient was Himalayan and my feet needed my hands to get anywhere. I got a couple of sweet hellos hollered over to me by diner regulars hard at work on other boats, the reticent turned boisterous now that their own habits prevailed. That was while I still strolled the deck. Eventually, I tucked myself into the front bench at the table up by the steering wheel. The GPS monitor looked like it should feature as a conceptual art installation, beaming pastel shades of meaningful pink, green and yellow. Joe was handling the boat like a stunt driver who never needed a second take. I could feel the *Darling Dolly*'s mighty thrust in her deep diesel rumble. We could have gone all the way to Iceland in the wrong mood on a good week.

It was a strange thing to actually see the crack of dawn. Cocktail-coloured light poured down on the grey water for a sunset amount of time, then morning cranked wide open and the shore reverted to brick-red with green trim. The McTeal buoys were confirmed as pink.

"We repaint them over the winter," Joe said. "At least I do."

"Do you make your own traps?"

"It's easy now they're plastic mesh. The old guys had to carve lathes and knit jute."

We had to shout over the engine; chat was entirely optional.

"What do you like best about all this?"

"Moving the traps around, I guess. Adjusting the dumps, figuring out where to catch not just the most stuff but the best stuff."

I knew that the protocol was to establish a lobster ground and stick to it season after season while engaging in daily minute variations therein.

"For someone not personally involved I guess it could get monotonous."

"If you get bored, Minnie, I'll take you back in."

"God no! I didn't mean it that way."

What a waste of sexual tension—to have acted too relaxed. Whence rectification?

"Hey, Minnie!"

I inched my way out to peek around the cabin wall. Colin was still busy with the gauge.

"Ever wonder how lobsters have sex?" asked the ever bothersome little brother.

"Um, NO!"

"Once the female senses a big strong male is available to her, she drugs him stupid with hormones. Then she moults and gives him her shell for a snack."

"How ladylike."

"He softens her up with some antenna stroking next and then he rolls her over on her back and shoots a ball of sperm down these little legs of hers, into the egg pouch under her tail, see right here?"

"I see."

"The older the female, the better the eggs, Minnie."

"Good to know."

"The lady lobster hangs out in his shelter while her shell grows back, stealing his food when she can. One night she sneaks out while he's prowling, lobsters love to prowl, they're real nosy types. That's when Lover Gal gives one of her girlfriends a chance to move in on her man. Only when she's good and ready does she unplug that old sperm ball and fertilize it."

"The things you men put up with."

"The important thing is that the female lobsters need the alpha males, Minnie. Otherwise they get confused and don't mate. Most of the time the males and females don't get along at all."

"How does a male get to be alpha?"

"Winning fights mostly, defending the best shelter. Staying out of traps."

"You're boring the poor girl to tears." Joe thumped the throttle into neutral and scooped his gloves back up off the cabin floor.

"I'm interested, believe me." I was most interested of all in the fact that Joe had called a forty-year-old woman a *girl*, wondering what woman wasn't a girl once Joe got a look inside of her. I sat back down to consider this.

Another haul, another dump, the eleventh of fifty. I was not bored, but I was sleepy. I was getting badly bullied by pitch-black sleep. I had sea legs, I had a sea stomach and I had leaden eyelids. The waves were so ridiculously rock-a-bye. I didn't just drift off—I was swept to unconsciousness like flotsam in the path of effluent. I woke up hours later, when Colin tugged one of my boots, from a nap that causes drool and grunting, from an embarrassment of sleep.

"One dump left, Minnie, my dear."

I was covered in someone's old jacket. The sun was as high overhead as a teacher at a school desk. The upside was the ribbing I'd get at the diner, the taunting fun for everyone. Yes, I'd slumbered through practically everything, but I'd also avoided vomiting last night's stirfry into the Gulf of St. Lawrence.

"I brought bear paws!"

"Oh, we got into those, Minnie, my dear. Joe did. He said you had to pay your way somehow."

The brothers' gloves were off for another day as well as their jackets. They had tobacco-brown arms and salt in their hair and crustacean juice soaked into their T-shirts. Joe stuck to the wheel while Colin sorted through gear. I said goodbye to the most open sea I'd see for a while. We stopped by the processing plant at the mouth of Tuck River to deliver the day's load of markets and canners. The buyer strolled the dock with a clipboard and his mouth full of pleasantries; so much of PEI's one-hundred-and-ten-million-dollar lobster catch per annum was up to middlemen. Colin unloaded while Joe sorted through his phone messages. I sat on the cabin roof swinging my boots and squinting. I had not bothered with a bra that morning, which I realized now had been a big mistake. Hot was getting hotter, the kind of heat that makes one's bones feel soggy. It was rude to strip down to one thin layer of cotton, but it seemed equally rude to assume anyone was interested in what I had to show for myself.

Joe kicked out of his rubber pants and hung them on their hook. I wanted to reassure him that the Strait wasn't the only place that had gone dire, that snow way up in the Rockies had also measured high for degrees of toxicity. But Joe was too good a person to be consoled by others' losses. Joe, at least, was pristine, a provincial park of a man. I wanted to lick inside his elbows. I wanted to thump my heels against fibreglass for the rest of the summer while the sun shone down and the brothers worked in sync. Eventually we putt-putted back to where we started.

"Minnie, my dear, I have to go into Montague to pick up the girls and take them to a birthday party. Joe's going to run you back."

"I can walk!"

"Joe doesn't mind. You sit tight, Minnie. He'll be off that phone soon. Either that or the battery will run out."

The tide had lowered so the wharf was now a lot higher than when we had set off. Colin anteloped his way back up there and Joe would, too. I would not be so lucky. Joe would have to haul me to safety by the arm that had not been broken. He definitely needed to get off that phone. My arms flexed at the thought of the effort to come. I studied my hands. They say there are brain cells in the gut but what about palms and fingers?

"Okay, Minnie, let's roll."

"Coming."

Joe leaped to the dock like a hurdler doing a warm-up. He trusted I would scramble up after him; I trusted he would not let me slip between the harbour wall and the pitching boat down into the soup. While Joe held tight to my forearms my boot toes scuffled with wet, chinked timber. Both my hands had reached up to him as naturally as panic.

"Terra firma!" I cawed when I could. My knees felt like they were stuffed with sponges, a sensation I tried to abate with a jig. My breasts quickly objected.

"I need to stop home for a minute, Minnie, and check on a fax. Okay with you?"

"Sure thing!"

It was hotter on land. Crickets were incensed, everyone's hair was bright metallic, Popsicles were an appropriate snack. I could see the Eat n' Treats' porch was crammed. Joe drove again: boat now truck. We zoomed into the densest huddle of village dwellings that studded the hillside upriver of the bridge.

"Recognize this place, Minnie?"

Joe's home was a concise two stories, authentically shingled, symmetrically windowed, a bit crooked if you stared for too long.

"No," I said. "Sorry."

The big brother was up to some mischief after all.

"Your mother was born here, Minnie. Once upon a time this was your grandparents' house."

"You bought it?"

"It's changed hands a few times since then, now it's mine. There's not much to see, but you can come in if you want."

"Yes!"

Very little in Joe's house went beyond the utilitarian, except for the television with a screen the size of a kitchen tabletop programmed to receive all manner of sportscasts. Colin was lured over most Saturday nights to watch boxing matches beamed in from Vegas. Elliot and Pierre were strictly forbidden to join in and the girls would be, too, once they knew what they were missing.

I had entered reverentially, hoping for poignant memories to report but no luck there. "Gosh, Joe, this is lovely!"

"Make yourself at home, Minnie. Let me know if I can get you anything."

Joe's sink was not full of dirty dishes, but his draining rack was perilously stacked with clean ones. His kitchen island was strewn with tide tables, licensing forms and phone books from PEI, Saint John, Halifax, St. Johns and Ottawa. The only art on the wall was a five-by-seven of a younger Joe at the wheel of a brand new *Darling Dolly*. The living room sofa was dented at Joe's end, but puffy where the view of the television was not quite so dead on. It was upholstered in sky-blue velveteen. I was compelled to sit down and rub the pile, the right way, then the wrong way, then smooth it again. Joe was scraping at his kitchen screen door for some reason.

"Come in if you're coming in," I heard him say.

A mournful meow, the fridge door opening, milk being poured into a bowl.

"I didn't know you had a cat!" Why that should be an accusation on my part I did not know.

"I don't."

"What do you call that?" It was a frail little thing, basically dandelion fluff with a face and tail and *how-could-you?* wail.

"I call this a stray that knows what time I get home."

"Wow, Joe, you're a softy." I was reproving again, keeping my distance vocally in case lust got the better of me.

"A softy, am I? Try telling that to someone who wants to go after bluefin first chance he gets."

"I hear you want to delay the start of tuna season."

"No point fishing up the quota while they're starving."

"More of them are migrating this far north, right? Because of global warming?"

"More of what tuna there is, Minnie, which is less and less."

Joe was opening up envelopes with a vengeance. Window envelopes and chunky manila ones.

"Fishing is pretty well ocean rape, isn't it? As things stand?"

Joe looked up. I heard matches flare beside my ears. Where my skin wasn't bare it prickled.

"Strong words for a strong thought, Minnie?"

"What I mean is, fishing can't afford to get too industrial. Too much effort defeats the resource?"

"Fishing large scale is hard to manage. You've got that right."

The kitty meowed, rubbing her flanks into Joe's denim.

"But how to stop what's started?" I asked this of the cat rather than Joe.

"I better get you home, Minnie."

"Don't let me get in your way."

My excuse to step forth and pat Joe on his back, a dauntless back, damp as if steam ironed. An anthropologist would have chuckled knowingly. I grabbed his keys from his cracked key bowl and tossed them over. Whatever was going on between us was to stay on a molecular level for now, I got that. Joe lowered both windows as soon as we got going.

"This truck is a standard, right?"

"Sure is. I like them better this way. More to control, more interesting."

"I wish I could drive. I'm a terrible driver."

"Probably because you don't get any practice."

Then we were at a complete halt, then Joe was out of his seat, at my window, jumping in beside me. I scooted over; now I was behind his wheel.

"Press in the clutch, Minnie, then shift her into first, now ease up on the clutch and push down gentle on the gas. That's it, there you go."

Whump, whump, whump. It was like the road was barfing the truck along in heaves. Herman honked as he overtook us, grateful that we were out of his way. I was too scared to blush. I was frightened of ditches, and stripping Joe's gears, and holding us up all afternoon in my attempt to drive one kilometre. I knew enough to thank God we had already crested the hill and were almost to Rex's road.

"Shit, shit, sorry, sorry!"

I forked shuddering left.

"That's it, Minnie. You're doing fine. Relax and you'll get a feel for it."

"I hate putting anyone else through this!"

Resonating in the hot bright air was the unspoken truth that a man should never try to teach his woman how to drive, that it is a fast route to recrimination and rupture. At least we were endangering our relationship before we had even got it started. Dosie was now in view, sceptical enough to consider us worth interrupting grazing time for. I felt sweat bead then trickle down to my waistband.

"That's it, keep her in second, Minnie, and slow her down. Easy does it."

I was not sure who I wanted to look at less, Joe or my frazzled self, my nipples hardened in the heat with fight reflex. Joe was lending me his vehicle, his means to be and do. But he had also forced a weapon into my hands, a ton of steel that could pop muscles open like grapes and squirt blood across the road like the Lord's ketchup. I stalled again halfway down Rex's lane. Joe said no aborting the mission: I had to park for real. Finally, it was over. Now I hated to let the wheel go. Joe was too pleased with both of us to care, looking like kite and kite flyer at the same time.

"I seen Herman's face when he drove by, Minnie. He couldn't believe it. It'll be all over the diner tomorrow."

"You *saw* Herman Walker?"

"I seen Herman gawking like a kid at the circus. He'll be letting everyone know what a tiger you are."

"That's good."

"You're a brave one, Minnie. There's no doubt about that. It's good to see."

I grabbed my jacket and sweaters from the back, and my smelly sandwich, and the baseball cap Colin had given me that advertised Ocean Choice. Joe patted my back this time before he climbed back into the driver's seat—with a hand that had as much soulful ballast as expected, a hand prone to good. Too bad I was queasy, insidiously so. I wished it was late-onset sea sickness or driving lesson nerves, but it was that deep in my brain I had taken poor Joe to Toronto, potentially, where I heard him turn into someone completely off-putting before I had even seen him do so. *Saw, saw, saw.* Who did I think I was, to cringe at Joe's backwoods grammar? No one I wanted to be. If we had been dancing some kind of local folk dance for the past few weeks I hoped it was over now with a curtsey and a bow.

"You take care, Minnie."

"Will do!"

I hurried inside for a hell of a whizz, and then sat on the toilet for so long afterwards that I burned a red ring into my ass. Happily, I would be seeing Rex soon, always a good cure for self-loathing. Friday after work Verna was going to trim my bangs and then we were going to drive into Montague and pay the Manor a call. Then we were going to hunt down the friend of a friend who could slip us some shine, take a nip or two as an aperitif, and make it to karaoke night at the Crab Shack.

"Minnie!" A child, out the kitchen window, now in the kitchen door. It was Elliot, holding a tiny green stalk. "Look! Mom said to show it to you."

"Holy moly, a four-leaf clover. That's wonderful, El. You're going to have such good luck your whole life long."

"Here, Minnie. You can split it with me."

Tiny dirty thumbs with nails that needed cutting, a moment of silence while the delicate task was underway, the stalk going mainly to one half, the half I got to keep.

"This is the best thing anyone ever gave me. I mean it, dude."

I had been wondering why perfumers never tout clover as a base scent. There were fields full of it smelling just the way sun-soaked purple ought to. Once Elliot took off with his characteristic sprint, I wandered down to the bottom of Dosie's meadow where clover was growing in mauve profusion. I tumbled into it. I literally rolled in clover until it was stuffed inside my mouth and pockets. Not that it was a soft ride. The field was studded with rocks and hillocks and possibly Dosie patties so I had to close my eyes and protect my head. I probably wasn't that far away from a snake; I had seen a few road-side while jogging, short, skinny little snakes that tempted towards misdeeds rather than out and out sins. I came to a rest and tried not to think about anything but the sky and how much I loved being under Rex's special tidy piece of it. And how far the ant up my pant leg was crawling. And what the hell I would say if anyone had caught me swooning through a clover patch like Isadora Bumpkin Duncan.

Tuna

6

Etta brought both sets of twins to the diner for end-of-school-year ice creams, as promised to the kids and to me. The girls and Pierre preferred soft serve, dripping fast in the scorcher. Elliot favoured a waffle cone packed with lurid blue Cotton Candy. He liked seeing me dig up to my elbows in the frost-frizzled bin for a final dizzy scoop. Eats n' Treats was hopping. Lots of other moms had the same idea now that elementary schools no longer condoned last-day-of-the-year pop and chips parties—the classroom blinds glamorously drawn, the teasing running high, the sugar rush playing into the holiday rush playing into the summer rush playing into joy, or at least the assurance that joy was enfolded somewhere inside all the excitement. Here was Christmas Eve's calendar counterpart. I was gathering how much fun it is to feed children. Not that I would ever feed a child a whole platter of fried chicken, fries with the works (peas, gravy, minced beef and factory mozzarella), large pop and a sundae to follow, heavy on the nuts. That was how many bulky Harbour parents often fed their zaftig children. "Child abuse," I would whisper to Trudy. She would shrug, a slash of shame twisting up her grin. Usually, I was dismissed before the mopping started. That Friday I stuck around to help scour the front counters, sweep the deck and shut off the appliances. Then Verna and I hauled a stool out to the bright, grassy Eats n' Treats rear yard. A poky bit of river sludged into marsh farther back, but the mosquitoes weren't yet out. Verna took the scissors we used to snip open bags of frozen peas to my forest-creature bangs.

"Just kind of hack into them," I suggested. "They're refusing to be neat anyway."

"So, like, post-modern hair then, Minnie?"

"Perfect. Tell me, who are we getting this moonshine from again?"

"A guy called Pat who we're meeting at the Crab Shack parking lot at eight sharp. I told him the green Yaris. He sounds okay."

"Don't say anything to Rex about dragging me astray. He'll never forgive you."

"That's better, Minnie. Do you want me to trim the rest of it, too?"

"No need. It hit my shoulders thirty years ago and stopped."

"It's a bit longer than that now."

Verna was wearing her black braids pinned on top of her head like a punk Heidi. She had on black velvet knickerbockers with pink polka-dotted black knee socks and a black ribbed undershirt with a heart outlined in safety pins. She was going to switch to black leather shorts, she said, once we were finished at the Manor.

"I had no idea lobsters lead such intricate lives," I told Rex and gang in the ground floor lounge while their dinner digested. "They're right or left clawed and recognize each other as individuals. They can walk hundreds of miles in a lifetime."

We had taken over the armchair pod farthest from the television, Verna and I perching on arms. Shirlene was in bed with sniffles but the ladies promised she always rallied fast. I had fetched Sally's white summer cardigan and felt Rex's hands to make sure they were warm. The Manor employed its air conditioning system cautiously, but needed to crank it on days like this when the local newscast doled out heat-wave survival strategies.

"Lobsters are industrious buggers, that's for sure." Rex held on to his cane like a tap-dance prop when he was seated. "That's as long as they've got some cobble to build a den. You tell Joe it's the scalloping in the Strait that's got to stop. Scallopers dredge the bottom of the Strait dead clean. Clean's no good for lobsters."

"That's what I told my dad." Verna had no problem chipping in. "Then he asked me if I want to go to university or not. I said we should just get rid of my brothers!"

Verna's mother fished lobster and scallops along with her husband, as did a few other sturdy Harbour wives. Most of them had long fuses and curt laughs and talked over their husbands' kooky inevitabilities in the same resigned tone they discussed the weather.

"Don was concerned about scalloping," Sally reminisced. "Tasty things, though, aren't they?"

Verna and I took our leave amid the flurry of scallop recipes, with Sally preaching garlic to the converted. Rex thumped his way out with us as far as the top porch step. He had on sneakers, old canvas lace-ups rather than anything swooshed. He was in flapping shorts that needed suspenders and a short-sleeved shirt that showed off his skin's many hues: pinks, whites, browns and even greens, a dozen different colours now rather than a sheen. Was Rex decomposing? He did not seem unhappy or unwell; in fact his face was extra placid.

"What are you young women up to tonight then?"

"Verna's taking me to the Crab Shack!" I was proud of my invite, knowing Rex would be happier for me the prouder I was. The Crab Shack skulked on the edge of Montague, wilfully repelling tourists.

"Minnie got us a room at the Shady Acres." Verna was excited about her first night ever of rental accommodation. I had insisted, based on my refusal to drink alone.

"Isn't that great," said Rex. "You two have a good time."

"Uncle Rex, no, no!" There were only so many no's I could utter before I had to accept the twenty-dollar bill that Rex was offering since there was one in it for Verna, too. Rex had obviously looked forward to his benevolence; who was I to mug it from him?

"Thanks, Mister Arsenault! First round on you!"

Whether Verna was very polite or it was the effect of average politeness in combination with her gloomy garb I was not sure. I took her cue.

"Uncle Rex, are you sure we can't take you back to the Harbour with us tomorrow morning?"

July first was the Tuck Harbour Canada Day parade, an annual filing past of antique fire trucks, Shetland ponies and a hodgepodge of floats that was the Harbour's sole bid for attention, followed by a strawberry social in the community centre baseball field. The young golfer was rumoured to be flying in for the day to participate. Trudy had arranged to put an old table with a gingham cloth, mugs, spoons and menus on the back of a flatbed truck to represent Eats n' Treats. Verna and I were slated to "pour" coffee up there for Herman Walker and Darlene MacDonald while Doris helped out back at the actual diner. I was sincerely looking forward to the flags and the crowds and the tuba toots from the Montague High marching band. I would have loved to wave at Rex and then take him back to the house for a mild early supper, holding his arm up the stairs, checking on Dosie and then turning out the kitchen light. Or take him to Etta and Colin's barbeque dinner; she was grilling asparagus, and promising me plum tomato-halloumi flatbread and seitan tofu skewers.

"I'll sit this one out, Minnie. You tell me all about it, dear."

"You bet."

Rex was shorter than me now. He was shrinking like a bar of soap, still the same shape, still smelling the same, but there was gradually less of him to get a hold of. I hugged goodbye after Verna so that mine would be the one he was left with. We were both sad to leave him, I thought. Then we realized we were both very hungry and very thirsty and very pleased about the implications of that. I liked the way Verna's decisive driving further eroded the age difference between us. The Tuck Harbour assumption seemed to be that coming from Toronto made me so different from everybody else that ordinary differences barely registered. Desolée, in any case, was amused that my best Tuck Harbour pals were shaping up to be over eighty and under twenty.

We parked in the Crab Shack lot almost on the dot of eight—a mere five minutes late, which Verna reminded me did not count for girls. The lot looked disproportionately big. The Shack was one storey, the dirty pink of cinnamon gum. The red neon crab scaling the roof looked to be stretching the limits of provincial signage legislation. Verna rolled up our windows and cranked Fat Cat 99.3. We needed to review our karaoke options. Both of us were leaning towards glam rock. I passed Verna her secondary makeup bag out of her glove compartment so she could reapply mascara while Black Betty had a child and the damn town went wild.

"How'd you get so good at the war paint?" I wondered, marvelled actually.

"Trial and error." Verna smacked and blotted, her mirror face several degrees more suspicious than her regular expression but still pliant. "There's always more where it came from so you can always start over. You're lucky, Minnie, you don't need foundation."

"That's because I need wrinkle cream."

"Do not!"

Verna had wonderfully thick eyelids, a nice tip to her long nose, and sombre vertical cheeks—a face just right for a fresco, tapestry or a stained-glass window. I was formulating an acceptable way to explain this when we both screamed—at the knuckles rapping at Verna's side window. In an instant she had the music quashed and was humming down her window; work in a diner had rendered her octopus dextrous.

"What's up, ladies?"

"Are you Pat?"

Patrick from the shelter was leaning into the car. His submarketplace subsistence had combined with my overage mischief to make for quite a coincidence. I recognized his frayed cuffs and sanguine wheedle.

"Patrick!" I leaned over Verna's black lap. "It's Minnie," I said. "From, you know, Toronto. We met there a couple of months ago."

"Minnie?" said Patrick. "How do you like that."

Patrick was ruddier now, no longer harassed into pallor. His eyes continued bright. I hoped he was doing altogether better, but his jeans and sweatshirt looked too hot in the summer in the same way that they had looked too cold in the winter.

"Patrick was out West for a while this past winter," I explained to Verna.

"Yup, Alberta bound."

Verna was truly polite. "Hope that worked out for you."

Patrick was too well travelled to be unsettled by Verna's macabre attire. "Ya, well, I guess no one ever does as well as they wanted. I stopped off in Moncton at a buddy's place for a while there. Anyhow, I'm back now. Had to go to the beach, eh? It's summertime."

"So you're the . . . *Pat* we're looking for?"

"Guess so, Minnie. Make it twenty and we're square."

I reached for my bag; I'd assured Verna this travesty of good sense was also on my dime. We had ordered only a mickey, a mockery of audacity really. Still, Verna nodded at the back seat. She was right; it wasn't like we were trading in yellowcake, but there was casual and then there was asking for it. "Here." I jumped out of the car and flipped my seat forward. "Hop in."

Patrick was a small man, but he still had to origami himself into Verna's back seat, diplomatically the middle. I took the flat, sloshing, brown-bagged lump from Patrick's front jean jacket pocket in exchange for a twenty, Rex's twenty, which gave me a bit of a pang, plus an extra five.

"Thanks then, Minnie. Much appreciated. I'm just the delivery guy, but every bit helps. If youse ever want some weed just let me know, but that's as far as it goes. Harder than that and you're on your own. Man alive, it's nice and cool in here. Oh well, nothing we can do about the weather my good ma always said."

"We don't have shine in Toronto."

"Not that you know of, Minnie."

"Can we take you anywhere, Pat?" Verna was a real Galahad with the Toyota.

"Fact is, ladies, I fancy a bite to eat. Is the doughnut shop on your way?"

"We packed a picnic, but we've got way too much food, right, Minnie?" Verna had caught the scent of the dispossessed. "Why don't you join us?"

"I won't say no."

My mind blazed with vicarious worry on Verna's parents' part regarding Patrick's reliability, whether it extended to informing him of our accommodation arrangements and, if so, whether he would give Verna her first orgasm and then steal all our money, forcing Verna and me to drive off a sandstone cliff in quirky hopelessness. There was nowhere any of us could hide from each other for very long in Montague. The Shady Acres was closer to downtown than the Crab Shack, but still peripheral enough to afford its double acreage. Verna zipped there in a jiffy, pulling up outside reception until we found out which yellow or green door was ours. I told those two to find a picnic spot while I checked Verna and me into the *family motel*. Obviously, the establishment was geared more towards the vacationing lower middle class than the local no-tell contingent. I was given a key to room 10 by kindly Marie, who told me the other key unlocked the pool gate, dear. I was happy to see Patrick snacking on carrot sticks when I got to the picnic table overlooking a utilitarian little swimming pool set inside a cage.

"Room key plus pool key." I dangled them like lucky charms.

"Shit, Minnie, we should have brought our bathing suits!"

Patrick could have but did not say one lascivious thing. He was probably too tantalized by something other than a day-old fritter, finally. Verna and I had paid Trudy staff price for sandwiches and she had tossed in extra goodies. We had begged her to come with us on the Montague adventure, a *girls' night out* far more palatable in

145

rural PEI than urban Ontario. But Trudy was dreading the Canada Day rush too much to party.

Trudy herself had made my cheddar and tomato on whole wheat, sub mustard for mayo, so thick with cheese my gums shirked at the sight of it. I handed it over to Patrick along with my slice of chocolate pecan pie. I did jab at some coleslaw and munch one of Debbie's biscuits. What I really wanted to do was crack my way into our schlocky six-pack of Anne of Green Gables Raspberry Cordial. Desolée had always sworn the ruby-red soda went great with vodka; now we planned to spike it with shine. With Patrick right there it didn't seem polite to test for contraband purity, and in any case Verna was assuaged by all their PEI connections. Patrick had gone to the same high school as some of her cousins and he was old friends with the bass guitarist from the only power punk band in Island history, long since tragically disbanded.

The moonshine was a perky chamomile tea colour, and almost healthy looking in that without a label the bottle looked extra clean. We poured shots into our pop and then poked at it with our straws. Patrick and Verna behaved as if this was a routine chore, but I felt like a nerd with a new chemistry set. Patrick explained to us ladies that he was job hunting for something steady in order to save money for the electrician course at the CCC Charlottetown Community College. We sincerely wished him luck with that. I strained but I could barely taste alcohol. Maybe something rubbing alcohol-like, but mostly I tasted ersatz cream soda. I should have eaten more than one little biscuit, but they were so buttery they made my tongue sizzle. There did not seem to be much harm in showing Patrick our Naugahyde and chenille motel room: with two double beds, two bath and hand towels, two curvaceous water glasses, one small television, one recliner, one wastebasket and one little desk with one complimentary Shady Acres postcard.

"Whoo-weee!" Patrick jumped on a bed and boinged back to his feet in a smooth cartoon motion. Hilarious.

"Aw look, there's little fishies on the shower curtain!" Verna smiled a *Santa came* smile as she peered in every confined direction.

She was garnering décor ideas for the Montreal student ghetto, despite the deferral she had been forced to request from Concordia University unless Archie caught a whack of tuna.

Patrick took a pleather seat while we ladies chose beds and took turns slipping into the bathroom. I went first, partly to slow down my passage through my second drink. It was me as usual in the mirror. Maybe the relationship between one eye and the other had gone a bit wobbly and I had to look down farther than normal to see my feet, my feet no longer completely belonging to my hands, my hands no longer completely belonging to my arms. At least I was smiling, a grin so stunned it seemed pointless to ask myself any further questions. Verna seemed to be doing well. Of course, she had eaten a chicken sub, a side of macaroni salad, her pie and all the watermelon. We still had one cordial left and half the shine.

"Go for it, Minnie."

Verna was more in the mood to slip out onto the motel room front step for a smoke. She had warned me drink made her go chimney. I thought I had detected stale tobacco once in a while, beneath the magazine perfume tester strips she regularly rubbed over her wrists.

"Thanks then. One more nippety-nip maybe. I think I'm getting more of a buzz off the sugar than anything else."

"Could be, Minnie. We Islanders drink to get drunk, that's what my good ma always said."

"I like wine," Verna poked her head in the door to mention.

"Grape juice mixed with priest's breath."

"Pat, I could help you get over that, swear to God. You just have to set your mind to it and you can acquire all kinds of tastes, right, Minnie? That's my plan. I love mushrooms now even though I never used to. Next step paté."

I felt bad for my generation that we had been so headlong in comparison to Verna and her fellow tacticians. I was doubtful we could have had it any other way, since coming into consciousness had meant acknowledging flower people, psychedelia and many,

many peace signs—the letters of LOVE written big and bubbly on every babysitter's binder. But I did not really want to be shrewd; too much shrewdness and I would have ended up as Frank's dentist. I had not realized how soft the motel beds were. The pillows were definitely vegetarian, stuffed with foam that had long coagulated. In between cigarettes, Verna opened all the windows and filled out the complimentary postcard to Patrick, wishing he was here. Patrick clicked through the basic cable; I thought I might have seen the city park episode of *The Urban Forager* flip past—my one true source of television pride, my production furthest from smirch. But by the time I registered that fact sufficiently to draw attention to it, Patrick landed on Buddy Donovan loosening up his hips prior to a golf swing. Just like his uncle Thane, Buddy was a redhead hosting a freckle festival—a recessive gene sadly doomed to extinction by century's end. Surely no one had ever worn tidier khakis or tucked in their golf shirt as mathematically. Buddy was bearing up well under more scrutiny than any of his fellow villagers had ever endured, even the ones who had travelled to the Souris wharf to sucker punch trawler crews unloading mass catches of herring. After a nice loud *thwop* he ignited applause that seemed more than polite. Patrick whistled.

Verna emerged from the bathroom. "Balls, shafts, holes, tell me it isn't a big huge substitute for something that Buddy Donovan never gets much of, that's for sure. C'mon guys, time to get this party started."

"I'm with you there," said Patrick.

Horrifyingly, I now wanted to stay sprawled on the bed watching young Donovan swish steel rods through the Fort Worth air. My solar plexus was weighing me down. My head, however, had been pumped full of helium. I needed to rouse myself, collect myself, and supervise the evening. My feet found their way to the floor in one of those decisions feet make on their own. Patrick wandered outside to wait for us gals while we finalized our girly prep. He kicked up pink dust with his withered sneakers, his frayed jacket left behind with our permission for later retrieval. Before Verna could follow, I reached for one of her slim arms.

"Verna, listen, Patrick was staying at a homeless shelter in Toronto where I volunteer. That's how I met him."

"So?"

"Just so you know."

"That's no reason to judge someone, Minnie. You shouldn't be helping out there if that's what you think."

This was what it was like to be a teenager nowadays, even in a tiny fishing village: you ran piping hot with justification, you refuted anyone's moral authority but your own, you deserved the best opinion—like all teenagers through the ages only more so. Verna had outgrown loving with her instincts; now she experienced love as mental process—buzz-saw love that demarcated the favoured. The warm washcloth rub of love wrung from the heart was yet to come.

"Right, fine. I just wanted you to know."

"So now I know. Can we please go before he figures out what you're saying?"

"Okay, Verna. I'm not the bad guy here."

Neither was I her mother so she could stop her stupid prancing. Even in flip-flops Verna was half a head taller than Patrick. Immediately they were snickering about something; Verna excelled at conspiratorial laughter. I took one last raspberry swig before I shut the motel door behind us and hurried to catch up. So much for being part of a duo. It was a quarter mile jaunt from the motel to the Crab Shack, a walk that was hot enough to quiet us down. It was one of the brightest nine-thirty's I had ever experienced, the sun still high enough in the sky for blue. Many of the cars whipping by were headed where we were. Island DUI arrests made it to the front section of *The Guardian*, the court columnist was diligent that way. I thought such gallows entertainment ought to catch on all over the place, all that death to reputation.

We penetrated the babbling scrum that was the Montague Crab Shack on the last Saturday night in June. Verna handed me a conciliatory glass of house red and then showed off by getting one for Patrick, too. The clunky bar and round waxy tables encircled by wide-hipped saloon chairs were filling up fast with keyed-up fishermen's helpers set free from their bosses with thousands of dollars for beer and child support literally in their pockets. And cocaine up a lot of their noses, judging by the jabber and concerted pitch of the drinking. Verna picked us out a table in a back corner from where she could survey covertly. She bent down to her straw rather than lifting her glass, her Merlot tasting just as good through plastic stripes she said, and with less effect to her gloss. I was glad she was not allowed to smoke inside, glad that no one was, now that one could not light up a butt indoors in Dublin or Marseilles either. Patrick sat between us, nodding his head no matter the tune.

"So, where are you settled?" I asked him, hoping he would completely disprove my point about his instability, but that Verna was listening if he didn't.

"My brother's place, but that can't last long. His wife is a nice lady, but I know she doesn't want me on their couch forever. I was thinking maybe I'd apply at the cannery, as long as they haven't given all the jobs away to Russians. Don't know how I'd get back and forth to work, though. Us local guys don't get a dormitory."

"I'm sure something will work out."

"That's what my ma used to say, 'Things have a habit of working out.' Nice attitude if you can keep it."

Verna stood up to whistle her approval of the first karaoke performance of the evening, delivered by one of the few other fortysomethings in the room, although this gal was maybe a wizened thirty, or a stubborn fifty, with roots that had been touched up crayon-yellow. She was wearing a deeply plunging, electric banana, puff-sleeved top. She had been born a rambling man. One more chorus and I was going to start worrying where I had rambled to myself. Weeks of belonging in a row and suddenly I had no proper part in things. Somewhere between the Manor, the Shady Acres and the Crab Shack, I had crawled under a rock and moulted.

"Your turn, Minnie." Verna was overdue for a smoke. "You promised to dedicate one to me, remember? Go now while there's no lineup."

Such had been our plan, made speculatively and in innocent camaraderie, a plan dependent on our mood and that of the joint at large. Now Verna had me tight by one wrist and she was dragging me up out of my seat from across the table—how did these people get so strong? The little stage was carpeted in moss-green shag. Maybe Verna had a point; best to get my David Bowie cover over with. I weaved past sticky tables full of loud men flirting with chubby chicks and vice versa, the most popular form of flirtation seeming to be a taunting denial of whatever the other person had just said. I reached the station up front over to the side where a sleepy-looking guy controlled the song selection; you picked, he scrolled and clicked and got you started. I asked him to turn to the Brit rock page, then I pointed a brave index finger down the bottom of the list at "Ziggy Stardust." I had downloaded the lyrics and practiced them on Dosie. It would be hammy, but I would wing it. I looked over at Verna and Patrick. *Go on*, she was mouthing, probably shouting. Patrick lifted both thumbs and jabbed the air above his head. The Crab Shack ceiling was low, too low. My eyes clenched the monitor. The lyrics to "Under Pressure" began to scroll.

I had known something was awry when I heard the opening instrumental: *doom-doom-doom, da-da-doom-doom*, instead of wailing guitar. Fine, I could remember just about enough of this spin-class classic to handle the Bowie bits. But Freddy Mercury was on his own. So I thought until Patrick leapt onstage beside me to handle the chorus and save the night. Because day could surely no longer be going on outside the smothered windows of a bar full of peppy hooligans begging right along with Patrick and me to give love one more chance, give love, give love, give love, give love one more chance. *People on the street*, Patrick had sung in an unearthly falsetto, his cheek smooth against mine while we jointly courted the mike.

"Guys, guys, holy shit, you were great!" Verna had hastily moved us to one of the last empty tables up front.

"Patrick gets the credit."

"Anytime, Minnie."

"C'mon, Minnie, you both rocked it!"

In her ebullience Verna had mistaken my full wineglass for her empty one. Now she had two upward red wine fangs staining her top lip. That was fine, I did not need any more to drink—considering I was going to be tanked for days on Anne and shine. The eighty dozen separate chemicals at work in my system were fully kicking in. I felt comical but reduced, like a character in a newspaper strip. In fact it was so loud in the Crab Shack that one's speech needed to get put into a boldface bubble to be heard. (*Not a chance! ... You idiot! ... For sure!*) Eventually I spent a lonely five minutes in one of the ladies toilet stalls, one arm stretched out to keep me steady, the other hand clutching my hair out of the way if need be. I was too disorganized to force the issue, although I would have if I had remembered to wash my hands on the way in. I doubted moonshine was going to be less of a depressant than ordinary alcohol.

By the time I made my way back out to our table—a task of difficulty on par with an introductory Polish lesson—someone had flipped on the house black lights. Everyone's eyes were Plutonian, Patrick and Verna's black shirts revealed ten thousand large and small specks and my white blouse had a frosty glow. I was scared to look at anyone's teeth. This was meta-drunkenness. I would survive it by doing my best to curtail my realization that when God had lost validity we had not as a culture made up for that by having faith in lots of other things, that for the most part we only pretended to believe in things: jollied into it by historic sites, national holidays, trials by jury, charitable foundations, self-penned vows and, most insidiously of all, liquor ads. We were too petulant for faith, now that we knew we were not loved automatically.

"God is dead!" I smiled brightly at Verna and Patrick to say it. Out of shine had come truth.

Hearing me wax so existentialist, Desolée would have known to cut me off and stick me in a cab, but Verna ignored me and Patrick gave a *what, me worry?* shrug. I was relieved to have had something to say, finally, having been as still as a cactus throughout the whole country classics set woman-handled by a hard-partying quintet in for the night from Rollo Bay. They had piled their purses on the table beside ours and started a tab for birdbath drinks. Certainly, I would have been more than happy to elaborate to Patrick and Verna as to the more problematic aspects of an absent divine. But now neither of them was paying any attention. Patrick because he was concerned about what had Verna so worried. Verna was looking up from her drink, looking high up over our heads, into the eyes of Fibby Trask.

Fibby had also chosen the Crab Shack as the best place to unwind that night on his way home to the Harbour from his Klondike hut at North Cape.

"Greetings, Harbourites."

Fibby's arms spanned all our chair backs. He had the savage bonhomie of a game show host. He smelled of drugstore hair gel and deodorized groin. Bottles of Coors Light hung from each of his little fingers. Verna rolled her eyes and slumped her shoulders, Fibby's cue to sit down beside me. I had a ragdoll smile stitched onto my face with only a few threads loose, which reassured him more than it should have. I had managed to dig a bit deeper into his failed romance with Trudy. It seemed he had never really done anything outright vicious, he had simply slowly and permanently oppressed Trudy with snide remarks about her knock knees or her weird laugh. Fibby belonged in the Beelzebub category of devil: too goofy to be truly satanic.

"So what's a fancy Toronto lady like you doing in a place like this?" Fibby leered.

I smiled in the blank new way I had just picked up.

"So what's a fancy Toronto lady like you doing in a place like this?"

Fibby's chops were right at my ear this time, his breath tangy with ferment; his arms bustling with musculature that had to have come out of a syringe. Now his ear presented itself front and centre for my response. I smiled at Fibby's surprisingly dainty ear, its whorls as precise as a carved cameo, the opposite of Rex's floppy saucers. Small ears, poor listener, ha ha. At which point there was a sudden toilet flush down in my gut, which then rerouted itself upward and filled my mouth with hot vomit. Not wanting to fill Fibby's ear with vomit in turn, I spewed it over his shoulder like a fountain programmed for dancing bursts. Not what the lady from Rollo Bay wanted, the one who had made a specialty out of Hank Snow tunes, the one who had curled her hair into sausages and then slapped on the kind of hat Oliver Twist removed when asking for *more*. I had spewed raspberry-tinted puke with a bit of biscuit for texture over this woman's tank top straps, bra straps, bare freckled shoulders, lap, and possibly all the way into her chocolate martini.

"Bitch! You fucking little bitch!"

Fibby took exception to that with Douglas Fairbanks Senior efficiency. No woman was all that big when Fibby had likewise thundered to his feet. I was still limp in my seat, my eyes at Fibby's fist level; his hands were expanding and contracting like combustion-fired anemones.

"She didn't mean it," he said.

Well, I wished I hadn't, but in a way I had.

"What kind of a fuckwit is she then? Come on then, just try and stick up for her, you fuckwit yourself."

My pride was assumed to be that of a simpleton, but theirs had become a serious matter. The woman was beckoning Fibby's fists towards her kisser with little flipper motions of her hands, a gesture that made her upper arms jiggle in alarm. Ominously, Fibby swept aside his chair. Now there was nothing between them besides world weary broadloom, fury, and a James Brown wannabee's loud vocal stylings—he felt good, he knew that he should ya. None of us wanted the bouncers onto us.

"Fibby!" Verna ordered. "Cool it!"

Patrick had found a wad of napkins and was passing them to

Rollo Bay women #2 and #3 who were wiping off Rollo Bay woman #1's immediate environment while Rollo Bay woman #1 rolled her shoulders like someone who would rather sting like a bee than float like a butterfly and was looking forward to getting her mouthguard in place. Fibby's eyes stalled for time by picking a fight with his eyebrows.

"Fib, chill out. It's not worth it!" Verna hollered.

Get up off of that thing. It was a whole James Brown medley. Really, what we all had to do was dance it off. I reached over and tugged on the irate woman's belt loop. She swatted my hand away. I rose to my feet.

"I'm so sorry," I began. I did not want to alarm her by leaning in too close, but I required her attention. I stepped between her and Fibby. Point form would do. "APOLOGIES! Your anger, totally understandable. A round for the table on me. Money for the dry cleaning. Shine, first time, big mistake. I'm *from away.*"

"Tell your friend here I'm the one who should be pissed off, not him." Quasi mollified, she dabbed at a splodge. Verna dragged Fibby away from the nexus of shame.

"I agree. So sorry. Words can't tell."

"I guess we put up with worse from our kids. I've had five of them puking all over me for the last fifteen years. Not something asshole over there would put up with."

Perhaps everyone thought I was tumbling to my knees in the classic beg-for-mercy position. I was actually rooting around for my bag with all my other twenty-dollar bills. Back on my feet, as dignified as a senator in a sex scandal, "Ignore that man," I advised her. "Nobody likes him."

Patrick came with me to the bar and helped with ordering six chocolate martinis—an extra one for my victim—plus delivery. He served the Rollo Bay ladies with enough gag flourishes to turn the whole event into a fond memory. Then he took over on Fibby duty. Verna was free to join the Rollo Bay gals. She explained that I was a fancy television producer from Toronto who had been crazy proud of herself for not puking when she went out fishing and how the mighty had fallen! From now on I was to take two Gravol whenever I got into the shine, so said everyone, taking their turn with the joke. Eventually, it was again my turn to deal with Fibby.

"You must feel like an idiot," he said, shaking his crusty head.

"Yes I do." My hands were chastely in my lap for the rest of the evening. "I hear you had a good lobster season?"

"Pretty goddamn good is right." Fibby was the kind of guy who took a gulp of beer as if he was accomplishing something. "Record breaking you might say."

"Are you going after tuna?"

"Soon as I can. Need to find a guy to go with me, though. The last loser I hired told me he's taking off, effective immediately. Wants to go work with his girlfriend at a call centre in Charlottetown, the pussy."

"Do you want to do something good?"

Fibby's eyes narrowed in suspicion. "Maybe."

"Take on Patrick. He's a bright guy."

"I don't know. He seems like a bit of a runt. I'm going after the big fuckers. I don't want any crybabies on my boat."

"Does he look like a crybaby to you?"

Patrick was chucking Rollo Bay woman #1 under her chin, both her chins, which made her snarl in pleasure and her chums mad with glee. Verna was giggling into her hands. Fun was being had by everyone but Fibby and me, who were not as good at it. Patrick would be doing Fibby the favour, really.

"Okay then," said Fibby.

I looked back at Fibby; Fibby looked down his beer.

"Okay what?"

"If he wants, I'll take him on. He's a lucky little prick. Right place at the right time. I've got a bunk at the hut. He can feed himself, mind you."

As soon as Patrick extricated himself from a frenzy of cougar jokes, I filled him in on his new opportunity. He didn't think twice, shaking on it with Fibby like a mayor with an industry captain. Patrick took another turn at the mike with "Purple Rain," and then Verna did, too, after incessant encouragement, with a mock version of "I Will Always Love You." Fibby refused despite all goading. It was one of those nights at a bar when time lashes out, presenting last call mere moments after midnight. Not that I was having such a good time, but I was having a warped time. Fibby really was sober enough to drive us girls back to the Shady Acres; after a cocky start his thirst had shrunk along with his Crab Shack machismo. Before the men could show us to our door in the chirping dark, the breeze still velvety, the chance of death by exposure hovering at nil, Verna grabbed the room keys out of my hand and scampered around the back of the motel. Even before we three rounded the corner, we heard the pool gate creak.

Mercifully, Verna opted for the old jumping-in-fully-clad shtick. What could the rest of us do but follow, one *sploosh* after another, Fibby giving off the most spray. Patrick tugged off his sweatshirt and track shoes first. There was some talk of us gals mounting the guys' shoulders for a round of pool combat, but thankfully the idea got splashed away. Patrick and Verna smacked water at each other in the shallow end. Fibby took over the diving board. I clung to the edge at the deep end after struggling through a length. Swimming was not something I practiced, not even when my gym had a pool. Patrick claimed to be no good at it either, not something I wanted Fibby to hear, but Fibby was too busy showing off his swan formation.

"You're too skinny to float!" Verna merrily excused Patrick.

Pocked and elfin as he was, Patrick was a beauty, as was Verna, as was even Fibby; they were proving it with all their beaver baby activity. Liquidly, I thought about how there was not only beauty in function, there had to be function in beauty, especially uncontested beauty like Joe's. We did something to each other with our beauty— we gave each other things to latch on to and recall. The more we were privy to beauty, the more we were connected to and by beauty and beauty made sense of us. Verna would soon be reminded that no mascara was 100 percent waterproof. She started to stud her talk with teeth chatters. After the first minute the pool had become warmer than the air above it, but now the water was getting cold. When I lay back to practice my float, the sky looked as if someone in the universe next door had been chipping ice.

I was the first to haul my dripping jeans up the deep-end ladder. I thought maybe I should sleep in them until they dried and fit me in the way that jeans ought to but never did. We offered the men the use of our towels before they left. I was glad when Patrick put his sweatshirt back on; his chest was not exactly delicate, but you would not have been surprised to see his heart beating through its thin walls. Fibby was going to drop Patrick off at his brother's place because it was on his way so what else could he do? Verna was about to contradict that until I pressed on her toes. One by one, we hugged and parted.

♋

Morning came in a melodramatically grumpy rush for Verna and me, which added to our solidarity because we could make fun of everyone else. Even sweet dumpling Marie at the motel front desk, after she said it was a shame we hadn't had a chance to use the pool. Verna took the shortcut back to the harbour: a road that was a bucolic version of a Hot Wheels track in its swooping ups and downs through miles of shipshape farmland held in place by bush. It was one of those very blue and green PEI days. No matter how despoiled one's perspective, the ocean cleaned most things up and spruce groves took care of the rest. Verna dropped me off at Rex's house in time for a quick sunny bath full of squeaks as I shifted from lather to rinse. With determination I had formerly employed to get on set in time to prep a crew of twenty, I flurried out of the house and onto my bike in time to make it to the Eats n' Treats float before the Canada Day parade set off.

Everyone who was parading was lined up along Tuck Harbour's only big side road. The Agri-Co-op had a float, and the Ladies

Auxiliary from both churches, and the Montague Rotary, and the volunteer fire department. I spotted a shock of orange atop the Astroturfed mounds belonging to the Ocean View Golf Course float: Buddy Donovan in the flesh and coif. It was a strange sensation to bike fast past a line of floats waiting to get going—a parade occurring in an odd new dimension—and it was extremely strange to see a youth who had straddled continental airwaves the night before now appear in the Harbour, grinning at kids too young to remember him fumbling at his locker before history class. I rubbernecked along with everyone else and got my own wave as a result. I waved right back, rode over a stone, felt my handlebars pick a fast fight with the road and came close to wiping out in front of the Boys and Girls Club float, who howled in understandable pleasure. And then moaned in ecstasy when I flipped them the bird.

"Minnie did a bad thing!" screamed Bette, Joan and Pierre.

The Fishermen's Association–Kings County South float was next in line and Joe had seen to it that both sets of McTeal twins were pretending to fish Tom Sawyer-style off the sides and back. Elliot gave me his fingers-in-the-mouth whistle while Joe reeled in his cork-baited rod. I waved at Elliot, which Joe mistook as a wave to him, a wave that I then tried to widen. But I was in danger of slamming into a chunky majorette, enough at her leisure to pluck at her hose where they had twisted around her juicy thigh while she waited for the sky to hand back her baton. This was the kind of woman that Joe belonged with, a well-intentioned young female who knew how to make rice pudding, march like a Lipizzaner and speak colloquially.

Eats n' Treats was two floats behind the Fishing Association, almost but not quite the tail end. Miss PEI Fisheries and the Queen of the Furrows were sharing a convertible behind us. Verna was slumped up against the stove in the sole patch of shade atop the flatbed trailer.

"So, Minnie, did ya take your Gravol this morning?" Herman Walker was grinning the grin of the informed.

I would have berated Verna for her loose lips if I had not been so worried she'd desert us for the truck cabin, leaving Herman, Darlene and me to act out all the fake diner activity. "Did you guys see Buddy Donovan?" I passed my bike up to Herman so he could hide it behind the stove.

"They say he flew in on a private jet!" In sunglasses Darlene MacDonald looked marvellously blasé even if she didn't sound it. "He chartered one special, just so he could make it to the parade! He's the youngest grand master in parade history."

"Whatever." Verna retained enough politesse to keep this to a mutter.

"You just missed him, Minnie." Herman was halfway through his first cinnamon bun before we had even set off. "He was after our Verna here. 'How are you, Verna? How've you been, Verna?' Someone has a bug up his rear."

"Who gives a crap about golf? Buddy Donovan thinks he's hot shit because he can hit a ball into a hole. There's way more important things to do than that." Verna's black pedicure had chipped overnight, which was likely depressing her. She had gone all the way into Charlottetown to get her toes done at the Delta Hotel spa.

"Sure thing, Verna Doiron, there are more important things in life than getting a golf ball in a hole. But not a lot of them pay so well." Herman shook his head in wonder at the way the PEI golfing industry had rejigged what would have once been mostly NHL dreams.

"I heard Buddy got a great big scholarship to that junior college in Florida. Saved his parents a mint." Darlene was already fanning herself with her menu.

Off we lurched, sparing Verna the need for further outrage.

Freak Trask, Fibby's gangly yet down-to-earth cousin, was doing the driving. He was called Freak only because he had said "freak me out" a lot as a kid. Normally, he drove potato trucks to the outskirts of Toronto and back. When the time came, I was considering asking Freak for a lift home along with a few tons of russets.

I saw Joe's float take the left onto Main Street ahead of ours. As usual, Joe had the composure of a soap opera villain showing up at a shopping mall for an autograph signing. Parents were pointing him out and getting their kids to wave. There were almost as many Tuck Harbour citizens manning floats as there were cheering, but lawn chairs had been unfolded curb side and flags of various sizes were stirring up extra breeze. Joe kept one hand on Elliot's shoulder while the other waved back. Elliot could have been his child. Elliot could have been our child. Joe would likely be the kind of husband who helps out the ob-gyn by lifting a leg and wants to see the head crown. There should be rules against that.

"Joe better not wave at my dad." Verna's chin dug into my shoulder.

"Why not?"

"My dad hates what he's doing, giving away what little power the fishermen have left. My dad says fishermen are the ones who really need there to be something left in the ocean and they know best how to keep stocks up if the government would stop regulating the hell out of them."

"What do you think, Vee?"

"I think we'd all be doing smack and crack if there was nothing to stop us. Grown-ups are even more insane than kids."

"Hey, get us some coffee over here, would yas?"

Darlene hauled us back to our pantomime. Mercurial Verna was now all cheered up. At the bottom of the hill she waved heartily at her parents, her little brothers too busy revving their ATVs in bronco circles. Archie Doiron had the turgid bulk and red hue of a man at risk of a heart attack who nonetheless kept going year after year, chugging out of the harbour before dawn, swatting at his kids with the newspaper when he got home.

There was a scary moment halfway up the hill when I thought our table might go sliding off the back of the truck, but Herman held firm. Colin and Etta were waiting at the top, patting bouncing heads once Joe passed down each kid. Freak pulled over to the side of the road. Herman passed down my bike. I tried not to say too many thank yous.

"Have fun, Minnie?"

Joe, with his eyes that smiled and mouth that didn't: my facial opposite. I wanted him to stick his hands under my arms, too, and lift. It would hurt, but I would feel the true weight of myself. I wanted the man to accost me. He made me want to ransack.

"Gosh, you bet. What a fun parade!"

"Bobby MacEachern said he seen you at the Shack last night."

"Oh, right. Well, that was fun as well."

"Minnie rocks!" said Verna. "Nothing stops her, man. Oh frigg, not again."

"Hey there, Verna. Can I give you a lift anywhere?" Buddy Donovan was now maintaining an honour guard of pageant winners. Possibly, he wanted to shake them, but that looked next to impossible, the girls were far too sinuous. "I'm taking the ladies here down to the diner for a cool drink. Care to join us?"

"You want me to serve you guys, is that it?"

"No, Verna, I never said—"

"I don't know what you bother me for, Buddy, when there's tons more fish in the sea."

"The ladies here have a car. We can drive you—"

"I can walk, for crying out loud. There's nowhere in this village that's too far to walk, but I guess you don't remember that. Minnie, hand me those menus. Trudy said to make sure to bring them back. Some of us have real jobs to do."

We could have all watched Verna stomp downhill, but Joe distracted Buddy with some man-to-man congratulations while I applauded Miss Fisheries and the Queen of the Furrows, the former buxom down to her teeth, the latter chubby-cheeked but otherwise skinny. I appreciated Buddy's courteousness and the anecdote value that would arise from this meeting for years to come, assuming Buddy went on thwacking his way to his success and I went back to Toronto.

"Welcome home, Buddy," I emphasized. Buddy's eyes invited forthrightness like ponds welcome stones.

"I love being home," he said. "Nice to meet you, Minnie. See you around, Joe."

"Minnie, c'mon!" No one tugged like Elliot. I reversed him and patted him away.

"Will you be at Colin and Etta's later?" I asked Joe. I dared to squeeze his elbow at this, turning my question into a request. I wanted to spend dusk with Joe McTeal on an evening when his cellphone was unlikely to ring with DFO guys on the line. His joint was nice and thick with bone.

"Absolutely, Minnie. I'll see you tonight."

Joe now answered my squeeze to his arm with one to my bicycle bell, punctuating our moment with a *brrrring*. We were in the middle of the biggest crowd Tuck Harbour had seen all year and would likely see for another year, but it was the most alone together we had been so far. Then a whiskery old guy with his wife in curlers beneath her scarf wanted to know if Joe was going after tuna. That I could only watch.

"Want to come with me and the kids to the strawberry social, Minnie? We're doing the playground thing afterwards. Etta wants to head home and cook while she's got the place to herself."

"Colin, hi. Gosh, thanks but no. I have a slight hangover I'm afraid. I don't think I could take it." I knew a bit about playgrounds. Boredom's knives would soon stab the back of my neck and sides of my head, then boredom's sledgehammer would pound my cerebral cortex.

"Don't you worry too much about your bout in the ring with the shine, dear. Most of us around here have had at least one of those. My granddad used to pour the stuff in a clean piss pot when the inspector was around, toss a few chunks of brown doughnut in there for good measure and stick it under the bed. Even Joe's been knocked around a bit with the shine in his time. Not that he's talking now."

"Were you two close growing up?"

"Joe let me help with his model airplanes, read me Snoopy cartoons, took me to the rink and stuck me in goal. He was good to me for sure. Better than most brothers would have been to a little pain-in-the arse like myself."

This was permission to seek out Joe's bright white T-shirt in the crowd, always an inviting blank. He was now holding court in a ring of elderly interested parties, all of them with their arms crossed in friendly simultaneity. "I can't say I'm surprised."

"He's a good man, Minnie. A woman could do a lot worse. A patient woman, mind you."

"Oh! I'm sure. I mean, I don't doubt." Panicky blanket affirmatives—both brothers deserved better.

"Joe needs a woman who knows what she wants. Who's got that in her and can act on it."

"DADDY!"

When it came to the girls, one twin's tears always increased the likelihood of the other's, not at all the case with the boys. Joan was crossing her legs in a way that spelled trouble. Joe had given them all pop.

"Hey, do you think Etta will put up with some help for tonight?"

Colin had a girl under each arm and knew better than to slow down. The kids were getting their choice of strawberry shortcake, pie or sundae: sundaes for the girls, shortcake for Pierre and pie for Elliot.

"Give it a shot, Minnie, my dear. You know what Lester B. Pearson said: 'Diplomacy is letting someone else have your way.'"

Besides Joe and myself, Charlie and Dolly McTeal were coming to dinner, and a couple of women from Etta's bank. Herman Walker had been invited in equal parts fondness and pity. Elliot charged up when he saw me leaving the parade. I promised him I would not go missing for long and was charmed afresh to feel like a corner piece of Elliot's puzzle. Family life drained and replenished, then drained and replenished again. So I considered as I pedalled back to Rex's, trying not to crush ladybugs. I had always enjoyed the suspense of not knowing who my very own family was going to be. Then came some suspense as to whether I would even have a family. I'd been sure my lollygagging had reduced its scope. Now I knew nothing.

A second bath of the day seemed called for but profligate. I rode my bike right up to Dosie's fence, which outraged her; Dosie seemed to rate the bike up somewhere with fire-breathing dragons. The beach was as empty as hoped. Far off in the distance I could see a white smudge in the sky—belch from the Pictou pulp mill. A white dot in the water constituted the ferry on its way to Wood Islands. I was free to strip.

It wasn't the temperature of the water that demanded courage, it was the murk. All I knew was that something silky was growing on the bottom, long enough to feel like it might wrap around my ankles if I stayed still. It was too early for jellyfish, thankfully. Desolée had the knack of scooping them up, and tossing them, the hussy. This was the first time I had ever attempted a swim at Rex's beach without her. I went down butt first, hard on the hair but good for the skin: impromptu antiseptic. I surged out to tread water. This was real-deal swimming, perhaps even more chemical than a pool, but with equations that dated back past the missing link. By the time I wore socks of sand on my feet and was frisking up the red cliff back in view of Dosie and my bedroom windows, I felt like I had a clean bill of soul health. I had to dry my hair fast before it clumped. Verna was right, it was no longer medium hair: provoked by who knew what, for the first time in years it had grown long enough for someone to dig in a hand, wrap it around their wrist and tug me to a cave.

7

Etta let me spear mushrooms, red and yellow pepper squares, tofu cubes, cherry tomatoes, little sheaves of onion and asparagus bits onto twenty skewers, everything slicked with seasoned oil that she had also wiped over a couple of chickens that were now propped on beer cans ready to be grilled. When Colin brought the kids home they hit the sack, taking miraculous strawberry naps. Joe arrived while they were waking up and exerted his avuncular repertoire—pretending to suck on his eyeball, and to detach his thumb from its knuckle, and that his hair was a poorly fitting toupee. I watched Etta's best friends from the bank—gruff Bev and doe-voiced Jan—take in Joe's nice way with kids. Bev's children were in the custody of their father for the day, which explained the marvellous precision of her pageboy and the hard set of her wide mouth. Jan was shorter, curlier, charm-braceleted and locket-necked, and mystifyingly said to have lost "a lot" of weight. Jan's primal energies expressed themselves in her cake making, her latest triumph a gleaming, white-and-red slab of Canadian flag on a tinfoil-covered cardboard rectangle. The kids poked fingers into it when Joe and I were the only ones looking. I had brought along several bottles of Italian bubbly for lack of anything French at the Montague liquor store. I figured I still hurt too much from the shine to drink for weeks, but Etta soon scoffed at that.

"It's my turn to get trashed tonight, Minnie, and I want you along for the ride."

"Declare this a transgression-free zone then because I will go haywire."

"A what zone?" Bev was a hoverer.

"Don't mind Minnie," Etta said. "She swallowed the dictionary."

I wondered if Bev and Jan spent hours scavenging Internet dating sites for mates in their general vicinity. The provincial government was luring bioscience development to the Island with as many tax breaks as possible and had gamely helped to construct a Charlottetown headquarters for a prospective IT industry. I could not think where else fresh men would come from, besides local marriages torn asunder like Bev's. Bev and Jan did not seem like the kind of women who would consort with brawny youngsters to tide themselves over. Not that it would be easy for such incipient matrons to lure randy youths to their weight-watching sides. I could only guess what I would do lovelorn among the shanties if it was me. But surely I could never have been Bev or Jan? We had all got our start in the same place, but I was a clock with a very different tick by now. For one thing, I no longer defined time by whether it was spent with a man or not, at least not as a matter of daily accounting.

"Dolly, these pickles are delish." For all her outward placidity, Jan enjoyed crunch.

"Oh, well, gracious!"

I would have complimented Dolly as well, but I'd noticed how much pain it caused her to get singled out even for praise. No one wanted to see her tremble.

"Mother's a fine cook when she puts her mind do it. Oh, she'll cook something for you lot whenever you want it. But not for her poor, starving old man!"

Charlie McTeal kept the ho ho ho's ever flowing. He was the

perfect grandfather, and a wonderful father, and quite possibly a great husband. One of his swooping hugs now rescued his wife. Charlie and Dolly had been high school sweethearts, a Tuck Harbour standard. Mating was probably easy in a small place when accomplished early enough: a fairly straightforward procedure that would make romance, however, extra tough.

"I hear another gay cruise ship is docking in Charlottetown this summer so that more American homosexuals can come here and get married. I say just because the federal government says it's okay doesn't mean we have to like it." Bev's frank testimony earned her a corn chip dipped in Etta's verdant guacamole. We were congregating around the kitchen table, the back sliding doors open to the yard with its scattered toys and kiddy pool.

"Civil unions should be good enough, right?" Jan peeked a sidelong glance at Colin as man of the house to make sure. "That should make them happy?"

"The way I see it, if people want marriage that badly they're welcome to it." Colin handed a beer to Joe, who did not have my problem with twist tops. "I guess they think they'll do a better job of it than us guys with kids to weary our bones."

"Lots of gay people are parents, good parents." Etta was happy to sit for a while as the fowl grilled. "I seen it on the television, a whole special. Made me cry buckets."

Secord wailed death sobs until Etta rubbed his belly with her bare feet.

"What do you think, Minnie?" Herman was ever keen to hear my Toronto take.

For the sake of the party, I socked it to them. "I think *only* gay people should get married."

"Minnie, honest to god, is it fun living in Bizzaro Land?" Watching Etta unwind was the best thing about the occasion so far.

"Look at it this way: weddings are camp, the gay scene excels at camp, ergo they should have their way with the institution."

"You're a funny one, neighbour, I'll give you that much!"

Etta thought I was hilarious, but I had squelched her in-laws and pals. Not her husband.

"Joe here got very upset when they legalized gay marriage." Colin had tipped back in his chair and narrowed his eyes, already narrower than his brother's. Joe was backed into a kitchen corner, waiting like the rest of us for what was coming next.

"See, Joe here was boycotting marriage on principle until the gays were allowed to get hitched as well. Now that the fruits can say *I do*, poor old Joe here doesn't have any excuse not to!"

Joe tipped the neck of his brew toward his brother and then consoled himself with a swig. Party mirth, relieved and explosive.

I sympathized with bachelors for the mockery they were lately incurring—jokes from which single women had finally been absolved. We modern spinsters had very understandably become confused as to where in life we most wanted to be, what with the way the culture had shifted so radically beneath our feet. Single men in their forties, however, were now suspected of being disturbed, of suffering from some irreparable emotional pathology and/or suppression. Of course, males play the dunce role lately and are the brunt of most jokes. Now that New York shades of ash and honey cost career women three hundred dollars a month in upkeep, men are the new blondes.

"Given the chance, 50 percent of divorced women would remarry the same man." I loved some statistics for their bramble ways and hoping everybody else would, too, I rushed ahead so as not to upset Bev. "But 80 percent of divorced men would remarry the same woman."

"Divorce is more humiliating for a man." Etta seemed to be speaking for Bev, who nodded her head yes as her lips compressed. "They're like wounded animals."

"Fifty-eight percent of men are happier after a divorce," I said as gently as I could. "But 85 percent of women!"

At Etta's instigation we girls did a cheers.

"Okay, Minnie, what else you got?" Lovely Etta had requested.

"The average person spends eighteen months of their life on the phone."

"Whoa, Joe! Eighteen years for you, right, bro?"

Joe took his cellphone off its belt clip, glanced at it and then tossed it out to the back lawn. The happy party whooped, although vigilant Charlie soon found it between a trike and a bike, wiped it off with paper towels and handed it back.

"Hit us one more time, Minnie girl, you can do it." I would blame Colin later for egging me on.

I took a sip from my plastic glass and set it down on the kitchen table, where I had forsworn taking up a seat. I clasped my hands in front of me and bent my head. I admitted, "The average person spends two weeks of their life kissing." Cece and Shelley had put *The Book of Lists* in my latest Christmas stocking.

Colin rose to plant a big, fat smooch on Herman's creased old cheek. Then all the kids had to kiss Herman, too. Elliot, sticky of hands, nose and mouth, planted a kiss on me as well, as victoriously as if he had just made me It in a game of freeze tag. Then he followed up with Secord, a cheek licker at the best of times. Overexcited Secord then bounded to the kiddy pool, jumped in and bounded back, followed by a mutty shake back in the kitchen. Enough madness, Etta had to check on the chicken. It was time for Colin to put on dogs and burgers. Bev had to dress the Caesar salad she had brought along, the homemade croutons filling a twist-tied baggie. Jan readied plates, cake plates, cutlery and condiments. Herman loaned Colin counsel by the barbeque. The senior McTeals supervised kiddy handwashing. Only Joe and I escaped without chores.

I had to credit Etta; the prosecco was going down caustic but cleansing, like detergent with grease-cutting capacity. I took a big scoop of guacamole to smooth things over intestinally. And to cover up the fact that I did not have anything particular to say to Joe. Neither he to me, I suspected.

"Let me know if you ever want another driving lesson, Minnie."

"Oh, god, no. I mean, yes, that would be great for me, but hell on wheels for you."

"I don't mind."

"Wow, okay. Consider it public service. I'm free any time I'm not, you know, slinging hot beef."

"I'll give you a call. 2533, is it?"

For a mad moment, I thought Joe was quoting my waist and hip measurements. But it was the last four digits of Rex's phone number, recited in a place so minimally populated that everyone shared the same prefix, hence dropped it. The area code went on for provinces.

"2533 it is. Maybe I can drive us somewhere for dinner. My treat!"

Any PEI restaurant that wasn't a diner had broadloom carpeting, upholstered booths, and forks for every noodle. There were a number of chefs afoot who took food seriously but nowhere that treated food sexually. I'd worry when the time came where Joe and I could go in search of a meal that was largely recreational. For now we had a barbeque to enjoy, Bev apologetic that there was anchovy paste in the Caesar dressing and me reassuring her that was only to be expected and I was going to take more than my fair share of beet salad to make up for it. Joe allowed me to spoon purple chunks onto his plate, too, beside his roasted thigh. I was warned all over again to prepare myself for vegetable garden donations, Charlie's beans were coming along beautifully if he did say so himself. Etta apologized for serving early corn, inspiring everyone at the table to give their front teeth a runaround. We were at the outdoor picnic table. The grown-ups had moved outside because as a special treat the little ones were allowed to watch an animated feature about a cheerful whale and octopus on the kitchen TV. Even so we were squeezed in tight. I wondered if Joe was brushing arms with Jan as well. Joe's arm was a reddish brown beside my Acadian yellow. He also seemed warmer than me, if only by a half degree.

"You were able to hold off on tuna season, right?" I asked this softly so Joe would not get stuck up on one of his platforms while on holiday. "Bought some time to fatten them up?"

"We need a premium product. Tuna is a complicated catch. You can't just haul it in, you've got to bleed it at the right temperature away from pollutants. That's what gets Japanese buyers helicoptering to the wharf. They take it real serious, so should we."

"So you want the guys here to, like, value add?"

"That's the way of the future, Minnie. We're never going to go back to the good old days, when everything we wanted to catch was right there waiting for us. The quantity is gone so now we have to deal in quality. We've got to fish selective if we're going to fish sustainable."

"I guess it's a big change for some people, to cope with all the management."

"Tuna's internationally managed now. It's in what you might call a crisis. You've got a market that wants more and more of it and stocks that are going down by the year. Meanwhile there's boats down south using airplanes and satellites and heat tracking and every damn technology you can imagine. Our guys work rod and reel in small craft, hoping for the best while they burn a hell of a lot of gas getting from here to Yarmouth."

Joe and I could not help it—our little corner of the table had gone hopelessly political.

"It's too bad the European Union is dragging its heels when it comes to reining in the Mediterranean fleets."

"Things reek of havoc all over. Lord help us if we don't help ourselves."

"Now you're scaring me."

"I have to, Minnie, I have to."

"Well, thanks for being a guardian of *our* coast. As best you can anyway."

I got a sharp look in answer to this. Under the grave circumstances the only alternative to going eye to eye would have been for us to draw our faces so close together that our eyelashes brushed each other's cheekbones. Not when Dolly McTeal had us in her sights. Joe's mother delivered a pretty gentle form of scrutiny, but I could tell she was puzzled by whatever implications I bore with me. I would rather have had poor intentions than such a lack thereof. Dolly McTeal was probably unused to the way a certain breed and generation of woman had no idea what she wanted while she went tearing after it anyway, depleting everyone's resources along the way.

Happily I could afford to foist champers on everyone, including myself. And I had brought bubble makings for the kids—long wands that sent giant, wobbly oblongs floating above the backyard before they popped wetly on the grass. Bubble blowing, chasing the dog, scraping away cobs and bones, drinks refills and loading both dishwashers kept everyone busy until sunset, when Colin had fireworks planned. Desolée had always enjoyed a fearless love of firecrackers, but I was too possessive of my fingers and eyes. The boys were thrilled that their old sandbox was being used for something so technical. The girls preferred to watch the pastel munitions from laps: Joan in Etta's and Bette making me proud by picking mine. I was not in competition with Joe to see who could garner more kiddy love; we both did all the fun stuff and bailed at the third sound of a whine. I was relieved when Bette crawled from my lap to Joe's. He had sat beside me again, one corner of the picnic table now substantially ours. Now our legs became as easy with each other's as our arms had been. It was barely worth stirring for a refill, but I did. Everything needed to be toasted: the evening air, the Catherine wheels, our full bellies, the T-shirt evening, the lovely, lovely man I had for company. Joe took a taste of my bubbly, finally: I poured it into his mouth snorting with laughs.

With Joe so nice and close, I was reminded of that most blessed aspect of coupling—that the whole world can be going to seed, pandemonium can have cut loose, widespread wars can be waging fiendishly and without righteousness, but for a tidy twosome all that is at a remove. A couple constitutes a mini world with circuitry all its own, a world that's metaphysically safeguarded. Side-by-side with

Joe that evening, I did not feel assaulted by the fact that bluefin were endangered, that reality television was taking a bite out of crafted drama, that Rex's strength was dwindling, or that my cousin was taking a big risk on an unknown baby. Joe was giving me too good a bulwarking for that. In the right mood, at the right time, with the right disposition, membership in a couple does not double one's problems, it halves them. I could admit that. With my fourth refill sudsing down me, I was able to forget that I quite enjoyed my problems, that my problems were actually dear to me, that I inextricably identified myself with my problems and felt I owed it to my world to do so.

"Joe," I nudged. Bette had gone to check out the Little Red Schoolhouse before it was toast. "Let's go down to the beach. I've never been to the beach in the dark. Want to?"

"Sure, Minnie. If you'd like."

"Bring libations!" I held the neck of a bottle in one hand. As soon as we were around the house and across the road, I held one of Joe's hands in my other. He gripped back tight, but that could have been because I was slurring slightly and swerving. Joe's palm was a hard rind as anticipated. I was laughing at anything and everything—the dark, the moon, the possibility of skunks and bats, the slosh of my spumante on meadow grasses, and Joe's dire need for a five-hour manicure, as I lustily informed him, then held on to his hand all the tighter when he tried to let go. I led Joe down Rex's lane and into Dosie's meadow. There was a moment that had us both awestruck when she loomed up out of the shadows, her hooves scuffing the grass, her head on high. That night Dosie was a stern and wary beast composed of eye glint, body heat, and materialized night. I guffawed at this, too, mocking poor Dosie her banishment to a pasture she quite rightly thought of as hers no matter the hour.

"Touch her, Joe, oh my god touch her, she is amazing, she is amaaazing this horse, because she is so PATIENT!" There was nothing for it but to give in to my ecstasy, my gunning, hundred-horse-power happiness. "I just wish I could reach behind her ears. Can you reach, Joe? Scratch there for me, would you?"

Joe gave Dosie a nice smack to her neck. I was pleased to see that his fishing skills had not overwhelmed his ability to manhandle a barnyard animal. It was a night to heap upon Joe every aspect of prowess going. I was going to celebrate Joe with the determination guerrillas show to an insurgency. I was going to blow this thing between us dark sky wide.

"Waves!" I crooned. "I can hear them, let's go."

"Careful, Minnie, there's a cliff here somewhere."

"There's an electric fence before that! Take your pick, under or over."

I found the posts where the fence dipped at its lowest, scissored over it, then edged out to the lip of grass that curled over the bluff. I plopped down, legs dangling. The tide was high, splishing against the tumble of rocks below—no shaking sand out of hair for days, unfortunately, after a wave-side romp. With the patience of an exceedingly dedicated mental health care practitioner, Joe sat down beside me.

"Behold the night, Joe. Earth spun on its axis, sunny side in. A little something I cooked up just for you!"

"No need to have gone to the trouble, Minnie."

"No bother at all, HA."

Joe had a gift for making it seem like one's jokes had not completely fallen flat while not openly laughing at them.

"The moon is thirsty tonight, Joe, wouldn't you say? I guess you have a sense of the tides, the way I know about, I don't know, skirt lengths?"

"I guess so."

"Not that I know a damn thing about the latest looks, don't give me any credit for that!"

Joe's hand was on my knee now: a tender loofahing. "Some women are beautiful no matter what, Minnie." Joe's gist in the face of my inanity.

"Some men are beautiful, too."

That hand off my knee now. "I don't know about that."

"Sorry, Joe, I'm used to city guys. They can't compete over lobsters so they end up competing over their looks. You'll just have to find it in your heart to forgive them."

One last firecracker. We looked back over our shoulders as it snapped its pink way up past Rex's chimney, then shrivelled.

"That would be my brother's grand finale. Good for him."

In the dark some of Joe's handsomeness went missing and I got a sense of his lovely simplicity. Then I was off my rocker again.

"Lilacs! There's lilacs, finally. The trellis up by Rex's front door. Come smell them for luck, Joe."

The grass had started to prickle. I had on a pair of khaki shorts Desolée had left behind during an army surplus phase. I had also dared to wear my black bra, knowing it would show beneath my tennis top. The bra came with matching briefs, true panties cut scanty. Obviously, I had been oozing with all kinds of ulterior motives even as I'd pretended to myself that Canada Day always called for the careful eradication of stubble and the urgent use of emery boards and perfume, brow pencil and lip liner. I felt about my mood the same way I had heard some women talk about chocolate: I could not get enough of it, I was stuffing it into my mouth as fast as it would fit, I was roaring.

"Lilacs are so, so, so ... pretty." I had to huff after my lope up the back lawn, as did Joe, his strength ordinarily coming from arms and legs at once, not legs alone. He had kept up with me. "God, don't you love them? Don't you love this planet, this beautiful planet that gives us beautiful lilacs? Beauty, beauty, BEAUTY!"

"These are real nice, Minnie. Stop and smell the lilacs, right?"

"RIGHT! Oh Joe, Joe, you are so, so, so, so, soo000o right. Here, take some." I had wanted to tear off a flowery hunk but now I was thrashing with the moist branch. "What the hell? SHIT! Sorry, Joe, am I scaring you? I so don't want to scare you."

"Just leave it, Minnie. It's okay."

"I insist!"

Finally I handed over a young bough that would have been bleeding if it could.

"That's nice, Minnie, thank you."

"Water, that's what we need."

I sped in the back door, no locking-up having been necessary. So it had felt when I left and no one seemed to have stolen anything in the meantime.

"Why don't you take in some water yourself, Minnie?"

Dear Joe, taking a glass down from the sideboard shelf with his own dear hands, his hands now turning on the cold tap, now testing it for coolness, now filling my glass to just the right level, now handing the water to me with his customary modesty despite the fact that pretty well everything Joe did was wizardly. It took me a reverent moment to reach out and take the water, bright like purée of diamonds beneath the kitchen light. I drank it down with froggy gulps that sounded off in my own head as a countdown. I finished the water and handed the empty glass back to Joe.

"I want you," I said.

Joe set the glass down on the kitchen table and put his hands in his pockets but he did not move away.

"Minnie, are you sure you're feeling—"

"Yes! God yes. What are we waiting for?"

I took off up the back stairs. I was wearing my silver sneakers that the kids loved; Joe just needed to follow the glow. The stairway twisted and then opened up right at my bedroom door. My blinds were thumping like ghosts at a séance. I hiked them high. I pulled the covers off the bed and crawled across it and threw my shoes into two corners. I assumed Joe knew that I wanted more than just tucking in, that I never needed tucking in. Joe in my bedroom. Up on my haunches, I stripped to lacy black.

"Happy Canada Day!"

I tipped forward on all fours, wagging my panties behind me. I groped for Joe's belt, caught it by the buckle and pulled. There are these various series of movements that women learn as we grow: how to tie shoes, how to braid hair, how to crack eggs, how to undo a man's belt and root through to cock. Joe's dick popped out at me with no pretence of reluctance, a sturdy prong by anyone's standards. This was how short men got to be Napoleonic, with this kind of strength bound up in their being. Happily, drunkenness had not dried out my mouth. I lunged, tongue first. Drooling, I sucked Joe in while I flicked, rubbed, plunged and then licked. Hot, smooth, vague onion, emanative again: animal mixed with vegetable, maybe even some mineral, ideally nothing predominant. I made satisfied little grunt noises, going after Joe's penis with the same zeal lovers in movies of the week devote to a French kiss. My usual technique was to continue all out like this for a decent interval, then move on to something more penetrative. When I looked up at Joe he was not dumbstruck but rapt. His hands were out of his pockets now, floating by the sides of my head like he was a faith healer. I reached for his T-shirt, clawed up two wads of it, and pulled him down on the bed.

"Oops, Joe, sorry, just one sec." I squeezed out from underneath him to yank open the top dresser drawer. "Desolée sent these. Shall I do the honours?"

"Sure, Minnie, okay."

I saw to it that Joe was now spectacularly naked: white in provocative patches. Judging by what I could see of his face, one side of his brain was manning the arousal department, the other deciphering a puzzle. I slipped off my panties, straddled Joe's body-builder thighs, clenched him between my knees like a Jell-o wrestler, and bit into the square of foil. That wet rubber aroma: sexual only by association. With laboratory calm now, I double-checked which way things were unrolling. I bent to give Joe one more lick, then positioned the safe, pinched the tip, and unfurled as if I was hoisting a sail that would hustle me out of the doldrums. I scooted forward and leaned down. My breasts inserted themselves into the conversation as if curious. Joe had been too polite to touch so far but he had looked. He was utterly erect. I throbbed high and low to see it.

"This is good," I said. "This is very, very good. Because I want us to fuck like crazy. Can we please do that, Joe? Can we fuck like mad?"

"Yes, Minnie. If you want."

Kissing was beside the point and in truth I was finding that tantalizingly whorish; there was no need to love up Joe's every orifice. What I wanted most was to wiggle backwards until Joe's prick was aimed directly at my nethers and then slither down on him bit by bit. Then slam down hard all the rest of the way: grounded, loaded and full of fisherman's cock of all insane things. Then came my cobra dance. Then came some pelvic volleying. Then came my coming, my hand frantically at work while Joe drove his hips on, in, up, in, on, in, up. I would have died if he had stopped before I could abandon myself to ten seconds of delirious pulse and gush. I thought I must have scared away every cat and rat for miles. I am not in that way quiet.

Then it was Joe's turn. I rolled over and he rolled along. His hips felt nice and sturdy between my loopy legs. I tucked up with my abdominals so he could smack against maximum surface to greatest depth. I had meant it when I'd said I wanted *him*. He did not get much more *him* than this. Gutturally, I was singing a hymn to him. Finally Joe also cried for God before a small death took him and he collapsed by my side, the small of his back slick with sex toil, his breath simmering between my ear and the pillow. I thought we should be proud of ourselves for executing a pretty well perfect first fuck. Finally, I kissed Joe: a peck to his damp forehead where it dented between his eyebrow and his curls. I stroked the back of his neck even though it was sopping. When I was sure that Joe was asleep I hunted for the top sheet. I drew it up to our shoulders and settled onto my own pillow, for my own dreams, which would surely fixate on the incredibility of coital action, on the way I had just begged another human being to dig a select portion of his anatomy deep inside of me. Sex was astounding, really, when one did not just assume it was natural.

I woke up first to open blinds and sun sear. Joe was freckled shoulders, a charming tousle and large feet hanging out the far end of the sheet. And a salty new smell in the air, sharper than mine, cutting through it. The morning light was lemony after the hot butter of the day before. I knew what I had to do and it had to be within my rights. Going for a morning run would put the perfect cap on things. It would give Joe a chance to compose himself and I would beat my best time for sure, propelled by the hilarity and joy of having gotten some. I eased opened the dresser drawer with my jogging clothes and chose my best tank and leggings. I was not going to mind if Joe was still there when I got back. I would make French toast or something equally breakfast festive and crack open a second choice of jam. I tiptoed out of the room while Joe lay sleeping on his stomach in the way that babies are not supposed to. I left a note on the kitchen table belabouring at my minimum: *Looks like a great day! Out for a run. Thanks for all. xM.*

Dosie was lying down when I got outside, always a disconcerting sight. She lumbered up when she heard me, hoping for last night's pepper cores. "Dosie, I had sex!" I whispered. "Remember that?" Evidently not. I plucked grass out of her water dispenser and scratched under her mane. Then I token stretched and took off. It was indeed a wonderful run. There was nary a cloud, Eats n' Treats was closed for two days, and Joe liked the cut of my jib. Forty years old and I still had what it took. Decades of sports bras with the correct degree of tensile strength had worked some magic there. I circled the wrong way around the village in order to take the hill on the way back. Verna's little brothers were already out on their ATVs, howling past me and some early churchgoers like we were slalom poles.

Joe had gone when I got back. My note was still propped up against the lilac vase. I crept upstairs but the bedroom was as surreally empty as it had recently been phenomenally full. Joe was the kind of man who made a bed when he left it. So I immediately told Desolée.

"You screwed the studly fisherman. Good for you, Minnie. Was he all Heathcliff?" Desolée took a sip of her coffee.

"Don't romanticize, whatever you do. Most of these guys wear track pants with droopy knees and—"

"Okay, fine. But has he got a Moby Dick?"

"He was very responsive, I'll put it that way. Joe has loads to show for himself. He's smart, he's cute. Scratch that, he's entirely handsome. It was a no-brainer really."

"You could be on to something here, Minnie. Women have to start marrying down. It only makes sense demographically."

"What are you on about this time?"

"Females are hardwired to go in search of a good provider, right? But nowadays women can provide really well for themselves. Finding a man whose socio-economic status is even higher than yours isn't easy to do. Besides, a lot of high-end males prefer to reach way down the food chain for a sweet, uncomplicated little piece of arm candy who isn't going to have her own meetings of the board. You're at the cutting edge of a new breed of professional women, Minnie, who are prepared to wed the proletariat. Trust me, class is the new race."

"For one thing the man is an accomplished administrator and activist."

"Ya, but he still fishes."

"For two, fishing is big business here. Fishermen are hotshots now."

"You know what I mean. It's an education thing."

"For three, slow the hell down. Who says I'm marrying him? All we did was bonk."

"You always say *bonk* when you like them, Minnie. You sugar-coat. My point is, I think you should see this one through. This guy could be good for you."

My jogging bra had suddenly become sodden and tight.

"I need a whole lot of things to be good for me besides a man. I must be crazy to have backed away from Myriad for this long."

"Nah. It's a power move on your part. Retreats are all the rage. They'll want you even more now. Buddy there can spend winters with you in Toronto."

"Would you stop? Just stop right there. You're making me dizzy."

Desolée had been the one to master chess when we were little; no matter how hard I tried she always stayed five moves ahead of me.

"Min, I found something for Rex's birthday and had it shipped straight to the Harbour. Do me a favour and gift-wrap it before the party?" I could tell from Desolée's latest slurp that she had found something extra special.

"What is it?"

"An old studio portrait signed *To Rex, with all my love, Rita Hayworth*. Don't you love it?"

"Rex will be over the moon and so will the ladies. Nicely done."

"Stash and I were thinking of coming out this summer, but the adoption thing is just so painstaking. It's like we're under a spell or something. We can't move."

"Rex will understand."

It had been decades since anyone had referred to Lee having a baby with a *darky*, at least in our hearing, but I had never been quite sure to what degree Desolée's PEI experience differed and continued to differ from mine.

"Besides, I don't want to screw with your momentum, Lover Girl. You've got to keep your net wet."

"Piss off, please and thank you. Love you. Goodbye."

Miserably, it seemed like Joe had given me a virulent pelvic infection; so it looked when I took a morning pee. Then I recalled the beets that I had dined on at Colin and Etta's and hoped Joe would, too, when he had his own moment of urinary drama. I was not sure whether we would joke about that when we saw each other again. I wasn't sure when we would see each other again or when I wanted that to be. Long enough to assume a functional attitude towards the sex.

The phone rang in a way that makes one stare at it for a moment before answering.

"Hello?"

"Minnie, thank God you're there." Verna's adolescent theatrics.

"Thanks again for taking me to Montague, Vee. Sorry I went a bit nuts. What's up?"

"Pat can make it to the Harbour tonight and get a ride back tomorrow. I really want to see him. I kind of miss him."

"Your father lets you have guys over?"

"NO! Can he stay with you? Please, Minnie, please, please, please?"

I asked the kitchen ceiling for answers plus the table and the view out the windows where the sun shone with indifference.

"Just one night?"

"Yup. Fibby wants him up at North Lake to do some work on the boat before tuna starts. They're going to be fishing off Shelburne for weeks if they don't hook up around here. This might be our last chance to hang out with Pat for ages."

"Fine, but no sneaking around Archie at my expense. You're sleeping in your own bed and that's that." I had been twirling as I spoke and now the phone cord was wrapped around my neck; I wondered if I should just take both ends and pull.

"Duh! Jeez, Minnie, get a grip. See you around suppertime?"

"You might as well come for dinner. I take it this means you didn't hang out with the lonely young golfer last night?"

"I ran into him playing pool in Joanne's dad's boat barn. He's not such a hot shit pool player."

"So he let you win, that was nice of him."

"Minnie! He did not. I won, but then he kept bugging me about what a great pool player I am. It was just a few stupid little games, Jeez."

"I think you should show the poor guy a little mercy, Verna. And careful not to show our friend Patrick too much."

"You're the one who got Pat a job!"

"Yes, and let's give him a chance to take first things first, okay?"

"God, Minnie, you can be weird."

"See you tonight."

After wrenching off the bra, I scrambled some eggs for lunch and then shot off a slew of emails. First was a chirpy yet penitential update to Gail. Most were to Myriad. I was hoping that a lot of holiday weekend activity would make me seem hyper-present. Luce fired one back before I could log off, subject heading: *Guess What??!!* I could not guess. It turned out Hardy and Nicola were prolonging their Maritime stay at their own expense. Now it would last an extra week: they were going to drive across the Canso Causeway from Cape Breton to the Nova Scotia mainland to catch the ferry to Prince Edward Island. I could expect them in my neck of the woods any day. In other words I could shortly expect them at Eats n' Treats, the only venue of its kind for miles. That was how I had become something of a local celebrity and how I would now get found out in an apron streaked with hot fudge. Could I drum up some pretext involving research? For a series about diners? Or should I quit now that I was used to holding court with a J-cloth in one hand? It was not belief in myself as a professional that I wanted to salvage. It was Hardy and particularly Nicola's trust in our cash prize. Not that they were likely to win that prize considering Hardy's boundless belly and Nicola's tendency to cut things down to size. But I could not let the chimera suffer. Not if I wanted Hardy and Nicola attending the finale with gracious loser gusto.

I replied to Luce with an equal number of exclamation points. But no winky or smiley faces or Luce would smell a rat. At least it was Hardy and Nicola invading my turf, not Mr. Device and Mary-Jane. Although the latter could have been relied on to stay in one of the Island's five-star inns a couple of golf courses away.

In preparation for Verna and Patrick, and soon Hardy and Nicola, I dusted, swept and scoured. I felt a few finicky stabs of resentment at the thought of sharing Rex's big house. No matter how large one's living space, one gets used to having it to oneself. I had in any case. On my way down to the cellar to rescue some of Rex's old lawn chairs, I discovered that I was not alone after all. There was a stooped, dark figure down there with a grotesque pin head in a tattered suit, menacing me with his callous immobility.

Actually, there was an old tuxedo down there, withering away on a clothes rack. What on earth had Rex needed that for? It wasn't like there was an annual fishermen's ball. I bounded back up the cellar stairs with three serviceable old lawn chairs, dooming the tux to another several dozen years of gloom.

To make up for my closet antisociability I planned a pizza party, defrosting crusts and chopping toppings. I knew Verna would imperiously allow Patrick first choice of anchovies, tofu pepperoni, banana peppers, et cetera. The green Yaris pulled up Rex's lane at seven on the dot, Verna having pledged to show up at six-thirty. It was sweet the way she slung her arm across Patrick's shoulders as soon as she could. I greeted them outdoors, Rex's breeze refreshing everybody. Early-to-bed crows had assembled to express their outrage. I had set up a serving table out back beside the lawn chairs, with bowls of baba ghanoush, rosemary crackers and kalamata olives plus a jug of cranberry and soda with lime wedges. Secord was in attendance, his tongue a pink banner of his delight.

"Thanks for the grub, Minnie," said Patrick. "It's always nice to have a strange bite according to my old ma."

"Tell me more about this mother of yours. What's her name and what does she do?"

"Her name was Violet and she's dead."

"Patrick, I'm so sorry."

"*Cancer*," Verna mouthed. I had put their two chairs side by side, mine opposite.

"The colorectal got her, Minnie. That's the way it goes. Life's fast, then it's over. Especially when it goes in dog years, isn't that right, little poochie pooch?"

"Don't bogart the dog, man." Verna also wanted to pat Secord's bony head, but Patrick was getting all the attention.

"Go on, doggy. Go visit the nice young lady."

I couldn't help myself, I had to further contemplate public toxins. "I gather agricultural run-off is what's mostly damaging the Strait?"

"My dad says the worst pollution comes from municipalities."

Verna's hair was in braids again but down this time, a dark Guine-
vere. She was wearing a black 1950s bathing suit with torpedo cups
under black jeans. "A lot of people that have no business being here
adding to the sewage, Dad says. Water eddies around Charlottetown
harbour, picks up all kinds of crap and heads out again. Then it
comes by here."

"The thing is, Vee, your father better hope a lot more people
start moving here soon or else his kids are going to have to leave
because the economy flat-lined."

"Islanders want people to love the Island all right, but they don't
want to have to love them back."

"Pat, that is so dead on."

If Verna and Patrick were adhering to the Duc de La Rochefou-
cauld's maxim that, *In any love transaction, one party loves and one
party deigns to be loved*, I wondered who was accepting and who
bestowed. Neither of them were used to olives and were too polite
to spit out their pits. I did, into the mint patch.

"The second hay's coming in good," Patrick noted.

"Would someone please explain to me what the difference is
between hay and straw?"

"Minnie, I can't believe you don't know that!"

"Pardon me, Anne of Green effing Gables. So what is it?"

"Pat will tell you."

"Hay is a grass that's used for feed, Minnie. But when a grain,
say wheat, oats, or barley, gets threshed and milled for flour, the leftover stalks are straw. It's used for bedding."

"Thank you, Patrick. Now I feel educated." Now we were all
spitting our pits. An updraft caught my latest and sent it record far.

"Minnie, you so rule!" I was to Verna's inevitable credit again.

"I RULE!" I hollered to be nice.

"Okay then," said Joe.

None of us had heard his truck. There was Joe with his hair wet
from a shower carrying a small paper bag. I had a choice—fluff,
bungle or surmount.

"Joe! Join the party. I'll get you a chair."

I kafuffled my way down to Rex's dank cellar without a flashlight. It would be just my luck if the tux came to life and assaulted me in anger over all the fun it had never had. I flailed around for plastic webbing and found it. I hauled a fourth chair up to the kitchen to wipe it free of cobwebs and ceiling dribble. By the time I rejoined the others, Patrick was talking about the time he had donned a Maple Leaf Foods hat and sneaked into a pork plant.

"They mist the hogs before killing them," he recalled.

Thanks to a CBC radio doc I'd tuned into while mopping, I had information of my own. "Pigs seek out moisture because of their limited sweat glands. It's not that they roll around in dung by choice. Given the chance they're actually clean."

"Did you stay to watch them die?" Verna asked.

"I figured I owed it to them. I thought twice before I had lunch that day."

"What did you have for lunch?" Verna was to-the-brim fascinated.

"A BLT."

"Did not!"

"Did too!"

"They train army medics for battle by using pigs," I said. "Americans shoot them in the face with AK-47's and then try to revive them. Then they shoot them again. Canadians tranquillize them first. Try some of this dip, you guys. It's roasted eggplant."

"Minnie is vegetarian," Verna explained. In Tuck Harbour this came off sounding about as familiar and justifiable as being a Scientologist.

"Nothing animal at all, Minnie?" Patrick pitched forward in his seat to the same degree that Joe leaned back. Verna's long legs were tucked beneath her as if to hide them. "Not even the sushi?"

"From what I understand, catching bluefin these days is kind of like hunting orangutans. It's bush meat of the sea." I was defiling Rex's backyard with my Toronto rhetoric. It wasn't clear how many social ups and downs we could take. We needed an up. "Who wants pizza? There's fixings ready to go in the kitchen and the oven's warm. Verna, why don't you and Patrick get us started?"

Patrick jumped up. "Homemade pizza! I don't know whether to shit or wind my watch."

The youngsters took their clamber indoors. Joe and I were left with a hundred seaside acres plus Nova Scotia heaving sighs across the Strait, and Dosie chawing in a pasture corner.

"You forgot your lilacs," I started.

"You forgot to say good morning." Not upset but not not upset either.

"I left a note!"

"That's right, Minnie, you did."

What a blunder. I should have waited until dark before grabbing us a moment alone. But dusk took its time this far north in early July. Without a doubt, I had changed latitudes.

"Joe, if you were a Toronto guy you'd be thrilled by a note. We'd bump into each again in about a month at an extremely tiresome book launch. If you were a Toronto guy you'd have left *me* a note and then run home to change your locks."

"I'm not a Toronto guy, though, Minnie, am I?"

"No and thank God for that. Thank you for coming by, Joe. It's good to see you."

It really was good, to see the way Joe's parts fit so well together: his bones, skin, organs and steady nature. I liked the way Joe's head tipped to the side every now and then when he was thinking, as if the questions he asked himself were extra weighty. I liked the way Secord jumped at the sound of Joe's voice, going home when bidden. Joe owned river sandals, his nice summer-day sandals. I had to stop staring at his feet. Joe's feet were as plain and innocuous as a Renaissance apostle's.

"Hungry?" I had jumped up the way I did when I was finished conducting a job interview. Drinking for a third night in a row was out of the question; instead I would get scatty on tarragon crust, sun-dried tomatoes and goat cheese.

"Hey, Minnie, got any mozzarella? This white stuff tastes like feet." Verna was smelling her hands.

"Better get used to the chèvre if you're moving to Montreal, chicky."

"Are you moving to Montreal, Verna?" Patrick looked up from sprinkling mushrooms on his pudgy crust.

"Maybe. I got into film school, but I deferred my acceptance for now."

"Cool."

"It *is* cool, isn't it, Joe?"

"I wish you the best with that, Verna. Sounds like quite an opportunity."

"I guess."

"C'mon, Vee, real women love opportunity. Screw the small time!"

I thought maybe I should have asked Dosie to come into the kitchen and take my place; it was like I had clumsy flu. I could only pray it was not contagious. Dinner progressed as necessary. We got the hang of getting the pies out of the oven before they were charred and then they were just right, the goat cheese winning everyone over once I whipped up a curry base. Verna held up the proceedings with some documentation; she wanted to digitally snap her clock pizza, dartboard pizza and pizza as self-portrait—heavy on the black olives. Everybody ate one more slice than they had really wanted and spurned the notion of dessert. Joe was somewhat confused at quarter to eleven when I explained that Patrick was my overnight guest and Verna was on her way home. Joe had to back his truck out of Rex's lane to let Verna out and then he kept on going, his departure discussed as minimally as his arrival. I hoped he had not been in search of *closure*. Desolée and I had maintained for years that closure was a myth perpetrated by the therapy industry to keep people hooked on advice sold in chapters. I had long concluded that to be human was to be wrenched open, no matter how hard one tried to tell oneself or anyone else to shut up.

Patrick was smitten with Dosie. After waving goodbye to Joe and Verna, the latter a horn-tooter, the former not this time, we coaxed her over to the fence nearest the house. She dipped her fifty-pound head to let Patrick scratch behind her ears the size of a rabbit's.

"Do you ever ride the mare?" Patrick asked between coos.

"God no! She's not trained for that. Not for anything, actually. My uncle Rex always had her just for the pleasure of having her. There was room for her here so here she stayed. Right, girl?"

"No one to stand with nose to tail in a hard winter wind all these years?"

"No and I guess it's too late now, she'd kick a pony half to death. Come on, Patrick. Let's get you a toothbrush."

Whatever Joe had left behind in the paper bag on his lawn chair was small and tube shaped. I tucked it under my arm without saying a word. Patrick and I stacked the lawn chairs against the back wall and finished off the dishes. I stowed him in the little bedroom with an atlas to browse since he claimed to love maps. I closed the door to my bedroom. I unrolled Joe's bag to find hand cream, extra strength. I dropped it back in the bag, rolled the bag up tight, and backed up against the headboard with my limbs curled against ghouls. I breathed through my nose for a minute or two because it was easier not to groan that way. To have Joe back in arm's reach, I only wished. I could have spread a white towel, donned a Hungarian accent and played spa. It was vital to let Joe know that it was fine, good, all for the best to joke around with me. Granted, watching Joe crack jokes was as precarious as watching one's father sing. But I would deal with that if he would let me.

⌒

Tuesday morning I was happy to have a job where tidying awaited. For a good hour there was only Herman Walker to serve, who had taken to coming for breakfast and staying for lunch. Clouds had gathered like an angry mob and now drizzle was keeping everyone away. I dragged a stool around my side of the counter to sit for five minutes.

"Did you fish tuna, Herman?"

"I tried to towards the end there but I hardly ever got hooked up. Waste of a licence, probably."

"They're hard to catch?"

"Hard to land as well. You can't fight with them or you'll cook 'em in their own blood. Most times you can radio a guy over from another boat to help. Having it out with a big fish like that can take hours."

"Do you kill them in the water?"

"After you've dragged them for a while, yes you do. Icing them is best, but it isn't easy getting eight hundred pounds of fish up on deck. Some guys have a boom so they can lift 'em."

All this had earned Herman an extra refill.

"How exactly do you kill them?"

"Slit 'em behind the tail, get a knife in a special vein there. Or rake their gills."

"What does that mean?"

"You poke a stick in the gill and jiggle it around until it smothers. Then you bring the fish into port and stick it on the scales. The buyer from Japan, he'll take a tiny slice of tail meat, looking for parasites and feeling for fat. He sets the price, then off it goes in a tuna coffin to Tokyo."

"Too bad for tuna they aren't more cuddly."

"I've seen some beautiful tuna in my time, Minnie."

"No doubt."

I was too melancholy for any further discussion regarding the differences between what was beautiful and what was merely attractive. Beauty can of course be a bully. The paper bag containing Joe's hand cream was weighing heavily in my own bag hung by the back diner door. I couldn't stop glancing over there like I had a nemesis at a cocktail party. Luckily, Verna's desire to keep her Patrick entanglement hush-hush had stopped her from breaking the big news about my visit from Joe. Women surely gossip because they are smaller, or at least supposed to be smaller, and consequently need as much information as possible for their protection. Dopamine and seratonin bathe our brains as soon as we hear *don't tell anyone but*, something every decent woman takes her turn saying. I thought I would spare Joe our feminine survival strategies.

The rain let up around half past noon. Trudy told me to take off, knowing I'd want to bike my way home no matter how sloppy to the ankles. I thanked her and set off towards Joe's. When I arrived the roll call of the day's obituaries was just ending on CFCY 95.1. I tapped on Joe's screen door.

"Ding dong!" I tried.

There was a perilous moment of nothing and then there was Joe, saying my name like it was a correct answer in a trivia quiz, telling me to come in, slipping Rex's old rain jacket off my shoulders, switching off the radio, offering tea. I saw he had lunched on instant macaroni and gherkins, Dolly's home pickling, of course. Crunchy food reduces stress.

"You forgot something last night." I held out the paper bag. Understandably, Joe did not want to take it. I shifted us to the living room couch. "Come," I said. "Sit." I sat down cross-legged and fished the cream out of the bag. I squeezed out a fat dollop and patted the cushion beside me. "Let's go, buster, hand over those mitts."

For what they were worth I began my ministrations, slicking moisturizer over Joe's left hand then right, humming as I did, risking the odd smile, relaxing into the bare motions. Roman senators had been similarly goose-greased by Roman matrons over the past couple millennia. Joe sat a bit lower than me in his TV hollow; nerves had straightened my spine to full length. For the first time, Joe did not grab his phone when it rang. I worked unguent into his crusty thumbs and his fingertips. I acted like massage of all kinds came completely naturally to me. And it would have been a nice and giving, if taciturn, interlude if I had not then realized that the unlatched screen door and the broad daylight and the dense village neighbourhood in combination with Joe's vaguely softened paws were all adding up to a superb opportunity for afternoon sex when anyone might walk in. An incautious fuck would put everything I had to say to Joe into a nutshell, really.

I gave Joe his hands back. I peeled off my cotton sweater and unhooked my plain white day bra. I climbed topless into his lap, and placed one of his hands upon each of my tits. I looked down to see what kind of picture this made. Joe's thumbs began to rotate, then he began to twiddle and pinch. For rather delicate objects, breasts can take quite a beating. Evidently mine loved this. My pelvis started scooping for more action. My breath got ragged like I was rushing up a rocky slope. Despite the general quiet I wanted to whisper. "All the way, baby," I leaned forward to say. "I want to do it."

Joe lifted me up and twisted me back down onto the sofa like he was dog-training me. He pulled off my clam diggers and underwear as briskly as a paramedic, kneeled beside the couch, dipped his head and began to lick. I lay back and tried hard not to think of myself as a health-class diagram, or hair pie, or unduly odorous, or a sexual charity case. Joe seemed to have a genuine appetite for lady parts—always a wonderful sign in a man, right up there with respecting his female relatives. Yes, I could be a feed if that was what Joe wanted. I was, my god, Joe's fatty fish feed, his Omega-3s, his amino acids. He was not moving until he was done; I was informed of that with captain sternness whenever I tried to budge upright. It was as if this was what Joe had a licence to go out and get; this was what he was after. Was this how women became fishwives? I was gasping in subverted alarm.

Then Joe's index slid inward. I was hooked, all of me, on Joe's finger. Now I was hopelessly, flagrantly engorged, I was exhibiting every single one of my sex characteristics. My thighs were pliant loaves, my crotch was a fry-up, I was basted down there. Joe's curls *tickled*. I was, if I was going to be honest with myself, madly, feverishly aroused by the intense discrepancy between this man and me, between this man's handsome face and where it was plunged, between how well this man and I did and would ever know each other, likely, and what it was that we were doing regardless. And then I could only be honest about the complete basics. I was coming like a train. I took two fistfuls of Joe's hair, burst into hoots, and seizured with the kind of pleasure that feels gravity-free, bliss that just blasts everywhere. The rain started up so soon afterward it made us laugh. This time Joe really did have to get the phone, wailing on the kitchen table.

The Atlantic Large Pelagic Advisory Committee—Joe was going to have to head to Halifax and wage another of his battles against the tyranny of consensus. I skimmed up my clothes and shimmied into them before Dolly or a neighbour dropped by. I slipped past Joe as he shuffled papers at the kitchen table. He raised a finger— my god, the same finger—to tell me to wait just a sec. I'd forgive myself later for pretending this was a wave goodbye. I flapped a little wave goodbye back and split.

8

One rainy week later, Verna experienced a rude shock at the diner. I'd come in to work that morning half-comforted—the evening before, partway through my dinner of hot, buttery new potatoes strewn with gobs of mint, Joe had given me the *call from the road* that every harbour-bound maiden holds dear. But our chitchat had been undeniably stilted. I had sidetracked Joe into an irksome discussion as to why I did not own a dog even though I would have loved one, blah blah, which went on a good twelve beats longer than it should have. But Joe had refused to tell me a single thing about the latest International Commission for the Conservation of Atlantic Tuna directives, or why he was sleeping so badly the guy in the next door room at the Halifax Sheraton had finally pounded on the wall.

Verna answered the Eats n' Treats phone just as the lunch rush was ending, expecting whoever was on the line to order fish burgers and shakes. It turned out to be a swag dealer from Ohio trying to interest the proprietor in a consignment shipment of *Home of Buddy Donovan* ballpoints. He was convinced they'd sell up a storm.

"How ignorant do you think we are?" Verna asked before

slamming the receiver back up on its hook. Then she stomped back to her mass bacon grilling.

"I don't see what you've got against young Buddy."

"Okay then, Minnie. There's nothing wrong with Buddy Donovan. And there's nothing wrong with Patrick either. Alberta goes boom in some people's faces. That doesn't mean they're losers."

"There's nothing wrong with Patrick and there's nothing wrong with you, Verna. You're going to do great things. Once you get out of this village you'll end up somewhere that people judge you by your actions rather than what they expect of you."

I edged up to Verna close enough to hug her but smart enough not to. She had not combed her eyelashes that morning and they were bunched into sooty spikes.

"It just burns me, Minnie, the way things come so easy to some people. Not to me and I don't need Buddy Donovan proving that to me for the rest of my life."

"Some people just make things look easy, Vee. Bet you anything poor little Buddy is shitting bricks right now about whatever the hell he's up against this time. The young ace from Tucson who grew up with a silver club in his mouth. Or the sportswriter who thinks Buddy will never get enough sponsorship to go big or go home. Everyone struggles."

The bacon was going to be extremely crispy, which was fine since that was a constant customer request. I hoped pig vapour was not getting in my pores. Verna's spatula was still slamming around and scraping. I focused on her frown, a backwards comma hooked into her profile. Her eyebrows were forward slashes. Trudy and Debbie were out back doing freezer inventory.

The front door dinged: my job to follow up as to whether someone wanted a table or directions to the *bathroom*, the demure North American implication being that voiding is never undertaken without a good soak afterwards. Gail had brought Desolée and me up to ask our way to the *ladies room*, but Lee said it was better to shoot straight for a toilet; they'd compromised on loo or john. Henceforth,

I thought of loo and john as a reasonably happy couple who were settled into one another after years of bridge partnership and passing the salt. Much like basil and rosemary, and frank and surely.

Verna had one last point to make before I bolted. "Just because Joe is Mr. Cheekbones Smarty Pants Fishermen's Association doesn't mean you have to like him either, Minnie. You're in my boat."

I would have in turn suggested to Verna that she do her best not to behave like the human equivalent of a severe weather warning, but Nicola and Hardy were out front. Nicola and Hardy were disrupting Eats n' Treats with their rampaging hilarity. At least Hardy was hullabalooing about how hard it was to retract the darn umbrella. Nicola said that the score was now umbrella fifty-six, Hardy zero, and would he please get himself inside so they could order some lobster buns?

"Hello, you two," I said and everything that I was doing and that Nicola and Hardy were doing was thrown under a microscope, into a spotlight and up on a vaudeville stage. Those two had less warning, but they recovered first.

"Minnie, here you are," Hardy said. "What a lovely surprise."

"Not a complete surprise." It was unlikely that Nicola was often truly surprised. "Luce told us this was your neck of the woods."

"Kind of!"

They definitely wanted a table. I showed them to a middle booth. I handed them menus and dared to tarry, order pad dangling. "So what do you think of my summer job?" I asked.

"Refreshing!" Hardy said.

Nicola was more curious, her eyes incorruptibly blue whereas Hardy's were a mulchy brown. "Is this a family business?"

"In a way it *is*, yes." Trudy was possibly my seventh cousin eight times removed. I focused on the menu, my area of expertise. "The lobster buns are great. Season's over, but it's fresh frozen. Start with a cup of chowder."

"Lovely, thank you for the suggestion."

"Yum, yum, yum! And may we have two pops as well, please,

Minnie? Orange for the lady and grape for me if you have it, otherwise anything citrus."

"Coming right up."

Hardy was going to love our fat straws. Verna put two cups of chowder in the microwave and helped me load a tray with saucers, spoons and biscuits. "Minnie, are you mad at me? You look like you're going to scream. We're both just PMS'd, right?"

"Contestants from my show just showed up. Can you believe it?"

Verna peeked. "Shit, Minnie, sorry, the lady just saw me looking. What are those two doing together anyway? They look like Olive Oyl and Winnie the Poo."

"That's the whole point. It's supposed to be funny that they don't belong together no matter how hard they try."

Verna whistled in doleful admiration. "Brutal."

Nicola and Hardy were staying at the Shady Acres. Nicola saw no point in frills. They were going to be around for five days or so. It did not depend on the weather; any weather was good weather.

Verna scored a proper introduction in between first and main course. "You should see the house where Minnie's staying, it's amazing," she mentioned before heading out back to tell Trudy and Debbie who was here.

"Yes, absolutely, you must drop by," I said to Nicola and Hardy with intonations that were all of a sudden very Zsa Zsa Gabor playing up Green Acres. "I'm just outside the village, totally seaside, couldn't ask for more."

"Is it your house, Minnie?" Hardy had such faith.

"God no, it's my great uncle's place. He's in Montague for a spell."

In the same way that other people were sure-footed, Nicola was sure-worded. "When exactly would you like us to drop by?" she wanted to know.

It was Wednesday—how to set a balance between working up the courage for this and getting it over? "How's Friday?" I asked. "Friday happy hour?"

"Friday works for us." Hardy's moustache dripped fishy cream. "We're off to the potato museum tomorrow." Even Hardy's tongue was round.

"And Founders Hall as well, darling. You promised."

Darling? That was laying it on a bit thick. There were no cameras in Eats n' Treats.

"Oopsie, that's right. I tell you, Minnie, this lady loves a good archive. The things she knows about ink and old paper."

Nicola had to remonstrate. "Hardy, darling, stop that flattery. No more."

I would have looked straight into Nicola's eyes at this point, but all eyes were now on the mountainous buns that Trudy was delivering to the table in person, an extra half scoop of lobster meat each by my estimation. Hardy was delight-struck by all the mayonnaise in reach. Nicola was comfortable making friends with her mouth full. Trudy was soon regaling them with all the local landmarks—scenes of shipwrecks, the prettiest roads, the winery and the weavery and the fully historic village. So much for sending them to Cavendish to play minigolf and pay Ripley to believe it or not. Nicola and Hardy must have been counting themselves very lucky for all the connection, information and consolidation. Their luck was far from my luck but luck can be grotesquely double jointed. No doubt Nicola and Hardy were as gracious with Marie back at the Shady Acres. I wondered if I could get away with calling Marie to ask if they were actually staying in separate rooms, or supposedly staying in separate rooms, or not. I saw that Nicola let Hardy pay the tab. Not that I blamed her; Hardy was the kind of man who made footing the bill part of the natural scheme of things.

"We're coming back here for lunch every day!" They got four bottled waters for the road, thereby cleaning us out. Nicola's biscuit was wrapped in a napkin for later. "No crumbs in bed!" Hardy winked. Verna giggled. Nicola shook her head with mock weariness before hitting the porch.

"Nice couple," Trudy said.

"What? Oh, right, for sure."

It would have been churlish to protest that Nicola and Hardy were a couple devised for sly reasons and that their union would remain misbegotten to the point of defunct. If not, *Marry Me or Else!* was headed for major branding issues. The sight of Hardy and Nicola *à deux* was unlikely to score us any press, promo or profile no matter how well they were made-up, dressed and lit. I thought of emailing Barry to let him know that things were looking dangerously lovey-dovey and remind him that Nicola and Hardy were killer when it came to audience passion. Then I warned myself to stop worrying. The ex-nun and vintner would prevail as planned, their combined backstory was simply too firm to buckle. Barry and Luce seemed to be enjoying a jolly summer, Luce's emails ever full of exclamation points, Barry's quoting one wise saw after another. All the more reason not to give them the impression I was drumming up dilemmas out in PEI.

Joe had given me all his phone numbers—cell, landline, boat—and urged me to call him if I ever needed anything. I thought maybe I needed something: I needed a stabilizing element at Friday's cocktail party. I needed the nervousness Joe possibly felt around me to balance out the nervousness I possibly felt around Nicola. Besides which I was honestly fond of Nicola and Hardy. The least I could do was show them an authentic Island time. . . . Considering I had no intention of delivering them *fifty grand, twenty-five each*. Not that either of them seemed to have credit-card debt or blackmailers to pay off. I had no idea why they were succumbing to our gambit hook, line and sinker, maybe dragging me under with them.

I dialled Joe's cellphone as soon as Halifax business hours were conceivably over. I heard it ring once, twice, three times, four. Was I getting the brush-off? I felt awful for Rex's digits—shivering on a call display, spurned and by now probably muted. Or Joe had entered my name in his phonebook. In which case I felt bad for *Minnie*, neglected for five rings, now six. Or maybe just my initials?

"'lo?"

"Joe?"

"Joe here."

"Hi, Joe. It's me, Minnie."

"Minnie? Hang on a sec, I'll pull over."

"Oh, no, that's okay." Who was I to tell Joe that he shouldn't protect himself from a clunking? "Okay then."

"I'm on my way home. Missed the ferry, but I should make the bridge in forty-five."

"So, did you, um, manage to get the provincial tuna quota you wanted?"

"Quota is diminishing all over the world, Minnie, but we're doing our best to be fair. Looks like the season's starting August first. We'll see how long it takes to fish that up, whether we have to take a break if the first catches come in light. If not, three weeks is my guess."

"Right." I could hear tractor trucks zooming past Joe's window. I guessed his distress lights were on. I was all out of fishery questions. Between us we had over forty years of adulthood under our belts; something had to be worth tossing up as a combined point of reference. Would Joe have shopped in Halifax? Was it too late to attempt anything hockey related? Had he heard that Island Call-In was cancelled, making way for *new country all of the time*?

"Are you okay, Minnie?"

"Oh, okay, the thing is, I was wondering, Joe, can you maybe drop by on Friday? Because I'm having these people over. Who I know, well, I kind of know them from Toronto. And I'm sure they would love to meet a real fisherman. Not that you're an animal at the zoo or anything! It's just that they're contestants in a show I'm producing and ... it's all kind of strange. Forget it, this is stupid. I'm sorry."

"No worries, Minnie. Friday you say?"

"Friday around five?"

"That'll work."

"Thank you so much, Joe. It'll be good to see you, by the way."

"Happy to help, Minnie. Happy to hear you ask."

The weather had the grace to spit its last and clear up. I thought I had better run—as far away from myself as possible. Either that or I was sprinting in fear from the Maritime hospitality tradition. I double-knotted my laces and hit the road, letting the spotless views scrub my mind clean. Garnet-coloured earth, amethyst lupins, emerald fields, lapis seas and sapphire skies—PEI resplendence presented itself as absurdly commonplace. I wanted to convert the jewel tones into lozenges and rattle them around my molars. Nicola and Hardy would go home feeling enriched. I would go home feeling proud of the way Secord had stopped yapping whenever I jogged past the McTeal lane, and the way that Herman Walker now knew just to drive past with a wave, and the way the crows were more irate than ever to see me. Worthiest of all was the concrete strength in my legs I had gained by scaling hills that needed to get climbed back down their other sides. My only recent affliction was recurrent prickly rash to the soul, which I seemed to be itching my way out of with sex. Sociologists, women studies profs and lady columnists would be hard-pressed to believe me when I assured them that I did not have self-esteem issues. Unless I had ended up with too much self-esteem? In which case it made sense that I would fuck some self-esteem away.

Nicola and Hardy did not show up at Eats n' Treats the next day or the day after. They were typically gorgeous PEI summer days, temperatures hovering in the mid-seventies and no higher. Tourist season was beginning in earnest. My Harbour accent was now thick enough to pass as local and I couldn't resist, to the great amusement of the regulars, who continued to dominate the barstools and left the booths for sissy visitors. Or the McTeal kids. Colin was bringing them by for lunch several times a week. Come herring season in September, Etta would take her time off.

"I want a salad like Mom makes for Minnie," Elliot said.

Usually the kids jostled over two large orders of fries with gravy.

"Dude, I'm honoured," I said. "For that you get to come out

back and help me toss a good one."

"Fine, abandon us then, Minnie." Colin turned to Pierre with a jutting pout. "The hot ones always go cold."

"You guys can hold the cones later when I pump the ice cream, how's that?" Pierre was too deep inside a comic digest to care.

"Minnie, are you going to stay here?" Elliot had followed me into the walk-in fridge when I went hunting for cherry tomatoes. "Are you going to stay past summer? Mom says you might."

"I'll stay for a while, Dodger." Elliot had a summer buzz cut in homage to his dad that only Joan and Bette were allowed to rub and only to make it up to them when he'd made them cry yet again by playing King Arthur or Aztecs too rough. Secretly, I was glad his dark mop top was growing back.

"For a little while, Minnie, or a big while?"

"Thanks for asking, El, but try not to worry about it. Let's seize the moment."

"Season the moment?"

"Yes!" I was shaking bacon bits into his greenery and I had melon-balled a ripe avocado and shaved in some carrot. I wanted to engage Elliot's palate as best I could. Charlottetown Community College boasted a top-of-the-line culinary arts department and he had the taste, looks, balls and brawn it took to be an executive chef. "Pass me the sesame seeds; dude, you are so going to love this."

Colin offered me an ice cream along with everyone else, but I declined and got a fiver from him for my trouble, which was almost as hard to choke down. I preferred tips from Americans, and tossing the McTeal kids' spilled salt over my shoulder always felt lucky enough. They reinvaded the minivan before I could give back the bill, Elliot in the back seat pressing a hand like a little starfish underbelly up to the rear window as they drove off. The kiss I blew felt wispy in comparison.

Friday dawned foggy, but by mid-morning it burned away to reveal July in the way that everyone pictures July in their dreams: sunny but for giant, white popcorn clouds on high doing a climatological gavotte. Trudy had catered some tidbits for my get-together: sausage rolls and mini quiches that I could cart home and add to Gail's devilled egg recipe.

"Trudes, honestly, why don't you come by as well?" I had invited her twice already and now I asked again. Trudy was wearing another local band T-shirt, this time The Loud Americans. I loved looking up to Trudy. She was even more willowy than when we had met, if willowy was a nice way of saying rake-thin. Her hair was down to her tailbone. She was too busy sorting, simmering and kneading to follow Verna out to the backyard with scissors, a towel and a stool.

"No can do, Minnie woman."

"But Joe's coming. He'd be so happy to see you. In all honesty I'm surprised you two never ended up together." True, Joe was six inches shorter, but that could have stopped mattering somewhere between thirty and thirty-five.

"Me and Joe? Nah. We used to crack jokes on the school bus, but that's about as romantic as Joe and I ever got. No point messing up a good friendship. It's sweet of you to ask me over, Minnie, and I would totally accept. But something's come up."

I was pretty sure I had permission to prod. "What gives?"

"Fibby wants to drop by. He begged. That Patrick guy you hooked him up with, he seems to be having quite an effect. I'm not sure how. Guess I'm going to find out."

"Trudy, you're not—"

"No. I'm not going to trust Fibby Trask any further than I can chuck him." Trudy's laugh: an owl with a machine gun, *hoo hoo, ha-ha-ha-ha.*

I needed to hurry home with my foil-wrapped treats before their bottoms cooled. Trudy had promised to dock my pay to cover the cost. I barely knew what I made so I hoped I could trust her.

"You know, Trudy, there aren't any rules. Remember that."

"Sometimes don't you wish there were, Minnie?"

"No, actually. I'm glad there aren't rules. I find the best things happen when one improvises."

"One better shake one's ass, one has company tonight."

I put back down my pastries and sallied forth for a hug that had the welcome quality of making me feel like Trudy was an antenna that would fine-tune my reception. I was glad for men that they had started to hug each other as a matter of course, although male hugs are brief and undercut with whacks. Trudy was right; I had to hurry if I wanted to squeeze in a bout of Pilates and freshen up before greeting my guests with my core strengthened and my hair brushed.

I decided to set up in the kitchen again rather than the dining room: less ironic, more sincere. I put out cocktail napkins, olive-green alternating with pimento-red, and a stack of side plates, and wine and water glasses, and, on second thought, the chaffing dish. I added a tube of SPF in case anyone was running low while the sun still glowed. Did I dare snip the last of the lilacs? Not when there were overwrought roses available that would look great crammed in the old brown milk jug, weeping away their petals. A car cruised up the drive. Joe was invited, Joe was on his way. This might have been him, but I had not heard enough gravel crunch. I was beginning to recognize Joe's tires.

"Magnificent!" hollered Hardy after an arms-wide pirouette. "Heavens above, Minnie. My oh my." Hardy probably owned a Sudbury manse with a sought-after view from afar of molten red slag rivulets coursing down dark heaps in the night.

"This suits you," Nicola said, one hand above her eyes ahoy style. "This is a strong house, Ms. Gallant."

"Come in, I'll give you a tour. Uncle Rex will be so pleased to find out he had company."

Nicola and Hardy were now a total team, that much was obvi-ous, complimenting each other whenever one of them aptly praised the house, or the grounds, or me. (*Yes, you're quite right, my love ... Well said, darling ... You've hit the nail on the head there, madame.*) Hardy managed to relight the pot of Sterno. Nicola uncorked the (not again) champagne they had brought, a beautiful French rosé that smacked of Toronto's triumphantly knowing liquor stores.

Hardy filled two plates with a little bit of everything while Nicola perused Rex's cassette tape collection for just the right big band compilation. They loved Rex's etched drinking glasses and hand-painted china. We visited Rex's parlour so that Nicola could assess the library. That was when I spotted Joe's red truck turning down Rex's lane. Joe, Joe's hands, Joe's chest, Joe's stocky legs. Joe's quiet way with details. Joe's essential decency when I had thought decency was for the most part overrated. Joe's grade-twelve English plus technical terms. Joe was here and immediately I was a slightly different person. No doubt we all alter each other in various ways, but Joe's effect on me was ridiculous.

"Here's the fisherman," I said to Nicola and Hardy as if he had been specially delivered. "You can ask him anything you want, he's very approachable."

"Approachable, is he?" Nicola had caught a glance through the windshield.

"There isn't anyone this lady doesn't find approachable, Minnie. She had us chatting to the captain on the ferry."

"Joe is a family friend. Hardy, will you do the honours with refills? I'm just going to say hi."

Joe had veered around the rental and pulled up in his spot. He was sporting his usual James Dean finery and strolling with his deceptively surly gait. He had hopped out of his truck, snapped shut his phone and headed towards the back door before noticing me waiting. Someone in Halifax had trimmed his curls and he had a low tide of hair now rather than wave after wave. It made him look a bit older, which did not hamper him; Joe would be handsome until he died. He was holding a dinner plate wrapped in a stiff white dishtowel.

"You didn't have to bring anything," I moaned.

"Mom's biscuits, no big deal."

"We're drinking champagne, but there's beer if you want. Thanks again for coming, Joe. You're a trooper." I was up on a grassy knoll; I shuffled us indoors where we could be eye to eye again. Nicola and Hardy were stalling in the library.

"Quite the spread, Minnie."

"Trudy totally helped. She's so great."

"Trudy's a nice lady, you got that right."

Joe placed the biscuits by the butter, then hung the white dish-cloth on the stove door rack. He knew just what to do with things; it was so respectable.

"What can I get you? Oh, here's Hardy. Joe, meet Hardy; Hardy, Joe."

"Greetings, sir!" Hardy thrust his chubby hand forward like a race baton. "Minnie says we can ask you anything we want as regards the high seas and you'll fill us right in."

"I don't know about that, but you can try me."

It was worth shadowing Joe like a yes man to ingest a full dose of his pheromones. Likely, we had immune systems that covered opposite ends of the disease spectrum; that was supposed to get a female heart racing as long as birth-control pills had not pilfered her instincts. It was good to hear Joe's abrupt but polite way of talking once again, his courteous acknowledgement of others that stopped short of deferential. It was nice to know a man who still tucked in his T-shirts. Etta said Joe grew a bit of a paunch in the winter, but it never took him long to get rid of it come lobster. Now it had vanished, not even his rurally high waistband—Joe was no hipster—could detect an ounce of it. For an awful moment I wanted to see Joe reduced to sobs, purely so that I could clasp him to my bosom and calm him in a special way that only I knew how. Hardy passed him a highball of champagne.

"Bottoms up, Joe!" I was always making the poor man drink.

"Down the hatch, folks."

If Joe came to Toronto he could make a living by sticking on a captain's hat and trooping around kids' birthday parties out-earning clowns, magicians and reptologists. Or he could steer buffet boats around Lake Ontario for lunch and dinner sittings.

"Now what might a swimmeret be?" Nicola had volume L of the old encyclopedia open at *Lobster.*

"Nicola, Joe; Joe, Nicola." Amazing to be in our forties, perhaps fifties, and still playing, still getting ourselves into a kick-the-can and musical chairs mood.

"You'll find swimmarets underside the tail, Nicola. They're little fins. But the male's top pair are more like prongs. He holds them together to siphon his juice down into the lady lobster. It took the scientists a while to figure that one out. 1895, I think it was. I seen it written down somewhere."

"My my, I'll have to look that up. Or take your word for it. Hardy, why don't you have swimmarets? I feel quite cheated."

Hardy squeezed his arms together tightly in front of him. Being Humpty Dumptyesque, this was not easy to do. When he flapped his hands, Joe tossed him a biscuit. Hardy caught the biscuit and passed it to Nicola. She ripped out a bite and we all laughed. The evening managed itself from there. Nicola and Hardy were interested to learn that Joe had fished with his father until obtaining the fleet on his own and that there was a time when he and his dad had been out on the water from spring thaw until the ice was gelling again, going for cod and hake as soon as lobster was over, and maybe some haddock and mackerel before herring. Charlie McTeal had made do with a compass and gas engine when he first started, now Joe echo-sounded and globally positioned and could find Hardy a quarter on the ocean floor that he'd dropped overboard a year earlier.

"With these diesel engines we got now we can pull a ferry. A small ferry, mind you."

"But still, old chap!" Hardy would have made a good tugboat captain.

Joe told us about the fisherman from Bay Fortune who had taken underwater pictures of malformed lobsters for years right where the processing plants dumped their waste water.

"Treated like a crackpot mostly. Now everyone's taking him more serious." Joe seemed to like champagne; I would tease him about that later.

"I'll hunt around for some pertinent papers for you when I get back to work." Nicola touched Joe to confirm it, one of her long fingers tapping one of his thick wrists. Syntax notwithstanding, Joe was highly attractive. Any woman could see that—no-nonsense or not. Of course, much of a woman's attention is geared to a man's record with other women. Thanks to Nicola, I was taking another look at Hardy's waddle. I could see how endearing it might be to have Hardy shuffling one's way with breakfast tea or that week's funniest *New Yorker* cartoon. Or toddling around the kitchen table to offer guests a nip for the road. Hardy had designated himself a driver and switched to cranberry and soda. The *cing à sept* stretched into more of a *cinq à neuf*.

"Can I meet that great big beautiful horse before we head off?" Hardy asked with a slap to his knees. I was happy to oblige and Hardy said no time like the present. Dosie trotted over as if she was twenty-eight in human terms rather than the horse equivalent of elderly, thudding so heavily she made the field sound hollow. Colin had promised to take me to the Agri-Co-op to pick up oats and a new halter. I could hardly wait to see the words Agri-Co-op show up on my credit-card statement. Hardy got it and congratulated me in advance. The sky blushed at my blather, swathes of pink dabbed with peach washing over the darkening blue. The last birds were possibly the first bats. The ocean was gently snoring. Hardy agreed that it would be marvellous to burst into tuneful opera whenever the mood struck.

"*La donna e mobile,*" he tried. Dosie huffed and plodded away.

"*O solo mio.*" I copped to my excessive vibrato.

"What's all this rumpus?" Nicola was out the door, Joe following. Her flat sandals swished through the grass; no flip-flop thwacks for Nicola. Hardy hurried over to offer his arm, but she sent him to say his goodbyes to Joe instead and made her way over to me. I was perched on Dosie's fence, the top rung still warm from the day.

"Joe is a good man," Nicola said, as seriously as someone wishing me off on a polar exploration. "I'm very happy for you."

"Oh, Joe's not, we're not—"

"May I say that he's very fond of you in return. We compared notes as to how persuasive you are, Minnie. I hope you don't object. We meant it well."

Nicola made for the passenger seat. "Back to Montague, Romeo!"

"Your grace!" Hardy jumped to it.

The driver's seat needed coming forward and the steering wheel needed to retract, but Joe helped find the right levers.

"I'll be going into Montague soon myself," I said while the car revved, keen to see more of Nicola and Hardy after all. I was drunk on sunset if not champers. "Perhaps we'll meet again."

"We'll see you in a few months regardless." Nicola was cool as can be. "Marry me or else, Hardy."

"Ah, yes, our chance to prove our love!" Hardy honked so loud and long that I was worried Herman Walker would rush over all keen on helping out in an emergency. I had rendered Rex's lane exceedingly gaseous over the summer; no wonder the crows hated me. Hardy swerved neatly back out the lane. Everyone was a good driver except for me. Joe and I waved for the duration of their reverse and their first burst of forward motion, then sauntered back inside.

"I admire you Toronto girls," Joe said at the back door.

"Why?" Too vehement, try again. "Why's that, my friend?" To bludgeon, bludgeoning, bludgeoner.

"You really get things done. Your friend Nicola there, she has that library charity, for instance."

"She does?" This prodded me somewhere better lit to hear more. I went straight to Rex's sink. I enjoy doing dishes—the way they present accomplishment as blunt fact while warming the hands.

"She raises money for libraries in Africa. It was interesting how she explained it. Books are donated here and her group pays to have them shipped there. That's the expensive part."

"They do? She does?"

Joe grabbed the dishtowel to start drying.

"Sure. Plus they produce textbooks in those languages over there so the people don't have to learn English same time as they learn how to read. She seems really dedicated."

"Wow, the love of her life. Now I get it."

I could see how respectful Hardy would have been of Nicola's true motives, probably offering to toss in his half of the winnings for such a good cause. Nicola was after filthy lucre like anyone else; hers was simply destined to stay clean until it got to Accra or Bamako.

"Now you get what, Minnie?"

"Don't trust us city girls, Joe, that was your first mistake. We've always got an eye on our advantages. The thing is, Nicola and Hardy are trying to win a contest that I'm running. The libraries are obviously why she wants the money and Hardy is playing along to help her."

"What contest?"

"Oh, to see who can get engaged and convince an audience they'll stay that way. It's all old maids and terminal bachelors. Pretty dumb, I admit."

Joe gave the whistle of a gumshoe coming upon a tawdry corpse. "If you don't mind me saying so, Minnie, pretty dumb is what it sounds."

"Well, not *that* dumb, actually. We're expecting a lot of great fallout. We'll be able to expand the template if this takes off, move on to spinoffs for retirees, maybe. And if the winning relationship never pans out, that's the audience's fault at the end of the day. To be honest with you I got a lot of credit for this."

"You made all this up, Minnie? Got all this started?"

"As a production executive I do a lot of development, yes. Advertising and sponsorship lined right up. I've got nothing to be ashamed of here, believe me."

Joe was standing by with the towel. I dredged up a jagged mass of cutlery from the bottom of the dishpan and dabbed at its tips and points. I thought if Joe had a problem with the kind of television I produced he should have looked into that before bedding me.

Everybody knew that reality television was the new *commedia dell arte*, a frolicking with archetypes, a wilful sham. Or knew it even if they didn't know they knew it. It was not like I expected Joe to watch the show, let alone like it.

Another damn whistle.

"I went lobster fishing with *you*," I said.

"Yes, that was nice, having you along, Minnie."

The dishcloth now hung over Joe's shoulder. At least Joe's arms were not crossed, unlike mine. My hands were wet at my elbows, dripping on Rex's pioneer planks. Now I was pacing.

"Maybe you should take a stand and forgo fishing tuna, Joe, if it's so endangered. Did you ever think about that? About not fishing for what isn't there?"

"People are hauling tuna out of the water all over the world, Minnie. Us small guys are the least of it. There's countries like Libya, Algeria and Tunisia that aren't signatory to any treaties. There's Japanese guys with twenty-five-mile long lines that can fit thousands of hooks. A seiner sends a weighted gill net around a school of bluefin a mile wide. Nothing stops a seiner, Minnie."

"You still haven't told me why *you* have to do it, Joe. Next thing you know you'll be clubbing baby seals."

"Fishing tuna's what I told my brother I would do this year so that's what I'm going to do. I bought that licence in good faith. Whether I will go after tuna next year or the year after is a question. A good question, you're right there, Minnie. I trust your judgement if that's what's got you so steamed up. I've always trusted your uncle a good deal and so far I seen no reason not to trust you." Joe was literally handing in the towel, neatly hanging it back up. "You go ahead and do what you've got to do, Minnie. You won't find me stopping you. No one in this province has an active seal licence by the way."

The cookie sheet did not really need a thunderous scrubbing. Joe *trusted* me, did he? I was going to find that hard to object to without sounding perverse. He was right, come hell or high water I did what I had to do. And so did he. "You guys eat some of the tuna you catch, right, Joe? You use it to survive on, like, an animal level?"

"No, Minnie, none of us here eat that tuna." Joe took a look out the window to check on the water that he knew so much better than I did, that he knew so much better than he knew me. "It's far too full of mercury."

I tossed aside my scrub brush. "Joe, that is depraved." My foot had to stomp, just once, then twice. I slumped on a kitchen chair, head in hands, bangs slopped.

"A little bit of that tuna gets sold back to the U.S. Minnie, to the snootiest Japanese restaurants, the ones you need to reserve a table at way ahead."

"God, why?"

Joe's hands were shoved so deep into pockets that his arms were stiff.

"The fish we catch around here make their way up the eastern seaboard, past Philadelphia, New York and Boston. Coal burning is putting mercury into the atmosphere the world over, a lot more now that China's industrializing. Bluefin is bad with the mercury, albacore, too. But they warned pregnant and nursing women about that on the news, right?"

"No, Joe, I mean why do we let ourselves get stuck doing these lousy things? And what's worse, doing them well?" I took the champagne bottle over to the chipped old sink and poured out what was left, then tossed out the last sips from my glass and grabbed Joe's glass and dumped it. Nicola and Hardy's glasses were already rinsed and dried. "Don't you think we better wonder what we've got to be proud of? Obviously, we're screwed." I could neither look at him nor stop there. "Now I get why people make such a damn big fuss over their weddings and offspring; they don't want to stake everything on their occupations. Sorry, I speak for myself. For all I know, Joe, you want to father a whole nursery school full of fisherpeople. In which case I'm a very bad bet. I am so far over the hill that I have no idea where the hell I am." I thumped Rex's heaviest platter into the dish rack where it could drip dry.

"I'm going to take off, Minnie. We've both had a long week. I'll see myself out. You get some rest, chase those blues away."

"Fine."

Joe did not furthermore instruct me to polish off the leftover curried eggs, but I did, each one more sci-fi than the last. I had spiced yolk and rubbery white in my mouth before Joe made it out the lane and when I dared to glance at myself in the bathroom mirror before going to bed I had ochre crud stuck to my face. That's what sex did; it brought back *stress eating*. My heart remained on red alert when I snapped out the light. I had thought of cracking open *Anne of Avonlea*, finally, but I had too much bile on the brain. I hoped Joe would not tell anyone what a gloomy bitch I'd been. My new girl-friends would understand, and Colin would laugh it off, but I would be ashamed in front of Rex. I got out of bed and left a message with Tuck Harbour Taxi. I ordered a cab for eight the next morning, in time to get to Montague and back before work. I would confess my sins to Rex over a filched waffle. The first one to name a sin controls it. I would tell Rex I was a nasty hag who had no business courting male attention except for that of her dear and great uncle who some-how put up with her terminal consternation.

Mornings usually dawn more pragmatic than the night before, as I was soon awake enough to appreciate. In the cab on the way to Montague—silent once I agreed with the driver that I worked at the diner then went monosyllabic—I thought maybe I ought to go, leave Tuck Harbour altogether and head back to Toronto. It would be a dirty break, and a sour start back home, but at least I could keep a closer eye on *Marry Me* post-production, making sure Nicola and Hardy's *Getaway* wasn't rough cut with too much charm or edited with too much promise. In Toronto my toxicity would be less unique and harder to trace. I would phone Rex twice as often to make up for out and out fleeing. Doris and Sally could handle the birthday party details on the Saturday of Rex's eighty-eighth. At this point in the summer there were direct flights on and off the Island several times a day, some of them charter cheap. Lately it was the arrivals that were packed, not the departures—full of families with extra bathing suits in their luggage, happy to escape smog warnings, pile-ups on the expressway and heat that wet their ribs.

I let my head bump against the cab window and ploughed nice views into my brain: fields, hedges, copses and distant sea. The potato plants were flowering: white confetti shaken over bumpy acre after acre. It would be a shame to miss the raspberries. Etta had promised to take the girls and me to a pick-your-own soon, back when I still had a soon. Thirty dollars of dales later I was in Montague. I gave the cabbie a big tip in case we were assigned to each other on the way back. I'd asked to get dropped off at the lights. I needed to march a bit before giving Rex bad news, summoning soldier courage. All the better when sidewalk gave way to ditch. Head down, I hustled to overtake another power walker.

"Hold up there, Ms. Gallant. You're almost unstoppable. Almost but not quite."

"Nicola?"

I would have wondered what was wrong with the universe, but it was not all that much of a coincidence that Nicola was out burning rubber and I had encountered her as such, wearing proper walking shoes with proper walking socks and a safari hat over her Spock ears. Nicola Chalice probably collected hiking guides wherever she went and had retirement plans to scale Kilimanjaro in between volunteer stints at a Tanzanian primary school. We were halted beside a front yard with enough bunnies, skunks, gnomes and rabbits to populate a children's anthology. Nicola had been going harder and longer than I had and was readier for a break.

"I'm just going to visit my uncle. I'm popping in. On impulse really."

"I'm sure he'll be pleased to see you. I'm doing my daily tramp before Hardy awakes. He's a night owl, I'm an early bird. We do our best to share the worm."

The owner of the ceramic menagerie exited her front door and grabbed a hose, understandably curious about the two women in their so-so prime conferring by her roadside. Two women intelligent enough to talk to each other without pussyfooting, so I decided.

"I know all about the African libraries, Nicola. About your charity."

"I'm glad to hear it. The more people who are aware, the better. Literacy is a good first step I would say. People who can read and write can be heard beyond their tribe."

We were stopped beside the McAddams' place, so it was announced on a wood-burned sign with a brass ring of rope twirled around its edges. Calgary returnees, probably, with kids who wanted to go to college out East.

"The thing is, Nicola, I can understand why you would get your hopes up, but between you and me I wouldn't. Even if you and Hardy make it through to the finals, it's a toss-up what will go down in the end. I wouldn't want to see you disappointed for, as you say, such a good cause. Maybe I can see about some kind of corporate donation on our end? Nothing close to fifty thousand, though."

Nicola Chalice was regarding me as if in trying not to beat around a bush I had trampled it to the ground. That azure stare demanded to be met. Nicola's blue never got hot. "I see," she said.

The McAddams' freshly tarred driveway was the shiny, jet-black of houseflies; no wonder Mrs. McAddam wanted to hose it pristine.

"My guess is that Hardy chips in no matter what. That makes it all worthwhile, right? I mean, I'm sorry if I've given you a bum steer here."

"What makes it all worthwhile, Ms. Gallant, is Hardy. And, yes, certainly what's important to me is important to him, and vice versa."

"Great. But at the end of the day you don't have to, like, pretend you want to marry him."

Mrs. McAddam was halfway down her driveway now, splashing in sweeping waves left-right, right-left, her thumb over the nozzle to maximize spray.

"Hello, lovely day!" Nicola sang out.

"Lovely day," Mrs. McAddam allowed.

"Nicola, I just don't want you to have to, you know, go through with this whole scenario when it doesn't necessarily make sense. When you don't really need to. I'm trying to do you a favour here. A favour I could get in a lot of trouble for if this doesn't stay strictly between me and you."

My best and final attempt at a revelation, delivered at the side of a road filling up with Saturday errand traffic and families who had planned a beach day. Nicola pulled me down into the culvert. A truck moaned past, half of its eighteen wheels close enough to ruffle our arm hair. It hissed up the hill and groaned into a turn, then Nicola had a word.

"In truth, Hardy and I don't feel like we need to win any contest whatsoever. We feel that we've already won, you see. Playing along with your television program is entirely for your sake at this point, Ms. Gallant. We thought we owed you that. Perhaps that makes you uncomfortable for some reason? Better pipe up if so, don't you think?"

"God no. Great. Please, you know, play along."

"At our age love is a result of fairly logical thinking, is it not? What will work, what won't?"

"I guess so." I climbed out of the ditch.

Nicola held her low ground. "Hardy and I think we work and what's more, we think we'll go on working. We've certainly worked hard to think that through. In fact, without each other nearby, we think nothing will ever work quite as well as it used to. It's as simple as that, really."

I had always and would always envy the kind of intelligence that made things simple. Nicola the fortunate seemed ready to move along. There was something I had to make clear or I would be talking to Nicola Chalice in my head for days.

"Nicola, I wasn't trying to be sneaky, digging around for dirt or anything."

"I don't believe you were, Ms. Gallant. I imagine you know very well that to live by taking very proper account of someone else is an entirely rewarding prospect."

"FYI, if you get married before the finale airs you'll be disqualified. That's in the contract, right? A fourteen-week season takes us up to next April. Hope that works."

"Disqualifying ourselves would be problematic for you and your team, I'd imagine?"

"No big deal, we could work around it. Listen, Nicola, I'm sorry but I have to go. I'm visiting my uncle up at the top of the hill there. I'm pretty anxious to show up."

"Take care, Ms. Gallant."

"You too."

Brilliant sun everywhere but for the thunderstorm now in my mind. Multiple precepts, conjectures and conclusions that I had thought of as stiff forts for years were now flat, wet cardboard. Fine, I had pulled a genuine Cupid on Hardy and Nicola—great, good for them, good for me. Nicola could transfer her pension to the Sudbury library system, maybe opt for full-time fundraising out of her new home office. Nicola Chalice had so much intelligence on the go, evidently, that her emotional intelligence levels were also fully topped up. She sure had told me, hadn't she? One thing I knew for sure: the studio audience for the grand prize finale was going to get coached like circus chimps. I wanted it full of clods like me who would not know true love if it smacked them in the face at the side of a quaint road. Meanwhile, I would steer well clear of the legitimately happy couple thanks to Prince Edward and his island. No need to inform Rex of anything drastic as yet. Happily so, because it was the first time I had arrived at the Manor empty-handed.

"Minnie, thank goodness, that was fast." Jenny was on duty on a weekend. Social work usually took place Monday to Friday.

"Fast?"

"Did you not get my message?"

"No. What is it?" I asked even as I bolted for Rex's suite. Donny was just leaving with a sad smile and a bunch of bundled up sheets.

There was a nurse at Rex's side, a *nurse practitioner* I later found out. She had one of Rex's wrists between her fingers and her eye on her watch. I gave her ten more seconds.

"I'm his niece. How is he? Please tell me what's going on."

In one downward swoop I saw Rex on his deathbed and then Gail and Lee's demise as well. Desolée had escaped the craggy Gallant profile and therefore this wheezing end. Rex's mouth had fallen open as if he was mid-sneeze. His eyelids were purple as if the strain of being open earlier had bruised them. His arms were stretched out over fresh bedclothes. Someone had changed Rex into a hospital gown. His mottled hands were clean. God bless universal health care when it mattered.

"Shush, dear, out you come, come out here to the hallway." I liked old nurses, the ones who knew something to look at it. What had she seen this time? This urgent portion of time that belonged so ineradicably to Rex and me.

"It's a lung infection, which is never good in someone his age, but there is no reason not to hope for the best. It's pooped him out. You're here now, dear. That's good. They'll get you a cot. Jenny, how about a cup of tea for the lady?"

Officials clustered around as if I was the one in crisis. Rex would want us both to get through this methodically. "I'm fine. If I could just use a phone? I have to call my boss."

Optimistically, I meant Trudy. She said to take as much time as I needed, in fact I could skip weekends altogether from now on. Trudy would let Etta know to either come get me on Sunday afternoon or bring a change of clothes. After breakfast with Lydia and Sally, each of them taking an extra cup of tea on my behalf, their eyes mouse bright, their reassurances tactfully low key, I called Gail and Lee and Desolée from Rex's room, tamping my worry down to a murmur. Gail snapped awake and told me she'd get on a plane the moment we needed her. Lee reminded me that Rex was tough as nails and I was a tough cookie. Desolée answered her cell and said she knew in her bones this wasn't it, but still wished to hell she was there.

Otherwise, the day was composed of many indistinguishable moments, yet possibly Rex's last two o'clock, his last three o'clock then four, every moment almost bursting the day apart. Finally it ended; Rex had barely stirred, but his wheeze held steady. The night was just as short-long-short. Whenever Donny or the night nurse whisked in, I slipped out to prowl the quiet corridors, tempted to bang myself up against the walls and take everything out on my skull like I was my own rag doll with a porcelain head. One thing I deduced on patrol was that as soon as possible I should apologize to Joe so that there would be one less miserable thing to worry about. I waited until seven-thirty Sunday morning. Many puritanical Harbourites had been up for hours.

"Joe, it's Minnie. I'm sorry I'm such a bitch," I started.

"You're not exactly that, Minnie."

"I know. Bitch is a shortcut. But I can't say much more right now."

"Trudy told me about Rex. I was in the diner yesterday looking for you, wanting to say sorry myself. How's he doing?"

"I'm not sure. What have you got to apologize for, Joe? Nothing."

"Well, I'm sorry about Rex."

"Thanks, Joe, I very much appreciate that. Do I do that enough? Appreciate? Rex is so, Rex is, Joe, he's ... awake! Oh my God, Rex is laughing at me right now and he won't stop. Rex, cut it out! Joe, come find me at the diner again soon, okay?"

"Will do, Minnie. Take care of yourself."

Rex was thrilled to rib me about my *gentleman caller*, and had quite a hunger on him he didn't mind saying. If it was Saturday, didn't that mean it was blueberry waffles? We all trooped in and out of Rex's room with beaming looks of pride on our faces as if he had just performed well in a grade school play. For reasons Rex did not quite understand, we forbade him to get out of bed. When it was time to watch Buddy Donovan do his best in Fountain Hills on Golf TV, I broke it to Rex that he had somewhat misplaced his Saturday, but all was well now, pneumonia averted. Rex accepted this after a pensive moment, his lungs bubbling.

"I'm sorry to have scared you, my girl," Rex told me.

"That's okay, Uncle Rex. *I'll* live," I said.

Rex loved that.

9

Etta picked me up on Sunday evening once Rex was settled down with cough syrup and a spoon.

"Etta, thank you. You're a brick." She had waited in the mini-van right outside the front door as if I was a very important person.

"Hell, don't think twice about it, Minnie. My man's on rubber-duck duty, meanwhile I'm hitting the road with Dire Straits blasting. Don't worry, I know you hate the prog rock. We'll take her quiet."

"To be honest, Etta, this works out well because there's something I've been meaning to tell you." Joe's rig had been parked at Rex's house often enough to merit an explanation. "It's been tough finding the right time and words." Etta drove with her fingertips, unlike my clenched fists. "Tact isn't my strong suit lately."

"Shoot, Minnie. Do your worst."

"Joe and I are dating, I guess. To the extent that one can do that in Tuck Harbour."

"Whoo hoo!" Etta slowed down enough to get us honked at. "Dating, Minnie? Is that what you call it?"

"As far as Rex is concerned we are. He came to this morning just in time to hear me googly talking to Joe on the phone. It was an awful night and I needed to hear his voice. Not that I deserved to. I had what one might politely call a shit fit the last time I saw him. That's our first fight over and done with anyway. I want to be good to Joe, Etta, to whatever degree I'm capable. That I promise."

"Good to Joe? That shouldn't be too hard."

"The man has the most minimal feminine side in masculine history, and yet there's nothing tyrannical about him either, don't you find? Don't you love Joe's eyes? I love eyes that set out to be one pure colour and do it. You're all right with this, aren't you, Etta? Because it won't be much fun if you're not."

"Of course I'm all right with this, Minnie. I'm happy for you, indeed I am. It's about time someone snapped up that man. Joe needed someone complicated, Minnie, no offence. Someone he can really think through. I knew the moment he clapped his eyes on you his wheels would be turning. He's got wheels on wheels, Joe does. He's more than you'd expect for a small-town fisherman, isn't he, Minnie? He's really got you thinking, too."

"Joe is extremely intelligent. I defy anyone to disprove that."

"That's my brother-in-law you're talking about there. Hey, you realize what this means, Minnie?"

"What?"

It was dark enough now for Etta's high beams.

"I always wanted a sister!"

"Holy hell, Etta, bite your tongue. Especially around Colin."

"If you say so, Minnie."

"I just don't want people asking me questions about things I haven't figured out yet, you know?"

"Something tells me you're a lady who only bites off what she can chew."

"Good taste is a virtue, I've always believed that much."

"Then remind me never to let you in on the ketchup budget at my house. I think I have ketchup for blood by now."

Etta's heart surely resembled a big summer tomato warmed to bursting red. She switched on the radio and punched around until she found something we would both like—a new country maiden hurtling from one octave to another as she detailed her romantic destruction and subsequent redemption, her man crawling back on bended knee. Night had come on in an artist's version: watercolour blacks blobbed with porch-light yellows. Some nights are permission to rest rather than hours of gruelling guesswork.

Rex's house looked almost sacred when we pulled up. After saying good-night to Etta I performed an inventory: kitchen sideboard, parlour knickknacks, Rex's snowmobile boots and winter shirts, everything was still exuding its Rex-like thereness. When I called the Manor to find out how he was doing I was told he was sleeping well, temperature normal. I wandered out to tell Dosie the good news. It took ages to call her over; Dosie had none of a dog's pleasure at going somewhere. But she was thrilled about the leftover apple porridge that I let her snuffle right out of the bowl. I poured boiling water in the bowl afterward; all I needed now was equine worms. The weekend had already scooped at my cheeks with teaspoons. Between my face and my hips, one day my hips were going to win big.

Faces were shining so bright at Eats n' Treats on Monday morning that I had to ask if there had been an excursion to a nuclear power plant while I was away. Everyone was thrilled that Rex had rallied. "And Joe's been great," I managed to add, focusing my gaze on the box of plastic cutlery I had to roll up into paper napkins for the take-out bags. I saw to it that Trudy's visit from Fibby Trask was the next order of business. Now that Fibby's boat was in working order he was inspired to get his house in order. His spiritual house; Fib's house in the village was actually quite tidy, an easy feat for a property without a single flower bed, shingle or shutter. From what I could tell, Fibby's sentiments remained wholly geared to his own needs, but Trudy detected progress.

"He says it's plain weird how things have worked out with his lobster licence and it makes him feel bad, but he doesn't know how to bring it up to anybody." Trudy was pouring raspberry filling into pie shells. That pie was going to sell in a ruby flurry; it made my teeth wet just to look at it.

"I can see how Fibby would have made a better peasant than aristocrat."

"Back when Fibby bought his licence for the north shore there were guys his age down here inheriting top-class fleets. Fibby paid fifty thou in '89 for the cheapest licence he could find and busted his ass to do it. Now a north shore licence is worth half a million easy and no one wants in on the south shore except maybe crab fishermen looking for a tax break. Some guys down here had to mortgage their lives away to get their licences and they're barely breaking even. They're pissed, Minnie, pissed and scared. It finally sunk in on them that they were getting somewhere, and now the Strait's cacking out once and for all."

Trudy was tamping down her pie edges with a fork, which I knew was a typical pie thing to do but had no idea why. This was not the time to ask.

"It's always bruising to a soul to cope with defied expectation."

"Still, it's not like Fib has it easy. He says I'm the only person around here who's ever been halfway proud of him. All his parents care about is whether he's going to buy them another trailer."

The pies were getting little pastry roses around their centres. I wanted Trudy to leave one on a windowsill for Tom Sawyer to steal. I wanted to eat one in a contest, followed by another.

"I get it, Trudes, I really do. It must be really hard on the psyche to work in an industry that developed all this expensive equipment and then institutes a bunch of handicaps to make up for it. *Controlled fishing effort*, Joe calls it. He spends most of his time dealing with out and out pain. I'm glad he's so good at it. I just hope he doesn't get re-elected forever."

"I met that little Pat fella, finally. He doesn't miss a trick, that one."

"Is Patrick in the Harbour?"

Verna marched into the back kitchen with a scummy gravy pan, black pigtails bouncing. She was wearing a cerise slip over a black bodysuit, and rolled-up black cords with black break-the-kitchen-rules flip-flops, her toes a freshly sombre burgundy. Perhaps I had been just as interested in my outfits back when I was that age, but all I could remember were interchangeable separates.

"For your information, Minnie, Pat is staying at Fibby's house until tuna starts. Fibby feels really bad because he's already lined up guys for herring, but I talked to my dad and he might take on Pat. My dad does real well with herring. All Pat needs is some money to think with."

Verna had a knack for blasting away at congealed substances with the kitchen tap without splashing her face with grease bits. I could wait for the spray to subside. My only table was halfway through a scallop platter and I had remembered the extra tartar sauce. Trudy shrugged as she egg-washed her pie tops.

"Thinking is good, Vee, that's for sure."

"What I think, Minnie, is you need to get an order off table four."

Table four, it turned out, was Fibby and Patrick. I served the lads with good grace and accepted a tip, a ten spot from Fibby's crowded wallet as I informed the ladies. The guys had each ordered a hot turkey sandwich, white bread, gravy on the fries. The raspberry pie was out of the oven by the time they were done and Trudy sent out two scarlet slices. Verna said to pump soft ice cream on each piece so she could film the procedure. Patrick did none of the paying and most of the talking, eliciting curt nods from his master when he made a good point. Fibby checked over his shoulder every time he sensed movement, but it was never Trudy. I wanted tuna season underway as soon as possible if only to stow Fibby and Patrick out of reach—an Island Mugsy and Bugsy with sunburns, slickers and singsong vowels. Once tuna season was over, Fibby would chug his boat all the way down around the northeastern tip of the Island back to the Harbour. Herring fishing was not demarcated by area, merely by province, so all the Tuck Harbour guys would be in it together. The inshore fishermen called herring *feed*. They caught it, but they wanted other species to be able to catch it, too.

My shift ended with no sign of Joe. I thought it served me right.

I biked over every pothole on the way back to Rex's to punish myself some more for Friday night's altercation. I phrased a correction to Etta in my head about how serious things had not in fact become. My formerly broken arm had been smart to ache all weekend—there had been a deluge overnight and now there was terracotta soup ladled out wherever there was a dent in the ground. Possibly, Dosie had been rinsed, but it was hard to tell. I thought maybe I would treat her to a brushing. I found a curry comb in the barn and applied it in the circular motion that Rex had taught me years before, dust rising off her flanks in a cartoon cloud. Even when I stood on an overturned pail Dosie's withers came up to my chin. Rex said no matter how hard I pulled on her mane she would never feel it. Dosie's knees were the size of cantaloupes. Her hooves were the circumference of dinner plates. She stomped the hoof I was trying to pick clean deep into a mucky puddle brimming with liquid brick. The splash was opaque; for an instant it looked like she had stepped in a gaudy hand-blown ashtray with scalloped edges. My Bermuda shorts were soaked fore and aft and my top looked tie-dyed. All the more reason to go ahead and muck out Dosie's barn as promised.

The boots were in for a desecration. Dosie's straw had been damp and gloopy for weeks. After an idle look at what I was up to she sauntered off to make more big fruity turds. I stooped and shovelled, unleashing feisty growls of iron on rock as I went. Out in the country something was always having to get heaved. Rex had said to wheelbarrow the manure out to the middle of the field because gardeners who swore by Dosie's output would eventually drop by. I slipped on a wet clod at one point and went down hard, gashing open my elbows on symmetrical pebbles. The mud that had splashed down my collar was going crusty between my tits. There was a streak of poop on my kneecap and gummy straw stuck in my hair.

Dosie spied Joe's red truck before I did, taking off like she'd witnessed an inner-city shooting.

My elbows were leaking red jelly. I looked like I had smeared my entire body with a mixture of blood and homo milk. I reeked. "Thanks for dropping by, Joe," I said. "Can you stick around a sec?"

Joe had a clean white hanky; I made a ruddy Rorschach of the linen.

"I was wondering if you wanted another driving lesson, Minnie. Guess not at the moment."

"Rain check," I said, then "sweetheart," I added as a statement of fact.

I went upstairs to take a bath, two baths, actually, since the first one resembled a pig wallow. Joe delivered a mug of tea by the time the second one was filling. He had a mug of his own to sip from while he kept me company, toilet lid down. The fact that I had an apology to complete did not stop me from displaying my breasts to their best advantage, soaping them distractedly like they were what most needed cleaning. I have PEI earth–coloured nipples, something Desolée had noticed at some point between puberty and university and never let me forget.

"You know, Joe, I've had enough close calls for now." I sat up and hugged my knees. "I almost just lost my uncle, and I guess I came close to losing you the other night thanks to my hissy fit."

"I'm not going to give up on you that easy, Minnie. Fishing's a complicated business. You have a right to ask questions. It does me good that you do."

The second bath was ass-scalding hot, but I still lay back and tucked everything underwater from my chin on down.

"I trust you, Joe. Usually, I trust men too little, so they trust me too little, the final result being that important things don't happen and stupid things do. I want to give this a proper shot, though. I really do. How about you, Joe? Willing to test the waters?"

"Sounds good me, Minnie."

"Then get in here, pronto."

It was kind of Joe to oblige me, considering that he had probably taken a cold shower at the same time of day, every day, for the past twenty years. I thought I might even be taking his co-bath virginity, which came close to making me shy myself. But Joe was not that large and the tub was a clawed beast. Admittedly, he had to take a phone call first from the DFO inspector based in Cardigan— naked but for his socks, doodling in the window mist. Joe's penis remained more alert to his public relations than the naked lady in the room, it had that much circumcision. That was fine; my interests lay in general proximity, in the kind of jigsaw interlocking that makes for a bigger picture. Then Joe got in the tub with the grace in motion of a sporty convertible owner jumping right in. Lolling in the bathwater at Joe's side I thought I was at my lifetime's coziest and for the first time, properly, I kissed him: an eight-hundred-word kiss with a thesis, antithesis and synthesis. I guessed that we each tasted warmly and wetly of Ceylon. Joe had finished his tea and mine was the first thing I had taken in all day. Then we backed off far enough to smile like simpletons. I wanted to respect whatever it was that proximity had going for it besides the obvious. Had Joe and I been cheating not just ourselves but some higher power by remaining single for so long? To whom did we owe what? Did the substantial differences between us elevate our intimacy to something extra creditable?

The bathwater was tinged pink with a rub of grit at the bottom. I wanted to add some hot, instead I kissed Joe six times in a row, canted left then right then right then left, like I was outlining an X on his lips. I provided heat, Joe provided heat, and when we warmed each other up we gave off even more. Not polar-bear-drowning heat but soft, raspberry-ripening heat, burnishing heat, liveable heat. I loved the feeling of wanting to protect someone their whole life long; of wishing I had protected Joe at seven years old and wanting to protect him again at seventy-seven. "Green eyes," I said, before we fucked up a storm in the tepid bathwater, splashing like brawling seals, holding fast to the edges to make things stick. Finally we stumbled wet-assed and droop-towelled to bed where we went straight for missionary. Joe started to get slippery with sex sweat again much as he got wet with lobstering sweat, hockey sweat and tire-changing sweat: a man who efficiently put out his own fires. I suspected Joe was a longstanding master of the withdrawal method—he aimed right for the belly button, filled and overspilled. Swollen, driven and momentarily outraged, I scooped up some of Joe's spunk to use as lubricant, followed him to the hollering place and then that was enough excitement for one evening. I made tomato soup and Joe made a stack of toast and we each took a nip of Rex's port. It was great that I had scruffed myself up with horse chores because now there was an in-joke between us (*Careful you don't over-Dosie, Minnie*).

Joe got dressed and left me on my own for the night because he thought I might experience post muck-out aching by morning and need the bed space. I agreed to drop by his place after work the next day and let him know how I was doing. Kissing goodbye at the kitchen door, I was a little shorter for a change, which we both enjoyed. At least Joe enjoyed it enough to let me grind into him a bit before terminating the farewell. Definitely, I had a truck going in and out of my lane.

Joe and I were staying over at Rex's place, but as soon as tuna started we would switch home bases, should I want to sleep over at Joe's house on those six nights out of seven when games blared from the widescreen and his alarm would be set for 4 a.m. Joe watched baseball, basketball and soccer; he liked games with balls up in the air. And golf, but only if Buddy Donovan was playing, which he had been doing well. I was no sports widow: if Joe had a match to take in I would go for a run, shifting my route to end up at his place with sweat darkening my upper back and dripping from behind my knees.

The village at large began to pick up on our complacency. Dolly grinned at me in the Clover Mart and helped me find Shreddies. The gals at the diner started to imply *you* in second person plural (*You drive over to Montague to see Rex yesterday? You guys hear that crazy thunder last night?).* The church ladies conferred in whispers whenever I served them their chowders and side salads with Thousand Islands Lite. Colin started calling Rex's place when he wanted Joe—to come over and catch the last inning of the Boston game, or help fix his ladder rack. Or to tell Joe that Archie Doiron was still grousing about the minimum traps per dump limit to anyone who would listen.

Colin was the one who shepherded the kids and me on our raspberry-picking expedition, calculating that it would earn him a couple of beers over lunch. At the *Pick-UR-Own* we each got a tub to hang around our necks like cigarette girls. We had missed the height of the season, but there were still woozily ripe berries nestled deep inside bushes marshalled like infantry. The boys and I wanted our own row; Etta had stoked our competitive juices. I felt pity, affection and scorn for the fuzzy little red jewels, hiding fruitlessly from our cereal bowls and jam jars. I'd promised Joe I was going to share my pickings down to the last berry as soon as I got everything home and washed and some cream whipped. Now that our mutual baths were getting to be a regular thing I was looking forward to introducing him to all the places from which fruit could be served.

Joe and I enjoyed raspberries in our spinach salad that night, with a fresh raspberry vinaigrette, raspberry-based fruit salad to follow with a raspberry-rum coulis. Joe was bringing over pieces of beef, pork or chicken to fry. I was getting used to fat sputtering and carbon scrapings; he liked meat well done. He had picked up extra toothbrushes for us in Montague, one for him at my place and one me at his place. "I wish I had my towels from home," I said that night, tired of Rex's hardworking linens.

"What do you call these then?" Joe was the type to rub dry like he was sanding himself.

"I mean *home* home. Toronto. I've got better stuff there."

"Okay, Minnie. I catch your drift."

Michelangelo would have added to David's allure by slinging a towel around his hips like this. Joe always shook dry instead of blow-drying.

"Would you ever come to Toronto, Joe?"

"I've been to Toronto before, Minnie. Sure I'd go again. Why not?"

"Do you like it?"

"For what it is."

Tarzan had never had to compute aquaculture production per unit of area or provide a regional newscast sound bite. I knew Joe would hold his own anywhere. He handed over my toothbrush preloaded with paste. I was comfortable enough in Joe's company now to brush for the full two recommended minutes. There seemed to be more room to let Joe in when I had cleaned myself out. I loved the way Joe sometimes pulled out of me *in medias res*, almost but not quite—then thrust his way back in deeper than ever. We both seemed to enjoy penetration best: the wet lurking and stiff prodding, then in, *in*, IN. We'd lie there with crisscrossed arms and legs for a while afterwards, the enormity of what we had just done never quite getting to be too much for us. I would wonder aloud whether there was enough milk for the morning or if Joe wanted anything thrown in with my wash. He said yes more often than no. Soon we would roll outward to the bed edges where the sheets were cool enough for sleep.

Despite all our leftover raspberries, Joe and I went to Eats n' Treats for breakfast together for the first time: baptism by fried eggs. Sunday breakfast at the diner was the Tuck Harbour equivalent of the Brazilian ball. I drove us there, haltingly and disruptively, but no longer feeling like an assassin. Joe said I had daylight conquered. Next I had to try driving in the rain and after that the dark. I did not have the heart to tell him I was not eligible to take a PEI road test, that I probably wouldn't be the one driving us all the way to Halifax at summer's end to take in a few dinners, a couple of movies, and in Joe's case meetings with the top brass at the Nova Scotia Fishermen's Union.

After some coffee sipping to start—Herman Walker holding court on the porch—we took a back booth because the counter was full. We had arrived along with the flood of churchgoers, who I always suspected of contemplating Trudy's pancakes and omelettes all the way through their sermons. Trudy now had a couple of her cousins' kids, Doris's oldest and Wendy's oldest, helping out on weekends. I grabbed a pen and pad from Madison, with her nine-carat belly ring and perma-sulk, and wrote out the order for Joe and me. Our eggs came so quickly we knew we had bumped the queue. Trudy had remembered to put my butter on the side and give Joe extra bacon.

"Looks like I got friends in high places." Joe accepted my second egg.

"You bet."

Joe said that when tuna started winding down we could go into Charlottetown to birthday shop for Rex. I jumped at the idea.

"Truth be told, Minnie, I'm almost too tired to go back out and fish."

I didn't doubt it. Since lobster he had fielded maybe a hundred calls from infuriated DFO guys and the fishermen they infuriated.

"There's a biblical resonance to fishing, sweetie. Think of it that way. Symbolically, it's much more powerful than anything corporate."

Joe wasn't so sure about that but he had to hand it to me, he never knew what I was going to come out with next. I fetched the coffeepot to refill his cup and did a round of the diner while I was at it. I ran out before I could make it to the porch. Trudy and Verna were in sight in the kitchen but too busy for chitchat. When a rush like this descended, it was tragedy to send one mushroom astray. Doris's Katelynn, older and bigger than Madison by one year and three cup sizes, was poking at the cash register when Joe and I got up there. She looked ready to cry when Trudy called out to her from the kitchen to remember my staff discount. I whispered at Katelynn not to worry about it.

"Food at three ninety-five times two," I said. "Tax button number four."

Joe took care of the bill and I took care of the tip; amounts that I could not keep myself from rendering pretty well even. Joe teased me about that as we sidled towards the door, shoulders brushing. Halfway out the door Joe turned to wink in reference to my earlier request for some afternoon delight. I'd said it was only wise on my part considering that starting Wednesday he would get home from work smelling like Jonah's whale had belched all over him. I was the one who got this tomfoolery underway so I was inclined to take the blame when Joe failed to look exactly where he was going and banged the diner screen door into Archie Doiron, who should not have been standing there.

"Sorry, Arch." Joe sidestepped and I followed.

No hot coffee had splashed anywhere; I still was not foreseeing a big deal.

"Like you care, McTeal." Archie was shaking his head at the church next door, or maybe all the way to the wharf where boats were shrugging up and down like merry-go-round ponies.

"C'mon now, Arch. No hard feelings."

I tended to forget that Joe was short. He always seemed simply theoretically short. Archie was of no more than average height, but his flab made him colossal. Archie looked down at Joe's outstretched hand like he was trying to decide whether it was recyclable or just garbage. Then he turned his head slightly to the side, gobbed and spat.

"That attitude is futile in the extreme and insulting to everyone including yourself." My inner grade two teacher had rushed on the scene. "I'd desist if I was you."

"You," said Archie Doiron as if he had spat again. "You keep your skinny nose out of things. You're the one who's got my daughter chasing after that drug addict."

"No I did *not* and no he is *NOT*." Now I was ecstatically angry, I was on a geyser high, I was radiant with invective. "I have NOTHING to do with your daughter's degree of compassion and neither, I doubt, do YOU. No matter WHAT, I suggest you be proud of her because you'll be LOSING her before long and won't that be sad, but only NATURAL?"

Herman Walker was pulling me backwards like I was a stubborn bantamweight who had jumped in the wrong ring. Tourists who had alighted from their cars with smiles were now returning to their vehicles. Darlene MacDonald and Freak Trask were whispering to each other out the sides of their mouths, their coffee cups retracted.

"Leave her alone, Arch." Joe stayed in handshake distance, holding steady to his Southern Kings County Fishermen's Association presidency. "Minnie has nothing to do with this."

"And you," Archie spewed. "You're holding back the whole gulf with your crap. Limit this and limit that. I've had it with your goddamn limitations and your government buddies nailing me with fees every chance they get. You're an arsehole, McTeal. You're DFO's arsehole and they shit right out of you."

"Someone's got to be MAN enough to deal with the real problems!" Me again. "How ironic that the FAT GUY doesn't have the stomach."

With that Archie Doiron's pudgy fist whipped out and socked Joe's fine cheek. I thought I also felt the molar-shaking wallop and tasted blood under my tongue. *Does it hurt, Joe? Only when I smile.* Without a fight master on duty, Archie Doiron's knuckles were probably in agony as well. There had been a widespread gasp of amazement as the fight went real, during which Herman Walker loosened his grip on my elbows.

I had never kicked a man in the balls before. It took me a demeaning scurry first, to get into position. Then I whipped up fast with one knee, the top of my foot making contact with the fatty wobble between Archie Doiron's beast-of-burden legs. I did not feel much, but Archie bent over double. I looked towards Joe. His hands were at his face, checking for dislocation. I was about to tell him not to say a thing, not for a second or two, when Archie butted Joe hard in the belly with his giant meat head. Joe went flying back into the Eats n' Treats front window, which cracked retributively but otherwise held firm. And then Colin was in the thick of things. Colin was going to smash apart Archie's windpipe and shut him up for good. Joe shoved himself between Colin and Archie, pushed his brother far enough away to do no harm, and got Archie into what men call a headlock. It was pay-off time at the rodeo. Archie brayed.

"DADDY!" Verna was out on the porch, floored and pleading. "Let him go, oh Daddy, oh, oh . . ."

"Arch, it's all over now." Joe could have been speaking to a tuna, five miles out and four hours in. "Take your father home now, Verna. See if he won't go with you. That's enough, Arch. Good man. There you go."

Joe knew fish; Joe knew human beings. Archie Doiron had a lot of strength, but little with which to deny his daughter. His arm sagged across Verna's bony shoulders; her arm snaked around his big back. They made their way across Main Street and up the hill. The Doirons lived in one of the Harbour's smaller houses, but on one of the biggest lots—an outer block bristling with pine trees. It would not take them long to get home.

"You should have seen this man of mine leap the truck hood. In one jump! I swear to God, Col, you cleared the porch railing with a foot to spare." Etta and Colin had been on their way back to the raspberry patch for one last pick when they saw the commotion. "He loves his flesh and blood, that's for sure. I guess we'll have to forgive him when he gets carried away, won't we?"

Etta beamed at us in turn, spilling relief.

I was patting Joe's shoulder like he was a Persian show cat, scared to touch him, but scared not to touch him.

"I knew Doiron was spoiling for trouble." Colin writhed out of Etta's grasp then hugged her back close. "He's been blubbing his head off all summer. You okay, bro?"

I caught the little groan before Joe made his composure public. "Sorry about that, everyone. Trudy, I'll see to it that window gets fixed first thing tomorrow. Show's over, folks. Let's keep things moving."

"Joe, dear, do you need the hospital?" Etta had a hand under Joe's chin now, lifting his puffed eye.

Joe refused to treat his shiner with anything other than top-class sirloin. Luckily, there was just such a steak at his place waiting for a reason to thaw. Doris heroically donned an apron because Trudy was going to be swamped with the curious for hours. Colin and Etta moved their van from where it was blocking traffic and then kept going. Joe drove us to his place. I did my best with ice cubes in a facecloth. I turned off his cellphone and lowered the blinds. I thought the living room sofa would be best, but Joe said no, the bedroom as planned. I swore he was off the hook, but Joe would have none of that, pushing me up his shiny brown stairs ahead of him, the rubber treads hard on my bare feet. The sex was undeniably good in its guarantee of tenderness and hint of perversity. I remained on top, pitched forward just far enough to lock eyes. Joe's face was elegant even when smacked-up and swollen. It was time to identify the look he gave me during our pauses for thought as one that belonged especially to me, a look bestowing equal parts bemusement, perplexity and concern. It was the look of an extremely smart border collie obeying a learning disabled shepherd. My own face bore something simpler I was sure. I felt the lid pry off my heart with a gaseous pop. We napped until dinnertime—steak for Joe, spinach for both of us, and lime sherbet. I left Joe his bed to himself and walked home, trying to do unto him as he had done unto me. Later I wished I had slept over, finally, and seen the same sun seep in his windows that had nudged my grandparents awake year after year.

10

I put in a few extra hours at the diner the following week because Verna was off "sick." She was back on the job by Thursday lunch and, yes, she had heard the good news about Fibby and Patrick hooking the first tuna of the season. They had made it to page four of *The Guardian* in their cut-offs, rubber boots and baseball caps, posing alongside the upside-down behemoth—its gills sagging, its silver eyes agog at the wharf concrete, its fin likely never all that blue. Trussed and strung up like that, all 630 pounds of it, it looked like it had been caught in Guantanamo Bay. They made it to the Eats n' Treats bulletin board alongside Buddy Donovan hoisting a ten-gallon trophy.

Joe felt better day by day. With typical subtlety he did not get a black eye, rather a slightly blue eye followed by a slightly yellow eye—the white of his eye its usual paint-chip bright. Trudy told us not to worry about the front window, her insurance had it covered. Joe and Colin were not proving as lucky as Fibby and Patrick with the tuna. On Friday they were going to knock off early. As soon as I was finished at the diner, Joe and I were going into Montague to pay Rex a call. Joe arrived on schedule. Whenever Joe visited me at work I waggled.

"Almost done!"

Now I was practically a burlesque act; wiping up as if I had a feather duster, sweeping as if I was doing the tango, bumping and grinding with a bag of trash. Joe agreed to a coffee; he could take in caffeine any hour of the day and still fall asleep at night. I poured him a cup and resisted the temptation to lean across the counter and lick his lips as I handed it over. I got close enough to inhale Dolly's fabric softener; with no need of Ocean Breeze she had gone Forest Fresh.

"I seen you sweeping the porch on my way home from the wharf, Minnie."

Caught unawares I knew I generally looked like I was *deep in my own little world.*

"Did you now? I can't believe you drive that short distance, you lunatic. In a city we'd walk that, no question."

"You're a hard worker, Minnie, aren't you?"

"So it seems. Hush, you, while I count the tips."

Joe was quiet for a sip and a head cock. "Verna home sick still?"

"No, she's here. Grumpy, but here."

"Better not forget her."

"What do you mean?"

Joe tapped the counter where I had coins and bills sorted. "You only made two piles—you and Debbie."

"Oh, Joe, quiet or the girls will hear. I don't take any tips. I haven't all summer."

"Why not, Minnie? The money's yours fair and square if anyone's."

It was the first time I had seen the bridge of Joe's nose furrow up like this, a bump jammed between his brows as if someone had slid a small arrowhead under the skin. I looked around for help. Desolée was far away.

"I don't need the money. Joe, you know that. My salary will be kicking back in before I know it. Honestly, it makes so little difference to me that I'd rather not. The girls will never be the wiser. Here, I'll take out seventy-five cents to pay for your coffee, how's that? Does that make it seem less weird?"

I slid out three quarters, popped them in the till and slammed the drawer. There was no point in mentioning that a coffee in Toronto cost seventy-five cents only when it was subsidized by a social welfare agency or sold in a neighbourhood where street whores might partake of a double-double. Joe passed the coffee back to me as if the cream had gone bad.

"I'll wait in the truck." His stool squeaked in alarm, the floor-boards grunted and the front door whined open.

"Joe, stop!" Better to tackle the matter dead on. "Are you mad?"

"No, Minnie. Not mad. Let's get you to Montague."

Trudy had to fix the front door; it banged shut like a gun.

I would have prolonged my goodbyes, but Verna was continuing November chilly in August. By the time I crawled into Joe's truck, he had decided to behave as if I had not spurned an honest, worthy, Tuck Harbour source of income all summer long in my metropolitan disdain. Apparently, he was driving us all the way to Montague even though I usually did the first leg there and back. Evidently, he cleared his throat over and over again when he was unwilling to go into matters. I wondered if the term *passive-aggressive* was in Joe's lexicon, which was a regrettable thought because I had worked for years to keep it out of mine. It was a good thing we were on our way to see Rex. No one stayed angry around Rex for long.

"Well, hello there." Rex spoke with freighted delight. His room was ajabber. Sally's grandson, Ralph, was on the Island and at the Manor. Sally's lips had been traced in special-occasion red and she was in her good cardigan, the one with the bow at the neck. Ralph was a twenty-eight-year-old doctoral candidate in marine ecology and I liked the look of him from the moment I saw him manhandling Sally's wheelchair. He was button-nosed, chubby-cheeked and sandy-haired. He looked like he would always be too moist to wrinkle. I could tell that Ralph wore a flappy button shirt over his T-shirt for the sake of the pocket. He made use of his cargo shorts pockets, too, for pads and markers and who knew what else. Ralph had just flown up from Maine.

"I was told there would be square dancing, but no." Ralph had no qualms about addressing a room, what with tutorial assistantships under his belt. "Every *second* Saturday you tell me. I've been robbed cruelly by you people; you've robbed a young man's dreams. Damn you and your adult diapers."

"Silly boy, let Minerva show you where to fill the kettle."

I understood why Ralph dominated Sally's panoply of family photos in his graduate robes and cap, the tassel looking like it tickled.

"Minnie, dear, could you put out a plate of those fig biscuits?"

"Will do, Uncle Rex."

These were Rex's favourites, but since he also thought that they were my favourites, it was hard to keep him from stockpiling. I took a box of them out of his mini fridge under the far window. I loved Rex's western view for its latecomer warmth. Rex was often in a wheelchair now, too, but this was not as injurious to witness as I would have thought. He still stamped his slippers with pleasure when the conversation surprised him, and now he always had armrests. He was allowed to switch to double canes if he was up for it. I left Joe with him to discuss the vagaries of cod once again.

Ralph and I hit the corridor. "Are you here for long?" I asked. Ralph had the kind of spring in his step usually seen in Walt Disney characters. He was waving at whoever he spied through a doorway. His bangs were Liverpudlian.

"That depends. I'd like to be here for a lot longer than I probably will be. It's up to the provincial fisheries guys, really. And the FRCC."

"The Fishery Resource Conservation Council?"

"Minnie, you've got a boyfriend. Stop turning me on."

I held the kettle up to the faucet while Ralph worked the cold tap. "What exactly is up to fisheries and the FRCC?"

"Whether they're prepared to buy into my idea about an underwater reserve, which would entail constructing and protecting appropriate terrain for a lot of lobster breeding."

"You want to build a lobster ranch?" I plugged in the kettle and hunted for a platter. Joe had brought along some of Dolly's Nanaimo bars, humid brown and shrieking yellow, to be sampled by those whose blood sugar was at liberty to skyrocket. I wanted to set them out with the fig cookies in concentric circles.

"Managed habitat is the idea, yes. What this Island needs are lobsters in amounts that match the number of people who can profitably succeed in fishing them, correct? We're talking about preserving a couple hundred years of culture here, that's what science has to understand. A mere 2 percent of spawn survive naturally, but in manipulated circumstances we're looking at more like 90 percent. So screw capacity-reduction schemes and screw fleet rationalization. What we need is a sub-surface Serengeti."

"Wow."

"Exciting, I know. You think the minister will share your enthusiasm? You think I could sneak an extra one of those chocolaty things before we go back to your uncle's room? He's been teasing me about my child-bearing hips."

"Have a word with Ralph," I murmured to Joe while I was passing around the treat plate and napkins. "He's really bright." Gladys had her bony old hands circled around one of Joe's tan forearms, however, and was not about to let go. Joe resembled Gladys's youngest brother, the one who had been killed by a drunk driver outside Pinette back in '72. I dragged over a stool and squeezed in between Rex and Sally.

"Really, there's got to be a beauty contest at this joint one of these years," Ralph was insisting. "I know my grandma would win hands down, but some of you gals could be runners-up, right? Rex, you're a shoo-in for master of ceremonies. You know how to keep these wild women under control."

Ralph seemed the type to leave a wake of giggles behind him wherever he went.

"That's a young man to keep an eye on if I've ever seen one," I whispered in Sally's enormous ear. It would not do to champion one grandson publicly.

"He takes after his grandfather in many ways. He has the same powers of persuasion." I had never dared to ask Sally exactly when she had lost Don. "Ralph will be visiting his grandfather while he's here, he's a good boy that way."

"His grandfather? He's alive?"

"Alive in body, but not in mind. Alzheimer's, I'm afraid. The last stages."

"Sally, I'm so sorry."

"Don't be, Minerva. Love always finds a way, love is never at sea. We were together for as long as we could be. Ralph will take me to see him tomorrow."

"That's nice. That's something?"

"Yes, Minerva, quite something. Now go pull that window blind all the way down, the sun is getting in your uncle's eyes. And give Lydia this cushion, please. I simply don't need it."

So many snacks were pressed upon Joe and me, the ladies poaching sweetmeats and meringues from their own larders, that there was no point going out for dinner after all. I suggested as much to Joe and he agreed. He drove the whole way back to the Harbour, but I kept my right foot busy with a phantom clutch. Joe had not gotten much of a chance to talk to Ralph, who had been busy organizing charades. Ralph's team won by guessing *Rich Man, Poor Man* thanks to his strutting and panhandling. Joe drove us to the end of Rex's lane, then put his truck in neutral. We had not spent a night together since tuna began. "Joe, are you coming in?" It was time for me to shut up about Ralph's progressive lobster sanctuary. "Can you stay?"

"No, Minnie. I feel bad about that stray cat. It meows all night long if I don't put food out."

"Joe, come on. Fuck the cat."

"Don't know if the neighbours will agree with you there."

"Fuck the neighbours!"

"Don't think so, Minnie."

"Is this about the diner, Joe? About me not bothering with tips?"

"Just because you're good at your work there doesn't mean you think of it as a real job, Minnie. I should have known better than to believe that. I'm over it now."

"At least come down to the beach for a little walk with me, Joe. It's such a nice night." I punched his arm like a sitcom character. The do-or-die atmosphere suffusing his truck needed masking. Joe agreed to stroll.

It was a lovely walk, anyone would have thought so. Daylight was dissolving, but the sand was still warm underfoot. We thought we heard seals smacking their flippers; Joe said they were curious animals and were probably wondering what we were up to. I for one was bouncing balls on my nose. I asked Joe if he had come to the beach a lot as a kid; his childhood had got us through many a conversational glitch before. Joe had preferred playing in the river when he was little. I asked if that was because the river seemed less full of concerns. Joe said no, it was just that it was warmer and if I wanted concerns I could go ahead and have a word with the Tuck River mussel farmers whose shellfish were lately overridden with tunicate, an invasive, globular invertebrate that grew all over everything and spread from hull to hull when people did not disinfect properly.

"Yikes, the night of the living sea squirt." This earned me a halt, a tug and a drawing in.

"Minnie, I want to say I'm glad you came out here." Joe was saying this mostly to the hair behind my ear and to Damson Island hunkering down for the night while the water darkened.

"I'm glad I came out here, too, Joe."

"You put a new light on things, Minnie, you really do."

"Speaking of, don't forget to use that waterproof SPF 30 I gave you, promise?"

Given the chance, I would chart Joe's freckles and moles like an air traffic controller. That was as long as I still had him in one piece, not decapitated by a propeller blade or rotting at the bottom of a kelp bed. *The Guardian* had recently cited fishing as the most dangerous occupation in Canada. Tuna fishing was not the worst of it; that was to come with herring as of September first. Several Tuck Harbour women had been widowed by fishing over the years: Rex had spotted a couple of them tramping the edge of his field, their eyes straining for one more glimpse of the boat they knew so well and their man had not known well enough. Bodies did not necessarily wash ashore in the Strait.

"We're cool, Joe, right?" I asked this by Joe's truck door after he had clasped me to his chest once more as if the TB had spread to my bones. Joe's chest: my treasure. He was going home and I was not going with him—no bedding down on his sawdust pillows, no inhaling his exhalations, no spreading my legs and expecting the best.

"I hope so, Minnie."

"Sleep tight then."

"You too, dear."

There was a message from Desolée waiting for me when I got in, haranguing me for not staying in touch. She picked right up when I called back. The moment I heard Desolée's voice Joe's off-putting retreat was glazed with a higher purpose and I had the happy feeling that he was going to be doing the right thing all of the time. Desolée was more interested that he had been sulking.

"A tiff with Hair Capitaine?" I had gone overboard describing Joe's tousles.

"Kind of."

"Is he sexy when he's mad? Stash definitely isn't, he just spits a lot and goes red. Oops. What's that, lovey? No, I said you're *cute* when you're mad. What? YES! Sorry about that, Min. Where were we? Ah yes, mutiny on the bounty. Is anyone about to jump ship?"

"I'm worried Myriad will think I've bailed on *them*. I haven't checked my email in days. I met a really interesting guy at the Manor today. A grandson of Sally's. I got his card. He's sweet and bright and funny and a committed environmentalist. Based at the University of Maine."

"Now I see which way the wind is blowing."

"Desolée, please. He's twenty-eight!"

"So? The other one buys diesel fuel."

"Ralph is great. But he's a bit, I don't know, Porky Pig."

"You're so rude about anyone with meat on their bones."

"I am not!"

"You're just lucky that every time you eat for comfort it's because you're so stressed out you burn it all up. Don't freak out when you see me again, Minnie. My pudge has pudge. I'm eating for two even though I'm adopting. That makes total sense, right?"

"I'm sure you look luscious."

"Guess what I read the other day—the happiest couples are childless."

"Happiness is overrated."

"But couples are statistically happier than singles. And they get more sex. I'm just saying."

Dark was definitely coming on earlier. A month before I would have been looking through rose-tinted windows. Now it was spectacularly lunar; the sky was so clear I could see the moon's entire outline even though it had waned to a sickle.

"Joe and I are still on the go, Des. I'm so nice and used to him now. I don't know what I would do without the fellow. Throwing this one back in the sea would be positively grim."

"Minnie, why do you sound like you're reciting nursery rhymes lately whenever we talk?"

"I do not!"

"Okay then, why do you sound like a puppet in a puppet show reciting nursery rhymes? Face it, you're all PEI'd out."

"Christ, Des, don't scare me. I don't want everyone at Myriad thinking I've gone to seed."

"Better check your email. There's a new picture of Bernard-Louis in there."

"How does he look?"

"Loud, like he's got some major pipes on him. Stash already

bought earplugs, but he promises to wear only one at a time. Jesus, Minnie, hit the hay. I can hear you swallowing yawns."

"Sorry. I miss you."

"Damn right you do. Nighty-night to your skinny ass."

Desolée had a point; it was time for bed. Winding up Rex's back stairs, I felt like my own madwoman in the attic. The dark was enervating, but snapping on an overhead light felt like it would be bad luck. I lay in bed for a long time, quiet and motionless, like I was posing for my own sarcophagus. Then I practiced lying in state, imagining my mourners. Gail would push Rex's wheelchair and for his sake try not to break down. Good old Stash had Desolée by the arm, otherwise grief had her crumpled. Etta, Colin and the kids were in their Sunday best. Then Joe parted the crowd to battle it out with the heavens, his arms outstretched in accusation until he collapsed on my chill loins to douse my burial wear with his hacking tears. Scratch that. Joe stood silently at the back of the room, drawing concerned glances. Until he bolted out to his truck and wept all over his steering wheel, thrashing out beeps.

I could never understand what the intense dilemma was in encountering one's own death, intellectually; I quite enjoyed the process and indulged in it at regular stages. The death of those near to me, however, was a chilling source of despair. I fought off my fear of bereavement now with flooding, teeming, undeniable love for everyone from old Rex to tiny Bernard-Louis, love that eddied warm around Joe as well, up past his knees and rising. Maybe Joe should cry at my funeral after all; it was the newly masculine way. I wanted to cry when I imagined Joe in a suit—tight at the shoulders and short at the cuffs with outsized lapels. It was the sort of wanting to cry that makes one laugh instead and bury one's face even though no one is looking.

I was right back in the jolt and hustle of office life the next morning when I opened my inbox. Luce had emailed me twelve times since Thursday with Barry close behind and Nate pulling up the rear. Our ex-nun and vintner out West had so far failed to engage, but a burly retired army colonel (her) and palpably unstable mental health nurse (him) had set a date, as had a Sicilian widower in the construction business and a manicurist with a heart of fool's gold. Barry was getting word from Juice that they were keen to go live with the finale. There was talk of a call-in vote brought to our viewers by a Viagra knock-off. Nate was all for it, but I dreaded the wisdom of crowds.

By mid-morning, I had dealt with a fraction of this—with Bernard-Louis minimized for easy reference so I could regularly thrill to his drool, mystification and dear little baby fingers. Rushing between my laptop and the diner for the rest of the week, I had coaxed everybody through the worst of our rough patch by the following weekend. With time left over to have Joe to Sunday lunch. I made us a frittata as colourful as a fruit cake that he pretended to like. Then I treated his freckled shoulders to a rub that went on for an hour, to the excitement of the bedroom blinds, which kept backing off and then billowing when their curiosity got to be too much.

As Island wisdom had it, the weather would turn towards autumn as soon as Old Home Week was over—the middlemost week of August. Homesick Islanders were now headed back to Charlottetown to bet on the biggest harness race purse of the year, maybe ride the Zipper, munch on a corndog and take in the dog show. Joe and I were giving it a miss. Quietly ministering to Joe's sore spots while he hovered just short of deep sleep, I was reminded that the true purpose of intelligence has got to be empathy. I had always loved language above all and now it occurred to me that what I enjoyed most about language is that it is love's cup. "Lovely Joe," I whispered, not to rouse him, simply to address him. But he came to and groaned and his spine reverted to being the thing that held him upright. Once Joe drove off in a massaged stupor I called Barry. He was on his way back to the city from his cottage and keen to chitchat on the handsfree.

"The brass know you've been a constant contributor, Minnie, doubt ye not."

I had shifted from vacation pay to a consultancy fee.

"I do doubt, Barry, absolutely I doubt. But I doubt selectively."

"They're convinced up top *Marry Me or Else!* is coming together, genius. Good thing you've got me brainwashed as well; it makes me much more persuasive under pressure."

"We've got nothing to worry about, Bar. Love always finds a way, love is never at sea."

"Someone's been eating Hallmark cards for breakfast."

"You, sir, can eat shit because that was very profound."

"Your fisherman friend teach you that?"

"To which fishermen friend are you referring, may I ask?"

I had sworn Luce to secrecy. So much for freeform inter-staff communication; from now on I was going to be a strict professional.

"Don't blame Luce, feisty. I needed a flower delivery so I called your cousin. Chicks yap, you know that. Don't worry, I haven't told anyone you're the catch of the day. Excuse me, catch of the summer. I don't mean to imply this thing of yours is, ahem, fleeting."

"Then don't."

"Barb is so jealous she's making me practice knots on the cottage dock. Figures you'd go for a rugged individualist."

"For the record, he doesn't smoke a pipe or wear a yellow hat."

After we hung up, I clicked onto my bank accounts for the first time in a long time, to make sure my postdated rent cheques were cashing. Luce's mother looked to be paying my utility bills as they came in. The consultancy business was profitable for as long as it went untaxed. Shockingly, it seemed Harbour life was saving me money. Especially if I was labelling it a research expense and tax deducting my transportation and subsistence costs. Consequently, Monday came as less than a completely rude blow.

The atmosphere at Eats n' Treats was already fraught when I got there. Fibby had come home to the Harbour on Saturday afternoon in possession of what was speculated to be a forty-ouncer of shine. After a liquid dinner and more boozing to follow, he had stumbled up and down every Harbour lane begging forgiveness from whoever did not have their windows closed. Trudy found him slumped over a garden gate at the corner of Main and Calhoun. Freak was summoned and together they dragged Fibby home to bed on the couch. Freak did night nurse duty and Trudy had heard nothing since. Fibby was not one to use his cellphone frivolously.

"Christly hell, what next?" I asked. "This place is cracking up!"

"Is that what you think, Minnie?"

I'd assumed Verna was still out back looking through the freezer for pattied hamburger. She unloaded the meat onto the kitchen counter with a clatter. Archie had hooked a big tuna a few days before and both father and daughter had regained their native pugilism since. Verna might not have begun the summer with a stare that could knock over a gravestone, but she had that going for her now.

"I meant it well, Vee. A lot of excitement is all I meant."

"Maybe there's too much excitement around here with so many of us working. Things will settle down from here on in, now that everyone from away is going home where they belong, isn't that right, Trudy?"

Accuracy got the better of Trudy. She muttered "yes" as if she was saying no; it was the best she could do. Then she fled to see to Herman at the cash.

"So what you're saying, Verna, is that this diner isn't big enough for the two of us?"

Please God, I was not going to laugh. If anyone hummed a Sergio Leone melody I was a goner. Debbie was madly buttering bread slices for a big take-out sandwich order due to be picked up in half an hour. I wasn't sure who got the white hat and who was stuck with the dusty black one, but I had no doubt Verna was fast on the draw.

"Let me put it to you this way, Minnie. If you don't quit, I will."

I had grown unduly fond of my Eats n' Treats schedule, I could see that now. Some days we had been so busy I had not even needed to run. I had become acquainted with a whole village at a blow and convinced numerous tourists that I was locally colourful. Once and for all, I understood why solitary confinement is a form of punishment rather than a reward. I would miss Herman and Darlene and the church ladies and the brash teenyboppers, even the entirely fat families. But I would have more time for Rex without my little job. And more time for Joe. No holding back on tuna season—the license holders were keeping at it until everything they were allowed to catch was caught. There were maybe three days left before someone scooped the last of the quota. Possibly Trudy had never expected me to stick around for this long, but had no idea how to lay me off.

"Fair enough, Verna. I'm out of here."

I doffed my apron and hung it back on its hook. It still had a good couple of days to go before it had to go home with Trudy for a hot wash. I hugged Debbie from behind, happy to have someone virally spreading my side of this story. I turned to Verna and aye-aye saluted her a snappy farewell.

I got exasperation in return, an eye roll plus a snort.

"Maybe it's not too late to head to school this year after all, Verna. I honestly think it would do you good. You could start off with a year of humanities."

"Whatever."

"Not whatever, your future. Your big idea. Your heart's desire."

"Ya, well, maybe you better keep an eye on the ball yourself."

Trudy was grateful, copiously so, telling me that I was a gem and unforgettable and she couldn't have asked for more. I reminded her I wasn't gone, that I would be in before she knew it, demanding service with a smile. And that Rex's big birthday party was on the twenty-fifth.

"Let me know what happens with Fibby," I begged. "Once he finds out who put that pail beside the couch." My hand was on the door.

"You got it, Minnie." Trudy was in long sleeves she had picked up at a Lonesome Sailors show. She waved goodbye, Verna scowled goodbye, and the door banged behind me.

Outside, the trees were having a good gossip. I buttoned up my cardigan. Summer was casting hints about its departure and here was my first real day *off*. It was time to sneak in another swim. The beach was as empty as hoped, completely so. The water was clear this time so I could keep an eye out for crabs and watch my knobbly white feet put on their show of bravery. It was hard to wade any farther than pubic but I managed by diving before the diving was good. At my deepest I could still tiptoe down to the bottom if I kept my mouth shut. Enough of that, I dog-paddled inland fast. I hopped into as few clothes as possible and dashed up the cliff, noticeably crumbled since May. I whipped through Dosie's pasture and into the house for a hot bath and shampoo. I was allowed to eat only potatoes for dinner again; they were no longer new, but the mint was at its peak. The sun set so beautifully quietly that I was compelled to watch it tumble, slippery as a yolk, behind something that land-locked Ontario never offered—a real edge of the world. Whoever had decided to call it evening was absolutely right. Even as, even so, even if . . . I was breathing evenly, I was evening things out.

Herring

11

I had good big news for Barry—a live finale for *Marry Me or Else!* was a definite possibility. The ex-nun and the vintner were surely good to go now that Nicola and Hardy were completely out of the running. On the morning of Friday, August twenty-fourth I received my invitation to Nicola and Hardy's New Year's Eve wedding, thus had they pre-emptively disqualified themselves. We would have to dump their shoots, quiz included, but we could easily pad out a full season with an episode of *never-seen-before* highlights footage of everyone else. My invitation to the wedding arrived in Rex's mailbox, in Helvetica on crisp Bristol board, with exhortations to attend only if convenient and to donate to Third-World libraries in lieu of gifts. Indeed I would donate, possibly all my Eats n' Treats salary. Nicola could earmark my dollars for libraries in Haiti so that while I was at it I could provide Bernard-Louis with a goodbye gift to his own island—swathed in strife and rife with degradation, but perhaps BL would help change all that one day with some true north strong and free equanimity. Nicola and Hardy were inviting each guest to bring a guest. I wondered what Joe would make of late December in Sudbury, of lakes the size of a small ocean but faster to freeze. He was too busy wrapping up tuna to call on the spot.

I was hoping Joe's association duties would keep his mind off the fact that he and Colin had not hooked a single fish. I knew the brothers were not alone in going empty-handed, but I still felt bad for them. And for Etta most of all: Colin's charm would now come forced for weeks to come unless topped up with Labatts Ice. I declined to head out with the brothers on the last day of the season. I was worried I would add my own luck to the tuna's luck and blow Joe's luck out of the water. Or worse, be obliged to watch a fish that had spawned in the Mediterranean twenty years prior and lived wild since then, with the ability to swim forty miles an hour in great gunning bursts, thrash to death before my eyes. Fibby and Patrick had hooked up eleven times in total, making their way back into the newspaper for a congratulatory sentence in the season-ender round-up. Prices had dipped the second week of August, then rebounded, but no one was in the habit of thinking they were what they ought to have been. I thought the average PEI fisherman would triumph in any given gripe-off—against a Las Vegas headlining comic, against a Fox News pundit, against Moses fresh off the mountain all peevish with commandments. Joe did not gripe, not gratuitously, but if I was going to stick around long term, I would have to learn how to reduce a lot of his complaints to moving-right-along dimensions.

If I was going to stick around long term?

Firstly, I had to ask myself what the hell kind of question that was. Did I plan on becoming Myriad's chief long-distance consultant? It was doubtful that Myriad or the zeitgeist would let me get away with that for long. Anything in PEI that did not have to do with fishing or potatoes seemed to occur as an echo—great if one's ears were smarting, but it made it hard to feel tuned in. I needed income from somewhere and I point-blank refused to fix up Rex's spare rooms as bed-and-breakfast accommodations—come for the homemade granola and stay for the beds that have seen eight generations come and go.

More and more often, I felt like a mad scientist exploring the physics of intimacy (love equals patience divided by bravery squared). I would picture Joe's belly with its layer of winter fat. I thought I might want to rub that belly come February when the Leafs were down a man in overtime. I wanted to feel that belly pressed up against my own, once it was softened by pie and who knew what else, Trudy's shortbread and Dolly's fruitcake probably. I would have to install a treadmill at Rex's house before snow drifted up to the windows and sealed me in. On good days Dosie's field would be blinding white and the sky refrigerated blue. I thought about getting hugged in the cold, how the wool from a handknit sweater would scratch when Joe forced shivers out of me by squeezing through to ribs. I knew from years of chatting to Rex that PEI seasons come upon each other as hard and fast as crimes and their punishments. True, summer would have burned us all out if it had kept on going. There were only so many blooms, bees and beans we could take, only so much growth.

Attention-seeking raindrops started falling about an hour after Nicola and Hardy's big invite arrived. I wondered if rain would ever go back to simply meaning I needed an umbrella. At this point I knew that rain would do the potatoes some good. The CBC weather woman had not warned anyone about the cloudburst, but as usual her tone betrayed no remorse. Rain would keep me from obsessively checking out the kitchen window for whales. Herman had assured me this was the right time. For once I was hitting the correct season for things. Blueberries were now turning up roadside. Trudy had promised me cobbler on the house. Missing her, I phoned her at Eats n' Treats, using Hardy and Nicola's big news as an excuse. I wanted to make sure she was managing okay because there were still golden-aged holidaymakers around and the autumn colours boat cruises were coming. Trudy answered. She was thrilled for the *happy couple* and doing fine at the diner.

"Actually, Minnie, I've been meaning to call. Get this." It was Trudy's first gossipy call: in a way I was sorry I had pre-empted it. "Fibby sent me flowers!"

"Get out! What, a whoops-I-almost-barfed-in-your-face bouquet?"

"Who knows? He's never done anything like this before. He spoiled the surprise some by calling to find out if I'd got them yet. I had to promise to call him back as soon as they got here. Pat helped him do it online at the Souris library. Getting Fib to use his credit card—that's a big deal right there. He's all cash on the barrel, that one."

"What did the note say?"

"*Sorry Fibby.*"

"That works."

"Verna figures a comma cost extra. Fib's going to want to curl up and die when he sees how girly the handwriting is."

I heard the diner door jingle; I owed Trudy a wrap-up. "I'm happy for you, Trudes. You deserve flowers."

"Come see 'em for yourself, Minnie. But not this aft. Soon as this rain lets up I'm going home to trim my hedges. I've been promising the neighbours for weeks. They hate not seeing me come and go."

"I've got plans myself. Don't forget, Rex's birthday party tomorrow."

Joe was coming to pick me up that afternoon for our big trip into Charlottetown. We were going to run a clump of errands and birthday shop. And in Joe's case have a word with the assistant deputy provincial fisheries minister. Rex's lobster suspenders had arrived in the mail, plus the Rita Hayworth glamour shot from Desolée, which I had wrapped in tissue and ribbon. Now I wanted to browse the downtown core for gag gifts and party favours. Plus Etta said the Charlottetown Superstore sold a mean chilli pepper hummus. Etta was dropping by the party with the kids, at least for the cake part. The girls loved birthday cakes as long as they each got a corner piece. With Joe's help I would pick up Rex's *gâteau* in Montague on Saturday afternoon: white with blue flowers and two big eight-shaped candles as opposed to eighty-eight little ones.

I double-checked my shopping lists; they had to be so premeditated in the country. Joe's red truck pulled up Rex's lane just after the rain cleared up, having it out with the puddles. Away from the diner it turned out that I saw less of Joe rather than more. But now here he was—my escort, my paramour, my Island guy. Joe had said he was going to treat us for dinner no matter how little I minded paying for a T-bone when my tab was all tofu. I was back to a place and time that considered the word *tofu* a punchline in itself, at least in McTeal company.

Joe was on his phone when he first drove up. That was fine because I had long wanted to fellate him, at least once over the summer, in his truck. I thought I had warned him about that. He was still damp from the shower so any reluctance on his part seemed uncalled for. I unzipped his fly while he discussed the possibility of briefly reopening the halibut fishery for the second time since July. Every penis has body warmth going for it, but Joe's was ideally spiced: a dash of salt and just a hint of pepper. I bent to slurp, to suck pride up into that head for five minutes, maybe ten. There was Kleenex in the glove compartment to cope with the consequences ... which did not result. Not with Joe's free hand shoving me back into the passenger seat, my mouth as empty as a guppy's. Joe was cupping my brains and pushing away hard. This was not play wrestling; force counted. I hurt.

"Ow, my neck! What?" It was the first time I had drowned out one of Joe's calls, or tried to.

"Right you are, Fred. Talk to you next week, yup, yup, got it. Okay then, good stuff. Bye then."

"Joe, come on, don't tell me you're angry?"

"No, Minnie, I'm not angry. But don't you have a lot to get done? You want to drive, you said. That always takes longer. I've had a long month, dear, you know that." Joe rubbed his nice face.

How the hell was one supposed to repay these people for all their door-to-door rides, handiwork, and fresh-picked carrots? It was a constant struggle. I clasped my hands tightly and shoved them in my lap, no church, no steeple, no people. "Fine."

"Don't *you* be mad, Minnie. Did you really want to do that?"

"Do what?"

"That?"

"Evidently yes, I did."

No man had ever seen me cry as much as Joe. No more tears, not this time. Not the day of our big date in the capital city of Charlottetown where all the houses still look like farmhouses and oncoming cars grind to a halt if you even think about jay-walking. Petulance was out of order, I knew that. It was a shame that I had to rack my brains to figure out what state of mind was appropriate. I felt Joe turn his gaze away from my ducked profile. Scientists would be intrigued by my ability to sense Joe looking at me from the front, side or back.

"Whale," said Joe.

"What, where?"

The sun had come out so soon after the rain that the sky was a clotted, dark blue. Dandelions were having a second go at the summer.

"Gone. Spout caught my eye. That's how you spot them from this far away."

"I can't believe I missed it! I want to show off when I go back to Toronto, whales outside my window and all."

"You'll see plenty of whales if you come out herring fishing, Minnie. Will you stick around long enough to do that, do you think? Stick it out here in the slow lane with us hicks?"

Joe needed to gun an engine. I thought I knew how to make him happy while we backed up.

"Joe, that top railing on Dosie's fence is loose. Will you help me fix that some day? I don't think I can do it on my own. She likes to scratch her rump on it and I don't want to leave nails poking."

"Sure thing, Minnie. I can help you with that. Just remind me."

Dosie nodded at us while we zoomed away as if she was saying goodbye, but she was probably just jerking flies from her eyes. She hated wearing her space woman goggles and I did not blame her; even the largest anti-bug mask was a squeeze for her two-and-a-half foot head. Dosie had eyes the size of Grade A eggs; flies came buzzing all day looking for eye juice.

"Oh, wow, Joe, I almost forgot. Nicola and Hardy are tying the knot! December thirty-first in Sudbury."

"Good for them. They seem to know what they're doing."

"Think about, you know, flying out for it. I'm invited and I think they mean by that you're invited, too."

"I'll think it over, Minnie, I give you my word. Look at old Herman, off to the diner. He wants lunch number two is what. Hope you didn't eat, Minnie? You promised you'd be good and hungry for supper."

"I'm ravenous, can't you tell?"

It was not simply a drive to town—it was a drive away from a time in my life when sex in a vehicle was a distinct possibility to a time in my life when it was not necessarily on. It was a drive to a place with double-lane traffic. A few months before Colin had manhandled the Charlottetown thoroughfares one-handed, but now Joe picked his way through them shoulders to ears. I tried to be a calming influence at the corner of Euston Street and University Avenue, but Joe's shoulder was damp to my touch. He was craning into the windshield at every turn and twitching, cheeks and trunk. No squeezes to my knee now, or ribbing me over my silver-dollar words, especially not after we got honked at. Finally, we herringbone-parked on Queen Street.

I told Joe that I would find a bank and a dollar store and just to meet me at the pub on Water Street for dinner. We were going to the one with the sign in the shape of a dory, a net nailed to the ceiling, and mini lobster traps on every table to hold the salt, pepper, sugar and vinegar. All this to lull tourists into the benign notion that fishing was still more craft than industry, that it took more than a dashboard fully equipped with sounder, plotter, radio, radar and auto-pilot to get it right, and that the fish on their plate had been caught in keeping with every high seas regulation. Joe dashed, but I ambled. The air in Charlottetown was as fresh as the air in the Harbour and just as sexless. Fortunately for Rex's party guests, Island dollar stores were awash in the normal flood of Shanghai trinkets.

I found a Dollarama in the basement of the Confederation Court Mall with cute honey pots, oven mitts, lipstick caddies, mugs, fridge magnets and lawn toys. Rex would have been mortified to be the only one getting presents. I grabbed a multicoloured stamp pad to make him a homemade card, the only way to go when it came to Rex and in Rex's case a card was essential. I could use a potato to cut hearts and stars. At Charlottetown's little Roots outpost I found Rex an updated lumberjack shirt in a digital check with a cozy fleece lining. And a waterproof wallet with Velcro fasteners because Rex loved the sound of a good rip. At the ice cream parlour next door they were selling old-fashioned lollypops the size of dinner plates. I picked up ten and called it a day. Then I went back to Roots and got Joe the same shirt in medium.

Joe had left the truck open. I stashed my shopping bags, locked my side and headed to the restaurant, early, but I would have a very weak drink while I waited: gin diluted with tonic diluted with soda. No Joe, as expected. I bellied up to the bar, a nice long one with a right angle. And there was Ralph around the other side, with his hand on a pint and his nose in a research paper highlighted in shocking blue.

"Ralph!" I assumed I was invited right over.

"Minnie, we have to stop meeting like this." Ralph shifted his bulging rucksack onto the far stool and patted the seat beside him.

"I'm not interrupting anything?"

"Climb on. I'm just going over some notes before my fiancée gets here tomorrow. She's on her way up from Maine. She's coming to Rex's party, actually. I want her to get in on the action while it's hot."

"She's very welcome. In fact I just got her a great big sucker."

"She's already got one of those."

"Stop."

"Trust me, I'm a sucker for the lady. No one charts scallop industry growth with reference to diminishing predation like she does."

Ralph's woman was wise to have kept an eye out for him. This was the best age at which to mate; older than thirty and everyone except maybe Hardy and Nicola risked mixing in too much relief. No wonder Ralph had a glow. Although that might also have been a result of his forehead, which bulged towards any light.

"What's this lucky lady's name, may I ask?"

"Felicia. I call her Fizz but don't you go doing that or she'll know we've been intimate."

"You, my good man, are heedlessly incorrigible." I imagined Ralph was infamous on campus for being the first guy to wear shorts every spring. "And you make your grandmother very proud."

"She's not the only one. I'm actually very proud of myself."

"Minnie, good, you found some company. How are you keeping, Ralph? I seen you over at fisheries offices earlier, but I was running late for a meeting. Glad you made it to The Wave and Oar."

"Joe, hi! Ralph was just telling me that his fiancée is on her way to the Island tomorrow."

The men shook hands. Twenty seconds and counting and Joe had still not placed a hand on me. I was curious how long that would take in Charlottetown. It was only fair that it take a while. Because I would maul Joe in public in Toronto for sure, but how I would handle him in the privacy of Concord Avenue after a long day of work was another question.

"The good news is that Fizz is nothing like me; she's extremely civilized. Joe, man, take a load off. You make me tired just looking at you."

Ralph's rucksack landed on the floor and Joe ended up on the other side of Ralph. He quickly tucked his feet onto the stool rung; Joe's length was all in his trunk.

"Nothing like you, huh? Well, gents, you know what they say about opposites. Word is they attract."

I reached across Ralph to brush Joe's forelock off his brow; unnecessary but the baboon in me made me do it. Joe's hair belonged in a British comedy of manners. He had a new white dress shirt overtop his usual white T-shirt. I would save his new shirt from me for another day.

"My theory is that opposites attract for a preliminary period." Ralph burped demurely. "The trick is keeping it that way."

"Joe, sweetie, we should get you a drink."

The pub served micro brew, but Joe went for something light and American. As soon as possible we did a cheers, the men's drinks toasted shades of gold and mine colourless. Ralph had treated, sliding a wallet made entirely of duct tape out of an upper pocket.

It did not take Joe and me long to decide that Ralph should join us for dinner. Knowing Joe would be hungry I made short work of my aperitif, sucking fast until the ice rattled. I sat beside Joe and across from Ralph at a table of chunky wood that would be hard to drag anywhere. I did my best not to get embarrassed by the mammoth menu, each page the measurements of a king-size bedsheet folded for a roomy linen closet. Joe ordered wings and steak. Ralph ordered garlic cheese bread and seafood lasagne. I asked for garden salad followed by smoked chicken rigatoni hold the chicken, extra roasted red pepper, baked potato on the side, no butter or sour cream, but olive oil if they had it, extra virgin. My fuss was endearing to Joe, who understood by it that I was really enjoying myself.

"So I hear we're going to be all out of fish by 2040?" Joe's free arm rested along the back of my chair. I leaned back, his elbow at my head. I wanted to thump my tail for him.

"Maybe not, brother Joe. Depends what kinds of international treaties on trawling get drawn up, or should I say who panics in time. Most governments still haven't accepted the fact that they can't fish their fast-reproducing species without screwing up their slow-reproducing stocks at the same time."

"Don't they know how to count?" I asked, chewing on a hunk of white bread that was irresistibly unresisting.

"Most stock assessments are based on fifty-year-old single-species models. The accurate, multi-species software just isn't there. Who knows if it ever will be? Sorry about that, that's my job."

"Fish bounce back." Joe could swig like Colin when he had to.

"You're right, some animals procreate more when their population is endangered." Ralph was probably too absorbent to feel his booze without really trying. "Unfortunately, that doesn't seem to be the case with cod."

"More cod sex!" I banged on the table with balled-up fists like I was cheering on my college team. Ralph banged along. Joe winced over his shoulder. Our appetizers were on the way. I thought maybe I needed to take a hoe to my salad. Even the croutons were huge and made a ruckus when I crunched them.

"Pretty well every ocean is screwed," Ralph munched on. "Most commercial stocks are down 90 percent since the 1950s. And you know what they say, anything less than 10 percent of pre-industrial numbers and you're looking at a complete collapse."

The more I knew about fishing, the more I respected Rex for having fished when it was more of a challenge and less of a massacre.

"Is the ocean *emptying?*"

"Good question, Minnie. Pass the salt if you would. There's as much biomass as ever, but you can start kissing all the palatable stuff goodbye. Lots of eels and worms and jellyfish left, all kinds of shrimpy stuff, but way fewer big guys to eat it up. You should see the shark numbers. Fin soup sells too high; it's worth it to chop off the fins and chuck the fish. Funny how people think pollution is the worst of our worries. The worst of our worries turns out to be progress. What's the matter with your onions, Minnie? Joe doesn't mind. He's a strong fellow."

"*Technological creep.*" For an awful moment I thought Joe had lobbed an insult across the appetizers, but the men were playing jargon Frisbee.

"Now you're talking. Boosted fishing effort eats away at stock projections every time. We're too modern for our own good. For the fish's good anyway."

I forked oily leaves into my mouth and shoved stalks in after them. "They're going to have to start colouring the oceans on maps red, not blue!"

"From what I hear from my nephews about global warming, the whole planet's on red alert."

"Joe, sir, you make a good point; things are critical all over. But I don't know if people really see the sea, or see deep into it."

"See the sea," I repeated, then with my eyes closed, "sea the sea," I intoned. I opened my eyes and smiled brightly at the men. Unfortunately, they now thought I was blotto. "Salad, anyone? I can't finish this."

Joe said no, but Ralph shoved aside cheese bread to make room on his plate. Joe ate quickly and Ralph ate slowly, but they both left debris: in Joe's case a pile of shiny little grey bones with shreds of fried skin stuck to the knobs. I could not fathom why Ralph was leaving his crusts; to my mind they were the best part. I bit my tongue yet again. One more drink, however, and I would be asking Ralph if I could sample those crusts, bite marks and all. Desolée had always given me hers: sandwich, pizza and pie. I ordered another drink when Ralph did, but Joe said he was driving and asked for tap water.

After Ralph finished his dessert—crème brulé that I had claimed to want a crack at but foreswore under the gun—and after Joe took care of the tab, paying with cash and tipping 10 percent, we offered Ralph a lift to his hotel, but he insisted he did not need a drive around the corner. We admitted we had no idea if the Charlotte-town Delta in-room entertainment menu included porn. Joe shook Ralph's big mitt, I kissed his big cheek, then we scooted for the truck. "I miss the Harbour," I told Joe. More specifically I missed Rex's road—the way the view made a clean sweep for miles, of sky and sea that were often the same shade of blue except that the sky was starched cotton and the sea was wiped glass. Or they were two separate shades of blue: one powdery, one shimmering. Or they were the greys of pigeon wings, baking sheets, cobwebs, botched laundry, or charcoal smoke. By the time Joe and I got home it would be dark. I wanted sleep to come long and hard—the kind of sleep that feels like downing liquorice cocktails—narcotic, system-flooding sleep that quenches every cell while giving rise to millions of new ones. I thought I could now attempt sleep that deep by Joe's side.

"Sorry our date got crashed, Joe," I said as we buckled in. "I kind of wanted you to myself. Greedy, I know." I had a tonic headache. Nowadays there was too little quinine and too much sugar.

"Ralph's a nice fellow, but you're the one I have time for, Minnie." A knee squeeze and jiggle; Joe was not as nervous in town traffic when dusk had rendered it anonymous.

"Shucks!"

With seedy contentment I sensed that we would be having sex again, for the first time since Joe's three weeks of thirteen-hour fishing days had gotten underway. When we hit the highway and picked up speed, I closed my eyes and felt the hills in my solar plexus. I thought about Ralph's contingency visions and wondered what I could do to help. Fifty minutes from start to finish, Joe and I pulled to a stop. I dared not ask if he was coming in and he did. I brushed my teeth twice as fast as usual and dove for the bed. As soon as Joe crawled on top of me I made a silent deal with him: if he was immediately hard enough to enter me, then I was immediately wet enough to enter. I wanted sex like addicts want heroin—I wanted it in me, I wanted to be plunged full of it. In my moment of greatest urgency, my legs were flung up into a wide, beseeching V. I was begging Joe to please, *please*, just pound away. "I want to fuck, I want to get fucked, I want to fuck," I kept telling him, with sad, mad notes in my voice like I was confessing a crime I had been forced into by lowlifes. Joe grit his teeth like he was rescuing someone who had pitched herself over a ledge. That frown bundled up his eyebrows again while he stared down at my latest waxing job. I had mismanaged and been left with a parallelogram. Finally the slap, slap noise of our groins smacking together turned me on so much that I came Hollywood style, as if I had been storyboarded into it. I shuddered through a nice little series of aftershocks while Joe lay back and drenched the pillow.

"Thanks." I had not meant this to be a weird thing to say.

"Minnie, you can be a strange one," I heard.

"I just meant, you know, you're understandably tired tonight so I really appreciate you pulling out all the stops."

"Maybe we both needed that, dear. How's that?"

"I was thinking this morning how you'll have the whole winter to kick back. Lots more time off."

"Some free time maybe, but there's still work to be done."

"Buoys to paint and traps to build?" I took Joe's near hand and started tossing it from one of mine to the other like it was too hot to handle.

"That and campaigning for another year of paperwork, Lord help me."

"None of it paid for, you might add."

"No, but I got the EI starting."

"You've got what?" I sat up in the dark.

Joe closed his eyes. "Employment insurance, Minnie."

Sometimes, I wished for men that they really did have a bone in there so as not to look so utterly vulnerable. Joe was flopped out nude and susceptible, but I still needed an explanation. "Pogey? You go on pogey, Joe?"

"Sure, we all of us do."

"Colin I can understand. But you, Joe? You own the boat and licence. An operation that continues to be fairly profitable and used to be tremendously so. By anyone's standards. Why you?"

Verbally, I was equipped for dirty talk or combat, whatever came along. Joe needed to fight me on this one. I was up on my knees now.

"This is a seasonal economy, Minnie. If the government wants this province to stay populated for seasonal work, then they've got to be held accountable for that." Joe's hand was at his brow the same way he had clamped mine earlier, palm over the eyes, thumb in the temple. This had the effect of pointing his elbow at my chest.

"But there are too many of you fishing as it is! Don't you think maybe Mother Nature and the marketplace are trying to tell you guys that the jig is up? Them's the breaks, Joe. Them's the bloody, goddamn breaks."

"Coastal economies are not just seasonal, Minnie. They're also traditional."

"Fuck tradition!"

"Is that what you really want to do, Minnie? Fuck tradition?"

It was the first time that I had heard Joe curse, if only by repetition. The idea that he swore around men but not women was another infuriation.

"Guess what, Joe? Television has seasons, too. But you don't see me whining about it, nor any of my colleagues. You know what? We deal."

"Maybe people deal in ways you aren't aware of, Minnie, ways they don't want to open up to you about because you can be a damn tough nut when you put your mind to it."

I looked out the dark window. "You people expect the ocean to be so adaptable."

"We do our best, Minnie."

"I know one thing for sure, Rex never went on pogey."

"In that case he's the only guy around here who didn't. Sorry, or woman. I'm sorry, dear. I'm just plain sorry."

Joe was now well enough used to my eruptions to crash while the lava hardened. He did not stir when I bounced right out of bed and jiggled open the dresser drawer looking for a T-shirt. I tugged on some underwear for good measure and then some leggings over those. I could no longer look right at him, this deep breathing and heavily subsidized seventy-kilo collection of organs and limbs who had become the *man in my life*. It was a damn good thing Joe had paid for dinner after all. With whose money I was no longer sure and the waitress sure hadn't got her fair share of it. When I got back into bed I was irritated that the sheets were warm. Unexpectedly, I slept fast, like a SWAT-team veteran blasting into a hideaway. I dreamed of Joe falling into Rex's well, which made me cry. Joe did not seem to wake up, which relieved me and sent me right back to sleep.

By morning—squint sunny but a breeze had frisked up—I was glad Joe was not the type to go off in a male huff. There was also something manly about the way he had little for breakfast, downing a quick cup of coffee and then hitting the road. Breakfast is the apex of coupledom; the proof that you can get through things and then plan more of them. I kissed Joe goodbye with a happy grunt, as if tasting a new flavour of ice cream. Until I left the province altogether, Joe wielded a seductive power over most of our departures. He promised to be back in a couple of hours to take me to Rex's party. He said maybe I should run off my party nerves in the meantime. I could agree with that.

I pulled on my track shoes and set off in the clothes I had slept in since it would have been impossible to compete with the dank, vegetable smack of low tide sneaking up from the shore—in its own way the opposite of sewage. I was further rewarded when a zeppelin-sized flock of starlings whooshed into action over Herman's fields. Sky fish, Elliot called them. The rustling black dots on high always looked to me like a vast spray of commas and periods left over from things left unsaid all across the township. I doubled back at Herman's house in order to jog all the way out to Tuck Point on the gravel road.

I made my bath quick so I would have time to trim my bangs. Desolée could do hers even without a mirror, but my hair was too straight to show my hand much mercy. Rex's kitchen scissors won out over my nail snippers. My first, second and third swipes went fine, then a jagged notch appeared over my left eye. I put down the shears—any excessive correction and I would trim myself into a Vermeer. As things stood I looked permanently eyebrow-cocked, like life was a question. Joe did not seem to notice anything askew when he picked me up at noon sharp. Touchingly, I smelled a fresh application of something coiffeur related on Joe's part. The man was some kind of Samson, the way his hair withstood parabens and stayed wavy. Joe made me drive the whole way. He said the Superstore parking lot was going to be good for me.

I stalled twice on the way out of the Harbour, but otherwise performed respectably. I even changed gears a couple of times without prompting, causing Joe some sweethearted surprise. Did the fact that I had no idea how to go about applying for employment insurance benefits explain my unwillingness to do so? That and the dagger blow to my self-identity as a competent and fulfilled person that would result if I ever signed my name to the sad-sack application form and promised to attend government-sponsored job search seminars. Of course, there are as many types of intelligence as love. I knew that I was bright, but I did not necessarily think that I was canny. Joe had an angle on a lot of things about which I remained obtuse. Was some acceptance called for? Or would that be moral slithering? Had I spent four decades up in the clouds until Joe showed me the way down into the breaking waves?

"Left at these lights, Minnie. Crawl out, wait your turn and go."

From the moment Joe had met me he had not stopped tending to me with precision and courtesy. Affection was a fume, obviously; once pumped through my heart, it made for my cranium.

"Anything you say, darling!"

Joe had no idea that I loved him, but I did. Somehow it followed that Joe had been loving me without me knowing. But now I knew that he did. Especially when he agreed to keep me company in the Superstore instead of tipping back the passenger seat and cranking sports radio. I knew Joe loved me when he hummed as we traversed the parking lot and then dislodged a cart from the chrome tangle. I knew Joe loved me for a fact when he headed off on his own initiative to find party napkins: cute ones with frogs on lily pads that I told him were *just right*, Lord help me.

Joe had found Rex a new jackknife for his birthday: a small one to fit inside his pocket when he was in his wheelchair. We met up at the in-store bakery. Happily, the cake had as many turquoise flowers as ordered: the bakery manager was a Harbour girl who knew me from the diner. She knew Joe longingly from afar from the looks of things; the sight of him made her eyes stutter. I gave Joe the cart to push and stuck my free hand in his back pocket. "This way, I can lead you around by the ass," I whispered. If Joe and I ever married we could bonk in grocery-store aisles. I took back my paw before he had need of a codpiece and Rex's party was no longer the most memorable thing about the day. I found whole wheat baguettes to slice and toast for the bruschetta mix I had diced up the day before. Big bags of blue corn chips were on sale for the guac and salsa. Sally would be pleased with all the party garlic. I grabbed thirty bottles of cordial and sixty matching red cups. Guests were expected any time after three.

"Well, hello," Rex crowed when Joe and I got to his room. Someone had helped Rex scrub himself clean as if to the bone.

"That does it, Uncle Rex, you are officially old." When I kissed Rex's shiny forehead I saw his sparse lashes flutter with country gentleman bashfulness.

"Where should these go?" Joe was bearing the gifts. I had food to organize, bowl upon plastic-wrapped bowl.

"What nonsense is this now?"

"Relax, Uncle Rex. People enjoy picking out little things for you so why deprive them? Presents over there, Joe, on the trestle table, I'll find a tablecloth in a sec. Can you grab the pop from the truck? Thanks. Hi, Gladys, hi, Lydia! Who wants a job?" Desolée always said if television did not work out for me, there was always the army.

Party spirit overtook everyone in turn as they showed up to arrange the treats we would soon be offering each other, party helpers morphing into partygoers as early afternoon shifted to middle. Ralph and dewy Felicity—with an auburn shag, one deep dimple, Betty Boop legs and a chuckle on cue—helped blow up the last of the balloons. I had forgotten my camera of all things, in my sock drawer all summer long. Ralph was happy to capture something other than squid. When Etta and the kids arrived, the mayhem was official.

"Mommy, can I have chips?"

"Chips, Mommy, chips!"

Joan and Bette had practiced singing "Happy Birthday" for days, but now they wanted a snack first. I reminded myself never again to produce a television show that aimed junk food ads at children. The girls were excited to be wearing Sunday shoes on a Saturday, although Bette had on two left ones and Joan had on two rights. The boys were jealous of Rex's wheelchair. With Joe and Ralph's help he settled into his armchair instead and now Elliot was climbing in there with him, too. Elliot had something small and clumsily wrapped to hand over. "Presents time, Rex, okay?"

"What might this be? Let me see here, let me see." Rex's arthritic fingers were going to cause a lot of suspense. "What do you know!" Rex held up a chunk of bovine jawbone.

"There's a tooth stuck in it!" Elliot wanted me to see as well.

"Gosh, El, that's a beaut."

I loved the way Elliot's smile apologized for itself, and the way his head now slipped into the crook under Rex's neck. "Secord found it really."

"It still counts, little man. Told ya he'd love it." Etta had been in on the big surprise, but had saved it like a good mom.

"For sure it counts." I reached around to hug Rex and Elliot both; Ralph caught that in a flash.

The girls gave Rex work socks. Pierre had picked out a geometry set with sharp little red pencils, a compass and a protractor. Etta made no bones about handing over a forty-ouncer of Bermuda rum. "That'll keep the visitors coming, don't you know!"

"Why, mama?" Elliot hated every sip he had sneaked so far.

"You mind your own beeswax, son of mine. This is Rex's big day."

I had neglected the alcoholic aspect of the catering, but Etta took charge of a round of rum-and-Cokes, and when that ran out, rum and Anne. The biddies daintily partook, Sally despite Ralph's feigned horror. She had purchased Rex his own subscription to *Readers Digest* for his birthday because he loved getting to the jokes first. More hoots as more socks popped out of more packages. Gail and Lee had couriered a package that turned out to be a framed label from a nineteenth-century tin of lobster, the lobster looking dapper in spats and a top hat by appointment to His Majesty the King. Desolée's big-bang gift incurred a roar, the grown-ups passing Rita Hayworth from hand to hand, but the kids not allowed to touch. Ralph had signed his and Felicity's names to a gag card (*You're not getting older, you're getting bitter*), a fact that made her becomingly pink when it was read out. Then she helped Doris to find wall space and hammer in nails for Rex's new artworks. Meanwhile the lobster suspenders were a big hit. The pocket knife from Joe was duly admired, the boys allowed to touch this time.

"Cake, shmake, pwake!" Joan hollered, rousing Bette from Trudy's lap. Trudy had arrived along with blueberry pie, one for the party and one for Rex's freezer, the fruit bleeding delicious violet.

"Has Verna forgiven me yet?" I asked as soon as I could sidle up to her.

"Not quite yet, Minnie."

"Hell hasn't frozen over, Minnie, as far as I know." Doris had likewise sidled.

Trudy looked more twiggy than ever in a skirt: a denim mini that she had fashioned herself by chopping off jeans at the hip and adding a flounce. The occasion had called for her cherished Ramones sweatshirt. I sensed the Crab Shack in her near future.

Doris, Trudy and I skedaddled to the Manor kitchen to fetch the cake. We paused outside Rex's door to get a good grip on it. Doris remembered to turn it around so that it was legible from Rex's direction. "Ha, hap, Haaaaap . . . " I began.

Too low, too high, too flat.

"HAPPY … " Trudy sang out in a voice that was far too melodious to ever make it to a rock-and-roll stage—no wonder she was so vicarious. Doris and I and the little girls jumped in from there, with Ralph, Felicity, Etta and the old ladies soon piping up. I was finally in tune when we got to *"DEAR REX."* Even Joe joined in or at least mouthed the words. I could not pick him out unless he was the one who sounded like someone moving a bed. The Manor timbers resonated: every hearing aid throughout the east wing spiked and buzzed. Rex smiled serenely all the way to *TO YOOOOOU!* Elliot was happy to blow out the candles in two ostentatious gusts that made him look like wind on an antique map. Rex cut while I plated and Etta and Doris passed around.

Halfway through his small as specified blue-and-white slice of cake, I looked over to see Rex rereading the left-hand side of the card I had made for him. In it I had thanked Rex for changing my life for the better time and time again. I had promised to do my best to figure out exactly how he did that so that I could do it, too, for others. But I told him no one could ever make the splendid, inspired changes that he did, or keep just the right things the same the way he did. Hopefully, my card had not made Rex uncomfortable by attributing to him the powers of a fairy godfather. He did not seem burdened, in fact the opposite; he was giving off the twinkle equivalent of a train horn. By the time he got to eighty, Rex had started to look like the kind of alien people like to imagine visiting Earth to spread sixth-sense technologies on behalf of cosmic peace.

"Minnie, dear, come over here. I want you near while I tell you something." Rex had spoken quietly, but the party hushed to listen.

Back in Rex's lap, Elliot swung his glance between us while I settled down on his footrest. I could tell that no one but Rex knew what was coming next, but it turned out that Gail, Lee and Desolée had known what was in store, as they called to say shortly afterwards, from Vancouver Island and Toronto. On pain of personal bankruptcy, under threat of gun, grenade or sex scandal, I would never have guessed.

"I'm treated very well here at the Manor as a lot of you know . . . Thank you, Doris, you're very good to all of us, dear, and so are your chums." Claps. "My life was pretty well hard work and trouble all the way, and it's on its way to ending, like it or not. I wondered if I could make myself one last home here, me and my old bones, and it turns out I could and I did. A lot of you who are here today have to answer to that—Sally, Lydia, Shirlene and Gladys. But I want to thank my grandniece, Minnie, especially, who gave up her fashionable life in the city to help out her old uncle."

"City, yes, fashionable I'm not so sure!" High spirits made for easy laughs.

"The fact is, from what I hear, Minnie has taken real good care of the house. No surprise there. Because she's a good girl and always has been. She knows I think so, but it's not often I get to show her so. Well, Minnie, dear, thank you for taking care of that house because that house is yours. I've talked it over with your mother and your aunt and your cousin and they all agree you should have it fair and square. Soon your name will be on the deed, I can promise you that. You do what you want with it from now on."

My head had been pressed to Rex's knee for the last half of this. "Oh my god," I said to his kneecap. "Rex!" Elliot ducked so I could embrace Rex properly, my arms around his hillock shoulders, my face hidden from everyone but Joe in the corner. "Thank you so much, Uncle Rex!" Joe's expression was guarded, although cheers and whoops had started. It was fine to make it a long hug, but I had to let Rex go before I put my back out and created another fuss.

Elliot popped right back upright like the other half of Rex's ventriloquism act. "I know what! I'm going to marry Minnie and move next door!"

I had to laugh as well, although it made for one of the most bouillabaisse emotional states I had ever had on the boil. I barely knew what to think, let alone announce to my Island social circle. Rex's entire property sold for less than the two-bedroom, one-and-a-half-bath condo in downtown Toronto that I had put off buying for years, my savings accounts lined up like antsy thoroughbreds waiting for the pistol. Nonetheless, Rex's gesture was profound. I had to say something memorable, fast.

"Does this mean I get Dosie as well?"

"No house if you don't take the horse!" Etta had delivered the piñata-cracking moment that got everybody off and scrambling.

Dosie was now ostensibly mine and I had to wonder if the wind, sun and rain that gusted around the property were also mine. The well was mine, as were the lilacs, and the apple trees out front, and the dark mysteries of the barn loft. The ocean view was all mine, that was safe to advertise. And the parlour and the shutters and the two stone doorsteps. I sought out Joe, now that I was coming to my senses, to get reassurance that he was going to help me take care of all this. I held his hand while I waited to talk to my mother. It would have been a misnomer to say that Joe's hand had softened over the summer, but now it felt more like skin than pumice. I tried not to sweat when Etta passed me Gail on the phone. It was sweat or cry.

"Quite the news, Minnie Bug, don't you think?"

"Mom!"

"Let it sink in before you decide how you feel."

"Right now I can't quite fathom it." Joe tactfully forked up blue icing roses with his free hand. "I barely know how to accept."

"Your uncle loves that house and he loves you. To him this makes perfect sense."

"Are you sure you guys are okay with this, you, Lee and Desolée? Wait, I bet that's her on the other line. Do you mind if I take it, Gee? Love to Lee. Sorry, I'll call again soon."

"Much love."

I did not mean to rush away pretty well every time that Gail and I spoke. It had been good to hear her voice; too good, it made me want to whine.

"Des, it's me. Holy shit, huh?"

"So that's why you headed out there this summer, you weasel."

"Come on, there's no way—"

"I'm kidding, Minnie, get a grip. We're all happy that you get this in your life."

"Why me?"

"Maybe because you seem to need it the most."

I smelled pity. "Because you have *Stash* and the *baby* and Gail and Lee have *each other?*"

"If you want to put it that way, shithead, then yes."

"But I have Joe. He's right here. Do you want to talk to him?"

"Minnie, cut the guy some slack. Jesus, Emasculation City—"

"Great then, here he is. Joe, my cousin wants to say hi. Go ahead and hang up when you're done."

I hoped Rex could not feel my heart thumping as I nestled up to him, or would presume it was overjoy if he did. Bequeathals often tear a family apart, but I was the first person I had heard of who had picked a fight after inheriting a lion's share. Penny the physiotherapist showed up with her fiddle as requested, and launched into sawing, nervy tunes that got the kids up and dancing. They had forgotten their step class moves, but invented new hops and kicks. I hoped the Manor understood that the party was tossed wide open. I was not budging from the arm of Rex's chair where I could feel him quietly presiding. Joe patted my shoulder on his way to rescue Trudy from Celtic purgatory. I withheld my glance and Joe knew why—one jot of sympathy from his direction and I would toss aside the composure I had been building up for decades to bawl at Rex's feet. I would beg Rex not to die and leave me with a hundred acres and small cliff a kilometre outside a southeastern Prince Edward Island hamlet with lobster traps stacked on the wharf. For the first time I realized how hearts are raw. No wonder we find each other tough to digest.

"Did you notice the whale this morning, Minnie?" Etta asked. "I seen it from our bedroom window while you were jogging. I thought maybe you caught it?"

"No, I didn't!"

Etta had no time to rub it in. "Yo, you, out of those cookies,

Daddy's making ribs for dinner. Sorry, Minnie, we best be on our way. Elly, I said not to put chips in your sister's hair, didn't I? No, she's not picking them out, you are. Van, now, the lot of you! Many happy returns, Rex. We sure do miss you on the Tuck Point Road."

Of course they missed him. It had not occurred to me how much.

Trudy was next to leave. First I dragged her aside. She had kept us all calm at the diner during some hideous July lunch rushes so she could calm me down now before the streamers got detached from the walls. "Hello there, um, neighbour."

"Minnie, your mind is blown isn't it, poor thing? You drop by tomorrow afternoon and we'll gab it out. I owe you."

"Confess, are you meeting Mr. Trask in Montague this evening?"

"Fibby and Pat. They rode Fib's boat down to the Harbour today."

"Is Patrick going to go back to Souris for a while?"

"No, didn't you hear?" My look was my blankest. "Verna and Fib got Arch to take him on for herring. Pat did so well at the tuna and Arch is a man short."

"Tides sure do turn around here, sheesh. Tell Verna I said hello."

"Oh, she's not out with us tonight, Minnie. I promoted her to assistant manager. Good for her résumé, right? She's opening things up tomorrow. She's taking that nice and serious."

"Say hello to the guys for me then."

"You and Joe want to join in?"

"Thanks, but no. He's bagged and I'm fried."

Joe sensed he was a topic of conversation. I smiled to let him know it was benignly the case. I hoped he would not mind if we did not go back to his house that evening as planned. I needed to take a second look at Rex's house now that it was as good as mine. I was praying that it did not need a coat of paint all of a sudden. I was not up for reconstructing the chimney or checking the foundation for cracks.

Gladys was intent on leading the other ladies in a clean-up, but I forbade it. One by one, Ralph promenaded them back to their rooms. Penny packed up her fiddle and then Joe headed out with her to the parking lot to take a look at her leaky radiator—that would do for karma. Sally rolled her wheelchair up to Rex's armchair for a final quiet chat, one octogenarian to another. Felicity helped me dump out the chip and pretzel bowls and collect dirty paper plates and plastic cups.

"Welcome to PEI, Felicity. I don't know if I've said that properly yet."

"Thanks, Minnie. It's good to be here. Ralph could hardly wait. I wish we could stay like you."

"Could you both find work here, do you think?"

"That would be awesome. We're applying for research grants. You never know."

"What on earth do I do with these?" I had an armful of balloons. It hardly seemed right to leave them underfoot in Rex's room where they would wilt like geriatric buttocks. Felicity grabbed half by their ribbons.

"I know, Minnie. Follow me."

We headed down the hall and out the back door, out to the lawn that tumbled down to Montague River like a geography textbook diagram. Felicity reached into her pocket. She had two nails left over, one for each of us. We guffawed like a laugh track as we popped one balloon after another with red, green, yellow and blue bangs. Felicity thought it was hysterical when my last two got away, somehow blown in different directions. After we were done detonating, the grass was strewn with thin shreds of primary-coloured rubber. Stooping actually felt good.

"What are you two nutcases up to?" Ralph called over.

Joe was with him, hands in his pockets.

"Cleaning up!" I said. "Every good party must come to an end."

"Not this one," said Ralph. "There's still some cake left."

12

Joe was reluctant to let me drive back to the Harbour, but relented when I beseeched. Left-hand turns, merging, overtaking: for a change none of it seemed taxing. Taking the wheel was my only chance going to approach a Zen state and without a Zen state, there would be no REM sleep. No REM sleep, no sanctity. Joe had a rule that I had to keep my mind on the road. My road. I now saw that the Tuck Point Road had potholes and tarmac patches and a couple of take-out cups strewn in the ditches. My lane needed mowing up the middle; as things stood, it was tufted. I braked the way that Joe did not like me to, with a contagious jounce.

"Joe, do you think you could come in?"

Inquired as if I needed his help lifting a heavy box.

The more perfunctory our sex became, the more it turned me on. We did it doggy style this time. I moaned at every slam like we were driving over bumps. Any match made in heaven surely correlates penis length to a lady's interior canal; Joe filled me without gouging, we were safely cushioned against each other. I loved the feel of his balls softly whacking the backs of my thighs. Joe had big, bright pink balls with barely a hint of dangle, the kind of balls a French butcher would put in the front window. It was an effort for

Joe to support himself by one arm while his other hand headed down to where the action was, I understood that. The Sea of Joe: dribbling all over me again. I called on God the better to let Joe know that he absolutely had to keep it all up—the sweat, the stiffy, the ramming, the diddling, the breathing down my neck. Otherwise I might perish of carnal greed. "Oh god, fuck yes. Do it . . . oh GOD, yes, do it, Joe, yes, YES." The pleasure hit home. Joe groaned as well, like Atlas tossing the heavens off his shoulders.

Wisely Joe sensed I wanted a bath to myself, in fact the bathroom to myself. The skinned old sink and rickety taps would have to be replaced, but the two-ton tub was a keeper. Wearily, I pulled the plug, then slumped on the side of the tub and applied lavender lotion with the brio of an underpaid bricklayer. That was when I realized my womb felt taxed and crampy. Month after month my brave eggs awaited tadpoles to no avail. They were no longer *good* eggs. They were autistic eggs and Down's eggs and eggs with a hunger for Ritalin: far better they get washed away with endometrial lining. Once and for all, I assured my eggs neglect, then popped a painkiller and turned out the bathroom light.

Joe was asleep by the time I crawled back into bed, the sheets on my side folded down just so. I was grateful: the drive, the fuck, the bath, the pill, sleep. I dreamed of mossy BC and its huge trees that had been baby trees while medieval architects were drawing up plans for big European cathedrals. Eight-year-old Desolée was trying to hide on me as usual, but I always found her, no matter how enchanted the forest. Then she would hide again.

Joe did not have time to stick around in the morning. Herring was starting at the end of the week. I promised that at some point I wanted to come along. Cellphone clipped to belt, Joe bent to kiss me goodbye, leaving me alone on my pillow as pale, bleary and hollow as a governess down with ague. Then, what the hell, Joe invited me to Eats n' Treats for a quick tea and sugar bun before he started working his phone for real. I scrambled to dress while he threw my bike in the back of the truck. Absolutely, I wanted out of the house.

And to practice parking before the Eats n' Treats lot was full, and to clap my eyes on Trudy.

The churchgoers were all still busy getting harangued for the way Jesus had wept. Joe grabbed his favourite stool at the counter. From beside him I could see Verna busy in the kitchen pre-frying onions. Tentative Madison hurried out back to ask Debbie to cut us two slices of blueberry pie. I had forgotten that Trudy was getting a rare late start. Finally, Joe reached out and stroked my crown like I was a spaniel. I smiled in a way that he would catch from the side: an old, sweet smile like I had poured it from vintage sherry. I was almost ready to ask Joe if he would consider giving up his place in the village and moving to the Tuck Point Road where he could keep a closer eye on the sky and the water and his brother and me. I had the right jokey tone prepared. I thought I could leave the body language up to my subconscious and launch right in. But then Verna was behind the counter, wiping her long fingers on her apron and facing my way. Verna was talking to me after all.

"Funny thing, when you left, Minnie, the tips stayed just about the same. They even went down a bit."

"Oh, okay then."

"You'd think, with one person fewer to divvy them up between that they would've gone up, right? Why would that be, do you think, that they didn't budge a dime?"

It took me a while to get from my smile to Verna's accusation. It was an odd and unexpected calculus.

"Verna, are you suggesting that I skimmed tips? Are you accusing me of *stealing?*"

"I'm not accusing you of anything, Minnie. Only you know what you did."

"Hold on there just a minute, young lady." Joe would be quiet no matter how angry.

"Joe, honestly, it's okay—"

"You are making an accusation, Verna, a real lousy accusation. And you're making a big mistake. This woman *gave* money to you all summer long. As far as I know, she did not take one single tip, let alone what wasn't hers. You, young lady, will be lucky if Minnie accepts your apology because you have just made a damn big unforgettable fool of yourself."

Joe had not shouted, punched or pounded anything. He did not mean to make all the girls cry. Verna's tragedy mask was dead on, a silent grimacing howl that borrowed energy from all the laughs she had kept to herself.

"It's okay, Vee. No big deal, let's forget about it, okay? You didn't know. We'll move on. Water under the bridge."

Verna ran. We heard the kitchen door slam behind her, then we saw her sprinting in her black clogs up the hill towards home, her apron tossed on the sidewalk. Joe went to grab the apron before it started tongues wagging. I asked Debbie to put the pie back in the fridge and please finish off the onions. I told Katelynn and Madison to get the booths bussed and ready for the rush. I put on the apron when Joe returned it, winking goodbye because I was halfway through a phone-in order for fish burgers and fries. Joe mimed handlebars and pointed out back where he was going to stash my bike. Right before eleven Trudy showed up in the miniskirt and an extra large *North Lake Bait & Gas* T-shirt. She apologized for Verna's outburst. Trudy said she had warned Verna that if the tips had not gone up when I left that was probably because I had scored extra big ones when I was around. It was nice to be trusted in the way that women usually trusted me. I told Trudy she was getting one last shift out of me and I'd collect in my own way once the stoves were off. I needed to take her up on her offer to *gab it out*. She let me slip Herman Walker a blueberry muffin à la mode and told Katelynn and Madison to handle all the milkshake orders. *Final guest appearance*, I kept telling the regulars. By Tuck Harbour standards, the tips poured in all day. In the end we decided to put aside my share for Verna.

"So how was the Shack last night?" Trudy and I were dealing with the dish pit while Debbie cleaned the kitchen and the girls tidied up out front with illegal downloads thumping in their ears.

"The Shack was good times, Minnie, thanks for asking. Fib wouldn't let me or Pat pay for a thing. Pat did a couple of Prince songs on the karaoke. It was pretty funny, I've got to say. You should have been there."

"I wouldn't have wanted to glower at anybody."

"C'mon, Minnie. Fib is just a friend." Trudy was scraping hardened dough off the big blades of the industrial mixer. "He's just an old friend. Funny to think of Fib getting old. Guess he'll always have some growing up to do."

"Fibby is incredibly lucky to have a friend like you, I'll say that much." I was sorting clean knives from forks from spoons. "All of us are."

"The thing is, once you're the scum of Tuck Harbour, you don't ever get to not be that. But I just don't think that's fair. At the end of the day, Fibby's an okay guy. He just needs to chill. I hope you can understand that, Minnie. You've got some perspective."

"Yes, I do. Which reminds me, why don't you and Joe get your act together and get together once and for all?"

"Minnie, would you stop with that? Honestly!"

"It makes a lot more sense than anything else that's going on around here."

"Aren't you happy, Minnie, with the way things have turned out?"

We stopped rattling for a moment, Trudy's hands dipped in the dishwater and mine bound up in a dishtowel. "*Have* things turned out, Trudy? Sometimes I worry they haven't and that's largely my fault. Pardon the megalomania."

Trudy shook her head slowly no. Then she faced me dead on.

"Minnie, I admit it. Fibby is more than just a friend. Calm down! I'm not saying how much more, mind you. But he's trying real hard this time. I can't help but feel for him."

"Good for Filbert. A for effort." I went back to whipping clean knives into their correct tray. "Maybe he'll be worth it this time."

"One day he just might be, Minnie."

"Be careful you're not attracted to him just because he's attracted to you. I think that might be Joe's mistake."

"Joe is very good to you, Minnie. That's plain to see. Doesn't that make him good for you as well?"

"Personally, no. I find it terrifying. Pass me the vinegar, these knives still look dirty."

"What are you so scared of?"

"Yes, Joe's wonderful. He's even age appropriate. But I refuse to take him for granted. Probably because I'm frightened he'll do the same thing to me, which could end up really hurting him."

"You're starting to miss Toronto more, aren't you, Minnie?"

"Right now I have no idea what I'm missing." I was finished with the knives and had moved on to spoons. "Don't you worry that you're in it mostly for the sex, Trudes? Besides the friendship, which you can get as well or better from friends and family, and the help, which in all honesty might come quicker and be less burdensome if you paid for it, and the fun, which really isn't all that unadulterated, don't you ever worry that you're just in it for some slam bam, thank you, sir, see you around?"

"God no, Minnie. Sex is a lot of work." Trudy was so tall that she could probably never give up and cling.

"But I like work! Not that I've given Joe a blowjob in, what is it . . . weeks. Not that he's gone down on me since, damn, how long is it since my last . . . Oh God! Trudy, I am *so* sorry. We Toronto broads are trashy maniacs. Shut me up right now."

Trudy was motioning out the dish pit door with her whole head as if a monstrous upper body tic had just set in. She was scarlet all the way down her centre part. "Yes, Minnie, let's just change the subject, shall we? We were just blowing off some steam. We didn't mean any of it, not a word."

I tiptoed to peek into the kitchen. Debbie was right around the corner wiping crumbs off the toaster, her head scrunched between her sloping shoulders. I recalled that Debbie was either Presbyterian or Baptist and made up for missing Sunday service by meeting privately with her pastor. God forbid I had alienated Trudy's chief bottle washer and dough kneader any time before Thanksgiving.

"Trudy, you're absolutely right, I don't know what came over me, but enough of that foolishness! How are your apples looking this year? Rex's are coming along great. Dosie's going to be pleased! Hi, Debbie, can I help you with that? Here, let me plug that in for you. Wow, I can see myself in this toaster, clean, clean, clean!"

I fled my gratuitousness.

I enjoyed my bike ride back to Rex's enough to follow up with a power walk on the beach. The water was nippier than it had been a month before, but still worth removing shoes for, the sand balling up beneath my arches, the jellyfish finally random. When lechery ran out, there would always be walks on the beach. When walks on the beach ran out, there would be little point in anything. Waves were lashing out at my shoes by the time I got back to them. I hobbled barefoot through Dosie's spiky pasture and hung my sneakers up by their tongues. I ate leftover guacamole for dinner, scooped up with a row of saltines. I fished the pits out of the bowl—Desolée had taught me to leave them in to avoid browning—and sucked them clean. I ate another row of crackers with crab-apple jelly for dessert, spooning the jam out of the jar with my finger, which I had to keep licking clean. It was just what I had wanted: a salt fix followed by a sugar crash.

Monday morning, bright and Toronto early, I leaped from bed, charged full of purpose. I needed to catch up on email and then surf the Web for information about property inheritance taxes. But someone had decided otherwise. Someone had made it their mission to profoundly disconcert me. So I discovered when I opened the back door to test the morning breeze while the kettle gurgled. I stepped right back inside to call Joe. I said to come over immediately, not to ask why, just to come. He soon did.

"Joe, I didn't move a thing. Take a look." I pointed to the dead fish deposited on my back doorstep, the very middle of the middle step. "I'm lucky I didn't wake up with Dosie's head in my bed!"

I'd had no idea there was a Tuck Harbour mafia so symboli-cally at work. Unless Verna's little brothers were taking things out on me on her behalf? I was sure I gave them the creeps by being forty. I had once heard one of them call me *witchy-poo*.

"What's the drama now, Minnie?"

"Gosh, Joe, the drama, unfortunately, is that someone has put a dead fish on my doorstep in a cheap attempt to insult and intimi-date me. Word sure travels fast around here, doesn't it?"

"That it does, I'll agree with you there. People like repeating what they've picked up."

"Someone is mad that Rex gave me the house because I don't really belong here? That's got to be it, right? I'm from away and kind of hated?"

"No, that's not it."

Joe had no business looking me over so clinically. I was hon-estly frightened, looking forward to an opportunity to be honestly angry. Meanwhile he was staring at me like *I* needed to be figured out, examining well past my charms to my inevitabilities.

"Damn it, Joe. Tell me what you know!"

"I know that no human being left this fish here for you."

"Great, Rex's house is haunted by a ghost with smelly fingers, is that what you're trying to say?"

"What I'm trying to tell you, what you dragged me over here to say, is that a gull dropped its breakfast on your doorstep. Not on purpose, mind you. I wouldn't take it personal."

Joe bent to grab the evidence, holding it as casually as a lawyer holds a piece of waste paper. Now that I saw the fish for itself I took in its astonishing silver. Its lidless eyes wore an expression of huge alarm, but perhaps it had no other way to look. With belated re-spect, I reached out to pet it. It was weirdly dry.

"Shit, I'm sorry, Joe. I thought it had something to do with Verna. I found that whole scene rather upsetting yesterday."

I gathered the doorstep was as close as we were going to get to being inside together.

"Not as upsetting as Verna did."

"What do you mean?"

"Debbie was over at my mother's this morning, telling her all kinds of things. Seems that Verna up and left for Montreal, the 6 a.m. flight through Halifax. She's going to shack up with a school friend for now and start school in the new year. Buddy Donovan is doing some training there over the winter so that will be good company for her. Archie's going to drive her car out there as soon as herring is done. Or he'll get Pat to do it on his way back to Alberta."

"Alberta?"

"Looks like it, now that he'll have enough money for first and last."

"Wow." Verna had left me the Harbour so I supposed I could give her Montreal and Patrick could take the tar sands. "This is all good news."

"I'm glad you're happy, Minnie. It's important to be happy when you get a chance."

Joe had spoken my name again, finally, a small way of owning me. We were at his truck door. He was touching the truck. I pulled my cardigan tighter around my nightgown and stepped from one foot to the other in the chilly grass.

"Will I be seeing you anytime soon, Joe?"

"Busy days coming up. We've got to get the herring deck put on the boat and every damn MP in this province wants to have a word with me all of a sudden. No one but the seiners wants the seiners up here. No more fisticuffs up at the Souris wharf if I can help it, our guys punching out their crews every time they unload. That'll take some doing."

Joe was avoiding me. It was the first time so it was obvious, avoiding me in the way that no woman can stomach and every woman tries to rectify.

"Can I come fishing with you next week, Joe?" Halted in his tracks while the balance of power tip, tippy, tip, tipped in his direction.

"Quota'll take longer than that to get fished, Minnie. No hurry."

"But I want to go before it gets cold. It's a full moon next Wednesday. You promised!"

"Okay then, if the weather's good and you're still into the idea." Loyal to Joe, the truck started up with a healthy hack.

"I will be, Joe, guaranteed. Bye for now!"

It turned out to be one of those mornings when I skipped breakfast because I was not convinced I deserved the sustenance. I chose coffee over tea. I switched on my laptop and scuttled in spirit to Upper Canada. Barry was happy to hear from me. We sent a spate of emails back and forth to track our latest brainstorm. Plans for the live finale were coalescing nicely. The Viagra knock-off was indeed sponsoring a call-in vote and the network had sprung for a dedicated website. Couples were getting engaged coast to coast; summer was enough fooling around now that the cash prize was in sight. The ex-nun and vintner had obliged. This was destination viewing, of that I was convinced. *Marry Me or Else!* or else. So I belligerently told the view when I eventually looked out the window. No whales, but whitecaps clean as snow. Dosie ambled by and nodded yes to the breeze before groping for grass. She did not need hay yet, but she would before long. If there was another hot day I would give her a hose down, both a comfort and a humiliation from Dosie's point of view.

Things were going as well as could be hoped at Myriad, but anxiety was still percolating in my brain stem and dripping into my aorta. Joe's diffidence earlier in the day got more irritating the more I remembered of it. He could have gone ahead and laughed off the whole ridiculous fish thing. Instead he had dealt with me at a minimum and grumped off. Well, now I had some breathing room. Granted, more than expected, but it was still up to me to fill it with quality activity. I knew what I needed to do before I was reduced to picking up *Anne of Avonlea*: I would have Ralph and Felicity over for lunch. I could show off the property they had cheered to see me inherit. And I could relax among allies.

"Yellow," Ralph answered.

The next thing we knew hospitality was scheduled at my place for the following day. I defrosted a loaf of harvest bread and got to work on a pot of curried squash soup. If it was sunny I would make lemonade in the pink pitcher. I set my alarm for early the next morning to mow, no matter how much that angered Dosie. The moment she heard the chopping whine, she trudged to the edge of her field; Dosie had long-suffering down pat. Joe still needed to see to that loose fence railing. That would be one way to get him over during herring. It was a Gulliver delight when Ralph and Felicity promptly arrived in a subcompact. Ralph honked out their arrival even though I was right there to greet them. He bounced out of the car like Silly Putty.

"Wow, I had no idea Rex had traded in one manor for another."

"Hardly. Although the view is quite good."

"Ya, I guess you can kind of see the sea from here. Sort of, maybe."

Felicity grabbed a grocery bag from the back seat against my instructions to bring nothing. "Minnie, this is incredible!"

Meek landscape artists might have felt taunted, but Ralph and Felicity were drinking it all in. The few clouds were moving on to snoop elsewhere. The grass bowed in the water's direction. The sun was paying special attention to this hundred-odd square miles. A bird actually tweeted.

"Welcome, you two. Thanks for coming."

"We brought baps and dolce de lecherous ice cream, Fizz insisted. She's into comfort foods. Do you think maybe I don't satisfy her?"

"Ralphie, honestly!"

Felicity knew I *got* Ralph and that she did not really need to dread whatever he was going to say next. In full letting-it-all-hang-out mode—something that having elderly relatives at the same nursing facility seemed to inspire—I told the two of them about the fish on the doorstep incident.

"That's not as crazy as you might think." Ralph grabbed a soft roll and cold cider. "Mafias all over the world are involved in fishing. The Casa Nostra is deep into Italian tuna farms. Taiwanese mafia control illegal shark fishing in Central America. Not to mention all the tribal leaders in unstable African countries selling off fishing rights to the EU. Fizz, will you be the designated driver please? I feel like getting afternoon toasty."

"I don't know how you two find the strength to keep researching everything that's gone so wrong."

Felicity puckered. She had gone straight for lemonade and was smart enough to hydrate before she ate. "Imagine if Nobu served panda steaks, that's what Ralph always says."

"Or mountain gorilla."

I stirred the soup just short of boiling. "Nothing suspect for lunch today, cross my heart."

"Hey, Fizz, why doesn't our new friend chuck in TV and come join the cause? Help us avert World War Three, Minnie, when the south barely has any fish left either and the north still wants protein."

"Could it come to that?" I ladled fragrant, steaming orange into three china bowls. I loved feeding friends and Rex's kitchen was such a great place to do so.

"Let me put it to you this way, lovely Minnie. Industrial fishing is probably the single most destructive thing that humans have ever done. *Bon appétit, mademoiselles.*"

"Thanks. By the way, I'm not much of a *mademoiselle*. I think I'm a bit too elderly for that."

"What are you then?" Ralph was darkening a long row of crackers with olive tapenade. "What's your genus, Minnie?"

"We better figure out something!" Felicity was so young that cream still seemed to go straight to her cheeks, deepening her dimple.

"I've got it . . ." For all his uproariousness, Ralph never spoke with his mouth full, Sally having drilled table manners so deep into his mother that they had likely kept on going. "Miss Minnie is a sylph."

"A what?" Felicity looked like she might be willing to kick her fiancé under the table after all.

"Minnie is an S-I-L-F."

"What's that?"

I would let Ralph say it.

"Spinster I'd Like to F word. Not that *I* would. Sorry, Minnie, but Fizz and I are everything to each other. I can only ever toy with you."

Felicity and I rolled eyeballs at each other, with velocity on my part. Then we tucked in energetically to our second helpings and butterscotch gelato. I absolutely had to walk the beach after lunch. The young scientists came with me, distributing Latin names for shells and seaweeds. I hated to send them back to their Charlotte-town hotel. I offered to put them up, but they thought the better of it.

"I snore," Ralph explained. "So it would be less embarrassing, actually, if you came and stayed with us."

"Maybe I should. Joe is busy with herring six nights a week come Saturday."

"Poor Minnie, you're like a fish without a bicycle."

I was impressed that Ralph's references extended to Gloria Steinem. He bounced into the car as well as out.

"Actually, I've got a bicycle. It's parked behind the barn."

"This place has everything!" Felicity beamed. I liked how the better she knew me, the more she had to say.

"Come back any time, Felicity, and bring Ralph if you must."

Friday morning, Etta picked me up at Rex's house. She was going to drop me off in Montague before taking the kids shopping for sharp new pencils in new plaid pencil cases and tops and pants that fit.

"Grade one, grade fun, grade bun," Joan was singing in the middle row. "Soon we're going to be in grade one."

"Grade BUM!" Bette suggested.

"Grade FART YOUR BUM-BUM!"

"Can it, you two little vipers." Etta's orders.

Pierre and Elliot were quiet in the back with the latest issue of *Owl* magazine fresh out of the mailbox spread across their knees. I had learned to expect Elliot to want all of my attention or none of it. He was not going to be getting many back-to-school clothes of his own; Pierre had gained a whole head on him over the summer. When Etta pulled up to the Manor to drop me off, the kids were outraged. Sometimes I wondered whether they thought of me as a spare kid, as more child than childless.

"Minnie's got an uncle just like you guys and she cares about him a lot," Etta hollered into the rear-view mirror. "Give her a break, would yas?"

"Rex cares about us a lot, too, right?"

"That he does. And Minnie is going to say hi for you, Pierre-o."

"Minnie cares about our uncle a lot, too."

Etta loved this. "Good point, sonny boy!"

"Yes, El, I do. I try to care about *everyone* a lot."

"Minnie, do you care about POO a lot?!"

"Later for you, crazies."

Elliot's nose was back in his magazine by the time they drove away. I thought maybe he should trounce brainy Pierre's destiny and be the one to head to the big city. I would gladly guide him when it came to Toronto.

"Minnie, dear, here you are!" Rex was twirling his cane like a wagged tail. "I seen Etta pull up out front and I thought, there's my girl."

It was early enough in the day for Rex to go without his wheelchair, but I hated to see him so out of breath. They were his breaths, of course; how he chose to spend them was his business. I just hated how they were now as easy to hear as to see. Rex was still in summer garb, his bandy legs bare to the breeze. Everybody's birthday socks were getting their fair shake.

"Uncle Rex, you could have waited in your room!"

"I could have, but I didn't."

"Now that you're up, let's go see Sally."

Sally had probably heard all about Ralph and Felicity's lunch visit, and she had probably told Rex everything, but I wasn't going to spare them my version of the event.

"Ralph and Felicity love it at the Harbour."

"So they should." Sally would be crisp to her dying day. I gently rolled her further into a sunbeam.

"When exactly is their wedding, Sally, do you know?"

"Next summer, so they say. It's up to them. I told them there was no point rushing things in this day and age."

"I've been thinking we should offer our place as the venue, Uncle Rex. Would you like that? Trudy could cater."

"Minnie, dear, it's up to you. You do as you like."

"I just think it would be such a nice thing to see. Don't you agree, Sally?"

"They haven't been hinting, have they?"

"Not a bit. The notion is all mine. I'm still cooking it up really. I wanted to run it by you two first. I didn't want to put them on the spot."

"There is no harm in asking, Minerva, there rarely is. There's usually only harm in not asking. Why people lack the courage to do so is beyond me."

Sally turned to Rex, but he had other fish to fry.

"Time was I thought I might be seeing you or your cousin getting married out here, Minnie."

"I'm sorry, Uncle Rex. It's not laziness, I promise." I had not held Rex's hand so much since the summer I was seven.

"Leave the poor young woman alone. They see things differently nowadays and they do them differently, too. Not that you ever got married yourself, mark you."

"Why is that, Uncle Rex? Do you mind me asking?"

"I don't find it easy to get lonely, you see. And I thought that might make a woman lonely. It seemed to."

Sally's suite was a bit smaller than Rex's, but truth can fit anywhere.

"Anyone in particular you'd care to mention, Uncle Rex?"

"Good for you, Minerva. Ask away." This from Sally.

"There was one special lady, but I can't say it's much worth going into. She didn't like my jaunts out West and I wasn't about to stop those. Jacqueline was her name. She was dainty to look at, but pretty fierce when it came to speaking her mind, that one. She wanted to live in town; she liked a good tea dance. She wanted to get married there, too, at the Armoury, with chicken à la king in *vol-au-vents* for supper. She married some fellow from Tignish in the end and moved out that way and had six children and sixteen grandchildren. I always got a Christmas card until she passed, three years ago now. Jack, her fella's name was. She liked that, Jack and Jacquie. That's how she signed the cards."

"Oh, Rex."

"Your uncle chose to do as he wanted, Minerva. As we all tend to do once we figure out what we want. Would either of you like a peppermint? Why people bring old folks mints all the time I do not know. I never could stand them."

Rex declined so I was stuck accepting. "Mints are good preparation for a kiss, Sally."

"No wonder I can't be bothered with them. You two are going to have to leave me alone now. I need my nap or I'll be a mess, I know that much. I will see you at supper, Rex, which I look forward to as usual."

I helped Rex to his feet and out the door. Then I turned back to help Sally to her bed. "To thine own self be true," I tried.

"Very Delphic, Minerva. Your namesake would approve."

"I'm no goddess of wisdom. I don't know what my mother was thinking."

"She was surely thinking that there is no harm in aiming high." Sally clutched at my forearms as she rose from her chair to pivot to her bed. "Minerva was also the goddess of art and war, don't forget."

"Art and war? That sounds like television to me."

"Then why don't you add some of your wisdom to your art and your war and do the kind of television you really want to, my Minerva?"

My warrior self had been slumbering, that much was obvious, because she was awake now, addled but roused. Soon she would be ravenous for inspiration; she craved labours of love. "Sally, I will, thank you. You make me feel like I can."

No matter what production I moved along to, Sally would have to provide regular feedback. I was looking forward to filling my speed dial with Maritime area code 902. Long distance was going to resume its excitement.

"Thank you for helping me get settled, Minerva, dear. Now go find your uncle before he keels over."

I left Sally's door ajar so Doris could glance in. I found Rex in his room setting up the checkerboard. Desolée used to get angry at the way Rex would never let us win, but I loved his clean play because it meant that I could gloat when victorious. I conquered five times in a row with a lot of pirate laughter on my part. Then we telephoned Toronto and BC. We left Desolée a message, a long one that would drive her crazy, but Lee and Gail were both available. Lee showered me with more encouragement to make the most of things. Gail let me know that her lawyer would find me a real estate lawyer, but what did I prefer, a Toronto lawyer or a Charlottetown lawyer? I hardly knew. "Toronto then," Gail decided. As usual, we did not ask about each other's gentlemen callers. I tried not to bump Gail off the phone yet again, but I wanted to get back to Rex before Etta scooped me away.

Doris stopped by to plump Rex's pillows before she left for the day. She made a point of asking after Joe.

"Joe is fine as far as I know." No doubt Joe was forced to report on my health, too. I could almost hear him say it: *Minnie's good.*

On the way back to the Harbour Etta reported that Joe and Colin were still putting in the extra deck they needed to store each net load of herring below. "Just in time, the nincompoops. It's all that Association business of Joe's keeps him so stretched."

"It's good for him, though, all the responsibility. He loves it."

"Joe's got a talent for shovelling the bullshit, if that's what you mean."

"Mama, you said bullsh—"

"Hush and count your new pencil crayons. It's a fright what Joe deals with. My husband couldn't deal with all that crapola, I'll give him that. Colin wouldn't play nice if you paid him."

"I just hope the fishing around here lasts."

"I waste no love on fishing, Minnie. Herring's a bitch. Colin doesn't much love it either. He does it because it's there to do, but he'd just as soon do something else. It's Joe who's got it in the blood."

"I'm going out with them on Wednesday night."

"Dress warm, you could be out there until dawn. Fishermen's Bank, they call it. Some bank. Want to come to dinner, Minnie? I'm sure Elliot will let you sit beside him. Pierre can take Daddy's place; he won't be home for ages."

I got roped into bedtime-story duty, one picture book per kid on rotating beds, the kid whose bed it was flipping the page, but not until everyone had taken a good look. Back downstairs, I had a cup of lemon tea with Etta while we waited for the kids to doze. Etta wanted me to see the way they sneaked into each other's beds and arms. Sure enough we heard pitter-patter and then calm. I loved the sight of their twined little limbs, their cheeks hot with each other's breath, twin with twin, love coming as naturally as consciousness. I expected wonderful things for Etta's children, as I did my best to whisper on my way downstairs and out the door. So much full-fledged optimism felt odd, almost an out-of-body experience. On my own behalf, I bargained for no more than one or two best-case scenarios per year at best. "Everything is going to work out just fine," I said aloud to myself on the way back from Etta's house to mine, mostly for the wry laugh that followed. The fields were ridiculously dark.

13

Early Wednesday evening—sunshine still glinting everywhere like a bargain jewellery department—I set out from Rex's place to the crows' distress and Dosie's indifference. The wind was ornery so it was hard biking. That was minor insistence compared to the major insistence it had taken to get Joe's permission to go out fishing as scheduled. The night was rough around its first edge, maybe rough all the way through. I made it to the wharf on time but winded. All the boat decks were now built up so high that there were barely railings and what railings there were looked spindly. I parked my bike behind a stack of traps, caught my breath and wended over to the *Darling Dolly*. I hopped on board without a helping hand. Joe looked happy to see me, our good old flammability in action. Then a breeze bullied its way between us. I quickly climbed on top of the cabin to take in the activity, wharf wide.

Immediately, there was a lot of teasing about Joe's new *decorative fixture*. Herring season lacked feminine influence. Joe and Colin fished so well together that they did not need a third man. I thought that was probably Joe's way to do his brother another favour—the labour and profit divided as tightly as possible between them. Colin and Joe were not tall men, but they enjoyed lengthy arm spans.

Every net full of herring would have to be winched on board and then shaken empty before it could get dropped overboard again: literal tons of fish fins, heads and tails stuck in the yards of mesh. No matter how much technology was at work, the inshore fishery still demanded something primitive of its manpower; from my point of view that was the thrill. Ralph had told me that if everyone who fished actually had to touch a fish to do so, the industry would manage fine.

"Hey, Minnie, are you going to help out tonight? Show these fellows how it's done?"

Freak had called over from Archie's boat. Patrick was on board the *Little Verna* as well, hustling to earn his cut. Archie was notoriously dead set on meeting the daily limit and rarely went home without it: 15,000 pounds or bust. Nonetheless, Arch was a captain who loved a cockpit and that was where he was staying put.

"Forget that, I'm not helping out with a thing. I'm a goddamn vegetarian!"

That was my good-sport crack of the night over with. I was not going to give in to the crowd and holler much or often. The truth was, I was dreading the way the little fish heads were going to be ripped from their bodies, and the *rat-a-tat-tat* of their flaps to death as their fluid world thinned and hardened. I did not want to die in sin and come back as a herring—captured, pickled, kippered or schmaltzed, sardined into a tin or smoked. I did not want to be dragged, red, across a path to throw off bloodhounds. I was dreading fish Armageddon. But I dreaded not being a part of it even more.

First came the call to battle. It was going to take sixteen miles of slap-happy cruising to get to where the action was. One by one the Tuck Harbour fleet was ready to rumble. We were all headed to the same place, the herring shoal at its densest, shot full of boats, the *city out on the sea*. I was looking forward to seeing whales gather like township dogs. Joe was looking forward to watching his sounder fill up with prosperous pink. It was fishing-boat rush hour, hallowed and inexorable.

As soon as we made it out of the harbour Colin offered me mixed nuts and cookies from the collection of snacks that had accreted on the bridge. I took one of Etta's oatmeal-raisins. She used a mix and added cinnamon, but I was the only one who was the wiser. Joe had power bars, but he knew better than to offer me a bite of cheap chocolate finessed with health. He had pulled on a sweater while the engine was idling, a crewneck frayed at the wrists that was such a bright shade of green it made his eyes look like olive lightbulbs. I left the brothers to their dashboard ways and stuck my head around the edge of the cabin from where I could taste spray and watch Tuck Point retreat. Someone had invited the moon out for sure; it was on high, white as a raw pie against the draining blue.

I waved over at Fibby when he overtook us. Fibby saluted back, his Popeye forearms bare in the wind. Two of Fibby's Souris buddies were fishing with him now, guys who knew Fib Trask as the braggadocio sort of go-getter with whom it paid to be associated. I could see how over on Archie's boat Patrick might be missing Fibby's endless excitement about things. The last I had seen of Patrick, he had been down on his knees scrubbing a mere hour before Archie's deck would be running with blood.

Joe looked over his shoulder at about the halfway mark and ordered me into a life jacket. The waves were like a steeplechase circuit. When I checked to make sure there was a spare vest available, Joe told me not to be silly and to grab the thing from the forward hold. It was not hard to find, burning chemical orange in the cramped dark. The life jacket smelled of hardworking man and cupboard. It rubbed loudly against my windbreaker if I moved my arms. No one else was wearing one. To be polite I pulled the straps tight, although with one big wave I would have been sucked right out of the thing. My fingertips were puce with cold already. It wasn't freezing out, but I was guilty of poor circulation.

When land was as good as gone in every direction, the whales showed up. Thirty-odd boats were zooming back and forth in the watery middle of nowhere and in between them, big, gleaming grey backs rose out of the water, crested and then submerged. It was nature-show perfection; I almost wanted a soundtrack and to see it in slow motion. The whales were scooping jawfuls of herring before the nets could snatch it all, the seagulls screaming in fury to watch. I had to work hard to spot the whales because their immensity was so casual. First I would hear a hissing sigh, the sort of noise one might make to indicate an irritated *beats me*. Then I would smell fish. For the whales it was just another night on the shoal with boat bottoms to contend with. For Joe and Colin it was time to knuckle down. For me it was provocation to be grateful: to Greenpeace for moratoriums on whale hunting, to Rex for bringing me east, to Joe for bringing me fishing and to myself for my capacity for adventure.

Joe was captaining the boat as deftly as a barrel racer, slamming into a halt whenever Colin needed help in the back. All night long, they were going to be in and out of their oilskins—net up, net shaken free of bloodied fish until the deck was ankle deep in them, fish swept below into storage bins, then overpants off, boat rammed into a new position, net down again. Everybody's work ethic was in place; I was the only tick without tock. Consensus had it that the night was too rough to fill up with more than 10,000 pounds. Archie got some ribbing over the radio for that. By midnight, the brothers' necks and faces were flecked with fish gore. They had herring blood in their eyebrows and probably in their lungs.

I stuck to the cabin while there was action on deck and to the starboard railing when the men were back in the cabin. The waves were continuing bronco, but my stomach held steady. There would be no going inshore now, not without ruining Joe's profits for the night and my reputation as a contender. I could see how addictive the routine would become, how Joe and Colin could never quite be sure how net would compare with net, but the gaining poundage kept them going when their arms, legs, backs and shoulders ached to hell, the more ache the better. The boats were all lit up like stages. The moon was a floodlight now, splashing glow down on the water.

It was hard to believe it was not our moon alone, that we were not the only ones out in the night doing something worth its interest.

"Last dump, Minnie," Colin told me by 2:30 a.m. "We'll haul this sucker up, then it's back to the wharf."

"Sounds good." I was still trying to be all eyes and no mouth.

Joe was not talking much either, at least not to me. "Rogue wave'll hit if we're still out here in an hour's time, guaranteed."

Colin agreed. "Look at Arch. He's listing, the asshole. One wave in that hold and he's down with Davy."

Everyone seemed to be working even faster, stalking their decks with the zombie gait that pitching induced. Fibby's boat was bobbing alongside Joe's, stern to stern with Archie's. Fibby and his guys were shaking out their last net of the night like it was a schoolyard game they would win if they just stuck with it. Joe and Colin were sweeping their last stiff, little, silvery fish below, with stained brooms they would never want to use for anything else. In true jackass fashion, it looked like Archie had decided to drop his net one last time. But then a small chunk of mesh got caught in his propeller. I could tell from the reaction on board that this was unwelcome but not unheard of. Patrick leaned over the stern to pull things loose before the *Little Verna* blew a gasket. I could see it all happening from Joe's deck when I stood up. Patrick grabbed at the lead rope and tugged, hard and then harder. It worked—the prop spat out the net and the boat jerked free. But inside that jerk, as a result of that jerk, Patrick sailed through the air in a perfect, diagrammatic arc and plunged into a trough between two four-foot waves as if he had been aiming for it.

I screamed, a curdled soprano with the red of my gullet in it.

Archie looked over at me, then back at his stern and slammed down on his throttle, his belly fat against the wheel.

"The rope, Joe, Joe, Patrick's got a hold of the rope!"

I prayed that was good. Because Patrick was going to surface any second brandishing the rope that would keep him attached to Archie's net until he was hauled on deck. There was no way for him to climb on board, no ladders built off the sides of fishing boats for water sports. Freak threw a life preserver where he thought Patrick would reappear. Joe rushed to back up closer to Archie and one of Fibby's guys did the same. Still Patrick did not surface. Colin shoved Joe's net back overboard as something extra for him to grab a hold of. I took off my life jacket and flung it. Freak was bent over Archie's stern with a spotlight, then Colin had another.

"His foot's stuck. He's caught under!"

That was all Fibby needed to hear.

Fibby hopped onto his railing, paused for an instant, and then dove like a gannet into the roiling spume. Upside down like this, Fibby made perfect sense. His boots thrashed at the surface while he tore down the net like a man battling a monster. Here was the task that Fibby's brute force had been waiting for all his life, the test his bare hands had been born into. In a meaningful yet measureless amount of time Fibby ripped Patrick free. He burst above the water with Patrick tucked onto his chest in standard lifeguard procedure. Patrick looked pale and pummelled.

"Over here!" Colin yelled.

Fibby swam our way. I scuttled down the stern to see Fibby clench Patrick between his knees, grab hold of Joe's lead rope and give a *let's go*. Patrick was curled up like a shrimp. Joe and Colin winched the two of them as high out of the water as they could, then the brothers reached down to grab hold of Fibby's underarms and Patrick's knees. They hauled so hard they danced, taking trembling backwards baby steps, then a final stumble. Fibby and Patrick thudded onto Joe's deck like something born in great veterinarian struggle. I rolled Patrick onto his back, ready to pinch his nose and place my lips on his. He was shaking and blue-lipped and obviously clammy beneath the soaking, but he was conscious.

"I didn't sleep with your daughter." We all knew Patrick meant this for Archie. Archie's boat was now rollicking alongside Joe's.

"That doesn't matter, Patrick." I squeezed his wet hand like it was a bellows.

"I'm gay. Verna is in love with that golfer guy. She's just scared he's a player."

"Don't worry about any of that right now, dear. *C'est la vie*, eh?" This was Fibby in his shirtsleeves, incapable of a single goose bump. "Love and learn, right? That's what you're always telling me, bro."

"It's supposed to be live and learn, but Ma always liked to get that wrong."

"Joe, what do you say we get this guy to a hospital? Just in case, Paddy. Put our minds at rest or we'll thump ya one. Me first."

Joe made straight for Souris where there was a small emergency department. I wrapped Patrick in a blanket, rested his head in my lap and fed him half a bottle of fresh water. He wondered if he was seasick for the first time in his life, but otherwise regretted only his lost boot. I offered to go with him all the way to Souris General, but Fibby wanted to take him.

Joe filled up the tank and we chugged off once more, this time into twinkly black. Contrary to Joe's predictions, the wind had calmed and the waves along with it. We all stuck to the cabin; Colin and Joe on their stools, me squeezed behind the table with my arms tight around my legs. Every question that came to my mind was too large or small to pose. Joe's focus was all on the wheel. Our life-saving high had worn off already. Colin tossed in the odd remark here and there—about the almanac's thoughts on the autumn weather, or the chances that the buyer would wait for us at the wharf until we got in. So much for Fib Trask being a total asshole, Colin had never thought he was all that bad a guy. And who would have guessed that Patrick was gay?

"Should we tell Archie?" Colin wondered.

I had a useful suggestion. "I know, why not tell Debbie? She blabs everything to everyone, right?"

That plucked Joe's glance from the black waves.

"Debbie has a habit of passing along what she hears, you're right there, Minnie. Some of it is hard to ignore."

My blabbed confession to Trudy about my potential nympho-mania must have served Debbie as quite the headline, perhaps massaged by her pastor into a handy object lesson in the evils of hedonism. Joe was looking at me less like a curiosity and more like an adversary. I would have congratulated him on his new cool if I had not been so cold.

"Remember, gentlemen, gossip is the first resort of the under-class."

That shut everyone up. I said no more for forty nautical miles. In a way I did not want dawn to come in case the night was going to get even more gruesome upon recollection. I wanted to make it to Joe's house while it was still dark and then empty my bowels, put on a pair of his pyjamas and lie down with him somewhere clean and motionless. The ground crew were waiting for us when we pulled up to the wharf. A youth with a dockside joystick saw to it that Joe's full tubs were hauled up and weighed and then another man shuttled the fish into the plant while a big guy with a clipboard jotted down the numbers that counted. Colin hosed the hold clean while Joe talked price. As soon as we berthed, Colin took off, with several juicy stories worth waking Etta up early for. I crawled onto the wharf and went to get my bike. Then Joe and I were alone in the parking lot. My gaze squirmed while his went what he knew to be east, or south.

"Quite the night, Minnie."

"No kidding."

Of course, Joe rarely kidded. He did not giggle or tickle; he took everyone seriously.

"I hope you're not thinking of riding that thing home?"

"God, no. Let's go to your place."

"I thought I would drop you off at Rex's."

The bike was out of my hands before I could protest. It was not an easy night to let anything go. Once upon a time, Joe had stashed my bike in the back of his truck with obvious care, now he just chucked it up there with the spare anchor and a spool of rope.

"Joe, tell me what's wrong. Go ahead and be surgical. Dig right in."

"We better leave things for now, Minnie. It's been a rough night and it's going to be a long day tomorrow."

There were all kinds of things that I wanted to fight out in the wharf parking lot, vaguely bathed in one of Tuck Harbour's few streetlights. But I was not the one who had to go fishing again in fourteen hours. I did not have to go out fishing again ever.

"At least let me drive. Keys, please."

"Minnie, it's too dark."

"No, it isn't. Look, it's dawn." The sky was cracking pink. "Come on, Joe. You wanted to teach me how to drive this summer and you did. Congratulations, I can drive. So let me drive."

No answer but the toss of Joe's key ring, heavy and sharp into my palm. I clenched their points and edges while I got into the truck, then my door and Joe's door *bang-bang*ed, shutting out the day's first *cheep*s. The birds seemed surprised to have us there. I found the car key and inserted it. I switched on the headlights, released the parking brake, depressed the clutch and reversed. A bit too fast; I braked, shifted to drive and turned up Main Street. Now I could step on the gas. I made it up the Tuck Harbour hill without problems or commentary. The little white churches had fought off their fear of the dark for another night. Main Street gave way to outskirts in a minute.

Joe was right; there was little to be said while the chilly fields played dead. Whatever we were going to discuss merited the clarity of an otherwise empty hour with some warmth going for it. Rex's place was not far off; there was mist in the hollows but I could tell from the way the road had straightened we were on the final stretch. I shifted down into second. Joe had switched on the heat in the truck and I felt it spreading upwards: nice for my knees, but too late for my hands. Still, it bore some promise of mercy. At any moment, at just the right moment, I could release my foot from the gas to turn and coast neatly into Rex's lane. If I arrived with enough chauffeur precision maybe Joe would stay overnight. We would wake up together bathed in forgetfulness. Then we could fuck like bonobos. Dutifully, I flicked on the turn signal; Joe was absolutely right about that, too: one had to follow the rules of the road no matter how empty the road. I was wondering if there was a polite way to commend him on all this when I caught sight of Dosie, not at all where she should have been.

Dosie was on the road, Dosie was right in my path. I saw her expression of dignified wonder in the headlights—her ears swivelled forward, her nose flared. Here was the world beyond her fence in all its enchantment and peril. I braked hard and heard the reactive clatter of Dosie's hooves. She veered to my left, I swerved to the right in a hot, squealing skid that was the second unforgettable scream of the night. Dosie provided the third. I managed to miss her forequarters, but I slammed into her hindquarters. Angry airbags exploded while the windshield shattered and the hood succumbed. I dragged Dosie along beside us for a grotesque couple of seconds and then I drove over her hind legs. The truck hit the ditch and halted. Joe and I took a second to blink glass from our eyelids and blow it from our lips. Then I punched at the airbag and tore at my seatbelt and pounded open the dented door. Glass tinkled, sliding off my lap and sleeves. I heard moans, one moan right after another, each with a sad, pained chuckle in it.

"Dosie!"

She was quivering. A haunch bone had torn through her skin and both of her hind legs were broken, one of them hanging by sinew. Her left front knee was split open like it had been axed. Her hide had been skinned off in ragged sheaves and there was more blood leaking out of her mouth. Her massive tongue was flopped out on the road. Dosie's eyes were far more alive to all this than nature ought to have seen fit. Possibly, she no longer had the strength to blink. I wept to see her as anyone would, the crows shrieking along with me. Joe was on his phone, pacing, dealing. "No, we're okay as far as I can tell . . . ASAP obviously . . . The horse is bad, hopeless . . . Will do."

"Dosie, I'm so sorry, girl, I'm so sorry," I whispered, now the only way to be gentle. Confused, Dosie half nickered back, like I was not the wretch who had just botched her execution, like we always met in the middle of the road. There was a horse and there was paralysis and it was awful the way the two things now went together.

"Listen up, Minnie. The police can't make it for about half an hour. You're going to have to wait here for a second. I'm sorry you have to be alone."

"I'm not alone, Dosie's here! Oh God, Dosie, I am so sorry. Please die, girl. Please, please die."

Joe thudded off. Dosie was gargling on stained foam. I kneeled over her head to keep the morning sun out of her eyes. Daylight was turning her blood from grey to red. Blood was coursing over the pavement in tributaries and sludging into the dirt beside the road. I stroked Dosie's head where I hoped she did not hurt. She was panting now, each breath making her groan. I prayed the pain was too mammoth to kick in, to ever kick in. Joe came running back with Colin and his hunting gun. When fishing was over Colin went after wild birds.

"Minnie, my dear, we've got to put this horse out of her misery. One last farewell and then we're good to go."

"No!"

Colin was handling the wretched gun like it was an umbrella in Mayfair. "This horse is in too much pain to live. You know that."

"Joe has to do it. I need you to do it, Joe, please!"

"Okay, Minnie. Just give me a second here."

Dosie was beyond following any of our actions and needs. I bent to kiss her giant, soft, red head goodbye—her nice long cheek, her slab of brow, her furry ears, her pretty mane. Dosie's inability to acknowledge any of this allowed me to back away. Really, she was already gone; she was shredded. I wanted to pat shut her massive eyes but I was appalled at the thought of frightening her any more than she already was and of angering the brothers by fussing. So I doubled over and cried as if I was hurling. My sobs chopped through the morning air in rough hacks. Joe conferred quietly with his brother over a few last details, then marched over to Dosie, aimed and fired. She jolted and then sank even flatter to the road. I smelled hot metal, blood and horse shit. Her brow was punctured now, and singed; she was dead in every way.

"Pull yourself together, Minnie." Joe patted me with one hand with the gun still in the other. He swivelled us around so I could cry into Rex's empty green fields. I could still see our bloody boot tracks intersecting.

When the young Mountie pulled up he told us that he had heard the gunshot from the other side of the Harbour. He also said that Joe and I were very lucky because horses generally crack like eggs. If I had hit Dosie dead on she would have gone careening onto the hood and exploded into the cabin, smothering us to death. The Mountie would see to it that transport and public works came to *dispose* of the carcass right away. I stonily agreed to that.

"That's good, right, Minnie?" Joe was attempting comfort.

"I suppose." I was not yet brave enough to take comfort or give it.

We filed the accident report, the forms belligerent in their need of facts without nuance. The Mountie's Ottawa Valley accent was raw in my ears. It was the first time my licence was scrutinized in this way, but I could not say that I cared. I thought if anyone congratulated me for good driving under difficult circumstances, I would slap them. Joe laid a blue plastic tarp over Dosie's corpse that didn't quite cover her. The Mountie was waiting for the clean-up crew before he signed-off on the *incident*. "The animal was dispatched at the scene," I heard him say to his radio and then the radio reiterated the information in a female deadpan. Colin towed Joe's truck into his lane. Joe called his insurance company, then asked me if I wanted to get checked for injuries because we had twenty-four hours in which to do so. I said that I was fine and please not to push me, to please leave me alone. Colin told me I was welcome to come over and have a word with Etta, but I said I needed to call Rex before he found out what had happened from someone else. It was fully morning now, an increasingly muggy one, September shoving our noses back into the worst of summer. Soon I would be sweating the way that Joe did. If Joe had not submitted to having a girlfriend for the summer, then none of this would have happened. He had to regret that.

"Sorry about your truck," I said.

"Don't apologize, Minnie. I don't blame you."

I turned and ran up Rex's lane. The fence was jagged. She must have knocked the loose top pole off and then crunched it in two when she hopped it. That would have scared her to death to begin with. I hurried inside to slump at the kitchen table and bawl into the nicked old wood. I was home and Dosie was not. Dosie was in a broken, leaking heap out on the road.

I cried some more when Rex forgave me.

"Minnie, dear, she was an old horse who should have known better. She was well taken care of as long as she lived and she knew that for a fact. Now she'll be glue."

I saw the Department of Highways truck pull up. They had a little bulldozer. Nonsensically, I was terrified that they were going to hurt Dosie. Rex told me not to watch, but I thought it might be worse imagined. The saddest part was seeing Dosie's hooves dangling over the lip of the shovel, those chipped old hooves that had always known where they were going. There was a sick thud when she landed in the dump truck. Then she was waste.

"She's gone, Rex."

"In a way I'm glad she's off your shoulders. It'll be easier figuring out what you want to do this way, dear."

What I wanted to do right away was sleep. Without taking a bath because I could not stand the thought of seeing myself naked. I woke up right before noon, groggy but compelled. First I dragged the compost bin into the apple orchard to collect the fruit that had fallen early; in a month, apples were going to be epidemic. Next I moved on to the barn. Once the stall was scraped clean I hosed it down and dragged all Dosie's tack upstairs to the barn loft. No evil surprises up there, just empty oat bins, rusty sleigh rudders, a decomposing plough and some spare fence poles. From afar, I heard the kitchen phone ring, but I ignored it. I was headed to Rex's tool shed to get a crowbar, a maul and some spikes. It did not take me long to fix the fence. The hammering was a solace, each nail with its own beginning and end. The phone rang again and I got it this time.

"Minnie, we just heard. We're so sorry." Felicity was handling this.

"Thanks, Fizz. You know what? You guys should take over for me here for a while. Really, I mean it. Live here as long as you'd like, get married here, start a think tank here. There are grants you could get, am I right? Other great people you could attract? Make this a research base. Let something take root here. Rex and I would love that, it would be a total consolation."

There was mumbling while this offer was conveyed mate to mate.

"Minnie, Ralph here. Don't let grief speak too soon for you."

"I'm not. Pack your bags, I mean it. I'll still come and go as I want, and so will my cousin and her family. But you and Felicity should stay here. I need someone to look after the place. You can see the sea from here. I know you love that."

"The See the Sea Foundation."

"Perfect. I didn't expect anything to be perfect today, Ralph, so thank you."

The sea would be a dreary grey some days, but Ralph would appreciate that as much as Popsicle-blue.

"Fizzy and I will give you a couple of days to think this over, then it's full steam ahead, how's that? Domestic bliss and ecological crusading."

"I'm happy, honestly I am. I'm very happy."

"Damn, Minnie, I don't know if I can do sorrow. We're both really sorry."

"It's just that the bottom field looks so empty, you know? I'm used to seeing Dosie out there, looking bored in horse paradise. I've barely made phone calls without her."

"Do you want Fizz back?"

"No, I'm fine. See you guys this weekend. Please."

"We love you for this, Minnie, and hopefully one day the ocean will love you for this, if I don't speak too strongly for my lady and the seven seas."

I had to go back to Toronto, I knew that now. But it would be good to spend a bit more time with Ralph and Felicity beforehand. I called Air Canada and booked a flight for late Sunday afternoon, choosing my departure and rattling off my credit-card digits as easily as if I was calling up a pharmacy to refill a prescription, which was surreal. Then I phoned Luce and left a message to say that I was on my way back, but I could stay with my cousin for a few days if her mother needed time to decamp. Then I called Desolée.

"It's me. It's over."

That got her attention. The store chatter subsided as Desolée headed to her tiny office and shut the door. For everyone else it was simply Thursday afternoon.

"How did he take it?"

"He doesn't know yet. I mean, he knows in his own way. We probably would have talked it over this morning, but then I crashed into Dosie with his truck and killed her, which was awful, and the truck is a mess."

"Oh my God, Minnie, are you hurt?"

"Airbags."

"So you're both okay?"

"I was shaky for a bit, but I'm better. He's fine. I'm going to miss him, of course. Or miss what I thought we had. Summer is over and so is playtime, I guess. For both of us."

I hated what I had to say. I was tugging on Rex's phone cord like it was caught on something. I hated what Desolée had to say even more.

"In all honesty you guys were doomed. According to the latest stats the highly educated marry the highly educated. That's how the rich get richer. Assortative mating, they call it. Secretaries and high school sweethearts are shit out of luck. Still, you seemed to be having such a good time, Minnie. Too bad."

I slid down the wall. "This seemed like my best hope so far. My crazy, last, best hope. But I couldn't even make that work."

"I'm sure he's upset, too, Minnie. But from the sound of things, he already has a lot on his plate, the way his industry's going tits up. It's hard for a man to commit when his income is in freefall. I can't believe he even tried."

"I know, I mean what was he thinking?"

"Sorry, Min, I know you hate cross-referencing love with money. You know me, I've been warped by the romantic-gesture business. Apologies."

"No, money is important, you're right. When it's all your own you can choose to be humble with it. Together, people become these acquisitive systems, family take all. Maybe I don't want it all."

Desolée meant her sighs well. The Mountie had told Joe that the smell of dead horse once stuck to his uniform for three days before he had it dry cleaned. I rubbed my forehead on my knees and dared breathe.

"Des, just so you know, I'm loaning out Rex's house."

"Jesus, Minnie, to who?"

"Those crusading young oceanographers. They'll do great things here. No one ever uses the parlour, might as well make it a command centre, right? Save the whales, save the kippers?"

"It's officially up to you."

"I'll still own it. We'll always have somewhere to stay whenever we visit Rex."

"For however long we'll be able to do that."

"Rex loves life, he's not giving up on it anytime soon. Not now that all hell has broken loose around here, thanks to me."

"There was always something kind of bitchy about that horse. Screw the horse, Minnie. And screw the fisherman."

"I should come with a warning label."

"You're not going to have a meltdown, are you? Think ice queen."

Sun burst through the windows, dismissing clouds like they were minimum-wage temps. I hoped it was sunny in Toronto, too, high above Desolée's concourse. That was sky I was going to drop my way out of soon, scruffy sky with less to go around per capita. I could struggle for my patch.

"I'm fine. It was nice to want someone for a while, but it's also nice to want no one. I admit it, marriage is an anthropologically weird thing to do in my mind. In the same way that reproducing offspring when there are needy orphaned children alive in the world might seem strange to future centuries."

"You sure sound enlightened."

"Lightened anyhow."

"I should let you go. Someone's in here complaining because their flowers died. Surprise, surprise, asshole."

"I'll see you soon. Do me a favour and call Gail and Lee and tell them what happened to Dosie."

"Will do, Minnie. Love ya."

I was flat on Rex's kitchen floor, receiver in hand. I had inched underneath the kitchen table and I wanted to kick it hard in the underbelly now, to make mockery of my country-wife shenanigans all summer long. But I spared the old butter dish and salt and pepper shakers. The floor was no place for a woman of forty. I had a lot to get done before I left; no running off to a fresh invasion before I had finished reconstructing. Then I heard mournful squawking. There was a crooked V of geese in the sky, flying south. They did not look like they badly wanted to fly south, rather like they were doing so because there was nothing else they could possibly do. I stepped outside to watch them go. I liked the look of the leader they had in place. I hoped they were going to make it further than a Florida city park. Then I spied movement in the lane. Not Dosie back from the dead. It was Joe, riding my bike. I had forgotten it in the back of his truck. The seat was high so he was straining for the pedals and I loved him for that.

"Keep it," I said. "It's yours." Neglectful of my implications, yet again.

"You won't be needing it, Minnie?"

"Joe, do you have time for a walk on the beach?" I owed him neutral ground. I knew Joe would spare us from fighting dirty.

"Sure, Minnie. With you I do."

We cut through Dosie's pasture. The humidity had burned away and now it was just bright. Seaweed had washed ashore overnight in morbid amounts, like there were dead bodies buried beneath it. I kept my boots on. Joe did not take off his shoes either, his running shoes although he did no running.

"You know, Joe, I think there are about ten thousand different kinds of love." We did not stop; I would not let us stop.

"Is that so?" Joe's hair was so shiny in the sunlight it looked like it had been licked.

"I feel about five thousand different kinds of love for you, Joe." It was tempting to stomp every seashell in sight. I was allowed anything in my direct path, but no swerving. "The kind of love that people sing soppy songs about. The kind of love that respects, really trusts and admires the other person's actions. But not the kind of love that's going to keep me here, I'm afraid."

"I seen it coming, Minnie."

"I know you did."

Of course Joe skipped stones well; that was where Elliot had got it. Joe sent a black rock scudding a good long way before it sank. He wiped his hands on his jeans. Those hands that had softened, that ass that had hardened. Those eyes as alive as vegetable garden lettuce.

"For a while there it seemed like we were going to work something out, truth be told."

We had to keep moving, it was our only chance at a conclusion.

"The thing is, there's this awful gap I tend to fall into between truth and honesty. The truth is that we would be great together, Joe, great. But at the same time I don't think it would be honest. Not of me."

"I don't flatter you, Minnie. That's the honest truth."

"Joe, you are dream-come-true flattering to me. But I have a limited interest in dreams. Dreams aren't really my thing."

"Not your thing."

We had ticked off a pair of blue herons. They flapped ahead to emptier shore. Joe wanted to follow.

"Joe, wait. Don't feel stupid for being happy. That would be terrible."

"I was never quite happy, Minnie."

"Oh. Good then."

Now we both stopped. We owed each other silence with enough syllables in it to include surprise, dismay and a hint of recovery. The tide was low. There were molluscs bubbling in the mud. The gulls looked sated and dopey. The water was as still as I had seen it.

"You know, Minnie, there used to be a channel between Nova Scotia and Cape Breton. Back when you and I were little. Then they built the Canso Causeway."

"Okay."

If we were going to take courteous detours like this, then maybe we could also go for some breakup sex, the sand serving as friction? Then again, it would be sex to merely make me feel carpentered together. Or worse, sex like a soother: popped in and quelling. If I was not too old for that, then Joe certainly was. I realized I had no idea what kind of sex Joe had ever really wanted, the tone had been all mine.

"They needed a cheap way to get coal to the mainland. They studied the currents in the gulf before they went ahead. There's a counter-clockwise flow. They thought the causeway would drain what it needed to and not affect anything much."

"I'm with you."

"But the siltification, it got bad and then with the fixed link it got worse and things are only going to go on swamping up. In a thousand years, Minnie, there won't even be a strait. This won't be an island."

"I'm sorry, Joe." I sensed mourning. "But would that be so bad?"

"Maybe not, Minnie. Maybe not."

I did not want to lay a hand on Joe in any way that would pain him as unwarranted. We knew to turn around now and plod back to the break in the cliff below Rex's field. Our talk went mundane, so thin I felt my blood thin, too. Joe said Etta was going to drop him off in the village on her way to pick up the kids from school. Yes, he was going out fishing that night, he and Colin were headed to the wharf to check the boat over. His insurance company was being cooperative, he was getting a new truck. Maybe another red truck, maybe not. Joe had left nothing lying around Rex's house that I had to return to him. He did not want a glass of water. There was nothing tangible I could do for him. And I needed one more favour.

"Joe, will you please not say goodbye? I don't think I could take it."

"I have to say goodbye, Minnie. But if you want another favour I'll say no more than that."

"Goodbye then."

"Goodbye, Minnie. Take care of yourself."

Fine to the end, Joe left. I saw his gaze stray to Dosie's mended fence as he went. I trusted him not to feel any kind of rebuke in that. There was such a brave set to Joe's head. I would forever love the way his dark curls kissed his neck. His arms rarely swung much. Joe's short legs, marching away. My guess was that his penis would survive the confusion. To call him back now would be idiotic. The trees were shushing me before my tongue even got to my teeth. It was a long walk for Joe down Rex's lane and up his brother's. Knowing he would not turn around I was able to watch him the whole way. Finally, Joe was a bobbing dot. I saw that the grass had grown again already. I would have to get in one more bout of mowing before I left.

I went indoors to make the bed, less punishment than I deserved. I refused to weep over the sheets. There was one helpful ceremony beckoning, however. At times like this, in love-gone-wrong's immediate aftermath, I needed to see my face. It amazed me to see the way something fell away from it and left it more open. I stared myself down in Rex's little white bathroom, the mirror small and blotched but clear enough. My eyes went to my eyes, then out to my whole face. I always looked more attractive to myself right after a rupture, as if my affair had been pasting one false expression on top of another, marring me, and now I had cracked free and reverted to purity. This time, however, I did not look pretty. Joe had carried that notion away with him and he was welcome to it. I was not about to abandon my sexual pride, but I'd had it with sexual vanity. There was no need to be pretty in order to mate with my own life. I looked tawny and bony and scratched, but resolute. I looked like I meant business. Once the coast was clear I thought I would go for a jog. It would do me a world of good. There was nothing whimsical about mobility, not mine at any rate. I loved running. I loved my own heart for beating even when it was sodden with lesser grief.

14

Friday I biked down to the Harbour to pick up some staples so that Ralph and Felicity could move in to a full larder.

Then I biked down the hill to the diner.

There was euphoria in the air. Fibby had decided to rechristen his boat the *Truly Trudy* and Trudy had decided to let him get away with it so Fibby had bought cones all around. Madison was scooping and Patrick was doing the handing out. Fibby had picked up Patrick in Souris, recovered from the dunk and a thorough favourite of the out-patient team. Then Archie showed up. He had a new pair of boots for Patrick from the Charlottetown Canadian Tire. Verna's little brothers looked on in wonder at the presentation: Archie shook Patrick's hand as curtly as if they were playing rock, paper, scissors. The boots were nice and old-fashioned with orangey-red trim, the kind of boots that looked like they had already been plodding around in PEI muck. Patrick said they fit so well that he just had to do a dance. Then Herman Walker jumped up to jig along, Darlene MacDonald and Freak linked elbows and twirled, and everyone else clapped like crazy. I felt a tap to my elbow. Debbie was handing me a neatly folded apron.

"Trudy said I could," she murmured.

The apron was mine to keep because Debbie had embroidered a red, swirling *Minerva* on the heart of the bib. I had teased Trudy all summer long that she owed us matching uniforms. When Trudy saw the big thank-you going on she came over. I dragged her right to a corner.

"You did it," I said. "You and Fibby got it together."

"Took us long enough."

"It isn't easy. Sometimes I think there are Einstein formulations at work."

"You have a way of making me feel smart, Minnie. Lord love you for that."

"Smart, you say? Then why, whenever I'm in a couple, do I simply add to the caseload of stupidity in the world? That explains the tail between my legs, by the way. It's a shame one can't sneak off an island."

"I'm going to miss you, Minnie. You're one of a kind."

"Between you and me, I'm worried I'm going to miss Eats n' Treats most of all."

"Good ole Minnie, you love slinging my hash. So do I, I suppose. I told Fibby we're keeping the bank accounts separate for a good long time and that's that."

"True love means getting to do your own thing. You cracked the case."

Then Fibby had to come along behind us, pick me up and twirl me like a toddler. The crowd loved it, especially when he set me back down and my world whirled. It was actually a nice moment of clarity. Patrick walked me out on his way to Archie's boat. I double-checked that he had my Toronto cell number.

"Nervous to hit open sea?" I asked.

"I want the work too bad to be scared of it, Minnie."

"Money comes and money goes. For everyone, Patrick. I mean that in a good way."

"Same with love, Minnie."

"Maybe so."

"See ya 'round. Hopefully not at the shelter."

"I'll be there regardless." I realized how relieved I was to be saying that and how much I would have hated the reverse. Leo would be a sight for sore eyes. I would bring Gabe blank canvases and buy some new cribbage boards and rent restricted DVDs for the movie room.

"I'll give Verna your love, shall I, Minnie, when I'm passing through *la belle province?*"

"Please do. Tell Verna I'll always be interested to know what she's up to. You, too, dear."

Patrick ran off, boots flapping. My bike basket was too laden down with foodstuffs to make it up the hill, but I did not mind plodding. The countdown had started: I needed to inhale as much Tuck Harbour air as possible before smog fouled my horizon. I had to get red dirt on my shoes and hang dry all my wash and take a close look at the night sky in sharp focus, the black a real black. I had to churn through all that was rural for forty-eight hours now that I was willing to admit how far away from the city I had been. And to take Herman Walker up on his offer of a lift for once in his life, just to keep him on his toes. I passed him my groceries and tossed the bike in the back. Before he drove off from Rex's I forced Herman to take one of my honeydews.

"I like a tin of pudding with my supper. It keeps me better company," he protested.

"A change is as good as a rest," I insisted.

Etta summoned me over to her place early on Saturday. She needed reassuring that I honestly did not want to go into Montague before I left. I said Rex and I would revert to phone calls a lot easier without a tearjerking last visit in person, me trying to memorize every age spot and Rex trying to excuse my hysteria. When I had called up Sally for a second opinion about this, she had concurred. Ralph's mother was apparently beside herself as regarded my "magnificent gesture" and was planning a visit from Winnipeg over Thanksgiving. To every loving act there are reverberations.

"I'll be back to visit Rex at Christmas," I promised Etta.

The girls liked the sound of that.

"Presents!" said Joan.

"Big presents!" said Bette. "Minnie is loaded!"

"These kids were sent to try me. Elliot, come here, sonny. Don't go hiding around corners."

Pierre was excited about my flight number, altitude and velocity, but Elliot was mopey. I had rendered the Saturday morning cartoons irrelevant, which was touching.

"Come here, El," I begged. "Let me feel your muscles." For one last time that summer, I received divine child weight into my lap. Children have such clean heads. "Pardon me, buddy? I didn't catch that."

"I said do you want to go, Minnie, or do you feel like you have to?"

An eight-year-old who already knew to measure self-interest against duty.

"Dude, what a question."

"She has to get going because she thinks she's too good for the likes of us, isn't that right, Minnie, my dear?" Colin was back for lunch. "Maybe old Ben Franklin said it best, 'Fish and visitors smell after three days.'"

"Etta, thanks for everything."

"Make your escape then, run for cover. Son, stop your clinging. No woman is ever going to respect you that way."

"Don't mind Colin," Etta said at the door. "He's just feeling for his brother." I could see the summer finely etched in Etta's face. Etta's vacation treat had been highlights; now she was even more coppery.

"I feel for Joe, too."

"Joe's a big boy. He can decide for himself who's going to lead him on. Maybe you and Joe were both too good for each other, how does that work?"

"Joe isn't mad."

"Oh no?"

"I did my best."

"You're a striver, Minnie. I'll say that much for you. Don't strive yourself to death."

Etta and I were good for one more hug.

"Take care of yourself, neighbour."

I cut across field rather than sticking to lane. I appreciated the trampling action and whipping noises; they went well with my reminder to myself that I never wanted to fly into a snit when some-one forgot an anniversary, disparaged my cooking or flirted with the waitress. Neither did I need to borrow anyone's razor, nor check to make sure it was okay if I bought a Cessna, a stake in a mine, or black pearls. I did not want to share all my moods between two or save for two. I did not want two futures on my plate or anyone subsidizing mine. By the time I got back to Rex's house I was a tor-nado of autonomy. It was my form of peace.

I was all packed when Ralph and Felicity pulled up early Sun-day afternoon. I had packed for Rex, too, a box of his personal effects for the young couple to take to the Manor on their next visit. I had put winter clothes in there and his favourite porridge bowl and the angel painting from his bedroom—an angel as husky as a McTeal. I showed the happy couple around the appliances, furnace, fuse box and woodshed. Rex would have fun answering further questions. I had intended to take a cab to the airport, my Toronto lack of thrift al-ready kicking in. Felicity refused to hear of it, however. Ralph was going to stay home and cook their first Harbour feast: lobsters, since I said I did not mind.

"I'm an opportunist, what can I say? I study them, I boil them, I dip them in butter." Ralph had a way with shrugs. And an American-strength bear hug. It was not hard to bid Ralph farewell because he would be at an *Islandness* conference in Toronto within a month.

Felicity insisted on helping me with my bags. I left behind the shiny boots and the whole Green Gables compendium. My laptop was back in its gash-proof case.

"I hope I haven't trapped you two into anything?"

Ralph could do many things genially, including closing a car door on someone. "Paradise is always a prison, sweet Minnie. It's one of the oldest paradoxes going."

I rolled the window down for one more shore breeze. "Don't rile the church ladies. They don't understand degradation."

"Look who's talking. Fizz, get the invasive species out of here before she spreads."

"Forget the Island, look to the water," I called out while I could.

"I'm deep that way," Ralph hollered back.

Felicity was not shy of her right of way or fearful of overtaking. She was willing to discuss her research speciality: the correlation between fishing effort and government subsidies.

"Either fish suffer or fishermen suffer," I gathered.

"It's one or the other. Usually fish. Fish don't vote."

It was comforting to scan Felicity's fresh profile rather than Kings County retreating out the windows and Queens County trading pine trees for gas stations.

"You and Ralph can vote for the fish—big, loud votes."

"Minnie, I hope you're not sad to go?"

"No more than I should be."

"I bet Joe is sad. Are you his one that got away, do you think?"

"Not if he takes proper stock of the situation, which I'm sure he'll do. I wasn't particularly right for Joe. Romance is best decided upon in the particular, not desired in general."

"I particularly love Ralph."

"You two base yourselves in circumstance rather than presumption. It's why I trust you so much."

"Love isn't exactly science, Minnie."

"No, but there's far too much casual mysticism clogging up our culture, don't you think? True love, chance and luck, they're all overrated to the point of affliction."

"Don't be mad if I wish you luck, Minnie."

"Hell no, I wish *you* luck, lots of it."

The Saint Dunstan's Basilica spires were taking a stab at poking a cloud. We accessed the Charlottetown bypass and then it was over.

Felicity's hug at the airport smelled of hyacinth and hydrogen; it was like April again. I got the porthole I wanted. I strained my gaze easterly as we took off. Etta was making sure Monday's homework was done. Herman Walker was cutting himself another slice of melon. Patrick was in his big new boots. Trudy and Fibby were probably in bed. Ralph was setting the table with Rex's seventies placemats. Rex was in Sally's room for a chat. Joe would be at his parents' house. Perhaps Dolly was taking a turn to say grace. The Island looked flat when I was not down there jogging its ups and downs. Every bright Island hue was so remorselessly on display that I felt taunted for leaving. One never really knows what anyone else's colours are; one only has one's own. I spurned New Brunswick to work on some email, all the way through the cocktail nuts to Ontario.

15

Concord Avenue smelled deliciously clean, courtesy of Luce's mother. This was home, unmistakably so. Toronto was chillier than the Island, with a faster claim on the fall. The East would catch up soon. Immediately, I biked down to College Street to pick up some cucumber and pickle maki for dinner, and California rolls hold the crab. I wanted wasabi punch and seaweed tang. Even Sunday-night traffic in Toronto made me feel gladiatorial. The sidewalks were full of bustlers and trendoids and the roads were full of two-seaters. I took a titanic shower before bed so I would have plenty of time to pack for work in the morning. I had lobster-flavoured potato chips and chocolate-covered potato chips for the Myriad kitchenette, plus mini wooden lobster traps with plastic lobsters for Luce and Barry's desks. And I needed gym clothes for Monday night's spin class. I took two streetcars to work, happy to transfer.

"The super producer returns!" Barry was also acquiring a jar of Dolly's preserves: ginger peach. I knew he had come in early just to get me alone.

"Yes, Barry, I'll hug you. But I've had enough damn hugs this summer to last me a lifetime. One more, that's it."

"Why, Toots, you've mellowed. I wanted you to come back sharp."

"I'm sharp all right. Sharp like a hook."

It was good to be back in Barry's office where the gravity was such that ideas bounced. I was actually half back in Barry's office. When things were at their best I merely leaned in the door.

"Talk, Minerva, I'm listening."

"See the Sea."

"Come again?"

"All over the world, Barry, oceans are failing. Fish stocks are plummeting, coral is dying, Atlantic, Pacific, Mediterranean, Arctic, there's trouble. A farmer gets better at farming, farming gets better. Not the same thing with fishing, not at all. The better we get at fishing, the worse it is for fishing, for us, and for the sea. It's a Catch-22 to the nth degree. I'm thinking Jacques Cousteau meets *60 Minutes*. Systems analysis but with spectacular underwater footage. Really diving in. Chances are we could get the Australian Broadcasting Corporations on board, maybe South Africa, too, let alone Europe and Asia. This is good, deep stuff, Bar."

"I need a host. Someone to stabilize things. Someone who knows what to look for."

"Good point, Barry. Very good point. In fact, I've got two of them for you, the cutest couple you've ever seen. And they're American. Be nice and I'll throw in my great uncle."

"I'm in. Sell it up top and you're off to the races. Think you could get more than one season out of it?"

"God yes. There are enough problems to last us for years."

Barry whipped his Nerf baseball at my head, which I was kind enough to return with a ladylike underhand, although I sometimes stole the thing and sat on it. When I got back to my desk I found a backup invitation to Nicola and Hardy's wedding in my stack of mail. I trusted Nicola Chalice to be up and on the go at this hour.

"Nicola, Minnie here. Congratulations. Is it bad form to accept a wedding invitation over the phone? I want to let you know I'm attending with pleasure."

"Good news can deliver itself any way it wants, Ms. Gallant."

"Joe is very happy for you as well but he won't be coming with me. I'm back home now."

"So I see. You're call displaying as Myriad Productions again."

"Don't worry, I'm not going to ask you to participate in any more crass displays of connection. But thanks for playing along for a while there."

"It did me good, as you well know."

I liked Nicola's tendency to announce things rather than just saying them.

"You've commingled souls, you and Hardy, haven't you?"

"Agglomerated, possibly. Hardy has great magnetism."

"I like having my soul to myself for now."

"Each to her own, certainly."

I flicked on the little Italian desk lamp. It was still beaming out comfort to the dedicated. No one had touched my stapler or my collected volumes of Anne Radcliffe. "You can congratulate me as well, if you'd like, Nicola."

"To what end?"

"It's my birthday. I'd ignore it if I could, but I'm guessing my cousin has something special cooked up while she still has time to fuss over the adults in her life. I'd like to get better at celebration, actually, now that I know it's largely my responsibility. I'm forty-one today."

"Will you accept my congratulations, Ms. Gallant, on being forty-one?"

"I'd love to."

Acknowledgements

Thank you first and foremost to my editor, Jane Warren, team-mate extraordinaire. Thank you to my diligent copy editor, Melissa Hajek. Thank you to Rob Howard, Daniel Rondeau and Jennifer Fox, with whose help I am sold and promoted. Thanks to Marijke Friesen for the great cover. Thank you to Jordan Fenn for putting all these people together. A constant, enormous thank you to my agent, Samantha Haywood.

Many thanks to those who assisted me with my fishing research, formidably Darren and Calvin Fraser, Stephen Chapman, Rory McLellan, Ken Campbell and Rick Williams of Praxis Research. Lorne MacKinnon was helpful on other matters.

I owe a big debt of gratitude to Leslie Merklinger for the close look she took at Minnie's working life. Blame any poetic license on me.

Desolée would never have become a florist without Susan Anderson and her gracious staff to inform me—thank you for my fragrant day at Black-Eyed Susan's.

Thank you to my PEI family who spare me no boon or kindness: lovely Sandra, Paul, Teresa and Frank Strain, spirited Joanne, Joan and Brendan McGinn, and Cathy Corrigan. My mother and father have made my writing possible by relinquishing their guest apartment for years on end and keeping me in olive oil and tangerines. I love you for everything, Margaret McCormack and Tony Sosnkowski. My brother, Andrew, will spend hours on the phone whenever my IT needs rise to the surface—I'd like to thank his wife, Rebecca, for that.

I have the whole Brehaut clan to thank so here goes. Thank you, Big Lorin, Big Shirley, Lynn, John, Claire, Jimmy, Dawn, Danny, Sarah, Eric, Little Shirley, Paula, Ted, Rachel, Leah, Stewart, the indefatigable Little Lorin, Isabella, Lori, Ryan, Whitney, Logan, Chloe, Scott, Dale, Sidney and Scotty.

Hal Roddy, Suzanne Copan, Jim Gormley, Kimball Lelacheur and Eber and Pearl Williams might as well be family based on how much I owe them.

So many people make my PEI days a joy, provocation and relief. Thank you to Kelly Scott and the whole frisky crew at Tink n' Ginger, Anna LaCroix and her fellow dance babes, movie buddy David Gallant, Joyce and Barb at the Delta gym, Debbie Denoon et al, Corena Hughes and Greg Arsenault, Kim Devine, Catherine Hennessey, Harmony Wagner, Erin Casey, Rosemary and Ed Schiller and Ina from Sunshine Farm. Phil and Alesia, you count as Islanders. Thank you to Erica Carragher for introducing me to Xiaoping Wang and Frank Huang. Thank you to Arlene MacInnis for introducing me to Rose and to Rose for introducing me to the Bluefield High School writing club. Thanks to all my pals at the glorious Confederation Centre Art Gallery: Ihor, Tamara, Siobhan and most especially, very especially, highly especially, Jon Tupper.

I have the gang at CBC Charlottetown to thank for a lot. If it wasn't an obnoxious option I'd copy out the staff list. Instead, let me especially thank Donna Allen, Laura Chapin, Brian Higgins, Rob LeClair, Paul Legere, Lloyd MacDonald, Laura Meader, Claire Nantes, Ian Petrie and Sally Pitt. Steve D'Souza, Andrew Sprague and Gary Cunliffe, you are great gentleman journalists. Sara Fraser, Sheila Taylor, Maggie Brown and Sophia Harris—you are more than colleagues, you are wonderful friends.

In the spirit of inclusiveness, I'd like to thank Gary MacDougall and Sally Cole at *The Guardian*. A shout-out to Dan Viau at CTV as well.

My Halifax "family" always makes me feel great: thank you, Ferne and Jim McCombe plus Karyn, David, Cody and Sam and beautiful Sheila.

Thank you to Kingi, Kim, Carole, Louise, Susanne, Angela, Susie, Christine, Leeta, Terry and Flavia, John, Morley and Michael for staying in touch no matter how far east I go. Thank you to Viia Beaumanis and Ceri Marsh for continuing to attach me to FASHION. Thank you to James Osborne for more website ministration than a girl deserves.

Desirée Andrew and Shekau Piwas—thank you for being such northern lights.

Research Debt

Besides *The Guardian* of PEI, I owe a great deal to several highly informative books and articles:

Charles Clover, *The End of the Line*, The New Press, 2006

Trevor Corson, *The Secret Life of Lobsters*, Harper Perennial, 2004

Alec Wilkinson, "The Lobsterman," *The New Yorker*, July 31, 2006

Elizabeth Kolbert, "The Darkening Sea," *The New Yorker*, November 20, 2006

Raffi Khatchadourian, "Neptune's Navy," *The New Yorker*, November 5, 2007

Nick Tosches, "If You Knew Sushi," *Vanity Fair*, June 2007

I also recommend the following websites:

www.endangeredfishalliance.org

www.msc.org (Marine Stewardship Council)

www.seashepherd.org

PHOTO: JESSICAH DUTTON

LOUISA MCCORMACK is the author of the novel *Six Weeks to Toxic*. She was born in Montreal, Quebec, and now lives in Charlottetown, Prince Edward Island. Visit her at www.louisamccormack.com.

The author is donating a portion of the proceeds from the sale of this novel to CODE, an organization that promotes and supports literacy in the developing world. For more information, please visit www.codecan.org.